SPACE RAIDERS OF THE FROGOPOLIS, AND THE CHAOS SINGULARITY

Tales from the Storystream

JAMIE BRINDLE

FREE BOOK!

For Matt and Charlotte, obviously.
Well, waiting 5 years for a wedding present isn't so bad, is it?

"That was close, EB," said the Captain, breathing hard, and double checking the scanner to make sure they weren't being followed.

Inside, the spaceship was small and cramped, festooned with papers and odd ornaments from the backwater pleasure-worlds of half the Galaxy, an inevitable chaos resulting from frequent artificial gravity failures. Outside the thin metal walls, a mind-boggling expanse of still, silent void stretched backwards towards the pin-prick light of the main-sequence star from which the good ship *Nippy-Whoas* was decamping at all haste.

"Relax," said EB, grinning through feline teeth, one paw resting lightly on the joystick. "You know I wasn't going to let those heathens catch you."

EB was small by human standards, which didn't count for much in the circumstances, because his provenance was decidedly non-human. A retelling here of his origin - which was complicated, unlikely, and bound to take more than an hour if one were to do it full justice - seems unnecessary at this point, as well as being a poor use of time, as something much more interesting is just about to happen.

There was a beeping noise, and the hatch to the engine room slid open, disgorging the Crew. The Crew consisted of one gentleman, dark hair speckled with a dusting of silver, slender, well-dressed with a tailored jacket and a gold-filigree pocket watch, and an air of damaged dignity which was the only sign of the frantic struggle in which he had just engaged with the ship's eccentric and utterly unique star-drive.

The Captain glanced over her shoulder, saw the Crew, and smiled.

"My hero!" she exclaimed. "How did you ever manage that? I thought we were about to be splatted!"

The Crew stomped forward and leaned against the metal bulkhead above the little hollow where EB sat steering the ship. He regarded the Captain for half a second, taking in her brown hair tinged with gold highlights, her sparkling eyes and warm smile. There was something about her, an ineffable animation in the way she talked, the way her arms and face moved, painting pictures, bringing life to the world of things. The Crew pondered, thoughtful. Then he blinked himself back to the present, and he shrugged.

"I kicked it," he said simply.

The Captain's eyes widened.

"You kicked the Chaos Drive," she said in a flat voice. "The most precious, the most highly advanced, the most elaborate piece of technology in the known galaxy. The one thing that keeps us safe and ahead of the game. *You - kicked - it?*"

The Crew whistled tunelessly.

"Pretty much," he said. "I might have shoved it a bit too," he added, at least having the good grace to examine his hands sheepishly.

The Captain stared at him.

Then she shrugged too.

"As long as it works," she said. "Which is further proof that we have perfected the division of labour."

The Crew frowned, paused in the act of rolling a cigarette, and fixed the Captain with a glare.

"We agreed," he said, clearly outraged. "Equal partners, remember?"

The Captain rolled her eyes.

"But you're so good at being the crew," she protested. "Look at how you got us out of there! There's no way I could have done that! You're a much better security guard than me."

"Stop it," said the Crew.

"And then there's the way you look after the engines," continued the Captain. "I mean, I don't know anything about the engines!"

"Stop it," repeated the Crew

"Not to mention how good you are at cooking," said the Captain. "Seriously, wow! You really are a man of many talents! While I, alas, only excel in the humble role of Captain..."

The Crew was shaking his head.

"Unbelievable," he muttered. Then he turned to EB. "What do you think, EB? Don't you think Charlotte should let me be Captain now? I mean, that was the agreement! Fair's fair, right EB? Right?"

But EB wasn't listening. Instead, he was staring with mounting disbelief at the small, ominously swift dot that had appeared on the screen of the scanner. The others had been too busy bickering to notice it.

"It's come through the Chaos," said EB, too puzzled to be really alarmed. "But how...?"

Matt - he who was so keen to relinquish the all-inclusive

title of Crew, and take up the role of Captain of the free-booter spaceship - saw that EB wasn't looking at him. He followed the feline's gaze, and was just in time to see the ominous little dot intersect with the centre of the screen.

"Balls," he said, and then they were hit by the missile.

❧ 2 ❧

There was a period of darkness.

It wasn't sleep, because sleep involves dreams; and it wasn't death, because death will be either utter nothing or absolute everything, and this darkness was too thick to be one and too thin to be the other. No, this darkness was closer to a...suspension.

In the darkness, something flickered...

...And in another place, the Chaos stretched, turned, pressing against the barriers that held it.

And found the hole.

The tiny, infinitely unlikely hole that something had ripped open, and which was closing swiftly.

It was too small for the Chaos to rush through. It was too tiny to unbalance the whole Universe.

But it *was* big enough for a...a movement.

The Chaos has no mind, not as such things are usually understood.

Nevertheless, as something slipped through, as an almost-impossible exchange was made...the Chaos was pleased.

Mischief was well begun.

𝔰 3 𝔰

Charlotte blinked open her eyes, and tried to remember where the hell she was. Everything was very silent and still. A constellation of small objects rotated slowly around her, drifting in a dull red light. The colour of the light was familiar. Charlotte felt that it should mean something, something quite important. She frowned, and tried to remember what it might be.

Where was she?

The wedding had gone off without a hitch, which was wonderful. Maybe that was why she felt so light, so sort of...floaty. She remembered the service, she remembered the cake, huge and resplendent, and admired by all the guests. And she remembered dancing of course, the dresses whirring and all the happy faces smiling back at them, and then...

Darkness.

What had happened after that? They must have carried on drinking, they must have really been putting it away. Why else would she be struggling to remember?

She peered upwards and tried to make sense of what it was she was looking at.

It was some kind of metal, a dirty greyish sort of bulk-head. It looked like a hull. Or maybe...maybe a portion of fuselage? Was it possible that she was on the aeroplane?

That must be it. She hadn't meant to get drunk, not really drunk; somehow, that intention must have failed. Matt must have got them both onto the aeroplane, they must be on the way to enjoying their honeymoon...

Charlotte frowned. That all made some kind of sense. The thing was, it didn't feel right at all. At that moment, her eyes fixed on one of the many objects that were spinning around her. It was a picture, a photograph of herself and Matt. She peered at it. It showed them, standing with big smiles on their faces, arms around each other, and behind them...

...behind them was what appeared to be the rings of Saturn.

Charlotte was just coming to terms with how weird this was, when the full weirdness of something that was so weird she had just taken it for granted until now, crunched weirdly into place.

The photograph she was looking at was rotating round her. Everything was rotating round her. And she herself was...

...She was floating. Floating, just as if she were bobbing up and down in a swimming pool that she was completely unaware of. As if she were suspended in water.

Or in space, she thought.

"Charlotte?" came a familiar voice from behind her. Charlotte was so startled that she tried to twist round, an act which only served to set her spinning gently end over end.

She made a noise that, while technically not swearing, conveyed something of a sense of concentrated sweariness. She tried to stop herself spinning, but found that she was unable to reach anything to brace against. She said something else that definitely wasn't a swear word.

"Don't worry, I've got you," came the familiar voice. Then a hand grasped her shoulder, and the world stopped spinning.

"Thank you!" said Charlotte. She followed the hand up, and her eyes locked on the face of someone who was almost Matt.

The bone structure was right, the roguish grin was completely familiar; but the hair had a little more grey, the eyes looked just a touch older, the whole was...unsettling.

"Matt?" breathed Charlotte.

"Of course, Matt!" said Matt. "Who else did you expect? The Wicked Witch of the West?"

"But you look..." Charlotte trailed off. "Where are we?"

"We're not in Kansas any more, that's a fact," purred another voice. Charlotte spun around, only avoiding launching into another set of rotations because Matt's hand was still firmly on her shoulder.

A pair of pale eyes swam out of the darkness, and a familiar feline shape floated gracefully into view.

Charlotte screamed.

"What is it?" shouted Matt. "What's the matter?"

Charlotte shot him a terrified glance.

"It's EB!" she said.

"Yes," said Matt reasonably. "So what?"

"But...But he's speaking!" protested Charlotte.

"True," said the cat. "I can't deny it. She's got me there."

Matt and EB were both staring at her now. Matt was looking at her as if she had gone mad. But EB's quick eyes were darting up and down, taking in her rumpled pyjamas, her hair, her eyes...

"But he's not meant to speak!" went on Charlotte, desperately telling herself that if only she kept calm, then the Universe was bound to start making sense again sooner or later. "He's meant to lay there and be stroked and look sweet!"

"Who says I can't do both?" asked EB reasonably.

Charlotte ignored him. She shook her head, and focussed on Matt. She took a deep breath.

"What," she said slowly, "the hell is going on?"

Matt had a smile on his face, but Charlotte could tell that he was worried. Very worried. She saw that he was looking closely at her eyes now, examining her hair and clothing, as if there was something very problematic about them.

He licked his lips.

"Where exactly do you think you are?" he asked, after a few moments of silence.

Charlotte shook her head in frustration.

"That's what I want to know!" she said.

"Okay, okay," said Matt, sounding like someone who is trying to sound soothing, but who, in fact, probably needs soothing themselves. "Well then...um...when do you think we are?"

Charlotte blinked. That was an odd question! When did she think it was? Well, that was obvious! Yesterday's date had been burned into her mind for the last six months, it had been the most important day in the year, the day that everything was building towards.

"Well, seeing as we got married yesterday, I think I should know what the day is!" She said, a little more acerbically than she had intended.

Matt raised an eyebrow. To Charlotte's chagrin, EB floated in gracefully from one corner of her vision and raised an eyebrow, too.

"It's Sunday the 19th of July, of course!" she said. "2015! The day after our bloody wedding! Now, will you please tell me what on earth this is all about!"

Matt and EB looked at one another.

"Oh dear," said Matt in a very small voice.

There was a long silence.

Then EB sighed.

"One of us has to tell her," said the cat.

"Tell me what?" demanded Charlotte.

"I thought this stuff wasn't meant to happen anymore!" complained Matt, completely ignoring Charlotte. "I thought the shielding was meant to prevent it!"

EB shrugged.

"Shields must have failed," he said simply.

Matt sighed, and turned to face Charlotte.

"It's kind of a long story," he said.

"I've got time," Charlotte answered promptly.

"Actually," put in EB, "I don't think you have."

EB had floated over to a small, green monitor screen. He was studying it with a worried look on his face.

Charlotte opened her mouth to ask why, and that was when the harsh, alien voice came booming out over the intercom.

❧ 4 ❧

Enmeshed in a thick, cloying substrate of algae and nutrients, Head Frog 127 regarded the image of the alien spaceship, and repeated his message.

"Once again, this is *The Pondwater*, a Tadpole-class super-fast interceptor, which has the honour to be engaged in His Majesty's glorious space navy." Head Frog 127 licked his huge lips and smiled in the darkness. "We can see from our scanners that we have knocked out your engines. There is no point prolonging the inevitable. Prepare to be boarded. If you offer your unconditional surrender and return the items you stole, His Majesty will grant you the chance of an honourable death. Resist, and...things will not go so well for you."

Head Frog 127 clicked his tongue, and killed the connection. He issued orders to his inferiors, and bent his gaze on the display. The alien ship, looking like nothing so much as a battered and broken tin can, swam closer as *The Pondwater* approached. The chase had been ridiculously easy in the end. Of course, Head Frog 127 had all the advantages of class and rank; his ship was by far the fastest in the whole of the

Frogopolis - if anyone had been going to catch the aliens, it was bound to be Head Frog 127.

There was a dull boom deep in the hull of *The Pondwater*. Docking had occurred. Soon, Head Frog 127 would be returning victoriously to his home world. He shuddered with pleasure as he thought of the accolades that would be heaped on him. Then a nasty thought occurred. He pondered a moment, agonising about what he should do. Then he switched on his communicator, and hailed his chief of security.

"This is Glob," came the hoarse, brutal voice. "How may I serve you, Chief Frog?"

Head Frog 127 frowned. The slip was deliberate, of course, a small piece of petty insubordination, meant to undermine the authority of Head Frog 127. He had never liked Glob, whom he suspected was probably plotting against him. Of course, Glob *was* plotting against him, just as every member of The Tadpole was always plotting against every other member. This was, in fact, normal behaviour for the citizens of the Glorious Hegemony of the Empire of the Frogopolis, a society which operated almost exclusively in shades of deception, mistrust, intrigue, and betrayal. Glob, however, was a most especially slippery customer, even by the notoriously slippery standards of the Frogopolis.

"Have you boarded the alien ship yet?" demanded Head Frog 127.

"No," answered Glob shortly. We're just about to go in."

Head Frog 127 scowled.

"Stand down," he commended.

There was a pause.

"What?" The voice of Glob was incredulous. "Why?"

Head Frog 127 coloured an even more vivid shade of green than was customary for a member of his species. Such outspoken disdain for the Head Frog of a craft was very rude.

"Do you think I have to explain myself to you, Glob?" snapped Head Frog 127. "Stand down! That's an order! I personally will be leading the boarding party."

Which means that there is no chance you will be sneaking your way into any credit you don't deserve, Head Frog 127 added in the privacy of his own head.

Glob started to protest, but Head Frog 127 killed the intercom. There, that would show him who was boss.

He croaked out an order, and a flurry of his small, attendant Froglings scurried forward to pull him out of his comfortable algae substrate, and lock him into the ornate Power Suit he used to explore inhospitable alien environments. When he was fully cloaked, he strode from his cockpit, making his way to the lowest deck, where he took personal command of the boarding party, dismissing a furious and glowering Glob.

"Now," said Head Frog 127, once Glob had stomped off, "everyone assume your positions. Prepare to board the alien ship."

5

"What the hell am I meant to do with this?" demanded Charlotte, holding up the small, silver object Matt had handed her. It looked a little bit like a fifty pence piece, though it was somewhat thicker.

"Put it in your mouth," said NotMatt.

"What?"

"It's a micro-respirator," chimed in EB. "It means you will be able to breathe. It will keep you alive."

Charlotte shot the cat a dark, mistrustful look.

"Why will I need help to breath?" she asked suspiciously.

NotMatt looked at her and shrugged.

"Look, we're about to be boarded by some of the nastiest, most untrustworthy, cruel, brutal, and just plain vile people in the known Universe," he said, in the tones of someone desperately trying to stay calm, and only just managing it. "In about twenty seconds they're going to finish drilling through the hull of our ship, and when that happens, the first thing we're going to lose is our atmosphere. All our air, gone!"

"But that will kill us," said Charlotte, reasonably. "They

don't want to kill us. Didn't you hear what the voice said? They want to grant us the chance of an honourable death! They can't do that if we're already dead."

"Yes, but in their book, dying horribly of asphyxiation in a breached spaceship *is* an honourable death," said NotMatt.

Charlotte looked from NotMatt to EB and back again. They both nodded at her encouragingly.

Then she gingerly placed the coin-shaped object in her mouth. It tasted pleasantly of aniseed.

"Very well," she said. "But I still want to know what's going on!"

"Sure, sure," said NotMatt, who was now struggling to pull some sort of retractable netting out from one corner of the room. "Just get yourself strapped in. There. Now, what do you want to know?"

Charlotte wriggled her shoulders inside the meshwork of netting between NotMatt and EB, opened her mouth to ask her first question, and the top of the spaceship exploded.

Or rather, it didn't explode. What it actually did was to bow inwards, and then get snatched out and away with a horrible tearing noise and a rush of escaping air. Charlotte felt her hair whip up around her, as the inside of the spaceship was swirled into a whirlwind of escaping atmosphere and chaotic debris.

She opened her mouth to scream, but the air was sucked out of her lungs in a single burst, and went dribbling away into the vacuum. She couldn't breath. Her hands went to her throat, flapping uselessly, as if vainly trying to call back the air.

Something grabbed her hand. Besides her, NotMatt was pointing desperately into his own mouth. Charlotte started at him for a moment, uncomprehending panic filling her mind. Then she realised he was pointing to the small metal coin that was lodged there. Desperately, she pressed her own hand into her mouth. There was a hissing, bubbling sensation. Suddenly, her lungs were filling with air again. Somehow, the coin was manufacturing air. Charlotte fought to control the beating of her heart, and concentrated on keeping her mouth shut, so the air would fill her lungs.

The structure of the ship shuddered again, then air was hissing back inside the craft. But whatever atmosphere this was, it wasn't normal. It smelt sour and was tinged with green, like a thick, muggy fog rising off a swamp. Charlotte was very thankful for the strange little coin.

"They've re-sealed the hull," observed EB, his voice sounding oddly deep and flat in the alien atmosphere. "That means they'll be boarding any second."

"But...but why?" asked Charlotte. "What do they want?"

"Oh, they only want their stuff back," said NotMatt, sounding much more relaxed now that they had survived the loss of the atmosphere.

"Well, that and the honourable death business," put in EB.

"What stuff?" asked Charlotte.

NotMatt waved a hand vaguely.

"Oh, you know," he said breezily. "Just some bits and bobs. A few artefacts. Some old bits of stone and suchlike."

All that sounded rather implausible to Charlotte, given the fact that they had just been hunted down, shot with a missile, and boarded without an overabundance of concern for if they suffocated or not. She was just about to point this out, when, with a great rending of metal, one whole side of the spaceship was peeled backwards, and a bright spotlight shot through the hole.

Charlotte shielded her eyes with one hand, and peered into the light.

A tall, bulky shape shouldered its way inside. It glowered at them. Then it pressed a button somewhere in the vicinity of its head, and the same voice they had heard earlier over the intercom boomed out.

"Greetings, alien scum!" it announced. "I am Head Frog 127. I arrest you both in the name of the Frogopolis, and declare you prisoners! You will be transported at all speed back to the home planet, there to await the pleasure of His Glorious Majesty, King Toadflaps III."

NotMatt turned to EB, and gave a hopeful smile.

"You hear that, EB?" he hissed. "Looks like this guy's overlooked you."

But EB wasn't looking happy.

"Take the humans into custody," Head Frog 127 ordered. As the bulky figure turned away, a swarm of smaller creatures swam inside the breached ship, and made their way towards Charlotte.

Head Frog 127 paused.

"And kill the pet," he added.

Charlotte's eyes widened in horror. She turned to EB. For one moment he stared back at her, his face sanguine and proud. One of his eyelids flickered. Then someone fired a gun, and the black cat vanished into a white ball of fire.

❧ 6 ❧

Matt stirred in the darkness. For a moment, his mind was blank, just filled with a lovely, gentle warmth.

They had done it!

They were married!

It had gone without incident - well, without major incident, anyway - and all the months of preparation had been worth it.

He felt himself relax, luxuriating in the sensation of the soft bed beneath his body, of the warmth of the woman he loved next to him beneath the sheets.

Things had gone well. The best man's speech had been less vicious than he had feared. No major fights had occurred, the food had been spectacular, and the dancing - the dancing had been great. He remembered the smiling faces, bodies jumping up and down, the band playing, heat and light filling the air, music and laughter and love...

How long ago was that? It seemed like a lifetime back, but it was still dark outside. It was summer, and dawn came early. The middle of the night, then. What had woken him?

He listened carefully. Outside, all was still. He could hear the tinkle of water running in the little stream under the window of their bridal suite. Otherwise, things were silent. No cars stirred the midnight air. It felt altogether special. Beside him, he could hear his fiancée - no, his wife! - as she breathed gently in and out. She sounded asleep, deeply asleep.

What had woken him then?

A sudden suspicion gripped him, and he gave his bladder an experimental squeeze.

Nope. That wasn't it. Still empty, even after all those glasses of home-brewed ale. He grinned in the darkness, silently congratulating himself on the capacity of his urinary tract.

What then?

Not that it mattered.

He decided to forget about it. He rolled over, putting an arm around Charlotte.

And froze.

He had been expecting to touch her warm skin, but instead his hand had encountered a rough, strange-feeling garment. It was very odd. It didn't feel like cloth, it didn't feel like silk. Not like cotton, or like a towel, or like...well, like anything, really.

And why was she still fully dressed, anyway?

This was one mystery too much for him. Matt was a man who misliked mysteries, unless they were of his own making.

He reached out and thumbed his phone on, filling the room with soft reddish light. He looked at the woman sleeping beside him.

His wife.

But his smile faded a little as he looked closer. Yes, she was wearing a very strange outfit. A jacket with mismatched lapels, and on her head, a jaunty cap. It rather suited her. But why was she wearing it?

He reached out and gently removed the cap. What material was this? It felt strange beneath his fingers.

He moved to put it back, and froze.

When had she cut her hair?

He stared, aghast. He *loved* her hair! It had been so long when they stood before the alter, when they danced in the middle of their friends, so long and gorgeous...

But it was half as long now as it had been a few hours ago! Had she done it just before coming to bed? How was that even possible? And - when had she had the blonde highlights put in?

He blinked in confusion.

Then he shrugged. His head still felt a bit thick. Perhaps he was still drunk.

Yes, that was it. He must still be drunk. He was sure there was a perfectly rational explanation for all of this. Furthermore, said explanation could certainly wait for the morning, when there would be a delicious breakfast and further merrymaking and...

Her eyes were open.

She was staring at him.

Matt started to smile...then froze.

Her eyes.

Her eyes were...blue.

Blue as crystals. Blue as the sea.

Which of course, wasn't right.

Charlotte had *brown* eyes.

He loved her eyes. He had always loved her eyes.

And those eyes certainly weren't hers.

"Where am I?" asked Charlotte.

And her voice was...

Her voice was *almost* right.

Almost. Not quite.

There was a little less husk there, a little more nasal resonance, it was all just...

Just *wrong*.

The woman who was nearly Charlotte sat up in the bed. She glanced around. Her movements were quick, abrupt, businesslike.

"I said, where am I?" the woman repeated.

Matt opened his mouth. Then he realised that, without meaning to, he had edged to the back of the bed, as far away from her as he could get without falling onto the floor.

"Um," said Matt. "The bridal suite?"

He didn't mean it to, but it came out as a question.

The woman who was nearly Charlotte nodded. She glanced around, and flipped a switch, filling the room with light.

Matt squinted in the sudden brightness.

"I see," said the woman. "And who are you?"

Her voice wasn't cold. In fact, it was quite friendly. Or rather, it would have been friendly, if it had been a stranger who was talking to him.

But it wasn't a stranger.

It was his wife.

Then he understood.

Matt broke into a foolish grin.

Of course. It was just like Charlotte, really. A little bit of drama. A little joke. She had probably been planning it for months. Her bridesmaids were almost certainly in on it. There might even be a camera hidden somewhere.

She was playing a game.

"Oh, it's like that, is it?" he said. "I see. Well. I'm your husband. I imagine you have amnesia."

She raised an eyebrow. There wasn't a smile there, not

exactly. But there was the hint that a smile was lurking, just beneath the surface.

That made sense. It was a joke. Just an elaborate joke. Matt felt himself relax.

"So you proposed in this version, then," said Charlotte. "Typical. Always seems to be the way. Every version but mine."

Matt smiled. The joke was more detailed than he had expected. Versions? That sounded inventive.

"So it's not amnesia, is it?" he asked. "Is it parallel realities then?"

NotCharlotte gave him a crisp almost-smile.

"Something like that," she said.

He opened his mouth to carry on with the game, but she was sliding out of bed. She paced up and down the room, exploring it, opening draws, looking out the window. For the moment, he seemed to be completely forgotten.

He slipped out of bed himself and stood, feeling a little cold in his best boxer shorts and nothing else but skin.

He had to hand it to her. She was really giving him the works A very committed performance. He looked on in admiration as she opened her cosmetics draw, withdrew a perfume, gave it a spray, looked surprised, sniffed, and drew back with her nose wrinkled.

"Wherever this is, you have some strange tastes in scents," she said. Then she shook her head, and continued the inventory of the room.

Matt loitered by the end of the bed, waiting for her to round on him, waiting for the next sign that the joke was continuing or - hopefully, he began to feel - was about to be wound up.

After a few minutes of being totally ignored, however, Matt decided things had gone too far.

He yawned theatrically.

"Well, this is all very nice," he said. "But we've got a long day tomorrow. Not that I don't appreciate all the effort you've gone to, fixing up this elaborate joke, but..."

He grinned as she turned to face him.

She wasn't smiling.

"It's no joke," she said.

But even though it clearly was, Matt found his smile faltering.

"It's not?" he asked.

"It's not," she confirmed.

He found himself getting annoyed now. Her inventiveness, her sense of playfulness were things that he loved about her, but still...there were times for such things, and there were times for other things.

Like sleep, for instance.

He could really do with a little more of that.

"Fine," he said. "You carry on being Princess Thingamyjink from the Order of Galactic Twerps, and I'll just get back into bed, and..."

But she still wasn't smiling. He was hoping to raise at least a glimmer of amusement.

"I'm not Princess Thingamyjink," she told him.

"Fine," he said. "Then who are you?"

"Charlotte," said Charlotte.

She paused.

"But not the one you think," she added.

"Yes, yes, of course," said Matt, sliding back under the covers and plumping up his pillow. "The other version business. The alternate universe thing. I remember."

"Not an alternate Universe," said Charlotte. "Not exactly. It's more about...stories."

Matt raised an eyebrow. That was a little different.

"Stories, is it?" he asked.

She nodded.

He shrugged.

"Well, you can tell me all about it tomorrow," he said. "My story right now involves sleep. Goodnight."

He laid down and closed his eyes.

For a moment, he felt a little bad. After all, she had obviously gone to a great deal of effort to put this whole joke together, but really it had gone too far. It just wasn't funny, that was the thing.

The pillow felt so soft.

He sighed contentedly.

Then her hand grabbed him around the ankles.

He opened his mouth to protest, and then he was being yanked out of the bed, pulled downwards with much greater strength that he would have deemed his wife capable of.

The sheets slipped under him, then he was flying out of the bed, shooting across the room and slamming into the cupboards opposite.

He slid to the floor in a battered heap.

"Ow," he said, with feeling. "Why the hell did you do...?"

But before he could finish the sentence, she was striding across the room. She grabbed him by the neck and hauled him into the air.

He dangled there. Several feet off the ground.

She was holding him there, seemingly without much effort.

He stared at her. He thought his eyes were about to pop out of their sockets.

He took in her short hair. The blonde highlights. The blue eyes. The bone structure that was *almost* right.

And then there was the superhuman strength, of course.

"Who...who are you?" he gasped.

"I told you," she said. "I'm Charlotte. But not the one you think."

She leant closer, fixing him with those piercing blue eyes.

"*Now do you believe me?*" she asked.

Matt found himself nodding, unable to speak.

She let him go, and he slid down the wardrobe to the floor.

"What's going on?" he asked. "Where are you from?"

"I thought I told you that, too," she said. Her voice wasn't unkind, now that she had his attention, now that he believed her. "I'm from a different version. A different story. A different version of your story. Of *our* story. There's been a mix up. *Again*."

She said the last word with an obvious sense of frustration.

"What...what are you doing here?" he managed to get out.

She shook her head.

"I'm not sure," she admitted. "But I have suspicions. We thought we'd ironed out all the bugs, we thought this sort of thing wasn't going to happen anymore. But it *has* happened. So we must have missed something..."

She trailed off, looking thoughtful.

Matt opened his mouth to ask what she meant, when a sudden, horrible thought occurred to him.

His mouth went dry.

"Where's Charlotte?" he asked. His voice was strained. "*My* Charlotte, I mean. My wife. Where is she?"

NotCharlotte gave him a sideways glance.

"She's where I should be," she said. "That's the way it works. Things get...mixed up."

"Is she...is she safe?" he asked.

NotCharlotte looked away.

"I'm sure she's fine," she said. But Matt didn't like something about the way she said it. She didn't meet his eye.

"But we need to get her back!" he said. "We need to!"

NotCharlotte nodded.

"We will," she said. "We always manage to sort these things out. One way or another."

She sighed.

Matt was frantic. How could she look so calm? How could she not feel the panic that was beating off him in waves?

"Come on, then!" he said at last. "How? How do we do it?"

But she just shook her head.

"It's not as simple as that," she told him.

"What?" he asked. "What do you mean?"

She hesitated, thinking.

"This world," she said. "This...this *version*. Tell me, you have a lot of...machines here, don't you?"

Matt frowned. What was she getting at?

"Yes," he allowed. "I suppose so. But what does that..."

"And most of those machines are made out of - what?"

Matt blinked. Why was she talking about this? What difference did it make?

"Iron, I suppose," he said at last. "Or steel. Or..."

But she was speaking over him.

"I thought so," she said. "When you live in a version like mine, you can always smell the iron when you end up somewhere else."

"Are you telling me there's no iron where you come from?" he asked.

"Oh, no," she said. "There's lots of it. Of a certain version. A certain *isotope*. But it's not the same as in your world. No, this world...this is an *inwards* world."

"Inwards?" Matt wrinkled his nose. "What do you mean?"

"I mean, this world, this version, this *reality*....it turned itself inwards. A long time ago. Probably hundreds and hundreds of years ago. That's what happens to worlds like these, one way or another. Iron. It always ends in iron, and lots of it. It...impedes things. It binds things in place. It prevents easy passage."

Matt squeezed his eyes shut and shook his head, trying to clear it.

"Look," he said at length. "Can you please just tell me - in very simple language - how we can go about getting my Charlotte back? Preferably in a way that doesn't include reference to elemental metals," he added.

NotCharlotte smiled at him, sadly.

"We can't," she said. "There's just too much iron here. There's no room for sliding."

Matt stared at her, waiting for her to go on. But she just sat down.

He moved next to her, tried to force her to look him in the eye.

"What, then?" he asked. "What do we do? I refuse to give up on the woman I love just because I drive an Astra!"

She looked at him.

"We wait," she said.

"Wait?" he repeated. "Wait for what?"

"For *my* version of *you*," she said. "He'll find me. Have no fear about that."

She hesitated. She frowned.

"Well, either he will, or my cat," she amended.

Matt slumped down, deflated.

"Fine," he said. "Fine. We wait. But can't we do anything?"

"Oh yes," said Charlotte. "Two things. And we must do them, or the whole business is bound to fail."

"Really?" asked Matt. "What two things?"

"First," said not-Charlotte, "we have to construct a beacon."

"A beacon? What good is that?"

"The Storystream," said Charlotte, then frowned. "The *Universe*," she amended. "The Universe is full of versions. So many versions, all jostling for space, all jostling to be noticed. If we don't set up a beacon of some kind, there's no hope of us ever being found."

Matt nodded. He was relived to find that this at least made some kind of sense.

"And second?" he asked.

NotCharlottes smile faded.

"The second thing is harder," she said. "Especially considering that we have to do the first, too."

"What is it?" said Matt.

"We have to *not* get noticed," she said.

"What do you mean? That doesn't make any sense. Not get noticed by what?"

"By the story," she told him. "Or by the people who look after the stories. By the Sheriffs."

"What are you talking about?" he asked. "What story?"

She sighed, as if explaining something simple to someone very stupid.

"This story," she told him. "*Your* story. The story of your life - yours and Charlotte's. We're all in one, you know. Like it or not, that's the essentially squiggly nature of reality."

"I'm in a story," repeated Matt. The words echoed around his head. They seemed to mean less every time they were said.

"Oh yes," said Charlotte. "And if it realises that something is amiss - or if the Sheriffs do - then we'll be expelled and cast out before you can say *just married*."

Matt put his head in his hands and sighed.

He could hardly believe that an hour ago the biggest thing he had to worry about was making the flight for the honeymoon.

Now he had to contend with a missing wife, an imposter version with superhuman strength, and the fact that he only existed in a story.

And not just any story.

A story that would throw them out if it realised something was wrong.

Life, he reflected, was much stranger than he had previously suspected.

❦   7   ❦

Charlotte watched as the swarm of smaller froglings scuttled back and forth, retrieving the hordes of stolen artefacts and treasures to their vile spacecraft. At least, that's what she assumed they were doing. It was difficult to tell for sure through all the tears.

"This is terrible," said Matt, shaking his head as much as the network of restraining wires would allow, and casting Dour Looks at every underling creature that came within range. The fact that the creatures seemed impervious to his Dour Looks only made him look all the more dour.

There were rather a lot of restraining wires involved. The froglings seemed somewhat fond of them.

"It's...it's awful," sobbed Charlotte, and she meant it. There was a hierarchy of weirdness going on at the moment, and just because her abrupt abduction by an alien, frog-based species was pretty high up the list, that didn't mean that she had no time to be concerned for the peremptory zapping of her friend. Or what amounted to some strange version of her friend. The whole thing was rather confusing, but that only made it more upsetting, really.

"When I think of the risks I took to get this stuff, and they just march it away..." Matt trailed off in disgust.

Charlotte paused. She stopped crying. She sniffed.

"I mean," she said, in a slow, poisonous voice, "about how they just killed EB."

Matt looked at her. An expression of disbelief passed over his face.

Then he burst out laughing.

Charlotte stared at him. There was perhaps a three second period of complete surprise before the outrage kicked in.

She tried to punch him, hard, but was confounded in the act by the dense webbing of restraints which imprisoned both of them. She settled for fixing him with a Deathly Glare.

"How can you?" she asked. "How can you laugh? He was our *friend*! He was our friend and they *killed* him!"

Matt stopped laughing, looked around to check that none of the frog-creatures were listening, and then leant towards her.

"Look," he said. "You have to understand that this sort of things happens to us all the time."

"It does?" asked Charlotte, momentarily wrong-footed.

"It does," confirmed Matt. "It's all a matter of...well, it's difficult to explain. It shouldn't be. I've had to explain it before, to other versions."

Charlotte found a tingling feeling was creeping up her spine. It was quite unpleasant.

"Other versions," she said, her voice low, hoping the words would somehow make more sense the second time around.

Matt nodded.

"Oh, there's lots of versions out there," he said breezily.

"Versions of what?" asked Charlotte.

"Of all of us," Matt said simply. "You. Me. EB. Everything."

"Ah," said Charlotte, feeling she was back on safer ground. "You mean metaphysically. Philosophically, there are all lots of different versions of us. We could all become someone different, given the right circumstances."

"No," said Matt happily. "I mean, really. There are lots of versions of the Universe, and of everything in it. An infinite number, in fact."

He tried to wave a hand vaguely, was impeded by the restraint netting, and settled for swishing a finger.

"The maths are complicated," he added. "But it was EB who came up with the machine."

Now Charlotte was really feeling lost.

"The machine?" she asked.

"Yes, the drive," said Matt. He caught sight of a particularly glittery artefact being offloaded from their spaceship and looked sad for a moment.

"What drive?" asked Charlotte impatiently.

"Oh, what?" said Matt, blinking at her, the thought of glittering treasure evidently still thick in his mind. "Oh, right, yes. The Chaos Drive, of course. That powers our ship. It's why we've never been caught. We're the fastest freebooters in the whole of the Galaxy! In the whole of the *Storystream*!"

He said the last proudly and winked, an effect that was largely spoiled by the restraint netting which held his eyelids in place.

Charlotte screwed up her eyes. Her head was pounding. Suddenly, it all felt too much. It was just too strange.

"What has all this got to do with versions?" she pleaded. "Or with why it's no big deal that our friend was disintegrated?"

"It's simple," said Matt. "We're the heroes, you see, and..."

But at that moment a klaxon horn sounded through the hold. The slimy little froglings all halted, snapping to attention. There was a hissing noise.

It took Charlotte a moment to locate the source. Then she realised it was the hole leading back into their breached spaceship. It was closing. Evidently the froglings had finished retrieving all the stolen treasure. She felt something catch in her throat. True, she had only been a resident of 'their' spaceship for roughly three minutes before they had been boarded, whereupon they had been spirited away to this horrid Frogship. But at least 'their' spaceship had looked vaguely human. There were seats that supported humanoid posteriors. There were buttons and controls suitable for human hands and fingers. There was *air* suitable for human lungs.

But this...

She watched in horror as the last glimpse of the *Nippy-Whoas* vanished behind a slimy, translucent skin that seemed to grow out of the hull of the Frogship. Then there was a deep shuddering, grinding noise. Something in the bones of the craft was moving...

Glimmering behind the translucent new skin of the hull, she could just make out their old spaceship as it drifted away gently into the void.

"Oh," said Matt in a very small voice.

"What is it?" asked Charlotte. "What's 'oh'? Why is this so bad? I mean, apart from the obvious reasons," she added.

Matt gave a thoughtful, tuneless whistle.

"You know those alternative versions I mentioned?" he said. "The ones that mean it's not so surprising that you've slipped into my Universe? The ones that mean there's some hope of recovering our zapped friend?"

Charlotte nodded, though really she wasn't quite sure that Matt had made all this as clear as he seemed to think.

"Well, all of that relies on the star-drive ensconced in our ship."

There was a beeping noise. It sounded quite urgent. Charlotte didn't like it one bit.

"Yes," she said uneasily. "But can't we...well, can't you just sort of, I don't know, get us free? And then we can just nip back to our ship and..."

The beeping noise rose to a very beepy crescendo, and then there was a roar deep in the bowels of the alien ship.

A spark of light flared beyond the translucent fresh-grown hull.

Something flared forward, shooting away, sliding brilliantly into the darkness of space.

It took Charlotte about a second to realise it was a missile.

"Oh no," she said.

Then there was an explosion, so bright the entire fresh-grown hull wall was illuminated, so bright that when it vanished a moment later, her eyes were filled with vivid after-glows, purple and red and gold.

And burnt onto her retinas, inescapable, undeniable - the image of the good ship *Nippy-Whoas* being blasted to smithereens.

"Agreed," said Matt. "Oh no."

There was an empty, hopeless pause.

Then, gradually, Charlotte saw some of the worry bleed off Matt's face.

"It's still there," he muttered. "I can *feel* it."

"What?" demanded Charlotte. "No, it's not. It was just destroyed, very comprehensively. We both *saw* it."

"It must have gone with her," said Matt, clearly not paying Charlotte any attention. "She must have gotten it away, somehow. That's good. That's..."

But at that moment there was an electronic whistling noise, a door slid open, and the horrible alien leader strode into view. Matt clamped his lips shut.

Even in his thick power armour, Charlotte could see the revolting froggy shape of their captor. It made her want to be sick, but she resisted because she knew that this would be an especially bad idea in a zero-gravity situation.

"Hello again, my disgusting human friends," said Head Frog 127. His voice was muffled and modulated, strained and electronic and very, very evil.

"We're not your friends," said Matt in a sudden burst of bravado.

"Yeah," said Charlotte. "At the very most we're acquaintances."

"Acquaintances on very shaky grounds," added Matt, giving Head Frog 127 a Withering Stare.

Head Frog 127 paused, head tilted to one side.

"My apologies," he said (but very evilly, in a way that signified he didn't mean it), "my galactic language translation hub seems to have got that one wrong. Instead of 'friends' I should have said, 'prisoners due to be put to death in elaborate and painful ways'. I do hope you can forgive the miscommunication."

Charlotte swallowed.

"Yeah," whispered Matt. "That showed him."

"I thought it only fair to keep you informed as to your circumstance," went on Head Frog 127. "Having destroyed your vile alien craft, we are now making at all speed for Froghearth, the home world of the Frogopolis. There you will be questioned. If you cooperate, it is just possible that we will allow you the honour of a painful death."

"Wait a minute," said Matt. "You already promised we were to be put to death painfully."

"True," agreed Head Frog 127. "But it's a matter of how honourable the death is. That it will be painful is a foregone conclusion."

"I see," said Matt with dignity. "Thank you for clarifying that."

"The transit time will be approximately five of your human hours," said Head Frog 127. "I suggest you use this time to accept your coming termination, and make peace with whatever fictitious, feeble gods you choose to worship. For now, goodbye."

And with that, Head Frog 127 turned and strode from the chamber. There was a collective drawing of breath when he was gone, and Charlotte realised that the assorted smaller Froglings were almost as terrified of Head Frog 127 as she was.

"Well, I suppose that's it then," she said. "Five hours. And then we die horribly."

She paused, reflecting on the fact that twenty four hours ago, the biggest thing she had to worry about was whether the wedding band would turn up on time.

Life was very odd. Priorities changed all the time.

She turned to Matt. To her surprise, he was smiling.

"What is it?" she asked.

He looked at her, eyes twinkling. His smile was infectious. She found she was smiling, too.

She couldn't say why, but all at once things didn't seem quite so bad.

"What is it?" she repeated.

When he told her, she didn't believe him.

Of course she didn't.

How was it possible that he could know something like that? And something like that...wasn't even *possible*, was it?

Was it?

But even though Charlotte told him he was crazy, she

couldn't help but feel a little - just a little - less completely hopeless.

After all, she told herself, stranger things had happened to her already that day.

Who was she to question one more way in which the universe had grown suddenly ludicrous?

8

Head Frog 127 removed his helmet and let out a long, weary sigh. He pressed a few buttons, and a pleasant hissing noise reverberated around his personal pleasure chamber, announcing the arrival of several jets of pungent swamp-gas.

Head Frog 127 relaxed, breathing in deeply.

Ah, that was better. The scents of his home-world washed over him, bringing back memories of his time as a frogling, the seemingly endless days of romping through muggy, putrid mists, the constant, beautiful fight for survival, the intricate webs of betrayal and intrigue...

Oh, childhood was such a wonderful time.

He smiled.

And yet he fancied his adulthood would prove more wonderful still.

He blinked his large, watery eyes, and held aloft the alien artefact.

It was an odd thing, about as big as a closed fist, but strangely heavy, spun about with glittering, flashing light and strands of circuitry. It had been housed in a battered old box -

thin metal with many dents telling of frequent kicks, if he was any judge - and he considered himself a judge of kicks indeed, having given not a few in his eventful life.

His lips slobbered and slithered, a fine, excited bubbling of mucous coating the inside of his mouth as he contemplated his victory.

At last! At last, he had achieved what he had been planning for so long! At one time, it had seemed such a far-off dream, such an impossible goal.

To win out over the notorious alien ship, the *Nippy-Whoas*! Freebooters famed throughout the galaxy, thought to be virtually unstoppable, untraceable...

And he had done it! Him!

Head Frog 127!

Oh, he would receive accolades for this, he would surely be heaped in glory. The nay-sayers would have to accept him now, there was no doubt. And then, there was the hand of the Princess to consider...

A mean little beeping noise interrupted his thoughts of glory.

The console at his side was flashing.

Head Frog 127 let out a hiss.

There was never any time! That was the problem. No time to enjoy his victories, no time to properly wallow in the anticipation of the larger victories yet to come.

But soon. Soon he would be in a position to avoid such nonsense. Soon he would be able to push aside the other pretenders, the fools, the tricksters - to push aside all those who sought to put him down, and take his rightful place as...

But no.

He mustn't let himself be distracted by dreams. Not yet. Things were too delicate.

And he couldn't afford to spurn the creature who had made all these victories possible. Not yet. No, for now he must still pretend to show respect, must give the impression of gratitude - of servitude, even!

He burped, the thought rankling in his gut like a rotten worm.

For a moment he choked, drool dripping from his lips, his yellow eyes glittering poisonously in the dim marsh-light of his boudoir.

Then he pushed the bile down, swallowed, arranged himself.

No.

He could not risk such flippancy. He must control himself at all times in his dealings with this one.

With the...the Prophet.

Head Frog 127 flicked the communicator panel.

"What is it?" he demanded, though he knew quite well who was calling. He had been expecting the call, expecting it from the moment the plan had worked, from the moment the fake, hollow treasure had been activated, disrupting the Chaos field, and allowing the missile to track the alien craft across the vast distances the ship had been fleeing.

A nervous voice croaked through the intercom.

"Um...please sir...sorry sir...but..."

The voice was hesitant, nauseatingly servile, disgustingly strained.

"Pull yourself together!" snapped Head Frog 127. "Are you a man or are you a frog? And to be clear, the answer better be, 'I'm a frog' or I will be personally seeing to the removal of your innards!"

There was a strangled, choking noise from the intercom.

"I'm sorry sir!" came the voice, sounding - if anything - even more flustered and petrified. "I'm a frog sir! I promise! One hundred percent froggy!"

Head Frog 127 paused, relishing the panic in his frogling's voice.

Then he sank back into his support pod.

"Good," he said, the words bubbling slickly from his mouth. "Good. I believe you. For now."

There was a sigh of relief from the intercom.

Head Frog 127 waited just long enough for his underling to think that the worst threat had passed, then stabbed his head forward.

"Well?" he hissed. "What is it? Why do you disturb my repose? I can have you stripped of muscle and gene-spliced back into a tadpole in thirty seconds, ensign! Don't think I wouldn't do it!"

The intercom made a terrified gurgling noise.

"Of course, my glorious leader!" rasped the frogling. "I mean, please, no, don't! But I know that you could. I mean."

The voice trailed off lamely.

Head Frog 127 waved one sticky hand vaguely. He grew tired of his sport easily these days. And who could blame him, given the great prizes now drawn so near, the horizons honing closer and closer...?

"Enough," he commanded. "Who is it. Tell me."

"It's a call, sir," came the voice. "From Froghearth. It's...it's..."

The voice faltered again, no doubt unsure what name to give the caller. This was not unusual. His underlings always treated the man with great suspicion, with trepidation. He was not trusted, certainly. Not that *anyone* was trusted in the Frogopolis, not really. But the Prophet...he was considered *canny*, even by the notoriously untrusting standards of the Frogopolis.

"It's the Prophet," said Head Frog 127 in a flat voice. "You don't need to beat around it, ensign. Put him through."

A sigh drifted over the intercom, the frogling evidently enormously relieved to be allowed to slink out of the conversation.

It was strange, Head Frog 127 reflected, as he waited for the call to come through. All the froglings on his ship knew that Head Frog 127 and the Prophet had a...*special relationship*. They all knew that Head Frog 127 had stood up for the stranger when he had first appeared at the home world, first applied for asylum. The Frogopolis never usually accepted requests for asylum, but Head Frog had pushed for it, pleaded and bribed in all the right places, and had managed - just - to curry enough favour to make it so. And he had done all this because of the promises. The whispers, the pledges...the mystical opportunities the Prophet had painted for him.

For the Prophet had known things. Many things, many strange things it was *impossible* for him to know. He had proven his worth time and time again. And now - this latest victory - the capturing of the human starship and the price-less, unique artefact that was the Chaos Drive...

It would have been worth laying his life and reputation on the line a hundred times. Head Frog 127 had no doubt that he had made the right decision when he had stood up and spoken on behalf of the strange human.

And yet.

And yet the froglings treated the Prophet as poison, something between a threat and a fool. An air of mystique hung about the man - for man he was, as human as these vile aliens so recently intruding in Frogspace - and his underlings did not like even to ferry his calls, for fear of some inchoate evil luck that might cling to them for doing so.

The screen blinked and sprang into life, and Head Frog 127 was suddenly gazing into the likeness of the man who had made all this possible.

The Prophet stood, tall and rather slender, a cowl over his head, his piggy little human eyes glinting somewhere in the darkness.

Head Frog 127 pushed his disgust down and plastered on a fake smile.

"Ah, my dear friend," he gobbled. "It is so good of you to check in on us."

The Prophet nodded, a spasm of impatience flickering over his lips.

"Yes, yes," he muttered. His voice was light and dry, his words forcing themselves past one another. "All the best to you, and you are very pleasant and so forth. But the thing is...*did it work*? Do you have them?"

Head Frog 127 started to snarl at the human's rudeness, then turned it into a yawn.

"Have them? Oh yes, we have them," he said. "It was easily. It went just as you said it would. They snapped up all the treasure, snapped it up just where we left it. They didn't suspect a thing. And they took the disruptor without a second glance. They thought it was a piece of gold! Oh, they are foolish! I must say, I find it rather confusing why you make such a deal of them."

Head Frog 127 peered slyly from under his brows. In all the last six months of his relationship with the Prophet, he had not yet managed to wheedle out exactly *why* it was that the human wanted the freebooters so desperately. It remained a mystery, and Head Frog 127 despised mysteries. He was determined to get the truth out of the Prophet before he handed the prisoners over.

A sharp smile slipped over the ugly human face.

"This *is* good news," said the Prophet. "And what have you told them? Of me, I mean."

"Nothing, of course!" said Head Frog 127. "That's what we agreed, isn't it? They know nothing of your involvement, they have no clue that the whole thing was a set-up. They don't suspect for a moment that we lured them here with all those disseminated whispers of the great wealth of the Frogopolis.

They simply think they are being transported back to Frog-hearth for trial and...punishment."

The Prophet paused, thoughtful.

"Good," he said, after a moment. "Good. You must keep it that way. It is vital they know nothing of me, nothing at all..."

Once again, Head Frog 127 had to push down the urge to berate the Prophet for his loose tongue. Did the man not know who the leader was here? Did he not understand that he only lived, that he was only tolerated to breath because of the intervention of Head Frog 127? Oh, such risks he had taken for the man, such terrible risks...

And yet it would be worth it. Oh yes. He was quite sure of that.

He found himself weighing again the alien technology, feeling it in his hand, and he couldn't keep a smile from drifting to his lips.

"And you got what you wanted, I see," said the Prophet, his gimlet eyes fixing on the shimmering Chaos-drive in Head Frog 127's hand.

Head Frog 127 blinked.

He had to watch himself around the Prophet. Why did he always forget? The human was sharper than he looked, much sharper. He hadn't meant for the Prophet to see how happy he was to have pilfered the Chaos drive for himself.

"It was where you informed me it would be," Head Frog 127 said. "It was not difficult for my froglings to disengage. And the ship...the ship is now destroyed. No doubt these humans you are so fond of will think their Chaos Drive destroyed also."

There was hissing noise from the monitor. Head Frog 127 blinked in surprise. The Prophet was glaring at him, actually *glaring*. He had never seen the man so angry before.

"They are no friends of mine!" he hissed. "No, after what

they did to me...Never, never call them friends! No, they will pay..."

Head Frog 127 watched as the Prophet visibly mastered himself. He took some deep breaths, he leant back, his cowl slipping further forward over his features.

"No matter," he said. "Words are nothing. The important thing is you have them. *Matt*," he went on, his voice dripping poison, "and *Charlotte*. Not to mention that ridiculous cat of theirs..."

Head Frog 127 shook his head.

"Not the cat," he said flatly. "The cat we terminated. We don't allow pets on *The Pondwater*."

The Prophet froze.

"What?" he said. His voice was icy cold.

Head Frog 127 shrugged.

"We killed it," he said. "Blasted the wretch. I gave the order myself."

The Prophet took several deep breaths. Head Frog 127 realised the man was struggling to master himself again.

"That was ill-done," said the Prophet at last.

Head Frog 127 couldn't keep his emotions in check any more.

He cackled loudly, his rough, wet laughter echoing around the inside of his pleasure pod.

"Oh, you are a strange one," he chuckled. "You hate these humans, yet you cry for their pet? It was a small thing, mangy and ill-kept. It's better off dead. The thing was an insult to the perfection of my race!"

The Prophet glared at him, unsmiling.

"You do not understand in what you are meddling," the Prophet said. "Did I not tell you to capture them *unharmed*? *All* of them?"

Head Frog 127 rolled his eyes.

"Yes, you did," he admitted, "but I hardly thought your words applied to that vile little fur-ball."

"That creature," said the Prophet, biting off each word, "that creature was the very creature who *designed and built* the Chaos Drive you've been so desperate to get your hands on. It knows secrets we can never even guess at, it created the Drive as an expression of it's own strange inner workings, it...It... "

The Prophet bit off his words in frustration.

"I just hope you haven't undone everything," finished the Prophet. He hung his head.

"Oh, come on," said Head Frog 127. "You can't be serious. It's a *cat*."

There was a pause.

"We say something on Earth about cats, you know," said the Prophet. "Something about how many lives they have."

Head Frog 127 found he was getting bored. He needed the Prophet, it was true. And he never would have gotten this far without him, never would have hoped to claim such a prize as the Chaos Drive, and there was no other individual - human, frog or otherwise - who was so privy to the extent of his plans and ambitious.

And yet...

And yet the man was tiresome.

"Whatever, Prophet," he said. "In any case, I am busy. I have many matters to see to. You should prepare yourself for our arrival. The moment you have awaited for so long is at hand."

The Prophet perked up a bit at that.

"Yes," he said. "Yes, that's true. I also have matters to which I must attend. Until we meet in the flesh, Head Frog 127."

The Prophet raised a hand in salute. Head Frog 127

thought it disgusting, with its long pink fingers and dry skin, quite devoid of slime.

"Goodbye, Prophet," said Head Frog 127. "We will be with you soon enough."

The connection died, and the image of the Prophet faded into blackness.

Head Frog 127 shook his head in distain.

The Prophet was clever, it was true, and he had several mysteries left to him, mysteries Head Frog 127 had not yet been able to work out. But he had no doubt that he would learn all the man's secrets, in time.

Just as he had learnt his real name.

"Goodbye...Philip," he said, speaking to the blank screen.

❧ 9 ❧

Charlotte managed not to be sick during the drop through Froghearth's atmosphere to the planet's surface, but that was only because she had been comprehensively sick during the journey through hyperspace.

Things had turned out to be much less messy than she had feared, however. As soon as she had opened her mouth to vomit, the little coin that had been quietly buzzing away and providing her with oxygen gave a shudder. Then it started sucking.

It was as simple as that.

She had blinked and tried to stare at the coin, something that was clearly impossible given its location inside her mouth. So she had settled for blinking at Matt in wide-eyed amazement.

"But...but where does it *go*?" she had managed, once the shock had worn off.

Matt had shrugged.

"Most space-faring cultures come up with things like that before they get very far out of their home systems," he had told her. "Cleaning up vomit in zero-gravity environments is not especially pleasant. Especially when there's lots of high-tech equipment about. Trust me. Carrot-looking bits end up *everywhere*."

Charlotte found herself nodding, and had only realised a few minutes later that he hadn't actually answered her question.

So that was something both her Matt and this version had in common, then.

They were both very good at seeming to explain things.

They were both exceptionally *plausible*.

Now, as the ship bucked and screamed its way through the thick atmosphere of Froghearth, as Charlotte's stomach heaved and pleaded desperately for something to be sick with, she found herself thinking of her Matt, and trembling.

What was he doing? What was he going through? Had he made contact with the other version of Charlotte, the one that belonged in this Universe?

If so, what were they doing?

She was pretty sure that whatever it was, it wasn't as unpleasant as this.

She missed him.

The ship gave a final, bone-crunching lurch, and silence descended. The only noise was the creaking and straining of metal as the ship cooled and contracted around them.

"See, I told you it wouldn't be so bad," said Matt. His hair was tangled, his eyes bulging out of the sockets. A thin sheen of sweat covered his face. He had obviously been making good use of his coin, too.

"Blurghhhphatarrrr," said Charlotte conversationally.

She shook her head, blinked a few times, and tried again.

"Awful," she muttered. "Just awful."

There was a beeping noise, and the doors slid open. A

work-crew of Froglings marched in and began unstrapping them both from the sticky restraining ropes. All the while, a host of other Froglings kept them covered with an array of large, shiny, and especially nasty-looking guns of the huge-and-terrifying variety.

"Oh, it was fine," said Matt. "Stop being melodramatic."

The Froglings finished unwrapping them.

"Ow," complained Charlotte. "Mind the hair!"

"Sorry," said one of the Froglings.

"We're not used to it, see," muttered one of the others.

They were marched through a seemingly endless series of dark, dank corridors. A thin green mist hung at foot level. Jets of foul smelling marsh-steam sprayed out on them seemingly at random. It smelt awful, but the Froglings seemed to delight in it. They were much more relaxed now, Charlotte reflected. Almost friendly.

"You know, you seem like good chaps, deep down," said Matt as they were bustled beneath yet another bulkhead. "I wonder if you've considered all your...ah...options. In the current circumstances, I mean."

They came to a set of huge metal doors. One of the Froglings keyed in a sequence on a pad, and the doors slid open, revealing a vast, derelict elevator.

"Oh, you know how it is," said one of the Froglings. "The vagaries of interstellar space travel. The loneliness of those in service. The relief at an unexpected chance at shore-leave. It puts us all in a good mood."

"Yes, yes, exactly," said Matt as they were ushered inside. The doors slid closed, then the elevator gave a shudder, and they were suddenly zooming upwards. "But what I mean is, have you given much thought to your position here? I am a rich man, you know."

Charlotte looked on as a single light rose up a columnar display in the wall of the elevator. They were obviously climbing rapidly. What was at the top, she wondered?

"We feel for you, we really do," said another of the Froglings, "the thing is, it's more than our skins are worth, to let you go free."

"That's right," said another. This one had a particularly evil-looking laser assault rifle. As he spoke, he used the barrel to scratch his broad nose. "And the other thing you have to remember is, we get such little entertainment on board ship."

"Sure, sure," said Matt. He was smiling, but Charlotte could see the sweat on his brow, the way his eyes darted around the inside of the elevator, as if looking for a way out. "But, look. I'm...I'm *connected*. You dig? Just tell me what you want. Money. Power. Girls."

"Actually, we're hermaphrodites," pointed out one of the Froglings, not unkindly. "At least, until we are fully mature."

"Ah, yes, right, yes," said Matt.

The elevator ground to a halt. The little light was right at the top of the column now. It was flashing. Charlotte wondered if that was a good sign.

"But what if...?" Matt started to say.

"Sorry, pal," said the first Frogling. "Even if you *could* make it worth our while to let you go, you don't think we'd want to stop the show, do you?"

Charlotte frowned.

"Make it a good one," said another of the Froglings enthusiastically. "I've got a hundred green marks riding on you lasting at least five minutes."

The other Froglings nodded encouragingly

"Yes, try not to die *too* quickly," said one of them. "*Please*."

Matt opened his mouth to reply, then all the Froglings were melting away, dashing backwards and through service doors hidden in the side of the huge elevator.

"Wait!" shouted Matt after them. "Just think about..."

But they were gone.

Matt shrugged.

"I nearly had the little one," he muttered. "Just a few more minutes..."

Charlotte was hardly listening to him. A feeling was growing inside her, a nasty, nasty feeling. The feeling that she really *really* didn't want to be here any longer. Not at the top. Not right at the top of...of wherever it was they had been brought.

She rushed to the service doors and tried them one after another.

Locked. They were all locked.

"Damn," she said. She cast around, looking for a way out, any way out...

And that was when she noticed the ceiling.

It was...changing.

At first, she couldn't put her finger on it.

Then she realised it was shimmering, *thinning* somehow, melting away. She remembered the strange gloopy substance that had sealed off the hole leading into the good ship *Nippy-Whoas*.

They used really strange materials here in the Frogopolis.

She glanced over to Matt, opened her mouth to ask him if he had any ideas, and froze.

Matt was sitting, cross-legged, seemingly totally at his ease. As she watched, he retrieved a tobacco pouch from inside his - considerably ruffled - jacket, and began making a nasty-looking roll-up.

"What," she said in tones of trembling, barely-controlled anger, "the hell are you doing?"

Matt glanced up at her, giving her an astonished, *what, me?* look, and turned back to regard the emerging cigarette.

"I tried my best," he told her. "And it didn't work. So we have to just relax and rely on plan B."

Charlotte marched over to him, hands on her hips.

"Oh, yes," she said. "The fabled Plan B. The one you were so happy to tell me about earlier. The one involving coded messages that only you can hear. Very reassuring, I must say."

But even as she said it, she found herself wondering. It sounded so, so unlikely. Impossible. And yet...

"That's the one," said Matt, seemingly oblivious to the sarcasm. "Don't you worry. He's gotten us out of stickier situations before."

For a moment she thought she was about to explode with anger.

Then she wilted.

"What the hell," she said, slumping down next to him and snatching the finished roll-up out of his hand. "I suppose things have been weird enough. Waiting for an invisible saviour that only you can communicate with is equally implausible, I suppose."

The light was changing. Above them, the layer of...of whatever the ceiling was made of was growing more translucent almost by the second. Peering up, Charlotte thought she could make sense of the shapes. It looked like...like they were at the bottom of a vast bowl? There were huge, sloping sides, leading up to rows upon rows of seats. She thought she could discern shapes, little froggy figures moving and jabbering away excitedly.

It was almost as if they were in the centre of a stadium.

Or an amphitheatre.

A sick little knot of fear twisted in her stomach.

"I have a bad feeling about this," she said, unnecessarily.

Something beeped in the corner of the room.

Charlotte jumped to her feet, frowning.

It beeped again. She walked over to it, Matt trailing along at her side, trying vainly to retrieve his apprehended cigarette.

A little red button was flashing urgently, next to a dark screen.

Charlotte stared at it suspiciously. Then she hit it.

At once, the screen gave an unhappy little fizzing noise and jumped to life.

Charlotte drew back before she could stop herself.

The face of Head Frog 127 was grinning out at her, huge and horrible, in definition so high it bordered on violence. His broad, oily lips slithered and slimed over one another, his greenish, cracked skin rolling and squelching as he masticated some horrible dainty.

"Ah, there you are," said Head Frog 127 in clipped, businesslike tones. "I do wish I had gotten a chance to thank you in person. But I am a very, very busy frog. All sorts of engagements beckon now, you see."

"Thank us?" asked Charlotte. "why would you thank us?"

Head Frog 127 grinned.

"For the elevation of my station, of course," he told them. "Why, before I captured you, I was just another Head Frog, fighting to be noticed amongst all my scheming brethren. Now, I have proven myself. I have been given a place of honour in the royal box. If I play my cards, right, who knows? There is always room for a competent, ambitious frog in His Majesty's inner circle..."

Charlotte couldn't put her finger on it, but there was something about the way he said that which made her think: *whichever Majesty he's talking about needs to watch himself.*

Not that she cared, of course. The whole of the Frogopolis could eat itself in an orgy of betrayal and intrigue for all she cared. But still...worth knowing, maybe...

"So that's it?" put in Matt. "You're just going to leave us here? To throw us to the wolves?"

"Not to the wolves, no," said Head Frog 127. "We never

evolved wolves on Froghearth. No, we evolved things that were so much worse..."

He leant back in his chair, and Charlotte saw that he was holding something in one of his horrible froggy hands. Something spindle-fine and intricate, with flashing lights and a vague sense of ephemeral elegance which seemed quite out of keeping with the technology she had seen so far in the Frogopolis.

Matt had obviously noticed it, too.

He was frowning. All hint of levity, of control had dropped from him.

"What," he said in a low voice, "have you got there?"

Head Frog 127 widened his grin, showing off rows of dark purple toothless gums.

"Oh, this?" he said, indicating the thing in his hand. "Do you mean your little toy? You didn't think I'd let *that* be blown up with your stinking spaceship, did you? The only thing of value in the whole rusty brig."

"It *didn't* go with her," Matt muttered to himself, clearly furious.

"What?" hissed Charlotte, but he ignored her.

"That," said Matt, speaking instead to Head Frog 127, "is not yours. Give it back. It's dangerous."

"Dangerous?" said Head Frog 127. "Oh, I'm counting on it. Very dangerous, to my enemies."

But Matt was shaking his head.

"It's not a toy," said Matt carefully. "It's the *Chaos Drive*. It's not just dangerous to your enemies. It's dangerous to the whole *Storystream.*"

A frown puckered at Head Frog 127's sinewy brows.

"To the what?" he demanded.

Matt shook his head.

"To the Universe, I mean. To the whole of the Universe."

Matt's voice had gone serious, deadly serious, more

pleading and sincere than Charlotte had ever heard it before. Head Frog 127 was scowling, a look of uncertainty on his face.

Charlotte could feel Matt by her side holding his breath, anxiety marking furrows down his face.

Then Head Frog 127 laughed.

"Oh, you're *good*," he said. "Very good. I mean, I'd heard about you, but even so you nearly had me there. That bit about it being not the Universe, that Story...whatever it was. Nice touch."

"No, wait..." Matt started to say, but Head Frog 127 leaned forward.

"No, *you* wait," he hissed. "I'm not listening to another word. I just wanted to make contact before the end. Not to wish you a noble death - we all know that's not going to be possible. No, I wanted you to know that I have your precious little toy. I wanted your last moments to be filled with the knowledge that *I* beat *you*! I wanted you to know that..."//

//and then the whole word shuddered and froze.

Charlotte looked around, blinking.

Above them, the figures behind the translucent curtain, all the froggy figures arrayed about them in the huge, rough circle...they had all frozen.

There was no movement. There was not a sound.

"What the hell is going on...?" asked Charlotte.

Matt shook his head.

Charlotte looked again at the screen containing Head Frog 127.

Only Head Frog 127 was gone. In his place was a strange tall figure, robed in black, a cowl obscuring much of his face. She thought she caught dark eyes glinting out at them.

The figure tilted its head.

"So," it said. "It appears I have been betrayed. Yet again."

"What...who are you?" asked Charlotte.

The man's face twitched, and Charlotte thought she caught a glimpse of a smile in the shadows.

"Do you really not know?" said the figure. He peered closer, examining them.

Charlotte started shaking her head in protest, but the figure was already leaning back. She could practically see the wheels spinning, whizzing round in his dark eyes.

"It doesn't matter," said the figure. "Just know that you have, ah, have a *friend*."

As he said the word, he smiled. It was a sickening sort of smile, the kind of smile that looked like it had been explained by someone who had no notion of what a smile really was, or why it might happen. Charlotte realised that she mistrusted this apparition already, whatever it said about being friends.

"A friend?" asked Charlotte. "What do you mean?"

But the figure was shaking his head.

"No, that's not the question. The real question is, how will I get to you, now that he's betrayed me? I mean," he amended quickly, "how will we *save* you. And then, of course, we must work out how to punish him."

Matt was nodding now. He seemed suddenly on board with the whole thing.

"Punish Mr Froggy," he said. "Yes, good. I don't know who you are, but I like the cut of your jib..."

"Oh, and I like *yours*," said the figure, bringing out his awful smile once more. "So we must make sure that this...this traitorous frogling doesn't punish you too terminally."

"What?" demanded Matt. "Why would he want to punish me? I'm delightful."

But the figure just shook his head.

"Oh, we will have time to talk it all through," he said. Then he paused. "Just see that you survive this, and I will come for you. I promise. "

Charlotte found herself wondering why she really, really hoped that this man did *not* keep that particular promise.

"Survive?" asked Matt. "Survive what?"

"Oh, you will see," he told her. "They are a brutish race, the frogs. But they are, shall we say...inventive..."

"Wait," said Matt, "maybe we can..."//

//but with a flickering, tearing noise, the figure was gone. Above them, all was movement and fuss again.

On the screen, Head Frog 127 was grinning at them.

"...to know that I won."

Head Frog 127 finished speaking. Then he gave them a little wave.

"Goodbye!" he said. "Try not to die *too* quickly!"

The screen flashed and went black.

Charlotte stared at Matt.

"What the hell was that all about?" she asked.

But at that moment a klaxon call rolled out, a huge swelling of noise breaking on them like a storm wave on a rocky shore.

Looking up, Charlotte saw that the final strands of the translucent ceiling had dissolved.

It *was* an amphitheatre. A great, wide amphitheatre. Row upon row of cheering, jeering Froglings surrounded them, shouting things, cursing, screaming in their horrible jabbering language.

The ground shuddered, and the lift rose up a few more feet, then the walls dropped away.

They were alone in the centre of the vast theatre.

Matt looked at her.

"So," he said. "Do you know any tunes?"

But she had no time to answer, because at that moment a horn sounded, huge and horrible. The next moment, a gate at the far end of the amphitheatre creaked open.

There was a roar.

There was one horrible, hanging moment, when Charlotte could see the darkness, and could feel the weight of *something* within, staring out at them.

Then it bounded out of the darkness, faster than seemed possible, huger and more horrible than any natural creature she had ever seen, ever imagined.

Charlotte screamed.

🦎 10 🦎

Head Frog 127 squelched back comfortably in his seat of honour. He couldn't wipe the smile from his face.

He was here! He had done it!

He glanced around, taking in the other occupants of the royal box. In the very centre, in the place of highest honour sat the glorious monarch himself.

King Toadflaps III was a vast, horrible frog, even by the notoriously horrible standards of the Frogopolis. He had once been tall and rather splendid, but the years had sunken his vast frame, so that he seemed to have been melted inside a sticky green froggy skin, eyes and nose sunken in folds of excess flesh, mouth out-turned and protruding. A thin stream of snot dripped continuously from his nose and lips, from whence it was sucked up by young, aristocratic froglings who fought and snapped with one another for the honour of performing such a role.

As if feeling his regard, King Toadflaps III turned slowly in his ornate, soggy throne and gave him a brief, unsmiling nod. Head Frog 127 bared his gums in a sycophantic grin, and bowed his head.

Oh, the old frog was *weak*. Head Frog 127 could almost feel the waves of decrepitude and vulnerability washing off the ancient king. This was the closest he had ever been to such exalted power, and the thought of all his carefully-laid plans being so close to fulfilment made him feel dizzy.

As he watched, King Toadflaps III frowned, turned away and coughed up a ball of green mucous. Head Frog 127 noted that it was streaked with blood, before it was slurped up by one of the attendant froglings.

Weak. Oh, ripe for the plucking.

All he had to do was bide his time, choose his moment, and...

But his eye was drawn from the hunched, mouldering shape of King Toadflaps, pulled away as if summoned by higher forces.

She was beautiful. Oh, so beautiful.

Tall and slender at the waist, with a comely sagging pot-belly, seductively half-hidden by her flowing silken robes. Her green skin was delicately brushed up with a subtle shading of artificial colours, and her pure, bald head sparkled in the red sunlight of Froghearth.

Princess Frogmella.

A dream.

A beauty to die for, a prize worth risking everything for...

...and, of course, the way to the throne.

Head Frog 127 realised he had stopped breathing.

He had seen her holo-likeness so many times, but still - to be here in the flesh, so close he could reach out and touch her...

He was aware of an annoying buzzing at his ear.

He frowned, shook his head.

"...I said, which one is the male of the species? I find them quite difficult to tell apart."

The voice came again. It was weak and quavering, but had an annoying undercurrent of urgency, as if it expected him to answer at once.

He swivelled, snarling, a sharp retort already on his tongue.

Then he realised who it was that was talking to him, and turned the sharp words into a coughing fit.

King Toadflaps. King Toadflaps was addressing *him*.

He had been so enchanted with the beauty of the princess, he hadn't even noticed the ancient frog leaning towards him.

"*If* you aren't too ashamed to talk to me, that is," King Toadflaps added, and Head Frog 127 realised with a nasty jolt that the ancient Frog was clearly still sharper than he looked. Of course he was. He had reigned as undisputed master of the Frogopolis for the last fifty years, something that would only have been possible by being subtle and sly and good at clinging on to power.

"My lord...my liege, I mean, I apologise most humbly," Head Frog 127 said, fumbling the words out. "I was just - ah - my mind was elsewhere..." he finished lamely.

King Toadflaps stared at him sternly for a few long seconds, then broke into a horrible slimy smile.

"Oh yes," he said. "I find my subordinates are often taken that way. Tell me, you have never met the Princess Frogmella before, have you?"

Head Frog 127's mouth had gone very dry, so he just shook his head, no.

"She is quite a sight, yes," said King Toadflaps, nodding his head proudly. "She will make some Froglord a fine wife one day, no doubt."

Head Frog 127 realised he was being examined keenly. He

could feel King Toadflap's cool regard on him like a physical thing. He felt like someone was peering into his soul.

He opened his mouth to reply, but King Toadflaps was already waving his hand, dismissing the matter.

"Now, what I want to know is, which one of these heathens you've brought us is the male?" King Toadflaps asked again. "They both look quite as ugly as one another, to me."

Head Frog 127 peered down into the arena, a strange mixture of relief and disappointment running through him. He thought he could talk of her for hours...though maybe not to her father.

There they stood, hunched in the centre of the stadium, surrounded by the cheering, jeering masses of Froghearth. The two aliens looked so small and helpless against the vast arena, Head Frog 127 almost felt sorry for them.

"The one with the streaks of silver in his hair is the male," he said, pointing. "He is taller, you see, his shape is different."

King Toadflaps raised an eyeglass and squinted, examining the aliens.

"Yes, yes - of course," he muttered. "Hair. How horrid. But a convenient way of distinguishing one from another. Tell me, did they give you much trouble? My advisors tell me you did a splendid job, recovering the treasure."

Head Frog 127 grinned.

"Oh, we will be the envy of the galaxy," he said, and it was true. "Of all the thefts these vile aliens have committed, of all the worlds they have plundered, we are the first victims who have ever got them! They put up a good chase, it is true, but they were no match for *The Pondwater*. Once we had blown up their engines, the rest was easy."

Head Frog 127 sat back in his chair and grinned, the kind of grin that was meant to say, *easy...but not for just anyone.*

The king nodded, satisfied.

Head Frog 127 looked back to the aliens, trying to seem cool and unruffled, as if speaking to kings and ogling their daughters was something he did every day.

He could see the panic on their faces, the tenseness, the fear. In a way, it was a shame to dispose of them like this. He had intended to give them to The Prophet, as he had promised. But the King had been insistent. He had demanded this sport at once, and there had been no time to make arrangements.

He frowned a little, and found himself wondering what The Prophet would do now. Surely, the man was not so foolish as to think he might get some kind of revenge on him, Head Frog 127. No, Head Frog 127 had made a deal with The Prophet...and he had betrayed him. And yet, the Prophet was just one man - a strange man, with strange gifts, true, but a man all the same. He was alone on an alien planet, and he could not afford to bring any kind of revenge to the one Frog of substance who had stood for him. Now that Head Frog 127 had what he wanted from the arrangement, now that he could withdraw his patronage, the Prophet would do well to slink away, get out while he could, get out and never be seen again.

And yet...

And yet Head Frog 127 could not shake the thought of the Prophet's angry eyes from his mind. He had messaged the man just before coming here, explaining the situation, even going so far as to offer a small, insincere apology. The Prophet had not had the good grace to accept it.

He had made threats.

Ludicrous threats, ridiculous threats.

But still, those eyes...

Head Frog 127 sucked his lip. Yes, he had done the right thing when he had ordered Glob to apprehend the Prophet. He had hinted that he needn't be too gentle with the man, either. Glob had never liked the Prophet. Perhaps things would escalate. It might be best that way. A dead Prophet would be much less of a complicating factor in the future, especially when he had finished unlocking the secrets of the Chaos Drive, when he was ready to put his plans in motion. Then the absence of anyone who knew anything at all of the matter would be desirable.

A warm breeze blew over the arena, carrying with it the distant animal roar of the thing caged beyond the gate. That cheered him up. Why was he worrying? Things were going well for him. Very well. He felt fortuitous, held in the hand of fate. What reason did he have to worry, really?

Everything was going his way.

"And tell me, where is your...your little *pet*?" asked King Toadflaps, as if reading his mind.

Head Frog 127 blinked, trying not to look guilty. Did the king know? Was it possible he had intercepted the coded transmission? Head Frog 127 had been careful, very careful when it came to setting up his communications with the Prophet. They had spoken of much that was...sensitive. *Could* Toadflaps have been listening in? If so, then Head Frog 127 was very much in danger. He had never spoken openly of insurrection with the human, but still...It would be better if the king had no idea of the secrets of the Chaos Drive, of the power it could offer...

"Oh, he knows better than to expect to come to such an esteemed gathering as this," Head Frog 127 found himself saying. "He did ask me, once, about being presented again to our great and our good. But after last time..."

King Toadflaps scowled, turning away, and Head Frog 127 silently congratulated himself for turning the conversation, for giving the little nudge it needed to fill Toadflaps' mind with unpleasant memories.

"That little weasel is an embarrassment!" snapped King

Toadflaps. "Honestly, the things he said - and not just to any old frogling - to some of my most noble Froglords, no less!"

Smiling inwardly, Head Frog 127 allowed himself a mournful nod.

"Yes, the Prophet really is most uncouth," said Head Frog 127. "Naturally, after that little display I made it very clear he would never be presented in public again."

"Oh! Is that what happened?" asked King Toadflaps, an angry glint in his eye. "The way the story was told to me, you were the only one protecting that ridiculous pole of a man from being ripped limb from limb."

Head Frog 127 spread his hands modestly.

"What can I say? I am, perhaps, too soft. I hate to see idiots suffer for their foolishness. The man was clearly delusional. It was my duty to protect him."

King Toadflaps gave him a long, level stare.

"Yes, you are the very model of mercy, I am sure," said the King. He gave a snort, dislodging another horrid ball of snot from a nostril and sending it careering down the vile landscape of his body and off into space.

"Oh yes, indeed," said Head Frog 127, ignoring the sarcasm, and thinking of all the effort he had gone to, him and the Prophet, the preparation, working out what would be exactly offensive enough. Talk that was designed and calibrated to stir disgust and outrage, enough to ensure that no other Frog of substance would spare the Prophet a second glance, give him another thought of patronage. No, Head Frog 127 had wanted the man all to himself, once he had realised how useful he could be. One of his conditions had been that the man play along and ensure his status as a pariah. Head Frog 127 had wanted the man dependant on him, and him alone.

King Toadflaps huffed and puffed his cheeks, evidently working out the nasty memory of reports that had come to his throne, reports of the shameful human and the Frog of substance who was vouching for him. Oh, that had been a risky game, and a black time for Head Frog 127. He had been most out of favour with the throne. If he had misjudged things, if he had upset one more courtier one iota more, if someone had spoken just a little more venomously against him...well, he would have lost everything. His command. His ship. His position. His *life*.

Yes, he had taken a risk in speaking for the Prophet. But it would be worth it. He was quite sure of that now. And remembering the risk he had taken washed away even the faintest tinge of guilt that still clung to him as to how he had treated the Prophet.

"And where is he now, then?" asked King Toadflaps, sounding somewhat mollified. "This man. This *Prophet* of ours?" He twisted the ironic honorific, the ridiculous sobriquet that the great and the good of the Frogopolis had given to the man.

"Where is he?" repeated Head Frog 127, as if considering the question for the first time. "Oh, I suppose he's just sitting somewhere quietly. Brooding on all the mistakes he has made."

Like trusting me, he added in the privacy of his head.

He thought of the broad, ugly shape of Glob. Thought of his head of security bursting into the Prophet's chambers. Maybe there would be a struggle. Maybe the Prophet would fight back...

Perhaps Glob and the Prophet would kill each other! Now that *would* be good! Head Frog 127 had been looking for a way to get rid of his chief of security for a while now. He never had trusted that sly little sneaker. Too knowing by half, and nowhere near scared enough of him.

Yes, they should both die. It was simple. It was...

But at that moment, a horn sounded out over the arena, interrupting his thoughts.

There was a moment's heavy silence, then a great roar went up from the assembled mass of frogs.

Before he knew what he was doing, Head Frog 127 found himself on his feet, arms pumping into the air, voice raised in a huge, hungry roar.

It was time.

The gate opened.

The beast was released.

❧ 11 ❧

Charlotte wondered who was screaming. It was so loud, so wild, so utterly, utterly terrified.

Then she realised it was her own scream, which made sense, because she had once had a nightmare about something similar to the creature that was bounding towards them, and at the time she had made a mental note to scream like hell if she ever saw one in real life.

The beast was...

It was difficult to describe.

It was awful, for a start. Really, really awful.

There were teeth. Lots of teeth. More teeth than the mouth was really meant to hold, and the mouth was *big*. The teeth protruded out at various angles, off-white spikes of an ivory-like substance coated with slime and ending in vicious screw-tips.

Then there were the legs. They were moving very, very fast, so Charlotte couldn't count them accurately, but there had to be - what - ten? *Twelve*?

She couldn't tell, but there were lots.

The thing was long and massive, bunched muscles moving under pert, slimy skin.

It was green, of course. Every living thing in this horrible froggy world seemed to be green. But it was striped with red, like a sort of nasty froggish tiger.

"What...what the hell *is it*?" Charlotte found herself hissing as the creature bounded towards them.

Then she wondered why she wasn't running.

She turned...but there was nowhere *to* run. The arena stretched all around them. There were no doors. There were no gates, other than the one the beast had rushed out of. There was nothing.

By her side, Matt scuffed the metal ground idly with one foot. He examined his fingernails. He peered up at the assembled frogs, a look of vague interest on his face.

"Well, I'm no expert," said Matt. "But if I had to guess, I would say it's a genetically engineered super-beast, spliced together from all the nastiest and most vicious examples of nature the Frogopolis have encountered in their long and brutal expansion through their little corner of the Universe."

The beast was roaring. It was closing on them. How long did they have before it reached them? Ten seconds? Five?

She opened her mouth to ask Matt why he seemed so relaxed, then changed her mind. He probably wouldn't have time to answer anyway.

She reached out and held his hand.

True, he wasn't actually *her* Matt, but at least he was *a* Matt.

That had to count for something.

She realised whatever she said next was going to be her last words. She wondered if they were going to be profound.

The beast bunched itself up, and leapt into the air.

It sailed towards them, claws outstretched, mouth a-snarl, teeth glinting in the red sunlight.

"Thanks for the smoke," she said.

Then it was devouring them.

Only it wasn't.

Charlotte felt the ground shake as the creature slammed into them.

Or rather, as it slammed into Matt.

Or rather, as it slammed into Matt's fist.

He had raised it at the last second, moving quicker than her eye could follow.

He had placed it at exactly the right point, so that it had slipped between two of the beast's outstretched claws, held at the exact point in space where the beast's horrible green forehead had arrived.

And the beast stopped.

For a moment it just hung there, hung in the air like an insect pinned in a collector's book.

Matt's arm didn't budge an inch.

Then its huge, horrible body was buckling around it, shockwaves of arrested momentum shimmering and sliding across the green bulk, reverberating across the skin.

Charlotte stared at Matt, mouth agape, feeling as if her eyes were bulging out of their sockets.

He looked completely relaxed. He didn't look as if he were dicing with death, he didn't look as if he were locked in mortal combat with a strange, hellish beast from beyond the ken of man.

He looked like a put-upon landlord dealing with an annoying - but ultimately harmless - drunk.

Then the beast was falling, sliding bonelessly to the metal floor. There was no blood, and Charlotte wasn't sure if Matt had killed the thing - killed it with a single blow, killed it with its own momentum - or if it was just deeply unconscious.

But that didn't matter.

Either way, they were safe. At least, slightly more safe. For a little while.

Matt flashed her a grin.

She just stared back at him. He looked completely unruffled, as if he had not just stopped a several-tonne beast in mid-pounce without apparent effort or injury.

He shifted slightly, moving his feet, and that was when she noticed the metal floor where he had been standing. It was buckled, pushed up around indents where his feet had been. And it was glowing. It was red hot. The bent, glowing metal was the only sign of the enormous forces that had been in play.

How the hell had he done that?

But there was no time to ask that, not now.

The astonished silence which had hung over the amphitheatre broke like an ocean slapping around the base of a mountain.

A great cry went up - a cry of mourning, of outrage, pouring from the lips of the assembled froglings, as if from the mouth of the Frogopolis itself.

Charlotte shivered, and suddenly she didn't feel safe anymore. Not at all.

She couldn't hear individual words, but the tone was clear enough.

Blood.

They wanted blood.

Not just any blood - *her* blood, hers and Matt's.

The noise was deafening.

She put her hands to her ears, but still it came at them - louder than a roaring train, more venomous, more cruel, more malign than cancer.

And suddenly she couldn't bear it anymore.

Why was she here?

What had she done to deserve *this*?

This wasn't even her *life*! She shouldn't be preparing to die in some ludicrous frog-based society, millions of miles from her home - not even in her own *reality*! No, she should be sipping cocktails on a beach somewhere and maybe - maybe - wondering if she had enough energy to go for another massage.

"Stop it!" she shouted, the words coming out before she was even aware she had decided to speak. "Stop it! Why are you doing this? This isn't right! This isn't *fair!* This isn't..."

But to her complete shock, they *had* stopped.

Everything was silent. So silent she could hear the creaking of the metal at Matt's feet as it cooled.

"Oh," she said, feeling slightly embarrassed. "Well, I wasn't actually expecting you to *listen* to me..."

Matt tapped her on the shoulder. She looked at him, and he pointed up into the crowded amphitheatre, to an ornate, raised box.

"Ah," said Charlotte.

A huge frog, bent and gnarly, bedecked in robes and jewels and finery, had risen to his feet. Every frog in the arena was looking at him, eyes wide, their faces solemn with respect.

He had been the reason for the silence. Not her words. Of course not her words.

"Who," said Charlotte, "the hell is that?"

Matt sucked his lip and made a humming noise.

"Well, I'd just be guessing again," he said, "but he looks even more horrible and even less pleasant than the other froglings. So I reckon he's probably their King."

And the King spoke.

❧ 12 ❧

Head Frog 127 could scarcely believe his eyes.

The beast had been floored.

And not by a huge, hulking hero, not after a long, glorious fight...

But by that scrawny little alien. And with a single punch.

He felt outrage curdling in his belly. In all his conversations with the Prophet, the man had never mentioned superhuman strength. Not once. It was the kind of thing he would have remembered.

He thought about how close he had allowed himself to come to the human and his scowl deepened. True, the man had been trussed up in restraints, true his froglings had had all manner of nasty weaponry trained on him at the time. But still...

King Toadflaps III got to his feet with dignity. Head Frog 127 was close enough to see the effort it cost him. His scrawny legs trembled under the weight of mouldering froggy flesh, his face was drawn with the effort...but still, the King rose.

He was weak in body, but not in will.

And when he spoke, his voice carried into the hushed silence of the Frogopolis.

"So," said King Toadflaps III, "you have defeated my beast. I hope you are proud of yourselves."

Head Frog 127 blinked, surprised at the gentleness of the king's words.

Down in the arena, the aliens shuffled nervously. There was a pause, then the male of the species – the one who had felled the beast with a single punch – shifted, shielding his eyes with one hand to his brow, and called back.

"Um, yes," he said. "Sorry about that. Didn't see as I had much of an option."

The king nodded slowly.

"Most of the beast's victims feel they have at least one other option," said the king ponderously. "That is to say, the option of being eaten."

The female alien raised a hand timidly.

"I did consider that option," she admitted nervously.

"Well, it's good to know you don't suffer from tunnel vision, at least," said the King. "And although I must admit to admiring your strength, I am disappointed with your lack of showmanship."

Down in the arena, the male alien frowned.

"*I* thought it was pretty damn dramatic," he said in a hurt voice.

A nervous titter went up from the stands. Head Frog 127 scowled. This was wrong. This was not going well. The aliens were actually being *endearing*. Surely, everyone could see it was a simple strategy? Surely, no one could actually *admire* these ghastly things?

"Oh, there was drama," agreed the king. "But you didn't exactly drag it out, did you?"

The alien nodded at that, accepting.

"True," he said. "I thought doing it quickly would make a point."

Now it was the king's turn to nod.

"And while I respect your decision to impress us with a swift, sudden blow," the King went on, "I must say I feel sorry for poor Tony."

The alien looked wrong-footed.

"Tony?" he queried.

"Tony," confirmed the king. "My beast. He does rather like a show. I can assure you, if the boot had been on the other foot, he would most certainly *not* have devoured you in a single bite."

"He wouldn't?" asked the female alien.

"No," said the King firmly. "He would have played with you. Made good sport. He would have given my people...a *show*."

King Toadflaps hissed the last word, and as he said it a sigh went up from the assembled froglings.

Head Frog 127 had to admit the king was right. Everyone had come here today wanting to see something special. They had wanted drama and excitement and - yes, ultimately - blood. For the humans to get a point or two would have been fine. But for the show to be so completely over so soon was...well, it was unforgivable.

"You want a show," said the male alien, frowning a little, as if trying to understand.

The aliens exchanged glances.

The female creature raised a hand.

"I can juggle," she offered.

King Toadflaps III smiled. It was a nasty smile. Even Head Frog 127, who was not in the smile's direct line of fire, felt his guts bunch up.

"Oh, I don't think that will quite do," said the King.

Even from this distance, Head Frog 127 could see the aliens were looking worried.

"What, ah...what exactly did you have in mind?" asked the male alien.

The King's smile broadened. Now it looked like a gaping slice cut through his entire face.

"A chase," he said. "A treasure hunt. One the whole of the Frogopolis can play."

A deathly science hung in the air.

"A treasure hunt?" said the female alien. "That doesn't sound so bad. What's the treasure?"

"You," said King Toadflaps succinctly, and a sigh went up from the assembled froglings as everyone understood.

"But...but what's in it for us?" asked the male alien.

"If you don't get caught, you stay alive," said the King.

The alien nodded wisely.

"I see," he said. "And if we do get caught?"

"Why, whoever catches you gets to keep the treasure," explained the king. "That is to say, you. Stuffed and mounted on the wall, in places of high honour."

"But that's not *fair*," complained the female. "How are we supposed to get away? And where are we meant to go, with the whole world after us?"

"We are not a total monster," said the king. "We will give you a chance, of course."

"Oh, right," said the male alien, perking up. "Well, in that case, I would like a ray gun for my weapon - one of those nice, big ones, like I saw on the ship, the kind that looks like it can vaporise a whole building with a single zap. And we'll need some food, and a map, naturally."

He put a finger to his lips, as if having just thought of something.

"And a spaceship, too of course," added the alien.

"Nothing fancy. Just something small and capable of inter-stellar travel. *Fast* interstellar travel."

The king was smiling again, and his eyes were amused.

Amused...but cold.

"That's not quite what I had in mind," said the king.

"No?" asked the alien. "Well, don't worry about the food, then. I'm sure we can rustle something up."

The King sat down in his throne again, and gave a sigh.

Then he leaned forward and pressed a button.

There was a deep groaning noise. It sounded like the bones of the earth settling in their grave. The ground shook.

In the far corner of the arena, a segment of wall had retracted into the earth, leaving a desolate, open pathway out...out into the hostile terrain of Froghearth.

"Here is your chance," said the King.

He closed his eyes.

After a moment, the other froglings in the arena realised what was happening, and followed suite.

Head Frog 127 thought about sneaking, about keeping his eyes open, but decided it wasn't worth it. What was it to him if his King wanted to play with the aliens? He would let this farce begin, then he could return to his ship...and to his inves-tigations of the Chaos Drive.

And the aliens? Really, who cared? He had what he wanted from them.

"Are we meant to...?" asked the female alien. Her voice sounded thin and worried.

"One," counted the King. "Two. Three..."

In the blackness behind his closed eyes, Head Frog 127 heard the desperate patter of departing feet.

He smiled.

They would not get far.

They never did.

✌ I 3 ✌

"**C**ome on," said NotMatt, not loudly, not even sounding especially excited. But there was a sort of icy, forced jolliness to his tone, and Charlotte could sense him concentrating very hard on not panicking.

Matt just wasn't right, she realised. The Matt *she* knew almost never flawed huge monsters with a single punch.

So she had decided the safest way to refer to him - at least in the privacy of her own head - as *NotMatt*. It felt more comfortable that way.

And if the person who had just floored a giant beastie with a single punch was concerned with not showing how panicked he was, Charlotte wondered if now might be a good time to panic, after all. She looked at the rows upon rows of frogs, hands placed consciously over eyes, mouths tight or hanging half open, teeth glinting out, drool forming there. There was an excitement in the air, a barely contained feeling of expectation.

Expectation of blood.

Of their blood.

Charlotte felt herself being pulled along, half-dragged

behind NotMatt as he hustled them towards the far side of the arena. Their footsteps echoed in an eerie silence, the only sound a horrible susurrus from the assembled frogs. She couldn't hear individual words, but she knew what they were doing.

Counting.

Giving them a nominal amount of time to get away.

But how long?

And did it even matter?

In this blasted, hostile planet, where was there even to hide?

They came to the segment of the arena which had been lowered, and NotMatt stopped abruptly. Charlotte came up next to him, and felt the colour draining from her face.

"Oh," she managed to say, which seemed totally inadequate for the sight that was before her.

She didn't know exactly what she had been expecting. A deserted road, perhaps; a few buildings, maybe somewhere to hide. Perhaps a vehicle, something they could try to jump-start and make an escape in.

But, no.

There was no road.

There was no solid ground.

Instead, the landscape swelled out around them, a stinking, fetid marsh, humid wisps of stinking gas whipping around them, and out across a seemingly endless expanse filled with algae and little tufty hills with diseased-looking, rotting vegetation. It rolled off into the deep distance, with not a building in sight, nor a spaceship or even what looked like a car.

But there were frogs.

Lots and lots of frogs.

They were laying half-submerged in the foul swamp liquids, perched in drooping trees, huddled together in dark, decrepit boats. They had their hands over their eyes, too.

Charlotte was struck by the great variation in the colourings of these frogs. Most of those in the arena had been green or yellow-green, like the frogs in the ship that had taken them. But there was no such uniformity here. Some were so dark they were almost black, with vivid slashes of red across their face. Others had lurid yellow complexions, and heavy sacks near their throats that looked ominously poisonous.

Charlotte looked to NotMatt.

Surely, he would know what to do?

He had to.

He would get them out of this.

Wouldn't he?

But NotMatt was bowed, head drooping, as if carrying a great and unexpected weight.

"This is...this is unexpected," he said, and he sounded so tired that Charlotte wondered briefly if his fight with Tony had drained him, somehow, sapped him of an inner strength.

In the distance, there was a noise. It came from the arena.

It was a sort of ascending note that sounded at the same time like the ticking of an old, damaged clock.

A clock that was pretty near to expiring.

And Charlotte understood suddenly - instinctively - that this was it. These were the last few seconds, the last few moments they would get.

It was a joke, a cruel joke. The whole thing. They were never meant to get away; they would never even be given a chance.

NotMatt looked at her, and took a deep breath.

"Oh, well," he said. "I suppose we better get on with it. You've still got the coin, right?"

"What?" said Charlotte, because she had been busy thinking about how those frog teeth would feel when they bit into her, and wondering if it would be satisfying, in a small way, to try and bite them back.

"The micro-respirator," NotMatt said. "It's still in your mouth, right?"

To her surprise, Charlotte realised that it was. It had lodged there, somehow aligning itself against her soft palate so unobtrusively she had almost forgotten it was there.

"Ye-s," she said slowly. "But why...?"

And then the clock stopped ticking.

And all at once, in perfect synchronisation, the frogs lowered their hands.

A thousand bilious, froggy eyes glared at them.

There was a single frozen moment, the sense of an indrawn breath.

"Press it with your tongue," commanded NotMatt.

Charlotte didn't even think about it, didn't even stop to consider why or what he was planning. A part of her brain took over, some deep part tasked with keeping her alive. It had evidently decided that this piece of advice was not some-thing it was in her interests to question.

She pressed her tongue into the coin, and her mouth was instantly basked in a flow of fresh, clean air.

And the frogs sprang.

They leapt towards her, jumping from every angle, leaping out of the filthy swamp-water, bursting out of trees and bushes, springing towards them with a horrid, unbearable silence.

She could see their dirt-streaked skin, sense the bulge of small, tight muscles beneath, and felt herself anticipating the grasping, slippery feeling as those clawing hands grappled for her neck.

And then NotMatt moved, too.

He span towards her, so quick and smooth that the ground beneath his feet actually rippled. Then his hands were against her, gripping her by the flanks, not hard, but completely, unstoppably firm. He pressed against her, held her tight. There was a sense of coiled tenseness in his legs...

...and they were springing upwards.

Charlotte felt the air driven from her lungs, and for a horrible moment she thought the coin would go sailing out of her mouth. But it was lodged there, somehow, adhering painlessly.

She felt her eyes bulging in her skull. Below her, the full extent of those that hunted her was revealed. They extended in ring upon ring around the point they had leapt from. Row upon row of frogs, green frogs, pale frogs with translucent skin and bulging purple eyes, red frogs with nasty little black-clawed hands...

Hundreds and hundreds of them.

And still NotMatt rose, and Charlotte rose with him.

They were high now, impossibly high, so high they were above the lip of the arena, and Charlotte looked in there, too, and saw the crowds surge forward, moving like a single, cancerous animal to the point where they had been given the chance to 'escape'. She caught a glimpse of their king, fat and horrible, and could even make out the cruel expression on his face.

And still they rose, so quickly that Charlotte felt her stomach would be expelled through the soles of her feet. And looking straight down, she saw that the first rank of frogs, those that had leapt towards them, had only now converged on where they had been but a moment before. They were gouging chunks of flesh from one another, so worked to frenzy that they weren't stopping to ensure they had the correct target.

They were so high up now that the figures were tiny things, small and rather dainty - if still obviously disgusting.

And Charlotte felt something relax in her.

She tasted the sweet air gushing into her mouth from the coin, and she understood.

"You can fly," she breathed, wonder trembling in her words. "You're going to fly us away! And we'll be so high, the air will be thin, and the coins will let us breath, and we will be safe and we will escape, and..."

Charlotte stopped speaking.

They seemed to be slowing their ascent now. The figures on the ground were getting no smaller. The air around them felt very still.

But if NotMatt could fly...why hadn't he flown them away to begin with?

"That would be nice, wouldn't it?" said NotMatt. "Much more comfortable."

Charlotte thought about this for a moment.

"You can't fly, can you?" she asked.

"Nope," said NotMatt. "Just jump. Very high."

"I see," said Charlotte. Something shifted in their movement. There was a tipping sensation, and then...

"And I can fall," added NotMatt. "I'm good at that, too."

"..." Charlotte said.

They fell.

The marsh rushed towards them. The figures, the thousands of horrible froggy shapes, were all getting bigger now.

Bigger and bigger.

Wind was in her face, blasting against her eyes so fast the tears came.

The frogs were watching them. They had marked them, could see their trajectory, were already - Charlotte could see - working out where they would land.

Charlotte could see, too.

"Oh, no," she tried to say, but the wind was too strong, and the words were whipped away.

NotMatt moved his arms, and Charlotte felt the wind flow differently around their bodies.

NotMatt was steering them, actually directing them like some kind of two-person kamikaze...straight towards an open stretch of swamp. There were no tree stumps there, no half-rotting boats, and Charlotte understood instinctively that it was deeper there, that it was a place where marsh ground gave way to something more akin to a patch of foul inland sea.

But they were going too fast.

They were hurtling towards the water now, so fast they would end up as a pinkish smear over the fetid liquid, she was sure.

They would smash into it and...

...and a sort of translucent canopy sprang up around their heads. There was a faint hazing of the air, but it was something she felt more than saw, felt in the way the air that rushed at them was suddenly deflected, felt in the way they lurched, slowing just a moment before they crashed into the water, and then...

...And then they were under the water, and Charlotte had the smallest, slightest impression of the water parting for them, just for an instant, then closing up behind them like a gown being zipped shut. She started to scream.

"Close your mouth," said NotMatt, and for a wonder she managed to do that almost before thinking it, which was only just in time, because at that moment the pouch of air that had followed them into the water abruptly shut off. Foul water rushed at her, clutching coldly at her clothes and flesh and eyes. It was horrible, much colder than she had been expecting, and the nasty brackish scent of it clawed at her nose, trying to break its way in. For a terrible moment she thought she wouldn't be able to stop herself opening her mouth to breath, and sucking in a deadly lungful of the fetid stuff. But then she remembered the coin in her mouth, and she realised at the same instant that it was bubbling away. It only took her a couple of breaths to work out what she needed to do - expel the used-up air through her nose and replace it with fresh air sucked in from the coin - but in that time they had already plunged far deeper than she had imagined possible, the momentum of their fall carrying them down, down, down...

They passed twisting filaments which she took to be roots from the drooping trees far above, wisps of slimy plant matter which clawed at them. Dark shapes darted in front of them as they descended, and for a nasty moment she thought they were frogs, but then she realised they were too small, and that they must be fish of some sort - though what type of fish would live in such putrid water she dreaded to think.

She felt pressure build up against her ears, and for a moment looked longingly up towards the surface, which she could see as a shimmering interface of white against the rippling water...

...and then she saw the foamy lines break the interface, and realised it was frogs, lots and lots of frogs, diving after them, leaping into the water to follow them, and she forgot all about the pressure in her ears.

She looked down again, still holding on to NotMatt. His eyes were darting around, quick and clever, looking for something. She followed his gaze.

The water was growing dark now, cloyed with algae and slimy plant growth. Faint rays of light from above struggling to penetrate through the thick stuff. But there were other lights down here, she suddenly saw. Little yellow-brown pinpricks, beating up at them from down below. She couldn't make them out clearly. They were too small, she thought, so impossible small. What were they? Some kind of luminescent underwater insect?

And then she blinked, her perspective shifting, and she understood.

This was no shallow swamp, passing on for mile after mile outwards from the arena. And they hadn't landed in one freakish part that was a little deeper.

This was a great, deep lake, or perhaps a shallow sea.

But it wasn't that which surprised her, either.

This was a city.

A great and horribly froggy city.

The lights she could see weren't insects, and they weren't small.

They were house lights and street lights, shining out from row upon row of submerged structures, slimed with pond weeds and - presumably - housing thousands more frogs.

She felt her blood turn to ice. Then, before she knew what she was doing, she was twisting in NotMatt's grip, pulling away from the light, trying to get away...but to where? There was nowhere to go.

They were trapped.

They would never get out.

They would...

NotMatt kicked with his feet, and Charlotte reeled in his grip as he pulled them under the lee of one of the buildings. He drew them in, close against a ledge which sloped upwards over their heads and ended in a little downward-curled ridge. NotMatt pulled her closer, and then slowly rotated their bodies so they were tucked in against what seemed rather like an awning. A moment later, froggy bodies started to shoot past, diving through the water where they had been a moment before. Charlotte couldn't see them clearly through the gloom, but they seemed intent on diving deeper, and none of them seemed to glance in their direction. She shivered, and tucked herself further upwards and into the little nook created by the awning. Up close, she could see that it was made out of a sort of pale, clay-like substance. The whole building seemed to be made of the stuff. It had uneven walls, and gave the impression of having been grown as much as built. But it was also very clearly a house. A rather big house.

And below them, she understood suddenly that there was a door, dark and a little forbidding. What was behind that door, she wondered?

She imagined a swarm of sticky, clawing frogs, ready to throw open the door in a moment and pour out at them. She felt her body tensing, almost involuntarily.

She had to get away from here. She had to. She...

"Stop wobbling about, will you?" said NotMatt, sounding a little irritated. "I think they've missed us for a moment, but if you are intent on splashing around like an injured fish, no doubt they will find us."

She blinked, not understanding how he had spoken while they were so deep under this thick, vile water.

And then she heard the hissing sound coming from NotMatt's mouth, and she realised. He had activated the coin somehow, turned it to full blast - and the air it was expelling was being trapped under the awning, so that their heads were now extending into a small pocket of air.

"It's a city!" she gasped.

"Yup," agreed NotMatt. "Their capital city, I believe. I should know. Wasn't long ago we were fleeing this place with a cargo of freshly liberated treasures."

He paused, a far away look in his eye, a slight frown on his brow as if balancing the joys of liberating treasure against the problems doing so had caused him, against the destruction of his craft, the death of his friend, and the swapping of his true love for Charlotte.

"On balance, we probably should have stayed in bed," he concluded, then peered down into the murk some more.

"But...but what kind of treasures could they possibly

keep down here?" she asked, trying - and failing - to imagine anything beautiful or valuable existing in such a place.

"Oh, brutish and violently expansionist races always manage to accrue rather a lot of goodies," said NotMatt idly. "The frogs are no different. You should see it as a manifest of the civilisations they've overthrown and plundered. We saw it as our duty to get that stuff and redistribute it to the wider universe."

"Redistribute?" asked Charlotte. "Like Robin Hood?"

NotMatt waved a hand vaguely.

"Bit like that," he allowed. "Only with more of an emphasis on selling rather than giving."

"Oh," said Charlotte. "But..."

"Perhaps we can discuss the finer points of economic morality later," put in NotMatt. "Once we've got out of here, for example."

Charlotte was about to answer, when a light sprang on below them. It was a much brighter light than the others, white and clawing, and it gave the immediate impression of having unfriendly intentions.

It darted around, spraying the underwater city with splashes of intensely white light, illuminating row upon row of buildings, shining through what she took to be windows and examining the inside of houses closely but swiftly.

She saw shadows moving about the source of the beam, and understood at once that this was a danger, an organised attempt to find them. She couldn't make out the frogs that were operating the light, but she was sure they were there, could imagine their pale, luminous eyes glaring out into the watery darkness.

But to her surprise, though the light was springing about seemingly everywhere else below them, it wasn't once pointed up towards the level on which they hid.

"Why are they looking down there, and not up here?" she asked.

"They think we've hidden in one of the empty houses," he said. "Makes sense. All the frogs from this area were up above, either in the arena itself or waiting for us to come out. So all their dwellings are empty. They think we must have hid in one."

"But we're not doing that," said Charlotte, not quite making it a question.

She found her attention drawn once again to the door immediately below their awning.

NotMatt had said the other houses were empty.

Did that mean this one wasn't?

What was inside this house?

"No," agreed NotMatt. "That would be far too predictable. See? They're convinced we would never be stupid enough to go into one of the occupied buildings."

Below them, the bright searchlight darted around. It completed an inspection of a layer of buildings, then paused for a moment, as if those who were operating it were consulting with one another.

"That does sound pretty stupid," agreed Charlotte. There was a horrible, sinking feeling in her belly. "We're not going to...?"

"Yup," said NotMatt with a bright smile. "Don't worry, you'll be fine. Now get ready..."

"But..." protested Charlotte.

The beam of light swung downwards for a moment, away from them.

"Now," said NotMatt, and he moved.

Charlotte was still holding tight to him, and he pulled her down abruptly out of the little bubble of air they had collected in the awning, and at once they were back in the cloying cold of the water.

The dark doorway loomed in front of them. It had a big metal doorknob, and a keyhole beneath.

She saw NotMatt wiggle his fingers, as if warming them up, and she thought for a moment that he was going to withdraw some kind of clever metal instrument from a pocket and attempt to pick the lock.

Instead, he reached out and slammed the doorknob into the door, hard, three times.

Charlotte thought her eyes were going to bulge out of her skull.

"What the hell are you doing?" she tried to say, forgetting for the moment that she was under water.

"Blagh gh galah?" came out instead, in a stream of incomprehensible bubbles.

But NotMatt paid no notice, instead pulling them down until they were floating below the door and slightly tucked under the gentle slope of the building above.

He held her still.

A moment later, the door opened, letting a slice of faded orange light leach out into the murky water.

A fat and rather stupid-looking frog peered out into the gloom.

It looked about questioningly, trying to find whoever had knocked on the door.

It kicked its chubby legs, and floated out a little way from the door...

...and NotMatt swam, pulling them both forward, darting through the doorway and inside, while the stupid-looking frog was still casting about, trying to work out what was going on.

They were in a sort of long corridor, Charlotte saw, extending away from them about thirty feet and opening out after that into what looked like it might be a larger room of some sort. The walls were slimy with pond life, and the ceiling...

...the ceiling contained air.

NotMatt kicked again, taking them up, and then they were clambering out of the water, and heaving up a set of stairs, ascending from the doorway past the mostly submerged corridor.

Charlotte wanted to ask where they were, but there was no time.

Below them, the frog that had opened the door was starting to move back inside, still not looking up at them, and NotMatt was pushing her on, one hand to the small of her back, urging her onwards and upwards.

The stairway was painted a sort of pale, insipid yellow, and - to Charlotte's surprise - sported various framed pictures showing rather bland landscapes. They were the sort of pictures, she thought, which you might find in down-at-heel charity shops, dog-eared frames and a faded, used-up look to the paper inside.

They came to the top of the stairs, and found themselves on another corridor. This one had a number of closed doors along it, and at the end an open doorway out of which a faint, tinny noise was coming. Charlotte could not make out what the noise was, but it seemed familiar, somehow.

"Hmm, wrong way, I think," whispered NotMatt, and they both turned to head back down the stairs. But the broad, slow frog that had let them in was starting to come up after them, eyes fixed in a placid, bovine way on the space in front of it. There was certainly nothing clever about the creature, nothing even curious - but Charlotte didn't doubt for a moment that if it saw them, it would recognise them at once as un-froggish.

"Bugger," said NotMatt. "Okay, change of plan..."

He led them onto the corridor, then tried the first door. It was locked.

So was the second.

And the third.

From behind them came a sort of sucking, splashing sound as the broad frog ascended out of the water level and into the air.

Any second now it would look up and see them. There was only one way left.

"Go on," hissed NotMatt. "No choice."

He crept past her, grasped her hand, then led them to the doorway at the end of the corridor and peered inside. Then he tugged gently at her hand, and she slid beside him, looking in.

The room was large, perhaps thirty feet to a side, and was decorated in a sort of drear institutional way which was instantly recognisable to Charlotte. There was something uniformly uninspired about the tatty, too-thick curtains, the thinning carpet, the threadbare sofas and armchairs that sat in a rough horseshoe arranged around what was clearly a sort of television.

And on the television was...them.

NotMatt and her.

She blinked, thinking she must have made a mistake, that perhaps she was going mad from stress.

But, no. It was them.

Them in the arena, what seemed like hours ago, but what in fact must only have been a matter of minutes.

She could tell by the hideously familiar shape of the beast, Tony, as it bounded towards them, then proceeded to get flawed by a single blow from NotMatt.

The footage was repeated a moment later, but slower, accompanied by a frenzied scroll of what looked like letters along the bottom of the display.

Then this cut away to an arial shot, looking down as NotMatt leapt them up into the air and plunged them into the murky water.

And Charlotte understood.

It was a replay. It must be a broadcast of the events in the arena. She had known that the show was popular entertainment for the frogs, but she hadn't expected this. To be beamed by some kind of broadcast to every home...every place...every...

She frowned.

Where the hell were they now, anyway?

A low muttering was coming from the sofas and armchairs in the room, and Charlotte realised to her horror that most of them contained frogs. They were so still, and the events on the display had captured her so completely by surprise, that she hadn't noticed them at first.

But they did not look like the other frogs she had seen. These were mountainous things of sprawling, placid flesh, pale green or sallow yellow or - in one case - a sort of faded, broken red colour; or else, thin to the point of gauntness, all flesh sucked away, with great, bulging eyes poking out, fixed myopically on the display. The scent that washed off them was instantly recognisable, too, though it wasn't quite human: dirt and waste, and other artificial scents used to cover it up.

Old. These were very old frogs.

Ancient.

"NotMatt," she whispered, as calmly as she could, "are we in an old frog's home?"

But there were footsteps behind them, and he didn't answer. Instead he urged her forwards and down, and she found herself bundled behind and then scrambling underneath an old, dusty sofa.

She wriggled, and then they were both curled up beneath,

and able to peer out from under the lip of the sofa. She had a good view of the room.

"Who...was it nurse?" creaked a withered-looking frog from the far side of the room. He was wrapped in blankets and had a thin, well-shaven face, which seemed like a ridiculous vanity given the explosive folds of wobbly flesh which protruded from his neck.

There was the sound of footsteps, then two stubby, hoary frog-legs were standing in front of the sofa.

"No one there," complained a voice from directly above their hiding place, which Charlotte took as belonging to the frog who had inadvertently let them in. "Must be all this excitement. It riles up the young ones."

"Despicable things," muttered another frog through a mouth full of gums and broken teeth. "The young these days...run around, behaving like tadpoles!"

"Would never have got away with it when I was that age," agreed a corpulent frog in the opposite corner of the room. This one wore a monocle and had a chest pinned with many coloured badges. "Discipline, that's what's lacking these days! Young froglings behaving that way...they should be marched to the mines and used for forced labour!"

"I concur, Major!" agreed the monocled frog. "It's that kind of dissolute behaviour which leads to a mess like this..."

And he waved a walking stick vaguely at the display, which was now showing a murky, underwater image which Charlotte recognised as being the depths they had descended through a little while earlier. As they watched, a great number of frogs were shooting down, diving into the deep water, streams of bubbles marking them. Many of them carried what were obviously sharp and rather unpleasant-looking weaponry.

"Oh, look, you can see our house," came the voice of the nurse above. "Do you see that, boys? We're famous."

There was a grumbling from the various ancient frogs.

"Bloody nuisance," said the well-shaven frog. "All this excitement. Quite unnecessary. In my day, we would have blasted the aliens and good riddance. None of this spectacle."

"Well said, Captain Fatleg," roared the Major, in a suddenly hearty voice. "It's all this bloody fool, Toadflap's, fault. Nothing like his father. Young upstart that he is."

Charlotte blinked, imagining the withered face of King Toadflaps, and wondering how old the Major was.

"And letting that idiot Head Frog into the royal box, no less!" Put in the monocled frog. "What's his number again?"

"127," said Captain Fatleg scornfully. "I knew him when he was an ensign. Always was a little sneak."

"Wasn't he the one mixed up in all that business with The Prophet?" said the monocled frog, and the others all laughed scornfully.

"Getting mixed up with filthy aliens," muttered the Major. "No good will come of it."

"As the tabloids said," agreed Captain Fatleg. "They got things right for once. Should have hung the both of them, that stupid Head Frog and his filthy Prophet, and good riddance!"

There was a roar of laughter from the monocled frog, which then cut off abruptly as something dropped away from his face and landed with a clack noise on the ghastly linoleum floor. Charlotte peered out from under the sofa, unsure what had happened for a moment...then something rolled beneath the sofa and bopped lightly against her face.

It was an eye.

Charlotte was so shocked, she couldn't have screamed if she had wanted to. This was, in fact, a good thing, as she did want to scream, and rather a lot, though she knew that this would be a strategically bad move.

"Oh, drat it!" cursed the monocled frog. "Bloody thing's off again!"

And he started to rise from the chair in a serious of arthritis creaks.

"Now, Colonel Slimeharbour!" reprimanded the voice of the nurse. "I've warned you about that. Don't worry, I'll get it..."

There was a noise from above her as the nurse stood up, and panic filled Charlotte, so thick she couldn't breath, she couldn't think.

They had to move, they would be discovered! But they couldn't get out from behind the sofa, not while the nurse was looking under it and all the other frogs were watching her do it...

Something tapped at Charlotte's shoulder. She turned, and was confronted by one of NotMatt's feet. It was wiggling at her nose, a little imperiously. She followed the foot to the leg, and then realised - to her horror - that NotMatt was stepping out from behind the sofa. She span around, hoping to perhaps pull him back down - but then she realised that the end of the sofa from which he was creeping out was directly adjacent to the thick curtains, and that he was pulling himself up behind them, under cover. She followed, and a moment later they were standing side by side, pressed tight against a cold, glass window. And not a moment too soon!

She had only just stood up when she heard the nurse give a sigh, and felt a stir of air from underneath, where she had been hidden a moment before.

"Oof," said the nurse, who was rather stout, and did not look like she was made for rooting around in narrow places. "Got it!"

Charlotte peered out from a crack between the curtains. NotMatt was pressed close against her, his head a little above hers. She saw the nurse stand, and hold the eye up to the light.

"You really must take better care of your glass eye!" the

nurse was telling the colonel, as she handed the thing over. The colonel made a noncommittal grumbling sound and half turned away as he pushed the horrible glass eye back into his un-monocled socket.

The nurse sat back down, and Charlotte felt her panic subside a little.

She let out a breath, and the back of her neck pressed against something cold. It took all her effort not to scream out or jump. Instead, she forced herself to turn slowly...

...and she was looking out into the depths.

They were pressed up against a full-length window of cold glass, behind which the swampy waters extended out as far as she could see.

From here, she could grasp the full scale of the search underway for them. From the images on the display, she had had a sense of many, many frogs diving down for them. But this was just...

It was ridiculous.

Thousands - literally thousands - of frogs were shooting past. Some were going up, some down, some sideways, all bustling about with a great deal of excitement and not much organisation.

She marked vehicles amongst the individual creatures, ugly submarine-like things with bright, seeking searchlights on top, and lots of nasty weaponry arrayed around them.

For a horrible moment she felt completely exposed, was sure they would be spotted at any moment. Then she remembered the dark windows she had seen on the way down, and realised there was no way the frogs outside would see them, not unless they had the bad luck for a searchlight to be shone directly on them.

There were so many frogs out there, it suddenly seemed impossible. The moment they got out there, they would be spotted and chased and taken...

"Phew, that was pretty close," whispered NotMatt in her ear. At least, it was nominally a whisper. The kind of whisper someone might whisper if they weren't really that committed to whispering properly.

Charlotte turned to glare at him.

"Be quiet!" she hissed, in a voice so tiny she could hardly hear it herself.

"What?" whispered NotMatt.

Charlotte swallowed, and peered through the crack in the curtain again. The frogs were all focussed on the display once more, a low, continuous drone of conversation rising up from them. If they had heard NotMatt's not-really-a-whisper, they gave no sign.

"Be quiet," she hissed again, then shook her head. This wasn't getting them anywhere. "I said, what are we going to do?" she demanded instead, making her voice just a little louder.

"Oh!' half-whispered NotMatt. "Yes, good question. Well, a lot of the bigger buildings have light transports docked. If we could get to one of them..."

"Great," said Charlotte. "All we have to do is sneak out of a room filled with frogs, and..." and then a thought occurred to her. "Hang on," she continued. "Why are we doing any sneaking at all? You smashed that big monster as if it were nothing. Can't you just fight us out?"

NotMatt looked a little shifty.

"It's not as easy as that," he whispered after a moment. "Doing stuff like that...it's draining. Not to mention, it might make us easier to find..."

Charlotte frowned. That didn't make any sense.

"But..." she started to say, but NotMatt put a finger to her lips.

She experienced a moment of outrage, and then her brain caught up with her ears.

Silence.

The frogs had gone silent. None of them were making a sound.

She peeked out through the crack in the curtains.

They were all staring at her.

No, she told herself desperately. They're all staring at the curtains. They can't see me. Can they?

Charlotte's nose was beginning to tickle, in the horrible way a nose tickles when it needs imminently to be sneezed through.

Oh no, thought Charlotte.

"I don't hear anything," said Captain Fatleg, a little primly. "You're all being paranoid."

"I'm not paranoid, damn your bile!" snorted the Major. "I'm telling you, I heard squeaking!"

"It's the mice," agreed Colonel Slimeharbour, sounding completely disgusted. "I saw one not last week!"

"We got rid of the mice," said the nurse, in the voice of one who feels duty-bound to defend a position, even while knowing full well that it was an unsound one. "I did the paperwork and everything."

There was a groan from the assembled ancient froghood.

"Well, that cinches it," said Captain Fatleg sarcastically. "If management has done the paperwork, there must still be mice."

Charlotte had one finger to her nose, rubbing gently, willing the sneeze to recede and depart unsneezed.

Gradually, the tickling in her nose settled.

It was working!

She let out a slow breath in relief, shifted her weight...

...and the floor under her gave a little squeak.

She froze, but it was too late.

There was a moment's pause.

"I did hear that," muttered Captain Fatleg, in a dangerously soft voice.

Through her crack in the curtain, Charlotte could see that everyone was glaring at the nurse. She looked back at them for a moment, imploringly, then shook her head.

"Fine," she said. "I'll get the poison."

"No need for that," said the Major calmly. He stood up, put a hand under his dressing gown, and withdrew it holding a sort of huge, ancient pistol. It had a thin coating of grease all over it, and looked as if it hadn't been used for the best part of a decade.

Still, it looked chillingly gun-ish.

It wobbled uncertainly in his shaking grip as the Major took a shuffling half-step towards the curtain.

There was a murmur of agreement from the other frogs, and suddenly everyone was standing up, and everyone was holding a previously concealed - but now entirely dangerous-looking - piece of weaponry. Even the nurse had a small snub-nosed pistol, though it looked like a pea-shooter compared to the entirely horrible and creakingly massive guns held by the ancient frog residents.

Charlotte ducked back behind the curtain, crouching down, hands trembling. She looked at NotMatt, who had drawn back to his side of the curtain. He glanced speculatively at the top corner, which was a foot or so above his head, then back at her.

From the other side of the curtain, an ominous silence rolled towards them, punctuated softly by the tiny noises made by people intent on violence moving very slowly.

NotMatt beckoned her urgently.

Come on, he mouthed at her, but Charlotte shook her head. She couldn't move. She was frozen to the spot. If she moved to him, she just knew that they would hear her. They would blast the curtain to pieces, and she would be splatted.

His eyes widened. He stared imploringly at her, and...

...and the curtains were whipped wide apart.

Moving without knowing what she was doing, moving faster than she had ever guessed she could move, Charlotte plunged down and backwards, forcing herself back under the sofa. But her ankle caught on something, and there was a searing pain in her calf.

Her foot had snagged in a piece of fabric under the sofa. She was flat on the floor, and most of her had got under the sofa - but her foot was stuck and she couldn't work herself further under. The top of her head poked out, leaving just enough room for her eyes.

She saw the horrible, jowly face of the Major thrust forward, bulbous eyes glaring to either side.

And behind and above him, Charlotte saw NotMatt leap.

He moved upwards, a desperate, sinuous strength in his arms. His hands grasped the curtain pole, and he pulled himself up, legs snaking up to wrap around the pole a little further on.

The Major turned his head, glaring for a moment at the scene beyond the window, his attention snagged for a just a second, before finally bringing his head round to stare at the curtain pole a moment after NotMatt had shimmied along it then pulled himself up and over it, disappearing from sight.

Relief flooded through her for an instant...and was then replaced by cold dread.

She couldn't move. She was stuck. All it would take was for the Major to glance down, and he would see her...

But the Major wasn't looking at her. A moment later, two other froggy faces hove into view above her. Captain Fatleg and the nurse had joined the Major, and all three were staring out at the scene beyond the window.

Charlotte was wiggling her foot desperately, but it was no good. She was stuck tight.

She wondered for a moment where Colonel Slimeharbour was, then realised she didn't care. The important thing wasn't the one frog she couldn't see...it was the three that could nearly see her.

"Quite a little search going on, isn't there?" asked the nurse blandly. "Wonder if they'll catch them."

She felt a cry building up inside her. It was so desperately unfair. If she could just get her foot free, she might have a chance. They might get away while these senile frogs were glaring out the window. But she couldn't do it. Every time she tried to pull her ankle free, pain slashed through it.

"Oh, we'll get the scoundrels," muttered Captain Fatleg darkly, and Charlotte realised he was talking about her and NotMatt in exactly the same tone that he had spoken of the imagined mouse earlier. A pest, vermin, undesirable scum to be hunted and exterminated, without mercy or hesitation. They would catch her. And they would kill her. And she would never see her home again, or her parents, her friends...or NotMatt. Her NotMatt.

And with that thought, something burst inside of her.

She gave a tremendous kick, and for a moment the pain in her leg was almost unbearable. Then something in the sofa gave soundlessly, and she was free. She scrambled downwards and out, sliding from under the sofa with a feeling off immense relief, emerging backwards and then standing slowly to her feet. She could see the back of the three frog's heads, as they stared out through the window. They were all kneeling on the sofa, looking bizarrely childish in such a pose, eyes pressed to the glass.

This was it. This was her chance. While the three frogs were distracted, she would turn and run out!

She turned...

...and remembered that there were four frogs, not three.

Colonel Slimeharbour was standing before her, one eye closed tight, the other glaring through its monocle.

But he wasn't glaring at her.

He was glaring at something in his hand, something held high up against his chest.

His glass eye.

He was examining it carefully, giving it a delicate rub with a little piece of tatty cloth.

She couldn't breath, she was so terrified.

Then slowly, with a dreadful inevitability, Colonel Slimharbour stopped his polishing, and raised his head to look at her.

Behind his monocle, his eye filled first with shock, then with disbelief...and then with a sort of ravenous, bloodthirsty joy.

Charlotte thought about running, about dashing for the door - but she was frozen, her muscles stuck rigid. She couldn't move.

Behind the Colonel, Charlotte saw something move high up in the corner of the room.

It was NotMatt. He was clambering on top of a bookshelf, moving towards the doorway through which they had first entered. Charlotte realised he must have clambered all the way around there from the curtain pole, across various pieces of furniture, remaining all the while out of the eyeline of the distracted frogs.

But they would not be distracted much longer.

Even as she watched, the Colonel was opening his mouth to draw in a big breath. Then he would bellow out the alarm, and the others would turn and they would see her and...

...and the colonel drew in an enormous breath...

...and the glass eye was sucked into his mouth.

There was a faint, sloppy glop noise.

The colonel stared at her in horror.

He tried to breath, but only a faint choking noise came out. His hands flew desperately to his throat, clenching and unclenching. His monocle fell from his face, and his one eye bulged desperately.

Behind the colonel, Charlotte saw NotMatt leap nimbly down from the bookshelf and land on the floor by the door. He beckoned her desperately, and Charlotte leapt past the Colonel. The door was only a few steps away!

She would make it!

NotMatt made it through the door, and turned to grin at her.

She would make it!

She would...

And the colonel made a soft and horrible noise, a sad and desperate and terrified noise...and Charlotte stopped.

She turned. The other three frogs were still staring out through the window, oblivious to the scene behind them.

The Colonel would die.

He deserved to, of course. He was set on killing her, she knew that.

She should just run off and leave him.

Of course she should...

...and she didn't.

Instead, she stood behind him, wrapping her arms around his midriff, and heaved.

Nothing happened.

She tried again.

Nothing.

Wasn't this the way you were meant to stop someone from choking? She was sure she had seen it in a film once.

Maybe frog's had different anatomy. This was useless. She would never save him.

He had turned his head to look at her. His single eye

looked at her imploringly, and on his face was a faint, hopeful smile.

Charlotte felt a stab of empathy rush through her, a warmth. He could see that she was trying to help him, he could see that she was - against all good sense - trying to save his life. She would save him, and then he would tell the others, and the frogs would stop hunting them and they would be friends, and...

...and she saw his hand raising up, and realised he was turning the gun he held so that it pointed straight at her face.

She saw his arthritic finger dancing desperately on the trigger.

Horror and revulsion rushed through her, and she dove away just as the gun fired.

She hit the floor and rolled.

But in her panic she had jumped the wrong way, back into the room rather than towards the door. She ducked and slid back under the sofa. A moment later, the Colonel hit the floor, his gun spinning away. She could see his eye. He had seen where she had hidden, and he was glaring furiously at her.

There was a thunder of creaks above her, and suddenly the Colonel's body was surrounded by limbs. The nurse, Captain Fatleg and the Major had all rushed to their fallen comrade.

"What's the problem, old boy!" demanded the Major. "Did you see the mouse? Did you get the blighter?"

The Colonel's eye was bloodshot now, and glaring balefully at Charlotte. But he could not speak, of course.

"He's choking!" said the nurse. "He's got something in his mouth."

The Colonel gave a final, convulsive rattle, then lay still.

There was a long, rather bleak silence.

"The eye," observed Captain Fatleg, just a triple smugly. "I always told him to get rid of it. Disgusting thing."

"We must do something!" demanded the nurse.

The Major gave a sigh.

"I concur," he said. "We really must call the undertaker. I detest it when the other residents die. Reminds one rather unnecessarily of one's own mortality."

Charlotte could see NotMatt, waiting just behind the door.

She was so close. The door was only a few feet away...but it might as well have been a mile, because the remaining frogs stood between her and the exit.

She could see he was wringing his hands, as if uncertain, as if undecided. She wondered what he was planning - what could he be planning? To run in and fight the frogs? But he had told her he couldn't do that, that - what had he said? - that it would be too much of a drain. But on what?

The nurse gave a sigh.

"Fine," she said at last. "I'll call the morgue and..."

"There really is no need," said NotMatt, sweeping into the room with a sort of unusual, rolling gait.

Except it wasn't NotMatt.

Charlotte blinked, trying to make sense of the images that slid around her brain.

She could see NotMatt there, looking just the same as he had a moment before, even if he was holding himself in an odd, stooped way//

//and she could also see something over him, a sort of shimmering overlay that cloaked his face and body, making him look...

Well, frog-ish.

He looked like NotMatt still, but a frog version of NotMatt.

Only now he was dressed in a long, rather formal dark

jacket with hints of a sombre suit worn beneath. On his hands he wore a pair of blue rubber gloves.

Charlotte rubbed her eyes. But when she opened them, the frog version of NotMatt was unchanged.

Somehow, she knew instinctively what it was.

It was a glamour.

An illusion.

It was something he was casting around himself, a field, something that played tricks with the minds of those observing him.

And it was working.

"Oh!" exclaimed the nurse, getting to her feet. "What...what are you doing here?"

"I'm from the morgue," explained NotMatt. "It's quite alright. We are just here to collect the body. Then we will be gone."

There was something to his words, a sort of humming resonance to them, and Charlotte realised that NotMatt was doing something special to his voice, too. Something to make the frogs think whatever he said the most reasonable thing in the world.

"From the...morgue," mused Captain Fatleg, chewing the words in his mouth suspiciously, as if concerned they might release some strange taste if only he could mull them the right way. "That seems..."

"Oh, the new system is marvellous," said NotMatt happily. Charlotte could practically see the force of influence he pressed into his words. "We get an alert very quickly. That's how we can be here so fast."

"Yes, you were very quick," said the Major, in a strange, hollow voice. "These boys must really know what they're doing, that's what I say."

The nurse nodded emphatically, and Charlotte saw a smile twitch on NotMatt's (disturbingly froggy) lips.

"Oh, we do," said NotMatt breezily. "Now, if you can just give us a hand with him, and show us to your launch..."

NotMatt moved forward, and made as if to start heaving the body away.

"Not so fast," snapped Captain Fatleg. He had turned to glare at NotMatt, his yellow eyes narrow and canny.

NotMatt froze, and Charlotte felt her heart give a lurch.

"Is there some...problem?" NotMatt asked. Charlotte could hear the austere, professional outrage he was going for, and she hoped the Captain fell for it. But she could also hear the uncertainty behind it, the fear. Looking at the others, she saw that their faces held just a hint of uncertainty now, too.

It all hung on this, she realised. If the Captain could see through the glamour, they were done for. He would lead them out of the illusion, she was sure of that.

"Something doesn't smell right," Said Captain Fatleg. "If you got here so quick, why do you need our launch? And how is it I've never seen you before now? It seems to me a resident dies here more or less every week. Where's the usual fellow? Where's O'Leery? That's what I want to know!"

Charlotte saw NotMatt hesitate, lick his lips. In that instant, she felt the glamour weaken, as if faltering in NotMatt's loss of confidence. She could see the suspicion deepen in Captain Fatleg's eyes, could see the questions forming in the eyes of the others.

The ruse was up. They were done for.

Unless...

She took a breath. She didn't want to do this. Really didn't want to.

What if NotMatt didn't see her in time? What if he couldn't cast a second illusion, anyway?

But such thoughts would get her nowhere.

If it didn't work, what had they lost? They would certainly lose if she didn't try.

So she stood up.

She saw NotMatt's eyes fly to her, just a moment before the others noted the movement and started to turn.

She looked into his eyes, and hoped he understood.

Then Captain Fatleg's burning eyes were upon her.

"Who the blazes are you?" He demanded.

"I'm O'Leary, of course," said Charlotte, putting on a broad froggy accent. "I thought you were getting old, but bloody hell! Can't you even recognise me?"

In the background, she saw NotMatt's eyes go wide for a moment...then flash to a look of profound concentration.

The room seemed to hang in the balance, suspended between two competing realities...

Then the scale tipped.

Charlotte had the strangest sensation of flesh sliding into place around her, a shimmering, diaphanous layer of insubstantial froggy flesh. She could feel it as much as see it, a wattled green and yellow skin.

She saw Captain Fatleg's eyes go wide for a moment, then relax with a sort of hazy, contented sheen.

"Oh, there you are, O'Leary!" the Captain exclaimed. Then he gave a laugh. "And just as much cheek as usual, I see! Who is this new boy? You had me worried for a moment there."

After that, it was easy.

The nurse helped NotMatt and her move the - surprisingly light - body of the freshly departed Colonel down to the lower level, where it could be slid easily through the water, and to a small, amphibious craft.

"Don't mind the Captain," the nurse told them rather anxiously, once they had the body packed, and the two would-be undertakers were sitting comfortably in the odd, ramshackle launch. "Some of our residents get that way. It's the advancing years, you know."

"Oh, think nothing of it, my good frog," said NotMatt. "Senility is a terrible thing."

"It is, at that," agreed the nurse, thankful to evidently be let of the hook.

"There is one thing you could do for us, though," NotMatt went on. "You know, to make up for this, ah little delay."

"Oh, anything!" Said the nurse. "Just name it!"

"It seems there's some kind of silly search under way," NotMatt went on, putting a hint of disgust into his voice. "Well, I'm sure it's frightfully important. But if you could be a good dear, and call the authorities, tell them you simply have undertakers leaving with body of a dearly departed..."

"Highly decorated," put in Charlotte.

"Yes, a military hero," went on NotMatt. "The body of a military hero, and we don't need to be interrupted by any of these tedious stop-and-searches that are no doubt being conducted...?"

"Oh, of course!" Said the nurse. "I will do it straight away!"

They waved her off, and waited until she had bustled away and the cockpit had closed.

Then Charlotte turned to NotMatt.

"How did you...?"

"I shouldn't have," NotMatt told her. "But glamour takes less energy than interfering with physical reality. I'm just hoping it was too little a trace for that Head Frog idiot to track..."

As he spoke, he flipped a number of switches above their heads, gave a joystick an experimental shrug, then sighed with satisfaction.

"You understand the controls, then?" Asked Charlotte, with some relief.

"Nope," said NotMatt. "Just enough to know how to initiate the automatic pilot."

He pressed a button, and the launch gave a low rumble.

A moment later, they were tossed forward as if by the hand of a giant frog, and then they were off, shooting through the dark, dingy depths of the Froghearth sea.

She just hoped that wherever they went, they would be able to leave this dank, underwater prison. She didn't know much about the surface of this planet, but how could it possibly be worse than this?

❧ 14 ❧

The warm summer rain thundered down. Matt scowled, and tried adjusting his coat. He succeeded in covering the weak spot at his breast, but in doing so he opened up a weak spot where his jeans met his tee-shirt.

He made a noise like an outraged cat, and pushed the coat back into its original configuration. Now there was hardly a square inch of him that wasn't wet. It was...it was *undignified*.

"Come on," NotCharlotte called back to him. She was marching on briskly, seemingly unaware of the driving rain. Water pooled in the gutters and flooded off awnings. The streets were near-deserted, though when he looked into the shop windows, Matt could see that they were jam-packed with bodies, trying to keep dry, trying to keep out of the vicious rain.

Which is what we would be doing if we had any sense, he thought to himself.

Or rather, what they shouldn't have any need of doing.

Of all the places they had planned to spend their honeymoon....

They had talked of Rhodes. Of the Caribbean. Of Mauritius.

All splendid options. All warm, and beautiful and - crucially - unlikely to be covered with the thick, eternal coating of British rain.

One place they had not talked of at all was Brighton.

Not that he disliked Brighton. No, it was quite a nice little town. Bit of nightlife. Bit of quirkiness. London-by-the-sea, and all that.

But not for his *honeymoon*. Oh no, that wouldn't be right.

No, they had both agreed absolutely on that - wherever they went, it would be out of the country.

Matt scowled.

Except, it wasn't *his* Charlotte who had brought him here. No.

His Charlotte was...he didn't know.

Anywhere. She could be anywhere.

His heart lurched in his chest. Suddenly, the rain wasn't the only water filling his eyes. The tears ran down his cheeks and into his mouth. They tasted of salt and lost hope.

Then a smallish, feminine hand came out of the rain and grabbed him by his collar.

NotCharlotte dragged him along without apparent effort.

"Hey, hey, hey!" Matt shouted, struggling to keep up and stay standing. "You can let go! I'm coming!"

NotCharlotte wheeled to face him. Her blue eyes burnt out at him, her shoulders set and determined.

Except it wasn't Charlotte. Not really. Not *his* Charlotte.

"How many times do I have to tell you?" NotCharlotte hissed at him. "I don't like this any more than you do. But I'm trying to sort things out. I'm trying to protect us!"

Matt attempted to brush her hands away, but they were as strong as iron vices. They didn't budge an inch.

"Well please excuse me if I'm not quite so good at dealing

with the extremely weird as you are," said Matt. He meant for it to come out scathing and sarcastic. Instead, it just sounded petulant.

NotCharlotte pulled him closer, until their faces were centimetres apart.

"Do - you - want - her - back?" she hissed at him.

He stared into her eyes. Fierce. Frightening.

After a moment he looked away.

"Yes," he said. "Of course."

"Then don't you think a little water is a small price to pay?" she asked.

"Yes, but-"

"It's *here*," she hissed at him, cutting him off.

Matt shook his head.

"You said that in London," he reminded her. "And in that forest in Scotland. And..."

"But this time I'm *right*," she said. "I can taste it. I can smell it. We are close, very close."

Matt thought about reminding her that this was exactly what she had said in those other places, but bit his tongue instead.

He thought of the market of Covent Garden in London, where they had gone first. He had to admit, the stall she had led them to had been...weird. It had definitely been weird.

He hadn't smelt anything, not exactly, not the way she had described it.

But there had been something in the air, something like electricity crawling on his skin. Everything had felt *thin* somehow. Everything had felt *possible*.

"I know, I know," said NotCharlotte, as if reading his thoughts. "It wasn't the guy who sold boomerangs. I was wrong about that."

Matt shrugged. The stall holder had been...odd. He had spoken to them, spoken in a way that marked him out as different. And yet, when NotCharlotte had tried to question him, had asked him about the thing she was after, he had looked at her blankly.

"He had some of it," NotCharlotte went on. "A small spark. He didn't even know it himself. He will have himself a strange life, I'm sure of it. But he couldn't have helped us."

"Neither could that woman," added Matt. "The one in the cave."

"True," said NotCharlotte. "She was ever further gone than the boomerang man. But we had to look. We had to ask. They both had enough of the blood to..."

She waved a hand in the air vaguely, her voice trailing off.

Then she frowned. The rain was starting to ease off, the thunderous fall of raindrops slowing to a steady patter.

She breathed in deeply.

Then she smiled.

"Oh, I can certainly smell it here," she said.

She turned, and without a backwards glance vanished into the maze of side streets.

Matt thought about turning away, about going back to the hotel. Really, all this talk of *versions* and *protection* and *beacons* was becoming too much. He wasn't sure how much more he could take. When he woke up in the middle of the night and looked at himself in the mirror, he had begun to see a madman staring back.

He sighed.

But then, what good was going back to the hotel? He had to trust her.

So he followed.

The Lanes was a higgledy-piggledy fairy-tale of back alleys and narrow passageways. Shop windows glowed out their wares, strange objects and beautiful things seeming to flare out against the darkening, drear streets. Matt struggled after her, hurrying to keep up as she darted this way and that.

Intermittently she raised her face to the sky and sniffed the air. All hint of uncertainty had left her now. She was like a preying animal.

She was following her nose.

The rain had come so heavy that Matt sent up a spray of water with every footfall. It was...uncanny.

Ever since the wedding, something had seemed not quite right with the weather.

First had come the winds. That was when they had left for London. Winds so strong that trees had come down all over the country (which wasn't so unusual) and cows had ended up blown across the channel and into France (which was). Then there had been the snow. Not that snow was so unusual in England, but five feet of it in the middle of summer was...

Again, Matt settled on the word, *uncanny*.

Now it was the rain.

When he had mentioned it to NotCharlotte, she had scowled and told him something incomprehensible about not playing by the rules of the story. Which didn't make any sense, because surely she was leading them on this wild goose chase because she wanted to keep them *safe* from the eyes of the story - whatever that meant.

All in all, it was very confusing. Matt had decided it was probably safer not to worry about it too much, and to concentrate on not being killed by a freak wind-swept cow.

Just keep his head down, and maybe, just maybe, he would get her back...

Matt rounded a corner and ran full-pelt into NotCharlotte. She had stopped stock-still in front of a shop window.

"Oof," said Matt, doubling up and trying quite hard not to be sick.

He still didn't know exactly what she was made of, but running into NotCharlotte was like running into a pile of bricks, only prettier.

NotCharlotte was staring into the shop window. From his doubled-up position, Matt tried to get a sense of the objects the shop was selling. It seemed to be a very eclectic mix. There were toys - a model train, a doll, some old-fashioned wooden animals, beautiful things that looked like they had been hand-crafted and painted at least a hundred years ago. But just next to the toys there were other things: a dagger with a cruel blade and a red jewel in the hilt, a bow and arrow, a mace.

A *mace*.

Matt tried to think if he had ever actually seen a mace before in real life. They weren't exactly common.

He looked at NotCharlotte. She was smiling.

"This is it," she told him.

Above the door, a beautiful wooden sign proclaimed the name of the shop in blue and gold, with stars and obscure symbols floating around the letters.

"*Fabian's Emporium Of Wonders*?" said Matt, reading the words with a cynical twist he could not keep out of his voice. "Sounds splendid. Very third-rate fantasy novel."

But NotCharlotte ignored him.

She pushed open the door and went inside, leaving Matt to hobble in after her as best as he was able.

Inside, the wares were even weirder. They seemed to be scattered about the shop without apparent overarching organisation. Ornate, plush cushions would sit next to crossbows, which in turn sat next to old, dusty books. Matt picked one up at random. It was printed in a language he did not recognise, which wasn't so odd he supposed.

He blinked.

He didn't even recognise the *alphabet*.

Apart from them, the shop was empty. Candles burnt behind the counter, giving off a dull yellow glow and an aroma of exotic spices.

Matt found himself nodding. This felt the same. He found he *could* almost smell it.

The same as the stall-holder in London.

The same as the woman in the caves in the wood in Scotland.

Only stronger. It was much stronger here, much more *real*.

He found himself wondering if he would have noticed it a few weeks ago, before the wedding, before his life had come so spectacularly off the rails. He wasn't sure. He didn't think so, somehow.

NotCharlotte was rubbing off on him.

A bell tinkled somewhere in the darkness at the back of the shop. There were footfalls, and then a shape loomed up out of some back-room that remained hidden.

Matt froze. He did his best not to gasp or draw back.

After all, that would be very, very rude.

The poor woman must get a lot of that, looking the way she did.

She was tall - taller than Matt, much taller than NotCharlotte - with thinning grey hair and a heavy build. Her face was old and weather-worn, and was quite the most horrible face Matt had seen for some time. When she smiled at them, he saw rows of blackened, stubby teeth. She walked with a shuffling gait, and he could see at a glance that her right arm was nearly useless, withered and contracted and bent into her chest. But her eyes were very bright, and her good hand darted around quickly, fingers always moving. And when she spoke, her voice was deep and rich, with no hint of shame or self-consciousness.

"Ah, young lovers, is it?" said the woman. "Here to sample the magical delights of the town? Of the city, I should say. It gets hard to keep up, when you get to my age. Anyway. I dare say I can help. What can I do for you?"

NotCharlotte smiled back. She looked very pleased with herself, like the cat who has not only got the cream, but who has worked out where the cows were kept, and had a basic grasp of pasteurisation, too.

"What a lovely shop!" she told the old woman. "I knew we would find something like this here, if we kept looking. I could almost - I could almost *taste* it in the air."

The old woman gave a little chuckle, but she tilted her head at the same time, and Matt thought he saw a glimmer of wariness start up in her eyes.

"Oh, yes," she said. "I flatter myself that you can find things here that might otherwise elude a curious traveller. What are you looking for?"

"You got that right," said NotCharlotte. "I am a traveller. I've come a long way. I need to go a ways further. The only problem is, the way I need to go is rather a strange one. I need to make sure that no-one notices."

Matt thought this just about made sense to him, after all the strange explanations NotCharlotte had given him. But he wondered what sense the old lady would make of it. She would probably think they were both mad, he decided. It wouldn't be long before she was talking about having to close up, and ushering them out of the shop.

Except she didn't.

Instead, she grew very still.

"Is that right?" asked the old woman, after a long, heavy pause.

NotCharlotte nodded.

The woman opened her eyes wide. She looked completely innocent, and it was at that moment that Matt - who knew something about trying to look innocent, having needed to do so rather a lot in his own life - suddenly decided that NotCharlotte was right.

There were no two ways about it.

This woman knew things. Strange things. *Weird* things.

Things that might help to get his Charlotte back.

Before he knew what he was doing, Matt was striding forwards. He put both hands on the counter and looked the woman straight in the eyes.

"Help us," he asked her. "You have to help us. This isn't my Charlotte, you see. My one has gone. I'm not sure where exactly, but I need her back. To do that we need a beacon, so that someone can find us. But then there's the business about the Story. It mustn't find out. If it does, the whole thing is over, and I'll never get her back, and then and then and then..."

Matt realised he was babbling. A moment later, he realised he was crying, too.

He shook his head, and mentally replayed what he had just said.

He couldn't have been making any sense. He looked up, expecting to see confusion - or maybe anger - in the old woman's face.

But instead, she was looking at him softly, with those strange, bright eyes.

"I see," she nodded, as if he had made complete sense. "A straight swap, was it?"

Matt opened his mouth, but NotCharlotte was already answering her.

"Seems to have been," she said.

The old woman nodded.

Then she shuffled out from behind the counter.

"You can help us, then?" Matt asked, but the woman walked straight past, ignoring him. When she reached the shop door, she locked it. Then she flipped the sign. She took a deep breath, and walked back to them.

"I thought it was probably about time," she muttered, rubbing her eyes. "Doesn't seem to matter where I go, there's no escaping the kind of work I do. Or the kind of people who need it."

She looked from one of them to the other, long and slow.

Matt - who had a finely tuned ear for an insult - found that he had come up with sixteen counter-insults without even deciding too. A moment later he realised there was no way he could deploy any of them.

"Please," he said instead. "It's not much, really, I suppose. Not to someone like you. A little thing to ask, right?"

He gave her his best Charming Smile. The old lady did not return it.

"Oh, *someone like me*, is it?" she asked. "What's that supposed to mean?"

Matt's smile faltered, limped gamely on in the face of massive facial opposition from the old woman, then collapsed with dignity into a subdued Friendly Look.

"Nothing," he said, a little too quickly. "Nothing at all! All I mean is..." he glanced about, looking for inspiration. "All I mean is, well, look at this place. Look at this...ah...workmanship. You must be...you must be very gifted. That's all I. That's all...Uh."

He trailed off under the force of her glare. He found that he was unaccountably looking at his shoes.

Next to him, NotCharlotte gave a loud sigh.

"Sorry about this one," she said. "A couple of weeks ago he was about to get married and the weirdest thing that had ever happened to him was doing a poo in the shape of the Virgin Mary."

"Hey!" Matt protested. "I told you that in *confidence*! And it wasn't *just* Mary," he added. "There was a wise man, too. *And* a sheep."

"Quite the nativity," said the old woman. "But I don't need to know the details, I assure you. I've met enough, over the years. People who know, and people who don't. I could see as soon as you walked in that I was dealing with one of each."

"Thank you," said NotCharlotte. "I'm Charlotte, by the way. This is Matt."

"Very good," said the old woman.

"And we should call you Fabian, I presume?" asked Matt, after a pause.

"Oh, you could call me any number of names," said the old woman. "But perhaps not that one. No, that one is for the regular customers. The ones who like the idea of magic, but who would run a mile if they knew the tenth part of the tenth part. No, you can call me June. That name has always gone with the work. I thought it left it behind more than once, but the work has a way of following you, so perhaps the name should, too."

"So you *have* done this kind of thing before," said Matt, unable to keep the relief from his voice. "I'm very glad. It sounds so mad. Stories and beacons and all. To hear someone else talk about it...it's reassuring."

"Oh, sounds completely mad to me," said June breezily. "Mad as spoons."

"What?" said Matt. "But you said..."

June waved him away.

"Don't worry," she said. "Different people have different names for all this stuff. Different frames of reference."

She shuffled past them, then led the way behind the counter and gestured for them to follow.

"No good talking business out there," she told them, leading them into a small, comfortable room. There were no eldritch candles burning with scents redolent of other worlds, Matt noted. Instead there was a sensible-looking angle-poise light, a neat, clean table, and several chairs well-stocked with cushions.

"Please excuse the normalcy," said June, who must have

noticed Matt's expression. "When you get to my age you begin to appreciate the benefits of good lighting. The set-dressing is all well and good, but I'm not trying to convince *you* that the world is a strange place. So we'll just sit and discuss this in comfort, if it's all the same to you."

She gave a sigh as she settled in amongst the cushions. Matt and NotCharlotte took the sofa opposite.

"So," said June, her voice slow and careful, "let's see if we understand one another. You sought me out because you needed my help. But you didn't know of me specifically. You needed *someone* who could help. From what you told me earlier, you've been sniffing me out, looking for someone like me, someone who lives on the cusp. Someone of the blood."

NotCharlotte nodded.

"And the fact that you *could* sniff me out means that you're not exactly normal yourself," June continued. "But you ain't got the blood. That much *I* can smell. So you must be...what? I don't sense any hexes or such, so we're probably talking augmentation of some sort or another."

NotCharlotte nodded again.

"Beneath the delicate beauty of this weak body beats the fiery heart of a warrior," said NotCharlotte. Then she stood up, and lifted the sofa (complete with attached Matt) several feet into the air with one hand. "The heart was mine. But yes - lots of augmentations. All manner of those."

She lowered the sofa.

"Strength in the limbs, then," said June. "Though that's easy to do. You see a lot of augmented bodies about, relatively speaking. But whatever it is in your brain...well, that kind of augmentation is much more difficult to pull off. Seen it done before. Often goes wrong. Whoever did that work must be a real artist."

NotCharlotte smiled lazily.

"All correct so far," she said. "An artist indeed. Without

his work-" here she tapped the side of her head -"We would have been well and truly buggered, pardon my Italian. But after the last time this happened, we decided being able to sniff out people who might help would be...useful. Very useful. So as soon as I found myself here - in this reality, I mean, this version - I knew what I had to do. So I started sniffing. We had a couple of other leads, but they both went cold."

"I'm not surprised," said June. "There ain't so many of us left, these days. Getting harder and harder."

"In what way?" asked Matt.

"In lots of ways," she told him. "Not many believe anymore. I mean, not many have believed for a long time. My whole life." She shrugged. "But it's getting less."

Matt found himself wondering how old June was. She looked to be maybe seventy, perhaps a little older. And yet...

"Then there's the iron," June went on. "Always more of that. More cars. More buildings. I mean, I work with the stuff, on occasion. I *have* to. But the wards are getting more difficult to maintain..."

"You've thought of leaving, I suppose," said NotCharlotte. Matt noted that it wasn't a question.

June nodded slowly, then looked away.

"Thought of it, of course I have," she said. "Be a fool not to. It's part of the same story, though. More iron, less belief in the old ways. This world's turning inwards on itself, and it's getting harder to walk away every year."

"But you still could?" asked Charlotte, and this time there *was* a question there. Matt blinked at her, surprised by the hunger in her voice.

June seemed surprised, too.

"I suppose I could, at that," she said. "Though where I would go - and if I would still be welcome...well, those are other questions. No, I'm here for the long haul, it seems."

Then she narrowed her eyes and leaned forwards.

"But I must say you seem very interested in that," said June. "A minute ago it was all stories and beacons and being rescued, and now - what? Are you thinking of running?"

NotCharlotte shrugged.

"If we have to," she answered simply. "But no, not really. Not ideally. But I need to be found. I really, *really* need to."

NotCharlotte glanced away, and Matt found himself noticing how tired she looked, how drawn about the eyes. He realised he hadn't given much thought to how she was coping with being here. Cast away from her reality, into a strange other *version*...She seemed so calm, that was the thing, so in control. From her manner, he had assumed that this sort of thing must happen to her all the time. But no. Of course not. She had been acting that way because she had to. Because otherwise, who was going to sort things out? *Him*?

"And a way out is a way in," said June. "Clever. Which is where this beacon thing comes in, I suppose."

"Nearly," said NotCharlotte. "But something else comes first. It has to. Before we can start sending out signals for help, we really need to cover our tracks. Or else..."

June closed her eyes, frowning as if trying to remember.

"Or else the story will find out and come and get you?" she hazarded. "That's what you said earlier, isn't it?"

"The story," agreed Charlotte. "Or one of the Guardians of Story. A Sheriff or an Epitaph or..."

June waved a hand.

"Nope," she said. "This is the point where those frames of reference I mentioned begin to get out of synch."

NotCharlotte smiled. Matt wondered why. It seemed to him that they were getting more muddled by the second. What was worse, he was beginning to get the mother of all headaches just trying to come to terms with one crazy bending of reality. To find that NotCharlotte and June did not, in fact, share this same view made things ten times more difficult. And what was worse, from the way June had spoken about *frames of reference*, he had a horrible sinking feeling that there might be other, even crazier ways of understanding the Universe.

"Look," he said, trying not to sound tetchy but instantly failing, "can't we try and keep this simple? For my benefit, if for no one else's."

June and NotCharlotte looked at him blankly for a moment then burst out laughing.

"Oh, but it's anything *but* simple," said June. "That's the problem. By definition, the universe is a weird, unlikely place. Everyone's got a different way of modelling it."

"Yes, but those models need to be *correct*," said Matt though gritted teeth. "Otherwise, what's the point?"

"Nah, that's not true," said June. "Haven't you heard of model-dependent realism?"

"Yes," lied Matt. "That's not the point."

"That *is* the point," said NotCharlotte. "Think about it. People have different ways of modelling something simple like what defines a friendship or how to drive a car. As soon as you start talking about *versions* or *parallel realities* or - yes, even *stories*...well, there's bound to be differences."

"Absolutely," chimed in June. "Add to that the fact that the very existence of different versions starts to make the Universe go all extra-squiggly, and you end up with the truth of the matter."

Matt sighed and leant back, with one arm over his eyes.

The headache was definitely getting worse.

"Which is?" he found himself asking, in a small, defeated voice.

"Different versions of different versions," said June and NotCharlotte at the same time.

Matt let out a long breath.

"Fine," he said. "It's easier if I just let you talk, isn't it?"

And they did.

It wasn't long before Matt found himself thoroughly, thoroughly lost.

There was talk of stories, and how that related to different worlds. There was talk about something called *The Grand*, which he had never heard of before, but which NotCharlotte apparently had, and which seemed very strange and mysterious. Then there was lots about being *of the blood* and about the trouble with iron, and about not being found by those who one didn't want to find you.

Matt just couldn't follow it. His headache was too pressing. The absence of his Charlotte was too sharp.

All that mattered was getting her back.

That was all.

The whole world could wrap itself in iron and bugger off to The Grand (whatever that was) for all he cared, as long as he could see her again. Just let him have her back, with her eyes brown again, the way they should be, her smile, her voice...

And then June was saying something that jolted him back out of his reverie.

He frowned.

What was it she had said?

Something that had made him sit up and take notice.

He replayed the last few seconds of the conversation in his head.

"Yes," he said, surprising both of the others by speaking, "we probably should talk about the cost, should't we?"

June was looking at him with raised brows.

"Ah, so you do have some use to you?" She asked.

"We had some money saved for the honeymoon," said Matt. "Obviously, this hopping around the country has taken a little, but it's much less than two weeks in Mauritius. How much do you need?"

June turned to NotCharlotte and gave a smile.

"Ah, they're so sweet when they're innocent, aren't they?" she said.

Matt rolled his eyes.

"Oh, here we go," he said. "Time to bring out all the little haggling tricks. Usually, I must say I would be bang up for this, but right now..." he shook his head. "Honestly, I'm not interested. I just want her back. So just name your price, and we can..."

June and NotCharlotte exchanged glances.

Then June chuckled and looked back to Matt.

"Whatever made you think I wanted your money?" she asked him. "After all this, after what you've seen, after what we've talked about, you really think money is any kind of use to me?"

Matt looked at her blankly.

"Then what do you want?" he asked her.

She told him.

15

"**O**h, a splendid throw, my lady!" said Head Frog 127 as he watched the javelin sail through the air. "You really are a natural hunter!"

The javelin glinted in the red sunlight, before descending gracefully and skewering the Kree straight through the middle. The huge herbivore stared in surprise at the metal implement which had sprouted out of its chest, made a baffled mooing noise, then toppled over, dead.

A cheer went up from the attendant servants, slaves and guards. Head Frog 127 was cheering loudest of all.

Princess Frogmella nodded and gave a modest bow. It set her delicate, beautiful underbelly wobbling in a most enticing manner, and Head Frog 127 congratulated himself once again on how splendidly life was treating him.

The attendants were arranged in a rough semi-circle around the royal chariot. The skinny little undernourished frogling slaves, the brutal, brawny elite guardsmen, and the various functionaries and servants of the court formed a shell of bustling activity around them, but really Head Frog 127 and Princess Frogmella might have been alone in the whole world.

The servants kept their distance, and Head Frog 127 more or less had the Princess all to himself. It was turning out to be a good day.

Another good day.

And what did it matter if they hadn't found the ones they were hunting? No, Head Frog 127 didn't mind at all about that. Let them run! Let them remain unfound! The longer the hunt went on, the more time he would have with the Princess, the more he could worm his way into her affections, win her to his cause...

And then, of course, it was only a matter of time before his scientists back at the ship completed their work. Soon, the Chaos Drive would be unlocked. Soon, all the secrets would be his...

She led the way, strolling through the long, dark grass of the rolling plane, towards the felled Kree. The royal guards shadowed them at a discrete distance, yellow eyes alert for any hint of danger.

"Wherever did you learn to throw a javelin like that?" Head Frog 127 asked.

Princess Frogmella tossed her head, making her green, jowly cheeks trembling in a way that he found most enticing.

"Oh, you know," she told him. "Father insisted I receive training in all types of combat. He said it was important I knew how to defend myself. It's a frog-eat-frog world out there, he always says."

"A wise frog," said Head Frog 127, though really he thought *cunning* and *devious* would describe King Toadflaps much better than *wise*. "Tell me, when we find the ones we hunt, will you skewer them dead straight off? Or will you make a sport of it?"

They reached the dead Kree. It was an odd sort of beast. Like most of the life-forms that inhabited Forghearth, it had been mucked about with in all sorts of ways on a genetic level, with the intention of making it pleasing and useful to the Frogling lords. It was about fifteen feet long, heavy, sturdy, with a set of udders capable of producing thick, delicious frogspawn, and great rump muscles that provided succulent cuts of meat. It was yellow-green and - of course - looked rather like a massive frog, only a slightly cow-ish one.

"Oh, I will make sport, of course," said Princess Frogmella, removing the javelin from the dead beast with a single, strong jerk of her well-muscled forearm. "After the way they treated poor Tony, they deserve to suffer, don't you think?"

Head Frog 127 looked out over the rolling plains. In the distance, the remaining Kree were charging away from their felled sister, which Head Frog 127 thought was a smart move. Over the last few days he had enjoyed the honour of many hours spent in the company of the Princess, rushing through the various environments of Froghearth, hunting for the aliens, trying to flush them out. And during those days, Princess Frogmella had shown herself to be very, very adept at killing things. She excelled at it. She revelled in it. For the Kree to get as far away from the princess as possible seemed like a sound survival strategy.

"Undoubtably," agreed Head Frog 127 as they strolled back towards the royal chariot. "They deserve death, but not clean deaths. No, their deaths should be long and splendid, and ornamented with all kinds of delicious, inventive sufferings." He gave her a roguish smile. "I'm quite sure you will be able to deliver that, my Princess."

"Oh, flatterer!" she told him, and slapped him round the head flirtatiously.

Head Frog 127 picked himself up. She was so strong! And she didn't pull her punches, which Head Frog 127 found deeply erotic. This was the third time today that she had knocked him off his feet. Things were going well. Better than he had dared to hope. King Toadflaps had clearly indicated that he was in favour with the court. And the Princess...she liked him. She *really* liked him.

They reached the chariot, and Head Frog 127 took the liberty of placing his hands on her muscular, slimy hips and helping her into the vehicle.

"Not flattery," he told her, "just the truth. Oh, when I consider the possibility of the aliens being caught by anyone other than you..." he shuddered. "Oh, it doesn't bear thinking about."

"Then we must make sure no one else beats us to it!" commanded the Princess. She turned to her attendants.

"Froglings, stop dawdling!" her voice was deep and commanding, full of all the authority of the Frogopolis. "Mercer, where to now? Any fresh leads?"

Mercer was the Princesses' equerry. He was tall and thin, with ancient leathery skin and a quick, darting manner. He held a tablet in one hand, which he consulted carefully.

"There is much chatter and excitement across the whole of the Frogopolis, my lady," he told her. "Most of it is likely nonsense, I fear, but I am keeping a list of those suggestions which seem more...plausible."

Mercer handed the tablet over, and the Princess scrolled through the list.

She frowned, displeased.

"Oh, but this is all poppycock," she announced. "Honestly, we were in the larvae district only yesterday. There wasn't hide nor hair of them."

She flicked through the list, shaking her head.

"No...no...no..." she said, her voice getting more and more dangerous. "This is all nonsense, Mercer! I want you to bring me facts, solid leads, not...not imaginings and fantasies!"

She tossed the tablet over her shoulder. Her face looked like thunder.

Her equerry - obviously used to such outbursts - steepled his hands and bowed his head.

"I am most sorry for this failure," he told her. "Just allow me a little more time and I..."

"Time? Time, he says!" Princess Frogmella snorted, and turned to Head Frog 127. "Time is the one thing we don't have! If we're not quick, if we're not first out the gate with every lead, then who knows who will find them? Probably some wretched common frog with no art in his soul and a penchant for giving simple, inelegant deaths!"

A thought crossed Head Frog 127's mind. It was a foolish thought, one he knew he would do better to forget. After all, the fewer people knew of his secret, the less chance there was of him being betrayed. He had already determined that. He was quite sure of it. No one must know of the device, no one must have any inkling of his plan.

And yet...

Her beautiful puffy face, the way her eyes bulged so wantonly from their sockets, the sweet swamp-breath that washed over him, warm and full of malice...oh, she was *splendid*. And right now, he wondered if he wouldn't do anything, anything at all, just to please her.

"There is...there is something I have that might help," he found himself saying.

She looked at him. A smile quirked her lips, but those beautiful yellow eyes of hers were full of hunger.

"Something? You have access to some information that even the royal equerry lacks?" she asked. There was a mocking edge to her voice. "Are you trying to tell me you have been withholding some advantage from the crown?"

Head Frog 127 wondered if he had gone too far. He should keep it to himself, all for himself...

But if he was to fulfil all his dreams, if he was to ascend to the very pinnacle of the Frogopolis and take his place by her side, well - they would do well to work together. Trust must start somewhere.

"It is a...a trifling thing," he said, trying to keep his voice nonchalant. He noticed the equerry was looking at him closely, following every word. That would not do at all. "Perhaps you would allow me to tell you of it as we make our way to our next hunting ground?"

Princess Frogmella smiled knowingly.

"Oh, you can trust Mercer," she told him. "He is father's most loyal servant, and you can rely on his discretion absolutely."

"I do not doubt it," said Head Frog 127, who doubted it very much. "But the truth of the matter is I wanted it to be rather a surprise for your father. Something I've been sort of getting ready for him. I'd hate for him to find out early, get his hopes up and then be disappointed."

Princess Frogmella stared at him for a long moment, flat and steady.

Then she smiled.

"How thoughtful of you," she announced. "Very well. Let us be on our way, and you can tell me all about this mysterious trifle of yours."

Mercer nodded and walked away, but Head Frog 127 was sure the equerry suspected something. That was one more frog to add to the big long list of people he didn't trust. It was a comprehensive list. It featured basically everyone Head Frog 127 had ever met, with the exception of his mother, and that was only because she was dead.

"So," said the Princess as the chariot trundled along, beginning to pick up speed, "what is this information you speak of?"

For a moment, he teetered on the edge. He could still go back. He needn't tell her the truth of it...

"It's an artefact," he found himself saying. "From the aliens. Something quite special. Something very interesting."

"Really?" she said, sounding disappointed. "What good is that?"

That stung Head Frog 127. He wanted to impress her, to make her see how useful he could be, to show her what they could become together.

"If my sources are correct, it could do us a lot of good," he told her.

She gave a little chuckle and looked out across the plains as they whipped by.

"Oh, father's always telling me of the plunder his captains bring back from the wars," she said breezily. "It's never any good though. What do you expect? They're barbarians. No culture, no taste. And judging from what I saw of them today, they could hardly be called *intelligent* life-forms, could they?"

"The Chaos Drive is different," Head Frog 127 told her, and it was done. There was no going back now.

She turned to him. Her face was still.

"What did you say it was called?" she asked him.

He repeated the name. Was he imagining it, or was there a glint of something there? Recognition, maybe?

But he brushed that thought aside. It was ridiculous. *He* had never heard the name, not before the Prophet had described it to him.

"What a curious name," she said after a moment's thought. "And what is this...this *Chaos Drive* supposed to do? Make a mess?"

Head Frog 127 tittered dutifully at the non-joke.

"If my source is right, it can do lots of things," he told her.

"Like what?" she wanted to know.

"It's how they got away, for a start," he said.

"But they didn't get away," she reminded him. "That's why they are currently sneaking and fleeing through our magnificent world, desperately trying to postpone their inevitable, horrible deaths."

"True," he admitted. "But they got away from a lot of people before they made the mistake of crossing us."

"And how is it you caught them?" she asked teasingly. "Apart from your deep cunning and strategic brilliance, obviously."

I got help, he thought. *I cheated.*

"Oh, my research gave me a few ideas," he said aloud. "I was able to block it, you see. I worked out how the machine worked, then stopped them using it. And now it is mine."

She smiled at him, and placed a warm, soggy hand on his cheek. The gesture was so intimate, so unexpected that Head Frog 127 thought his head would explode.

"*Ours*, you mean," she told him. "It belongs to the crown, just like all alien plunder."

He blinked at her. He was trying to concentrate on what she was saying, but it was very difficult to focus through the thick fog of erotic tension.

"Of course," he said. His voice was husky, barely controlled. "That's what I meant."

"Good," she said, leaning away again and removing her hand. "Anyway, I still don't quite see how being able to...to escape from things is going to help us find those vile creatures."

Head Frog 127 felt his mind clearing. It was so difficult to think sensibly around her. Perhaps he had made a mistake, bringing up the matter of the Chaos Drive. It would be better if he did some back-peddling, played it down a little.

She gave a sigh.

"No," she said, as if having made up her mind that he was a silly frogling spinning tall tales, quite out of touch with the real world. "I'm afraid you're just like the others, after all. Nothing special. What a shame."

Head Frog 127 felt his stomach turn to ice. He saw his golden future slipping away. True, he could use force, just use the powers the machine would grant him. He could use the machine as he had planned, make the interventions he required, and power would still be is.

But her eyes, he thought. *Her beautiful eyes. Her damp breath. That lovely red tongue, sticky and splendid...*

No, he wanted her. He wanted to rule - and he would do - but he wanted her, too. And he wanted her to love him of her own accord, without having to use the powers of the Chaos Drive to achieve this through artifice.

"You're wrong," he told her.

Her head snapped towards him.

"I'm what?" she demanded sharply. "That is not the way you talk to me, frog! I am your Princess, not some...some stupid tadpole of a girl with moss for brains who you can contradict as the whim takes you!"

"My Princess, I apologise," said Head Frog 127. "And yet...you *are* wrong. This machine...it will change everything. *Everything*."

Her lip curled. She tilted her head back and looked down her nose at him.

"Prove it," she told him.

Head Frog 127 smiled.

"Gladly," he said

He told her where the device was, and she nodded her understanding.

"We go to your ship, then," she said. "But I warn you, sir. If this wonderful boon of yours turns out to be so much hot air...I will be disappointed. *Most* disappointed. You can wave farewell to your glittering military career. You'll spend the rest of your miserable life mucking out the *Pondwater's* latrines rather than captaining her."

"I assure you, my Princess, you will not be disappointed."

Head Frog 127's voice was confident. Last night, his chief science officer had finally succeeded in cracking the main lock which kept the Chaos Drive from being open to him. Head Frog 127 had congratulated the science officer, promised him a glittering future, then - prudently - shot him in the back. You could never be too careful.

He was sure that now, with the main defences broken, it would not take him long to get the machine to start spilling its secrets.

What better way to put the Chaos Drive to use for the first time, than in the company of the beautiful frog he loved?

He would show her, he would demonstrate the powers that were now his to command.

Then she would love him. He was quite sure of that.

16

Charlotte shivered in the damp, moist air of evening and tried to block out the unfortunate smell of rotting mushroom.

"How long before we can get going again?" she asked, knowing already what the answer would be.

"We should wait a few hours, at least," NotMatt told her. "Middle of the night would be safest. After the moons have gone down. The darker it is, the less chance we have of being spotted."

Charlotte sighed and looked away. Even a few days ago, she would have protested. She would have talked about the dangers of staying in one place too long. She would have mentioned the need to find some food, or at least some water. Their supplies were running dangerously low, and it was difficult to keep moving - to keep thinking straight, even - when you were tired and hungry and hadn't eaten for what seemed like forever. Most of all, she would have talked about the awful, nose-melting smell.

It was like a physical thing, tendrils of dripping, stinking marsh-gas, slime-slinking their way through the air and forcing itself into their nostrils. The whole vast structure they were nestled in was rotting, apparently. It was difficult to breath without vomiting. It was difficult to *think*.

But now, after the best part of three weeks on the run, after being hunted and chased, shot at, screamed at, and not having been able to get more than an hour or two's sleep in one go for fear of being spotted and dismembered...well, the fight was going out of her. She was losing the will. And so instead of pointing out all the problematic aspects of their situation and demanding NotMatt do something to remedy it, she simply settled down in the soft mush next to him.

She hated to think about how much easier things had been while they had been underwater. She hated even more to think how much easier she had assumed it would be when they got out onto dry land. It made her worry that perhaps, however awful she felt things were at any given moment, they were only going to get worse.

She wondered again why the hell they had left the (relative) comfort of the little launch they had stolen from the old-frog's home, before another part of her mind reminded her acerbically that it was because the vehicle had been reported as having been hijacked by fugitives a mere forty five minutes after they had made off with it. At least this fact had answered her unasked question about how long Matt could hold the influence of his glamour after they had departed.

Not to mention that it had given them the vital chance to get away from the immediate vicinity of the arena, and loose themselves in the vast, foul-smelling, and altogether noisome environments of Froghearth. *Small blessings*, she reminded herself. *Be thankful for them. Even when they mostly just smell awful.*

"So they have huge, rotting mushrooms in the Frogopolis, right?" she said with forced brightness, trying to push the the thoughts of how hopeless it all was from her mind, and pretty much failing,

This was, of course, a redundant question, seeing as how they had both just climbed up into the disgusting architecture of purulent fungi a few minutes ago. Still, she felt she had to at least mention the matter. After all, it was increasingly possible that she was going mad from lack of food, water, and basic sane things happening to her. Perhaps she was only imagining the whole mushrooms-as-tall-as-a-skyscraper thing.

"Yup," said NotMatt, much to her disappointment. "Well, on this world at least. I'm not sure about the rest of the Frogopolis."

Charlotte was silent for a moment. She stared out across the darkening landscape of the planet. Huge mushrooms like the one they were currently bedding down in dotted the view, springing up out of the swamplands like a vast, ugly dermatological condition on the skin of the world. The red sun glowered at them as it sunk behind distant mountains. Strange, terrifying birds wheeled in the sky - the same birds which made travelling during the daylight hours inadvisable, on account of their propensity to swoop down and try to turn small, unhappy humans into dinner.

It was an...an *interesting* view, at least. Only a fool or a madman would call it beautiful (or even pleasant) but at least it was novel. Charlotte could never have imagined the existence of a place like this. She wished she still couldn't.

"I thought this horrible place *was* the Frogopolis," she complained. Not because the confusion on this matter really bothered her, but more because she really, really wanted to be complaining about something, and this seemed a good enough target.

"Nah, this is Froghearth," said NotMatt. "The home world of the glorious - and really rather unpleasant - Hegemony of the Frog. Which is also known as the Frogopolis, you see. The Frogopolis is what they call their whole wretched society. It's not a single place."

Charlotte thought about this. Around them, the darkness thickened as the sun dipped below the horizon. The huge, horrible birds went away, and were replaced by smaller (but equally horrible) froggy bat things.

"What," she said slowly, "the hell are we going to do?"

Matt shrugged.

"What we have been doing," he told her. "Not get caught. Find food. Stay alive." He shrugged. "It's nothing new, really. Life has been doing basically that for as long as it's been around."

"Life?" snorted Charlotte. "You might call this life, but I don't."

She expected him to turn away from her then, to go off in a huff. But instead he reached out a hand and laid it gently on hers.

"I know it's tough," he told her. "We just have to hang in here. We've done alright so far, haven't we?"

"That depends," she told him. "If by, *'done alright so far'* what you mean is, *'not actually been killed yet'*, then I suppose I see your point."

She screwed her eyes up tight and gave them a rub. In many ways, this was a mistake, because every time she closed her eyes, her brain started working through slow-motion replays of some of the more horrible things that had nearly eaten them over the last few days. There was Tony, of course, the huge claw-and-teeth monster in the arena. But actually, Tony had been a doddle next to some of the nightmares beasts they'd come across. There were the birds - wingspans over forty feet and huge, broad mouths filled with hundred of sharp, diagonal fangs - birds that had a strong, inevitable resemblance to terrifying flying frogs. There were the little

143

spider-like things, vile little critters that had eight legs and narrow, flickering tongues that stuck to the flesh and burnt like acid when you tore them off. If you were lucky enough to tear them off, that was.

And that didn't touch on a tenth of horrible the hunt had been, because that wasn't even considering the worst creatures that were after them, i.e., the frogs themselves.

They were everywhere. There was no safe place on the whole planet. Of course there wasn't. Their images had been beamed to every inhabitant of the Frogopolis. The whole world was out to get them, scouring every inch, from the broken industrial factories to the filthy, damp cities where frogs were packed together like rotting weeds at the bottom of the compost heap, to here - to the deep countryside, the most recent place Matt had recommended, leading them away from the built up urban centres and into the wild...

And even here, the frogs were everywhere, out in force, teeming, searching for them, always searching...

The fact that they hadn't been caught so far was...

Well, it wasn't luck. Not really. No. she had to admit, it wasn't luck.

It was NotMatt.

He was...

She was reluctant to use the word *magnificent*, mainly because if she did she had the sneaking suspicion that then he would never, ever let her drop it again, whichever version of Matt it might be.

But he had done well, for both of them. He had kept them alive.

Sneaking and sliding away whenever they could, turning and fighting when they couldn't...somehow, against all the odds, Matt had kept them alive.

But how much longer, she wondered? How much longer could they hold out against a whole world?

As if reading her thoughts, Matt gave her hand a squeeze.

"It won't be long now," he told her. "We just have to keep safe, to lay low. Soon. He will find us soon. I know it."

And as simply as that, the spell was broken.

Charlotte closed her eyes, and pulled her hand back. She took a deep breath, and concentrated on not crying.

It was always the same. Every time she began to let herself hope that they would survive, that NotMatt would get them out of there, it always ended up coming back to this delusion.

"I haven't heard from him for a while," NotMatt went on, oblivious to how much his insistence on the fairy tale of rescue was upsetting her. "But that doesn't mean anything. It's a difficult business, transcending and crossing his way here. Probably doesn't have time to keep making contact. Don't worry. We can rely on him."

NotMatt smiled, his teeth glimmering in the growing darkness, and suddenly it was too much.

An image of her beloved cat rushed through her mind.

EB, black furred and wet nosed, purring, rubbing against her leg.

This pleasant image was swiftly overtaken by a second image: the EB of this universe, of this *version*, sat upright and dressed in an assortment of strange, human clothes, sitting in his place on the good ship *Nippy-Whoas*...and then the noise the gun made as it fired, and the flash as the bolt of energy hit the brave feline...

"Stop it!" shouted Charlotte, jumping to her feet and spinning away from him. "Just stop all that! It's not just nonsense, it's actually delusional!"

Her voice echoed through the fronds of the vast mushrooms. In the distance, the cry of a hunting frog-bird cut the air.

Charlotte kept her eyes pressed tight, but that didn't stop the tears escaping. They were warm as they ran down her cheeks, and once they had started, she found she could not turn them off. They weren't just tears for EB anymore - not the EB of this world, who she had known for only a few minutes before he was zapped - but for the EB of *her* world, the cat she had known for years, raised from a kitten, and who was now lost to her, lost along with every other person she had ever known, lost like her whole world, her whole *reality*.

"I'm sorry," NotMatt was saying, standing at her shoulder, speaking gently. "I know this is difficult. Of course it's difficult. I know that maybe you don't want to here one more weird thing amongst all this crazy stuff, but really, *honestly*, he's coming."

She wheeled on him.

"Coming? How can he be coming? He's *dead*! We both saw him die!"

NotMatt nodded.

"We did," he agreed. "But you have to understand, EB is not...he's not exactly *normal*."

Charlotte snorted. There was that word again. *Normal*. She tried to work out what the last normal thing that had happened to her was, and gave up.

"Nothing about this bloody place is normal," she muttered. "It's all weird. And not in a good way."

"Some of it is good," said NotMatt. "I promise. And of all the weird things you have ever met or ever will meet, EB is the best of them. I promise you that, too."

And there was something about the way he said it, a simple sincerity to his voice, no bombast, no attempt to convince her with outrageous claims or so-called evidence. He believed it himself, she realised.

She gave a sigh and settled down again.

"Come on then," she told him. "If we have to spend the

night here, you can at least make it interesting by telling me about him."

NotMatt sat next to her. He put an arm around her shoulders, and she snuggled into his warmth. Safe. It made her feel safe. She knew it was an illusion, but right now she would settle for an illusion of safety over the grim reality off their situation. At least for a little while.

The sun was gone now, the last traces of red light leeching from one corner of the sky. Opposite, the first of the two yellow moons was rising. They had a good few hours to kill, before the moons had traversed the sky, plunging the world into a short period of blessed darkness, the only time when it was relatively safe to travel.

NotMatt scratched his brown-silver stubble, and pursed his lips.

"Well, the first thing you need to know is that he is a cat," he told her.

"Yes," said Charlotte, her mind remaining decidedly unblown by this revelation. "I gathered that."

"Good," said Matt. "The next thing is that he's always been special. Always been clever. Even before he ate...."

"Ate?" she said. "What did he eat?"

"I'll come to that," he promised. "But you have to understand, what EB is, what he became...well, that wouldn't have happened to just any cat. No, EB was special. He had...*potential*."

NotMatt breathed the word out in a long sigh, an effect which was marginally spoiled when a fly took the opportunity to enter his mouth and try to explore his trachea.

"Gurph!" said NotMatt, embarking on a long and comprehensive coughing fit.

When he had finished, he stared sadly at the tiny fly, stuck to his hand with a globule of phlegm.

"Even their bloody *insects* look like frogs," he complained, and it was true.

Charlotte shook her head. She wanted him to start answering some questions.

"Special?" she repeated. "Special how?"

In the sky, stars began to come out, their reflections dancing in the lake at the bottom of the giant mushroom.

"Well, even when he was a kitten he was very understanding," said NotMatt. "He knew what you were asking him to do. Not that he always did it, but he always, always *knew*."

"That's no big deal," said Charlotte. "Our EB, our version of him - he knew what was expected of him when you told him to get off the sofa."

"Yes, but would your EB be able to post an advert for the sofa and arrange collection?" asked Matt.

Charlotte shook her head.

"Ours could," he said simply. "He did all sorts of things. He was special. We loved him more than anything. He came everywhere with us. And then one day he was gone."

"Gone?" asked Charlotte. "Well, cats do that sometimes. They need their space. Probably wandered off to have a mooch around the neighbourhood or something."

"Usually, that's what I would have thought," said NotMatt. "But you have to remember, this was on a spaceship. Mooching opportunities were few and far between. And EB was nowhere to be found."

Charlotte stared down at the lake far below. The reflections of the stars danced and shimmered. Were one of those stars her own home? But then - no, of course not. Even if through some unfeasibly unlikely quirk of fate her eyes had alighted on the sun of her home-world...well, it still wouldn't be her home. Of course it wouldn't. This wasn't her *version*. There was no home for her, not here, not on this side of reality.

She wrinkled her nose, forcing the unpleasant thought down.

"Where could he have gone?" she asked. "Surely he must have been somewhere."

"You would assume so, wouldn't you?" said Matt. "But no. We looked everywhere. All the small, sneaksome places. Underneath vents and inside every nook and cranny. We even opened up the holds we used for smuggling, and there was no way he could possibly have got into them, because they were sealed shut behind vacuum chambers and designed to be unscannable. No, he was gone. Simply gone."

"What did you do?" asked Charlotte.

"I had a brilliant idea, of course," said NotMatt modestly.

"Really?" asked Charlotte, who had a sneaking idea that if the idea was that brilliant, it was probably the other version of herself who had come up with it. "What was that?"

"Cameras," said NotMatt. "It was obvious. Couldn't believe we hadn't thought of it sooner. The ship's replete with cameras. It's stock full of them. Very important, that. Caught out more than one stowaway. Not to mention the main reason for having them, which is to make sure that your crew don't go sampling the goods when you're not looking."

The stars down below twinkled and rippled on the water. The wind must be getting up down there, Charlotte decided.

"So you thought you could watch back the recordings, find out where EB disappeared to," she said, and NotMatt nodded.

"Exactly," he said. "Only thing was, when we watched the tape back, EB didn't slink off down a service shaft or under the bed. He just vanished. Pop. Gone. Not a trace."

"That's...odd," said Charlotte. "Even given the abundance of odd things your version of reality seems to be filled with."

"That's how we both felt," said NotMatt. "So we were

very relieved when we went to the place on the ship where EB had been a moment before he vanished."

"Really? Why?"

"Because that's where we found the rift," said NotMatt.

"A rift?" asked Charlotte. "Like...like a hole?"

"Yes, absolutely, exactly like a hole," agreed NotMatt. "A hole that led from the inside of our nice, cozy spaceship to somewhere else. You couldn't see it at first. Then we worked out the angle had to be just right. Approach that little patch of space from just the right direction, and you ended up falling through a doorway and coming out somewhere else."

Charlotte sat up straight, looking at NotMatt with renewed interest. A magic doorway that led to another world? That sounded interesting. That sounded...well, it sounded reassuringly *relevant* to her current situation...

"Where did it go?" she asked. "Did you find yourself in a world of ever-winter, surrounded by talking animals?"

"No," said NotMatt.

"Well, did it lead to a different time?" she asked. "Perhaps you wandered through and bumped into Jesus, riding a dinosaur and working on a plot to assassinate Hitler?"

"No," said NotMatt. "Not that either."

"Oh," frowned Charlotte, slightly disappointed. "Where did it lead, then?"

"Bournemouth," said NotMatt promptly.

Charlotte blinked.

"Bournemouth?" she repeated.

"Bournemouth," NotMatt confirmed.

There was a long, baffled silence. It was followed by a slightly shorter, but marginally more baffled silence.

"Fine," said Charlotte. "Um. Why?"

"Why not?" asked NotMatt. "Bournemouth is perfectly fine."

"I'm not having a go at Bournemouth," clarified Charlotte. "It just seems...well, I was expecting something more..."

She waved a hand vaguely.

"It was Bournemouth," said NotMatt firmly. "Or at least, it *looked* like Bournemouth."

Charlotte let out a sigh of relief.

That sounded more like it.

"In actual fact, it wasn't even a very good copy of Bournemouth," said NotMatt. "Not when you started looking into things. No, it was like a dim reflection of what someone who had never actually been there might imagine the place was like. A bit like the reflection of those stars in the lake down there," he added, gesturing down to the twinkling lights below. "You see? If you just glanced at it, you might think *down there* was the night sky, whereas actually..."

NotMatt stopped speaking.

There was a silence.

As silences went, it was quite a nasty one. Charlotte could tell that immediately. It was full of all kinds of unpleasant things that weren't being said.

She could tell that, because she was looking at the twinkling lights too, and was herself partaking in the creation of the silence.

It was a silence that said things like: *actually, those stars aren't just twinkling, they're* moving.

And: *why are there so many more stars down there than up in the sky?*

And most worrying of all: *why are those stars getting bigger and bigger ?*

"I think we will have to finish this story another time," said NotMatt, getting to his feet, and looking around for an escape route.

The problem was, there wasn't any.

The mushroom led in two directions. Upwards, the fungal

groove they had ascended in continued towards the summit of the giant mushroom. They were perhaps two thirds of the way up the enormous fungi. And if they reached the top, where would they go then? Charlotte wasn't absolutely certain that NotMatt wasn't hiding a set of retractible wings - after all, he was the proud owner of an apparent plethora of useful augmentations - but she thought it was pretty unlikely. And while she had always been fairly good at falling off of things, she was notoriously bad at landing when she hit the bottom. It was the landing that always hurt. She thought that would probably be extra true when it came to falling off of giant mushrooms.

That left the direction of 'down', which did not seem especially promising either, on account of what was coming up the mushroom towards them. Now that she had realised what they were looking at, the reality of the shimmering lights was obvious.

Torches. Hundred of burning torches. Maybe thousands of them. And each torch held aloft in a strong froggy hand; and beneath each torch, yellow froggy eyes and wide froggy mouths, filled with sharp teeth and slithering tongues.

They had been found once more.

Of course they had.

The frogs were coming for them.

Well, neither option seemed especially enticing.

But while 'down' seemed to end inevitably in a mob of crazed frogs, at least 'up' involved going away from said mob, even if this was only a very temporary solution.

They looked at each other and began to climb.

17

"What is the meaning of this?" demanded Head Frog 127, spittle flying from his lips, eyes nearly popping out of their sockets.

To his great chagrin, Glob didn't cower and gibber. Not even a little bit.

"I am simply patrolling the ship," said the chief of security aboard *The Pondwater*. His eyes flickered from Head Frog 127 to princess Frogmella and back again. There was a pause. Then he rolled his eyes and, "Captain," he added.

Head Frog 127 was so angry he wanted to spit. He felt as if an explosion was going off in his chest. The nerve of the frog! The *nerve*!

As if daring to sneak around Head Frog 127's private quarters wasn't insult enough, his underling hadn't even the grace to look terrified. More than that, he was offering him *lip!* Him! Head Frog 127, captain of the ship, most esteemed in the King's favour, accompanied by the Princess no less...and here was Glob - fat, ugly, hulking Glob - peering and sneaking where he did not belong - and he was daring to speak back to him.

"This is quite unacceptable," hissed Head Frog 127. "You will *not* address your commanding officer in such a way, are we clear?"

Glob raised an eyebrow. He looked entirely unimpressed.

"Are - we - clear?" Head Frog 127 repeated. He took a step forward, pulling out his ceremonial baton of office. It was a heavy ebony stick, about ten inches long with a weighted head shaped in the likeness of the King. It was a fine piece of workmanship, and all captains of the line had the honour of carrying one. It was useful for making dramatic gestures when one sat in the captain's chair...but the real reason Head Frog 127 was so fond of it, was on account of how useful it was for hitting people.

Usually he would issue a warning before doing such a thing, but now the rage had him, gripping him too firm and tight for him to think about warnings or second chances. He raised his arm, swung the baton. There was a heavy, satisfying *ca-thunk* as the baton hit Glob on the side of the head. The chief of security grunted, but didn't cry out.

He wobbled, but didn't go down.

"Thank you, captain," said Glob. "I am so - so - sorry to have spoken out of turn."

Head Frog 127's eyes went wide.

That was it. It was time to dispose of his head of security. He had meant to do so for some time, he had been well aware that he couldn't trust the fat, brawny frog. He preferred elegant solutions - for Glob to be quietly disappeared would be preferable to something that could be traced back to him - but then, maybe he had been too soft on his crew. Look at the way this treacherous bucket of frogspawn was daring to stand up to him! No, he should have made an example of the frog long ago.

He raised the baton again. Every muscle in his body was tense. He would not pull his blow this time. And he would not stop, either, not until the offending chief of security was down and broken, not until his froggy face was a green stain on the gangway floor...

He tried to swing his baton, but it didn't move an inch.

Confused, he followed the baton from where his hand gripped it, along the shaft, to the bulbous, heavy end...

...and froze.

The hand that held the baton steady was delicate and smaller than his, but the grip was stronger than the bones of a mountain.

It was Princess Frogmella.

Head Frog 127 blinked. In his rage, he'd quite forgotten where he was or what he was doing.

Or who he was with.

Sudden shame flooded through him, shame at how he had been spoken to, yes, but shame also at his own conduct, of how he had lost control of himself.

"Please, captain," said the Princess. "I can see that your chief of security has been a frightful bore. Nevertheless, what good would killing him serve now? Even if it is justified, think of all the paperwork it would generate."

She smiled at him, and though her voice was gentle, the grip in which she held the baton was absolutely unshakeable.

Head Frog 127 took several deep breaths.

All the while, Glob stared at him impassively, as if his life had not just hung in the balance, as if it had not just been saved by an intervention from the Princess.

At that thought, Head Frog 127 felt his shame soar even further.

Why? Why had Frogmella saved this wretch? It didn't make any sense.

"Come now," said the Princess, speaking to him as if trying to talk down a child who wanted the whole cake to himself. "Let this silly frog go about his business, and you can get on with showing me this device you think the world of. Or perhaps you are having doubts? Is that the reason for this show - to distract me from the wild promises you made?"

Head Frog 127 pushed down his ire.

She was right.

Of course she was.

She was talking to him in code, surely that was it. She was reminding him that the business they were embarked on was much more important than the life (or death) of an insignificant wretch like Glob. Killing him here and now really would entail a lot of paperwork.

Not to mention a mop.

That was all she meant. That was why she had interviewed.

He was sure of it.

And yet what was the sneak doing here?

Head Frog 127 felt the rogue thought twist its way free of his mind. It bobbed about in the back of his consciousness, making a nuisance of itself.

He let out a long, slow breath.

Then he managed a smile.

"Of course, my Princess," he told her, trying to make his words light and casual. "You are right, as always. I was thinking only of your honour, you see. The wretch insulted you with his wanton manner."

"Oh, you are *such* a loyal servant," said Frogmella, brushing one hand to Head Frog 127's cheek. "What have I done to deserve such subjects? No one could ever doubt your loyalty."

Her hand was warm against his skin, and Head Frog 127 breathed in the scent of her. He felt his muscles relax.

She smiled, and released her grip on the baton. Head Frog 127 tucked it back into his belt.

"No, do let this frog go," she told him. "I'm sure he has

other duties to attend to. As do you," she added, meaningfully.

Head Frog 127 turned his eyes to Glob and frowned.

"Go on then," he told his chief of security. "Get out of my sight. Count yourself lucky that the Princess has a tender, caring heart. If she hadn't stood up for you..."

He trailed off, trying to make his words as threatening as possible. But if Glob felt any fear, he hid it well.

"Very good, captain," he said, insouciantly. Then he turned to Princess Frogmella. "Until we meet again, my lady."

To Head Frog 127's horror, the disgusting fat frog gave a low bow, then reached out and took the Princesses' hand - actually took her hand! - and planted a slobbery kiss on her knuckles.

Head Frog 127 glared, open mouthed. He waited for the Princess to explode in fury, waited for her to take back all her favour and defence of the horrible frog, to ask - no, to demand! - that Head Frog 127 execute the vile creature immediately.

But no such thing happened.

Instead Princes Frogmella gave a little smile, and waved the chief of security away as if this was the sort of thing that froglings were expected to do every day, and not something that in most circumstances would get the kisser shot.

"I..." Head Frog 127 started to say, but he had no words. His outrage was as big as mountains, and words were far too small.

"Enough wasted time," said the Princess. "Now - show me!"

And she was right, Head Frog 127 realised

Of course she was. As he unlocked the door to his private chambers and let her in, he realised that none of this mattered. Not one iota.

Soon such concerns would be left behind, far behind.

With the power now at his disposal, he could take whatever measures he saw fit, he would be able to bend reality itself, to sit proud at the top of a pile of slippy, slimy frogs, and lead the Frogopolis onwards towards endless glory amid the stars.

He would sit atop the pile, and she would sit beside him.

The chamber was dank and deliciously humid. He indicated for the Princess to be seated, gave her his biggest, broadest smile, and unlocked the hidden safe with the correct sequence of eye movements.

He lifted out the device, careful not to disrupt the delicate flickering of harmonic fields as they danced around the surface. His chief scientist had been quite clear about that. It would not do to interrupt the fields. The machine would be difficult enough to control in any case, until it became fully synched with his neural patterns. Any rough movements or fumbling could be disastrous.

His chief scientist had been a gifted, brilliant frog; he had explained the basics of utilising the machine, and Head Frog 127 had smiled and thanked him and then shot him in the back.

No good having loose ends. It made things untidy.

"It's...it's beautiful," said Princess Frogmella, and there was something in her voice that made Head Frog 127 look closer, as if seeing her for the first time.

There was no artifice to her voice, no royal manner or hauteur. There was simple, frank wonderment. He studied her face. He saw behind the makeup, behind the glamour of her station. She was just a frog, he realised suddenly. Another frog, just like him, only raised differently, brought up from a tadpole to inherit the reigns of power. The insight unsettled him. He had always seen the Princess as someone apart, a figure of almost unreachable power, a symbol of everything he desired, everything he wanted for himself.

To see that she was just flesh and blood, the same as him,

to perceive suddenly the simple, open astonishment in her eyes...

He shuddered and pushed the uncomfortable thought aside.

No, he wanted the artifice. He wanted the Princess, not the frog beneath.

And then she caught him watching her, and the moment vanished. As quick as it had dropped, her guard was back. The strong, unreachable princess stared back at him, ineffably high, unreachable again, a symbol of all he wanted.

"I mean, for something constructed by heathens, it has a certain charm," she amended, a sneer creeping into her voice. "But really, I wonder now if it isn't just a bauble. Are you sure it has any real power?"

Head Frog 127 frowned, roused by her doubt, determined to prove the usefulness of the device, and through it, of himself.

"It has power," he growled, surprising himself by daring to speak in such a tone to the Princess. But it was odd. Now that he held it in his hand, now that he felt the activated energy of the machine, now that he could feel it reaching out to him, tendrils of eldritch power brushing against his consciousness...

He felt strange. He felt bourn aloft.

There was no other way to put it,

He reached out with his mind, instinctively, for it felt right to do so.

At once, the machine responded. The shimmering, dancing lights brightened. He felt them align themselves with the movements of his own mind, and the thought delighted him.

It worked!

The machine worked, and it was his to command!

And yet, even though it bent to his will, even though he

could feel it syncing deeper into his consciousness with every moment, still he felt a resistance there. It was difficult to pinpoint: a kink in the machine, an alien sensibility quite at odds with his own.

But that was to be expected. After all, the machine *was* alien.

His mouth moved into a strained smile.

That would be no problem. He enjoyed bending things to his will. The machine would be no different from the countless froglings he had taught how to obey.

Even as the thought came, he felt the link between him and the machine shift, as if some final resistance had been overcome.

A light was in the room.

To say it came from the machine didn't quite fit, for the light didn't seem to come from anywhere or even - in a very real sense - to *exist* anywhere.

It was as if a second reality was projected over the dim familiarity of his chambers, a spectral otherness that didn't so much exist in the same world, as besides it. At first, there was no sense there. Just light and shade and colour swirling and shimmering around the room, dancing, confused.

Head Frog 127 wondered if the Princess could see it too, but when he glanced at her again she was staring about her in wonderment. He watched her eyes move, watched them trace the same hallucinatory glimmerings that he could see himself.

"The device creates a field," he heard himself saying, explaining things in much the way his chief scientist had explained them to him. "It interrupts the normal flow of reality, interacting with those around it."

"Where are the controls?" asked the Princess, and Head Frog 127 smiled.

"Right here," he said, tapping the side of his head. "Even

as we speak, the machine is synching with my consciousness. We don't need a control panel."

"Then these lights we're seeing...?"

"Projections of that synching," he said. Then he leered at her. "You're seeing the inside of my head."

That wasn't true, not strictly speaking. The display was largely coming from the machine's own background hum, it was like a screensaver being displayed while it tried to make sense of the impulses and commands coming from Head Frog 127. Head Frog 127 had the instinctive suspicion that any projection of the inside of his own mind would be nowhere near as beautiful as this.

Quite the reverse.

Still, the Princess didn't need to know that.

She looked at him, impressed

"I never suspected you were so...elegant," she told him.

He bowed his head modestly.

"What can I say?" he murmured. "Still pond-waters run deep."

She opened her mouth to ask another question, and the display abruptly changed.

Head Frog 127 frowned, trying to make sense of what they were seeing.

Darkness was spread all about them - an odd blackness that superimposed itself on his chambers, blotting out the details of his room - and below them, far below but coming closer, what looked like hundreds of little fires were streaming up towards them.

"What is this?" asked the Princess. "What are we seeing?"

If he had just seen the images on their own, Head Frog 127 thought he probably would have remained baffled, too. But the fact was, light wasn't the only stimuli that was reaching his senses.

He could feel something else leaching in too, something tugging at his mind.

Thoughts.

Thoughts that were not his.

They were syphoning back into the machine, and echoing into his own mind.

Nasty thoughts.

Alien thoughts.

Thoughts that belonged to the machine's previous owner.

"It's them," said Head Frog 127. "The ones we hunt. This is where they are."

Princess Frogmella moved closer, peering, trying to work out where exactly what they were looking at.

"It looks like...the view from a mountain..." she said, speaking softly.

Head Frog 127 nodded.

"Close," he said. "I'd think that too, if I couldn't feel the softness under my feet. And the smell. The smell quite cinches it."

She looked at him, opened her mouth to ask what he meant, and then stopped. A look of wonder passed across her face.

"Yes," she said. Then louder, "Yes, you're right. I can feel it too! The ground is soft. And I smell..." she wrinkled her nose. "Mushrooms."

Head Frog 127 wondered that it had taken the Princess so long to notice it. But then, the sensations were leeching into his head, not hers. She was probably only getting a dim reflection of them.

"They are in the fungal blooms," said Head Frog 127, and he knew it was right, knew it not just from the light or the smell, even, but from the awareness that was growing in his mind. He could feel the male alien, could feel the direction his mind was in. It pulsed at him, like a small, horrible sun sending out tendrils of brightness into the hungry void.

He blinked, then smiled.

"And they are aware of us," he said. The words tasted delicious. He could feel the alien's horror, its fear. "He has realised what I have done. He knows that all is lost. Not only have I wrested his machine from his mind, but he is quite undone; now we know where he is."

Even as he said the words, the image shuddered. A scream seemed to build behind the other senses, a shrieking, an alien cry of anguish. It was delicious.

"He is trying to shake us off," said Head Frog 127. "He thinks that maybe if he severs his last connection to the machine, we won't find him. But don't worry. He is far too late. He can try and close the connections, but it is *I* who have the power now."

And with a thrust of his mind, Head Frog 127 sent a bolt of power spinning from the alien device. The image shuddered, held for a moment, then began to reform, stronger and more vivid than before.

The alien cry intensified. To his lasting delight, Head Frog 127 realised that he was actually causing the alien psychic pain. The alien was actually *resisting* him! But it was quite useless. With the machine now firmly adapted to his neural patterns, there was no hope that the alien could withstand him.

The room shuddered, and the image suddenly leapt in intensity. Now Head Frog 127 could feel the wind sluicing off the lake below, could taste the salt tang of the marshes...and he could hear the sounds of the coming mob.

"You say he's too late," said the Princess, and she was suddenly at his ear, speaking urgently, a fire in her voice. "But *we* will be the ones who are too late unless we move swiftly!

Look! They are nearly caught already! Oh, I must have them as my prize, I *must*!"

Head Frog 127 frowned. Again, there was something in her voice. Something that wasn't quite right. Something...he couldn't quite put his finger on it.

But what she said was true.

Even as he watched, the angry mob of lower-caste froglings honed into view. They were riled up and angry, filled with excitement at having been the ones who had located the prized aliens. They would tear the aliens to pieces, he realised. As soon as the first blow landed, there would be no stopping them. Not that it mattered to him what happened to the aliens in the end, but he wanted - needed - to show the Princess how useful he was to her. Which had never been the plan to begin with - no, he had meant to impress her with his obvious superiority, then swoop in with the powers of the machine if she resisted him. But something in her, some ineffable power that he could not quite grasp, had shifted his mind on that. Oh, he wanted her still, wanted her as much as any one frog could want another - that is to say, ferociously, greedily, and with a need that would not be stayed or put-off. And - to his utter surprise - he had found that he needed her to want him back. To *really* want him back. To *choose* him.

If he simply used the machine to accomplish that it would be cheating.

He looked at her again, hunger in his glance...and caught her staring at him, too.

Was it hunger he saw reflected in her eyes, then? He couldn't blame her for wanting him, he was sure that must be what was coming to pass...and yet a little, sneaky, wary voice in his narrow froggy mind whispered at him to beware.

What did she want? What did she *really* want?

As if reading his thoughts, she cupped his cheeks in her hands and hissed him.

"I - want - *them*!" and then, as if in a desperate show of emphasis, she kissed him.

Not on the cheek.

Square on the lips.

A green haze descended.

Head Frog 127 thought his heart might catch fire, which was strange, because everyone had always told him that he didn't possess one, and he had always agreed with them, sometimes whilst shooting them in the head.

But it seemed he did have a heart after all, and it was beating fit to burst.

The kiss ended.

"Now," the Princess crooned at him. "Take me to them. *Please*."

And that was that.

He really didn't need to be asked again.

And all thoughts of treachery and caution forgotten, Head Frog 127 turned to the shimmering projection around them

He focussed.

There was a sizzling noise, the smell of ozone filled the room and...

And something *shifted*.

❧ 18 ❧

Charlotte stumbled again. This time NotMatt went down completely.

He laid there, bonelessly, eyes wide and staring and not at all present.

She wanted to scream in fear and frustration, but she couldn't on account of having to use every ounce of breath just to keep moving, just to stay alive.

She glanced back. Behind them, at the bend less than a hundred metres away, spots of brilliant light suddenly shone out as the froggy mob rounded the corner.

"Up!" she panted, hauling on NotMatt. "Up! Come on, we have to run!"

This was the third time he had fallen since their mad dash began, but it was by far the worse.

What was wrong with him?

He had been fine at first, leading the way, running quicker than she would have thought possible, darting forward in the gloom of night. He had even shared a joke and a smile!

And then...

Something had gone wrong.

She couldn't say what exactly. But she had felt it too. It was like a rug sliding under her feet, like a buzzing in the head...but if it had felt uncomfortable to her, it had been much worse for NotMatt.

He had stopped, slack-jawed, fear filling his face. He had mumbled something incomprehensible about chaos, and then sweat had started pouring off him. A look of concentration twisted his features, and then that was replaced with pain, and the he cried out, as if all the toys in the world had been broken.

That was when things had changed. That was when Charlotte had realised that if they were going to get out of this alive, it was she who was going to have to organise the getting.

So she had hauled him up, and on they had run. Up, up, up. The gloopy, stinking twists of the huge mushroom were soft under their feet, and it was like running in a nightmare where the ground tries to suck you under. Still, they had managed to stay ahead of the mob, just. Whenever they rounded a corner, Charlotte had expected to find that they had come to the top - and no escape, just the darkness beneath, and far, far below, perhaps, the twinkling of the lake.

But no.

So far, the only thing that had followed each twist of mushroom was more mushroom.

But how long could she keep them going? She couldn't run much further.

And now, with this last fall...

She tried to shift him again. He trembled, a shiver running through his legs. He raised his head a little, then grunted dropped back to the ground.

She glanced back. The frogs were close now. Very close. They were no longer running. They could tell the chase was a nearly over. In the red light of their torches, she could see their horrible faces leering. Their eyes gleamed evil yellow and their teeth looked very sharp.

So this was it.

She would die here.

She would die in another world.

Far from home, far from everyone she had grown up with and ever loved.

On a giant mushroom.

It was just too stupid for words.

"No," she said. And as the word formed on her lips, she realised it was true.

She wouldn't give up. She wouldn't die here, not if she could help it.

What about Matt - her Matt, the *real* Matt? She thought of him, back in the real world, thought of him looking for her, never giving up the search, never giving up hope.

Who was she to deny him that hope? Who was she to give up, when she knew he never would?

"No!" she said again, louder, and then she was on her feet, hauling the stunned NotMatt up with her. She didn't know where she found the strength, because a moment ago her limbs had felt like jelly. Now they hardly felt like hers at all.

Adrenaline, she thought.

The last desperate surge, for whatever good it did her.

But then, wasn't that always the case? Life only led one way. There was no escaping the grave, and all living things grew cold in the end.

What could you say to that?

Only one thing.

"Not today," she told the Universe.

And then they were running, and for a miracle, NotMatt no longer needed supporting. His head lolled and he stumbled, but he seemed to be recovering somewhat.

Behind them, a roar went up from the froglings as they realised the chase was on again.

"What - the - hell - was - that?" gasped Charlotte between breaths.

Matt looked at her, eyes wild, specks of spittle on his lips.

"He won," NotMatt gasped back. "He's taken it."

And to her shock, his voice warbled on the last word, and he was near tears.

"What?" she said.

The path narrowed. Now they could no longer run abreast. She shoved NotMatt ahead and pushed him after her. The path took a slow bend round the side of the huge fungus. Charlotte glanced to her right, and was appalled to notice that the path no longer had a side. A sheer drop plummeted away, countless hundreds of feet down. The wind gusted, and she ducked instinctually into the fungal wall, fearful of being blown off. But then the roar of the froglings caught up with them, and she wondered if jumping might not be better.

"The Chaos Drive," moaned NotMatt. "Head Frog 127. The bastard who took us. He's somehow overridden the defence mechanisms. It's synched with *his* brain now. I felt him tear it off me. It was...it was *horrible*."

Charlotte opened her mouth to demand more of an explanation, but then they rounded the corner.

It was as she had been fearing from the beginning.

They had reached the summit.

And NotMatt would have gone over the lip, all the while looking back at her and moaning nonsensically about machines and synching, not noticing where he was going, if she hadn't reached out and snatched him back.

For a moment they teetered on the edge, then Charlotte's grip won out and they tumbled backwards.

The path had opened out a bit at the last, and they stood now on a broad ledge, perhaps ten feet across. Above them, a final overhang of fungus gave a slight shelter from the rain. But ahead and to the side, the void beckoned.

"Perhaps if we went back, we could hide?" NotMatt hazarded hopefully.

But they were already too late.

Even as he said it, the froglings began their final march round the bend. Now that they saw their prey was cornered, they came on slow again, deliberate, shouting out horrible taunts and curses.

"You know that super-strength thing you did earlier?" asked Charlotte.

"Yeah," said NotMatt.

"Any chance of using that now?"

NotMatt frowned.

"I wish I could," he said. "I'm nearly drained dry. I was counting on channeling a refill from the Chaos Drive if it came to the crunch, but now..." he trailed off.

This gave Charlotte a few useful seconds in which to ponder this incomprehensible information.

She thought about it carefully for a moment, then came up with: "Huh?"

NotMatt shook his head, as if to say trying to explain things now wasn't worth the effort, on account of how little time they probably had before being dismembered.

"I could probably summon enough strength to fight a few off," he muttered. "But with this many...there must be hundreds here."

And then the world *shifted* and someone at Charlotte's ear said: "Thousands."

It was a horrible voice, full of slime and smugness.

Charlotte recognised it at once.

She spun around, but she knew who she would see.

There, seemingly stepping out of the solid wall of fungus, Head Frog 127 strode towards them. At his elbow stood another frog, smaller, slighter, but still moving with a dangerous grace and purpose. Something was different about its face and the shape of its body. It was female, she realised.

I've seen that one before, thought Charlotte.

A moment later she remembered where.

"The Princess," she said aloud. "In the arena. In the royal box."

"Oh, this one remembers you," said Head Frog 127 to his companion. Behind them, Charlotte thought she could see the lambent outline of another place, a room somewhere, somehow apparently occupying the same space as the fungal mountain. But even as she watched, it faded away.

"I should think so," said the Princess. "I am difficult to forget."

And she smiled at Charlotte.

But it was strange. Although the smile was nasty, was - she was sure - meant to be quite as horrid as Head Frog 127's, at least was meant to look that way at a glance, there was something about her eyes...

"It worked, you see," Head Frog 127 told the Princess smugly. In his hand, he held a very strange - a very beautiful - thing. It was slab-like, thin and achingly delicate, with spidery gossamer threads of colour tracing across it in sparks and shuffles.

She started to ask what it was, then realised she knew already.

"That's *mine*," hissed NotMatt. "Put it down. You don't have the right! No *right* to put your stinking, slimy hands on that! My *cat* made that!"

And as if those words had galvanised him into a sudden desperate strength, NotMatt leapt forward. He moved fast, faster than Charlotte would have thought possible, and for a moment her heart leapt up.

He was lying, she thought. *All that talk of being drained. It was a lie. He's fast, he's strong, he's going to kill that horrible froggy...oh.*

Because a moment before NotMatt would have connected with him, Head Frog 127 made the smallest gesture. The machine in his hand glowed, and...

...and NotMatt was back by her side.

He blinked, for a moment unbalanced. Then he roared and jumped again...

...and again he was back where he started.

"You see," said Head Frog 127 to the Princess, quite ignoring NotMatt and Charlotte. "With this machine, there is nothing we cannot do."

The Princess hesitated a moment, didn't turn. Her eyes went from Matt to Charlotte and back again. There was something in them, some...some doubt, some conflict...Charlotte couldn't place it.

"I do," said the Princess, finally turning back to Head Frog 127. "But...but *what* exactly was that you did?"

"Rewrote reality," said Head Frog 127 smugly. "Re-wrote the *story* of our reality. That's what the machine is. "It erases things. It re-writes things. That's why these alien scum have always got away in the past. They've *cheated*."

"That's not what it does," growled NotMatt. "It's much more complicated than that. It's far too subtle for your little froggy brain."

"This froggy brain," said Head Frog 127, tapping the side of his skull, "is exactly the same froggy brain that outwitted *you*. I beat you, I took this from you. Now I will use this, and with it I will rule..."

But at that moment, several things happened at once.

First, something flared, and a bolt of red light shot towards them from the mob of froglings.

They've grown tired of this waiting, thought Charlotte. *Now they're shooting at us.*

But that wasn't all.

Princess Frogmella had raised a hand. There was something in it. Charlotte couldn't quite work out what it was. It looked heavy. It looked like a weapon.

And the weird thing was, she wasn't looking at either of them. Not at all.

No, she was staring firmly at Head Frog 127. In fact, it looked for all the world like she was about to brain him.

Which didn't make any sense.

But Charlotte really had no time to think about any of these things, because the third thing that happened in quick succession was//

//everything froze.

The Universe shuddered.

Charlotte thought it felt the same as the sensation one had when you were on a train that had just stopped: a moment of suspended force, of suspended time, and then a rolling, lurching movement as things settled.

Only instead of things rolling on around them, everything was frozen absolutely still.

Well, not quite everything.

Beside her, she could hear NotMatt gasping in deep, ragged breaths. But their assailants were all frozen, arrested to a frog in various acts of gloating or violence. Charlotte looked around, trying to make sense of things, trying to find a source for this strange event.

She glared over the side and into the void, and saw individual raindrops frozen in the act of dropping, their glittering forms shimmering in the reflected orange light of the torches.

"Matt," she whispered, half-afraid of speaking louder in case it broke whatever spell of silence had halted the dangerous flow of time. "What the hell is happening."

"I told you I had been betrayed," said a voice. Charlotte had heard it before. Of course she had. How had she forgotten? It was the same voice that had spoken to them just before they had been released into the arena, the same voice that had apparently been responsible for freezing time previously. She had meant to talk to NotMatt about it. It was the kind of thing one made mental notes about.

But life had been so full of running and hiding and hitting things since then, the appropriate moment had never seemed to arise.

"Who said that?" demanded Matt. "Show yourself."

A figure strode out of the darkness.

This wouldn't have been so impressive in and of itself, but the thing was, it strode out of the darkness *over the precipice.*

The man was walking on thin air.

For a man it was, Charlotte saw, a tall, rather thin man, with long limbs and a well-tailored suit which looked quite out of place amid the rain and desperation of their current circumstance.

"Who...who *are* you?" said Charlotte.

The man smiled.

"Philip Frogmore," he said, taking a bow. "At your service. And I think you need it."

His voice was rather rich and plumy. If they had been back on Earth - on *her* Earth - Charlotte would have thought it rather posh. Well-educated, used to being right, used to being listened to.

She couldn't say why, but she was suspicious of that voice at once.

Even if its owner was - apparently - in the process of rescuing them.

"Philip *who?*" asked NotMatt, wariness thick in his voice, too.

"Frogmore," said the tall stranger. "I know, I know, a terrible coincidence, and quite suspicious really, but the thing is, we really don't have time to worry about that now. My device is strong - stronger that yours, Mister Mathew, or should I say, stronger than *his*, now - but it can't hold out forever. Not against narrative inevitability as strong as this."

"Narrative...narrative *what*?" asked Charlotte, but Frogmore just shook his head.

"No time, my dear, there is no time," he told her. "Not now, at least, though I'm sure we can talk of it more later. No, right now, the thing to do is...*escape*."

Charlotte looked at NotMatt.

There was a considering light in his eyes, and a set to his jaw that made her think that NotMatt did not trust this stranger very far at all.

But after a moment, NotMatt bit his lip and looked away.

"Fine," he said. "We go with you. After all, what choice do we have?"

"None that don't involve falling to your death or being torn limb from limb, I'm afraid," said Philip Frogmore. "Options which, dare I say it, have rather the ring of finality to them. Whereas what I can offer you is so much more *interesting*."

He held out a hand. It was a long, bony hand, adorned with many rings. Charlotte hesitated.

"Quickly, dear, if you please," said Frogmore. As if to emphasise his point, their world//

//flickered.

The bolt of light zipped towards them.

The heavy object in the Princesses' hand fell towards Head Frog 127.

The rain fell, and the world//

//flickered again.

"Now, in fact," said Frogmore, a note of strain in his voice. "Now would do nicely."

And then Charlotte was reaching out, grasping the long,

thin hand in one of hers, and turning to NotMatt, and grasping him in her other.

Philip Frogmore was right.

What other choice did they have?

Charlotte blinked against the rain, and//

//and the world shifted again.

When Charlotte opened her eyes again, they were somewhere else entirely.

❧ 19 ❧

"**I**t's closed," said Matt blankly. "We can't meet with her. We can't get it."

And in his mind, the corollary of that: *she can't get what she wants, either*.

They stood, ankle deep in slushy snow, staring into the darkened shop window.

Was it disappointment he felt? Or was it relief?

From the moment June had named her price, he had felt apprehensive.

It was so vague, that was one thing.

How could you know what you were getting yourself into, with a price like that?

And who asked for wishes anyway, these days?

"There's a note here," said NotCharlotte, holding up a hand, and peering carefully at a scrap of paper stuck to the inside of the window.

"What does it say?" asked Matt, stepping towards her, and nearly slipping over. He tensed, whirl-winding his arms like a cartoon character, and just managed to avoid falling flat by grasping NotCharlotte firmly by the coat.

She scowled at him.

"Careful," she reprimanded.

"Sorry," he said. He stepped cautiously away from her, careful to steady himself against the shop window. He peered at the note, but had only managed to read the first couple of words before NotCharlotte was off, marching through the snow and out to the Lanes like a soldier on a mission.

Matt scuttled after her, trying to keep his feet, negotiating snow drifts piled up against shop fronts like miniature mountains.

For a second, he thought again about how weird this was.

Snow.

In *August*.

And not just a little flurry, not just a few flakes falling out of an otherwise clear sky.

No, this had been days of steady snow, heavy snowflakes falling from clouds that seemed to brood over the whole world, and a wind sweeping always from the North, cold as ice.

It was not like summer at all. Matt didn't know what it was like, apart from something wrong.

"Hang on a minute!" he shouted, catching her up. "What did it say?"

NotCharlotte marched on, not glancing back at him.

"It told us where to go," she told him shortly, and Matt made a rude face at her back.

Why was she being this way to him? Ever since she had arrived, she had been short, perhaps even a little bullying. But lately she was sliding from *'hectoring'* into *'downright rude'*. Matt would have called her on it, if he wasn't just a tiny bit afraid she would rip his face off.

"Oh right," he said. "And where's that?"

They rounded a corner, passing out of the network of

higgledy-piggledy streets that formed the Lanes, and the scent of the sea hit Matt like a physical thing. A few more steps, and they could see it, waves riding high and crashing in the wind, across the street and beyond the other side of the promenade.

NotCharlotte stopped so abruptly he almost walked into her.

"The pier," she said.

Matt looked up, and saw the off-white paint of Palace Pier glaring at them under the brooding sky. Waves crashed at the base of the long structure, sending up a fine mist of surf mixed with melting snow.

"Palace Pier," said Matt doubtfully.

There were no lights shining along the long structure. Everything was dead and silent, and clearly closed.

But NotCharlotte shook her head.

"Not that one," she said, and pointed over to their right.

Matt followed her finger, over an empty expanse of crashing waves to the burnt-out husk of West Pier. Matt swallowed. He remembered when he had first come to Brighton, many years ago, when he was just a kid. He remembered sitting on the beach on a fine, sunny day, trying to skip stones out to the wrecked remains of the old pier. Which had been impossible, of course, because what remained of the wreck must have been hundreds of feet out to sea.

"But...but we can't go *there*," said Matt, trying to keep his voice reasonable. "It's been derelict for forty years! It was destroyed before I was even *born*."

It was true. The West Pier had once been a glittering mirror of the structure that remained, until it was claimed by fire in the mid-'70's. Now it was just one more dying landmark, crumbling slowly back into the ever-hungry sea.

NotCharlotte shrugged.

"If June can get there, then we must be able to," she said.

Her voice was hard, almost vindictive. Matt's frown deepened.

Then NotCharlotte was stepping out into the road, leading them through traffic that advanced slowly through the snow, honking and swerving to avoid them.

When had she become quite like this? Matt wasn't sure. It had happened gradually, during the week of waiting after they had first met with June. The old woman had assured them that she could make what they needed, but that it would take a little time. And then, of course, there was the matter of the price...

Matt shook his head, trying to clear his head of that nasty little thought.

Now they were walking along the beachfront towards the stranded remains of the pier. The pebbles were slippy in the slushy snow. Slippery, mouldering pillars of wood stood up out of the waves in a rough causeway of stepping stones, the blackened bones of the ruined pier peeking out from below the waves. As he watched, Matt saw them alternately swallowed and revealed by the broiling waves.

He had dared to hope that things would begin to get better, that NotCharlotte would relax now that the bargain was struck, that she would become more friendly - or at least, not be as unfriendly as she had been recently. But no. Every passing day had left her in a fouler mood, more prone to brooding silences or violent outbursts. It was upsetting. Matt understood this woman wasn't the Charlotte he knew and loved, but the fact remained...she *almost* was. The whole thing was so strange, he felt so off balance all the time...

NotCharlotte stopped so abruptly that Matt walked into her back. She peered out to sea, eyes slitted against the wind and freezing rain, blowing in horizontally off the waves.

"What now?" asked Matt, having to shout against the wind.

NotCharlotte peered, examining the situation.

"There's a boat," she said.

Matt frowned. He hadn't seen a boat. Then he saw where she was looking, and realised there *was* a boat - a tiny little husk of a thing, bobbing alarmingly in the waves in the lee of the pier, hundreds of feet away across the stormy sea. A thin-looking length of rope tied it fast to the burnished wooden slats, and next to that, a rope ladder had been thrown over the side.

"June wasn't joking," said Matt. "She must have gone out in the boat and clambered up."

But he said it doubtfully, because it was hard to imagine an old woman with only one strong arm navigating a choppy sea in a tiny rowing boat, and then clambering up a slippy, unsteady ladder. And anyways, how would she row the damn thing, with only one working arm?

"It's a test," said NotCharlotte. "She's testing us. Seeing if we can get there."

"But we *can't*," said Matt. "There's no boat. We certainly can't swim out that way...and even if we could, why would she *want* to test us?"

But even as he said it, he knew why. Her price. What was the point of having wishes in your pocket if the genie had no power? This was her way of blooding them, making sure they were worthy. It was a challenge. A test.

Unfortunately, it was one Matt was quite certain they weren't up to.

"Well," he said, scratching his head. "I suppose we could...could we get another boat from somewhere? Or maybe if we threw something out to her boat, a grappling hook or something..."

But even as he spoke, his voice died, because he knew that was pointless. Even if they had a grappling hook, how could they possibly get it across that expanse of water?

He was expecting a sharp rebuke for such stupidity, but to his surprise, she held his hand instead.

He blinked, touched. Her hand felt warm and strong in his.

"A silly idea, I know," he said, turning to face her, smiling foolishly.

But she wasn't smiling. She was looking determined.

"What are you...?" he started to say.

Then she grabbed his leg.

Then she picked him up. There was no apparent effort, no sense of straining.

"..." said Matt.

Then she started to run.

"Wait!" he said, a horrible suspicion forming in his mind. "No, don't! There must be another way..."

But it was no good. Her legs were slamming into the pebbles, and every step sent a jolt through Matt, driving the air out of his lungs.

He tried to wriggle free, but she held him tight. The world titled crazily from his vantage point, balanced on her shoulders. The sea came up to meet them. She was nearly at the surf, she would run into it and falter and they would both drown and then...

At that moment, NotCharlotte put on a last desperate burst of speed...then leapt.

Matt gasped as they sailed through the air. Wind was in his face and snow was in his eyes, and the blue-green sea glittered up at them, like a huge tongue, a mouth glistening, gaping wide to swallow them up.

Matt tried to scream, but it was no good. All the air was gone, and he had nothing to scream with.

The sea rolled closer. They would hit it and be swallowed by the icy waves without a trace...

There was a thump, a reversing of momentum as Matt was crushed further against Charlotte's back, and Matt gaped as he saw slippy, slimy wood under her feet.

She had landed them perfectly, landed them on the first rotting beam, standing out of the ocean like a crooked tooth. But he hardly had time to register this, because they were bouncing up again, NotCharlotte kicking with her legs, sailing off into the air once more...

She was doing it, Matt realised. Quite how she was doing it was another question, but she was getting them there, bouncing them across the huge divide of hostile ocean by jumping from one wooden pillar to the next, skipping across them like stepping stones.

He laughed despite himself, tension bubbling up and away. The sea sparkled as it stretched out below them, huge and brooding and beautiful.

A smile surfaced on his face. They would make it after all! They would//

//and the world shivered//

//and NotCharlotte's grip faltered, and Matt slid sideways, half toppling away. He tried to scream, but no sound would come, nothing at all. He was too scared. The ocean rose up to meet them, and NotCharlotte's head lolled, a wild, distant look in her eyes. They had shifted off their course, and now the beam they had been heading for was a little to one side.

They were going to miss it. They were going to smash into the water. And water, Matt knew, only *seemed* soft. If you hit it too fast, it would be more like hitting concrete.

The sea roared closer, up, up, up...

At the last possible moment, Charlotte stirred, an arm shooting out as much by instinct, Matt thought, as by design. There was a terrible lurch that crushed Matt into her shoulders and made him want to vomit, then a moment of horrible suspension while NotCharlotte dangled one-handed from the slippy wood. The sea twisted sickeningly below them.

Then she cried out, and an instant later she was hauling them up, the wood splintering under her fingers. Matt slid off of her shoulder and they stood, side by side on the wet, untrustworthy wooden pole, far out into the sea.

The pole was perhaps three feet across, and there was no room for comfort. Below them, the waves crashed and tore at the wood. From above came the everlasting snow.

"What the hell was that?" asked Matt.

NotCharlotte looked at him, something wild in her eyes, and for a moment she didn't answer. Matt wondered if she would ever answer, if she even *could* answer. Fear was rolling off of her, so thick and cloying that he could almost taste it.

Then she calmed, her breathing becoming more regular, eyes closed. When she opened them, her eyes were clear and lucid again.

"It's broken," she said, and the words held so much dread, so much hopelessness, Matt felt his body wilt even though he didn't know what she was talking about.

"What?" he demanded. "What's broken?"

"The Chaos Drive," she said. "It's...someone's taking it. I can feel..."

And she shivered, a look of horror on her face.

"The Chaos what now?" asked Matt.

She turned her eyes on him. She looked devastated, as if someone had soiled the most beautiful thing in the world.

"Not broken. Breaking. The Chaos Drive is..."

She scowled, half turned from him.

"It doesn't matter," she said quickly. "There's no time. We have to go."

"Go?" said Matt. "Go where?"

"To the pier, of course," she said. "And quickly. Before it comes again. Before it shuts off completely, and I'm left stranded without any help at all."

"Jump again?" said Matt. "Are you mad? If you jump now, you'll kill us both!"

"If we don't go now, we'll be stuck here. How long can you hold on?"

Matt licked his lips and watched the furious ocean crash and churn beneath.

"But that's no choice!" he wailed. "That's no...hey! No! *Don't*!"

But it was no good. NotCharlotte's strength was unstoppable, and Matt kicked his legs like a kitten as she lifted him effortlessly into the air, put him back on her shoulders, and squatted low.

"Put me down!" Matt demanded indignantly. "Now, please! Now would be gooooo..."

And the word was lost, the air forced out of his lungs once more as NotCharlotte leapt.

There was a sharp snap from beneath them as the wooden pole splintered and crashed into the ocean, collapsing under the force of her kick. And then they were flying upwards.

For a moment they hung beneath the black sky. They seemed hopelessly far from the next wooden pole, and so high up that it was just a tiny dot far, far below. Then they fell, and Matt squeezed his eyes shut, sure they would miss it and crash into the waves.

But they didn't miss it.

The landing was worse this time, more jolting, more painful.

Matt screamed in pain but if NotCharlotte cared she didn't give any indication. A footfall beneath, then they were off again...

And again...

And//

//the Universe stuttered again, but this time it was worse. It was like a vast hammer had been set to crash into the Earth, to the sky, to the whole of everything. It sang through Matt's teeth and reverberated in his bones and//

//they were falling once again, and Matt gasped, terrified and elated for he saw they had reached the pier! They had reached it, the worn, greyish slats coming up to meet them, and if I roll, he thought, if we both roll when we hit it, then maybe we have a chance...

Beside him, NotCharlotte sailed through the air, face blank, and not an ounce of sense in her eyes. She had loosed her grip on him, and they separated a moment before they hit the wood.

Roll, thought Matt.

But it turned out rolling was impossible.

The slats were rotten and wind-worn and worked through by the salty gnawing of the sea.

As Matt hit the slats, they shattered, dissolving into a million sodden pieces.

Pain lanced through him, more pain than his mind could hold.

They crashed through the rotten wood. Matt tried to raise his hands to cover his face. He had a vague sense of Charlotte beside him, tumbling and crashing through the withered bones of the old pier. Down they went, past layers of cross-hatched wood and then - somehow, impossibly - it was done and the water took them.

All sound was banished.

Time seemed suspended. Matt hung in the freezing water. Salt failed his mouth, and blood, and light crept in slow waves through the shimmering greens of the ocean.

He felt his consciousness shrinking, screaming away from the pain that filled his body.

He felt warm now. Warm and comfortable and tired. So tired.

Perhaps if he just closed his eyes, this horrible reality would melt away, and he would find himself waking next to Charlotte - next to the real Charlotte, *his* Charlotte - and the whole thing would be a dream. He felt sure this would happen. Of course it would. It was so ridiculous anyway, so crazy...

No, said a little voice deep inside of him.

No.

That way was a lie.

He would never find her, not if he let himself be dragged into thoughts like that.

It was simple, he realised.

If he wanted her back, he would have to fight for her. Fight every inch.

And he *would* fight. He would fight and fight and fight until he had her back...or until he died.

There was no other option.

And with that thought, awareness came rushing back into him like a tidal wave rolling through a valley. And with the awareness came pain, terrible pain, pain in his arms and body and legs, and most of all in his head. He blinked, but the sea water was thick and dark, and he had lost his bearings in the fall.

Where was the surface? Which way was up?

Air was running out. His body was screaming at him, screaming that he needed to open his mouth and breath in. His heart thumped in his chest.

He tried to see which way the light was coming from, but it was no good. Each direction looked just as grim and uncertain as every other.

Not meaning to, he let out a sob, and with the sob came a burst of hot air escaping from his lungs.

He watched as the bubbles crept over his face and shot away, seeking the surface.

It took him a moment to understand what this meant.

The surface! The bubbles would find their way to the surface more surely than his sense of direction ever could.

All he had to do was follow the bubbles.

His gaze followed the shimmering ball of air as it shot upwards, and he caught a glimmering shadow of the surface.

His eyes widened. It was there! All he had to do was swim that way and he'd be safe!

He kicked out, relief flooding through him...

...and his feet struck something.

He twisted in the water, and saw her there, floating below him.

Her clothes billowed around her still silent body, making her look like a giant jellyfish.

NotCharlotte.

She was quite still and silent, unmoving.

Matt's lungs screamed at him. He had to get to the surface. He had to!

As he watched, she began to fall softly, drifting deeper beneath the waves.

He had to get her. He had to save her.

And yet.

And yet...was that the right thing to do?

Thoughts flashed and tumbled through his head. The way she had treated him, the way she had spoken to him. Grabbed him, bashed and bullied him, hurt him, even...

And he wasn't sure he even had enough air to get himself to the surface. His lungs burnt like fire. He could feel an ominous blackness tugging at the corners of his vision.

He could just let her drop. No one would be able to criticise him for it. If he went down for her, they would both drown. But he was at the pier now. If he went up, he could meet June, he could talk to her, he might carry through with the plan on his own. His own Charlotte was out there, and he would get her back, and he wouldn't even miss this horrible version of her, not after what she had done to him, not at all, not at all, not...

But his body made the decision for him.

Matt turned in the water and kicked.

Down.

He felt pressure build in his ears. It grew and grew, until it felt like his brain might explode.

She was still sinking, but he was moving faster.

Down, down, down...

And then she stopped, and it took Matt a moment to realise why.

The seabed.

They had reached the ocean floor.

It was dark now, very dark, the small amount of light that crept its way down here was scattered and dim. But still he could see her, laid out, unmoving, utterly, utterly still.

But the die was cast now.

All or nothing.

Knowing that any second he would lose the battle against his lungs, that any second he would be powerless to stop himself opening his mouth and gulping in a lungful of terminally salty water, Matt groped for her. He pulled one arm around his shoulder, then her leg.

A moment ago this was how she was carrying me, he thought.

Then he was kicking out, kicking against the ocean floor...

And it wasn't enough.

They floated up a little way, then stopped.

His lungs screamed.

He tried to keep his mouth closed, but he couldn't stop himself.

His mouth opened, and air rushed out, bubbling up to the surface.

He gazed in horror as the bubbles shimmied away. His ballast. The last chance he had to get up to the surface, the buoyancy of air - lost.

He had moments to live, he realised.

He turned to NotCharlotte.

She looked more like his Charlotte now, it seemed to him.

With her eyes shut and her hair dancing beneath the silent waves.

The blackness was closing in.

A kiss, then.

Die with a kiss.

Why not?

She wasn't his Charlotte, but she loved the other version of him, perhaps even as much as he loved his version of her.

He would die with a kiss.

He moved closer. The last flickering of his vision faltered, but he felt her lips press against his. They were still warm, beautifully warm against the salt kiss of the ocean.

Her lips slipped open...

...and something fell out into his mouth.

It was like...it was like a coin.

A hard metal coin.

With bubbles coming out of it.

He held it in his fingers. He could see nothing now, could hear nothing now but the thumping of his blood in his ears.

His fingers were going numb.

Not sure quite what he was doing or why he was doing it, he felt his fingers squeeze the coin.

Harder.

Harder.

Harder...

...And the coin seemed to *burst*...

...And the bubbles exploded in a jet, forcing down into the ocean floor, the coin punching upwards into his chest, punching upwards, and they were moving, they were flying upwards, flying towards the surface, and...

Everything went black.

❧ 20 ❧

Charlotte had never believed in giants. She hadn't really seen the point. Giants were just one more pointless thing to believe in, like goblins, or honest estate agents.

It was very difficult not to believe in something, however, when it was looming over you, looking as if it would like nothing more in the world than to reach down and gobble you up for an after-dinner mint.

This particular giant didn't actually look that terrifying in and of itself. It was female, with a brown cowboy hat and faded blue jeans, sharp, bright eyes, and a glittering badge in the shape of a star on her shirt. In fact, the only thing that really made the woman more than moderately alarming was her size.

The size counted for a lot in this case, however, as the woman stood at least three thousand feet tall.

She loomed over them. She filled the whole world.

Or rather, she filled the whole of the place where the world had been.

Now, to Charlotte's further alarm, she found that the

world was gone - or was going - fading and crackling behind them, closing in a dark wedge of light. And before them, peering at them - the giant.

Charlotte didn't even know that she was screaming, however, until there was another *tug* from Philip Frogmore, where he gripped her in his cool, dry hand, and then//

//they were hanging in empty nothingness.

There was a sense of the air changing, as if the pressure had dropped suddenly.

Charlotte looked around.

Nothing. White, rolling, empty fields of nothing.

Nothing at all.

No trees, no mountain, no screaming hordes of angry froglings waiting, at any moment, to tear them limb from limb.

No giant, either.

Which had to be a good thing, Charlotte reasoned, even if she hadn't looked like an especially evil giant.

Philip Frogmore released her hand. He looked at her expectantly for a moment.

She stared back at him.

He frowned slightly, and tapped her on the shoulder.

"Would you mind awfully if...?" he shouted at her, blinking encouragingly.

"What do you mean?" Charlotte tried to say, then realised she couldn't on account of all the screaming she was doing.

She stopped screaming.

It felt odd. Screaming seemed quite appropriate.

"Thank you," said Philip Frogmore in a more normal voice.

"Where...where are we?" asked Charlotte.

She looked questioningly at NotMatt, but NotMatt just shook his head, morosely. His lips were pressed tightly shut, and he looked ominously subdued.

"Somewhere safe," said Philip Frogmore. "Somewhere that wretched Head Frog 127 won't be able to find us. Or the blasted Princess. At least..."

He trailed off, a pensive look on his face.

Charlotte found she was looking at NotMatt, waiting for him to spring to life, waiting for him to ask what Frogmore was talking about, demand to know where they were or what that ominous 'at least' meant.

But NotMatt didn't say anything. He was staring around now, but there was a hollow look to him, an emptiness. He looked younger, she suddenly thought, younger and older at the same time. His face seemed more smooth, his eyes less knowing. And yet the streaks of white in his hair were more obvious, and he held himself uncertainly.

Charlotte realised if anyone was going to find out what that ominous, 'at least' meant, it would have to be her.

"What do you mean?" she demanded, trying to force some authority in her voice. "Are we safe here? Or aren't we?"

Frogmore scratched his nose. If he was impressed by her sudden attempt at being assertive, he made a good job of hiding it.

"Safe is a relative term, I always find," he allowed. "But yes - we are safe - for a little while, at least. Head Frog 127 has only just got his hands on the Chaos Drive, you see, and it will take a brutish runt like him a little while at least."

"A little while? A little while to do what?" demanded Charlotte.

"To find out how to use the thing," said Frogmore. "Oh, he's synched with it alright, and that didn't take long. And he got his head around the basics quick enough. How to plough through the story, how to alter the narrative flow. But you must understand, it can be a very delicate matter, undoing the weave of a story, threading in and out of it, not upsetting too many things. And he's a bit like a toddler playing with a paintbrush for the first time. He thinks his work is oh-so-elegant, but when his mother comes home and finds the living room covered in paint..."

Charlotte frowned. To her surprise, she found she was almost following what Frogmore was saying.

"The giant," she said, the suspicion forming in her mind instinctively. "That huge woman..."

"Not a giant," said Frogmore. He leant back in the soft nothingness, pulled an apple from a pocket and began chomping away. "A Sheriff. A Sheriff of the Order. Indigo Shuttlecock if I'm not very much mistaken, and that means one thing."

Charlotte, to whom this all meant very little indeed, shook her head.

"A Sheriff?" she asked. "What Order?"

Frogmore waved a hand as if dismissing an irrelevance.

"Not to worry, my dear," he told her in his crisp, plummy voice. "She is not our problem. Which is good to know, because Sheriffs can be very large problems for the unwary traveller, wending his way through the Storystream. Very bothersome. Very meddlesome. And that one - that Indigo Shuttlecock - is more bothersome than most."

"Is she - is she dangerous?" asked Charlotte.

"Oh, extremely," said Frogmore. "Most dangerous. And most untrustworthy."

And something in Charlotte's mind spoke up and said: *not as untrustworthy as you*.

Still, what good would it do now to act on that? They couldn't get away from the man, not now at least.

Frogmore finished his apple, and tossed the core over his shoulder. It landed in a pile of nothingness behind him. As Charlotte watched, it sank slowly into the white fluffy land, melting away and vanishing.

She blinked, and looked suspiciously at her feet.

To her great relief, they were not melting away into the whiteness, at least not obviously.

"Don't worry, girl," said Frogmore, who had caught her concerned glance. "You won't melt away as easy as the apple core. You and I have too much narrative potential. We are too anchored to ourselves, even in this empty place. We won't slip away. Not unless we want to."

Charlotte scowled. She found that she was liking her saviour less and less. She had never liked being called 'girl', and there was something wet and unpleasant about Frogmore's eyes, something smug and smirking, behind the friendly smiles.

"I see," she said, trying – and nearly succeeding – in keeping the annoyance from her voice. "And where, actually, are we? If you don't mind telling us, that is?"

"The Place Between Stories," said NotMatt

Charlotte turned to NotMatt. She had almost forgotten he was standing there, he had been so silent. Now, however, he was looking around. She was happy to see him seeming to take an interest in things again, even if he didn't look fully engaged.

Frogmore gave NotMatt a cheery grin. It didn't touch his eyes though, she noted.

"Very good, young Mathew," said Frogmore. "You have visited here before?"

NotMatt shook his head.

"No," he said. "But I know about it. Always meant to come out here. It was on our list."

He glanced around and gave a little noncommittal shrug.

"Doesn't look like much, though."

"Oh, but it *is*," said Frogmore. He strode forward a couple of steps, looking like a tall, ridiculous antelope stalking through the puffs of nothingness. He took NotMatt's elbow, turned him round with an elaborate gesture. "The glory of this place is twofold," he went on. "Number one is the emptiness. A very thin place. Very thin. You can make substances here out of almost nothing. Out of memories and moonshine; and a little narrative potential will go a very long way..."

Philip Frogmore, reached out and grasped Charlotte with his other hand, and spun them round.

"I don't see what..." Charlotte began, but Frogmore made a *shushing* noise.

And then he did a strange thing.

He turned some more.

Which should have been impossible, without coming back to where he had begun the turn.

But instead of completing the turn, the nothingness shifted and...

...and suddenly a grand house stood before them. It was made of white brick and strong, black beams. It reared over them, four stories high, honeysuckle and wisteria climbing up the elaborate frontage. Apple trees stood in a courtyard, bedecked with tinkling fountains and the sound of birdsong.

"How did you do that?" asked Charlotte, astonished.

"My girl," said Frogmore annoyingly, "we are in the Place Between Stories now. It is a very empty place. Very empty. The one thing it has a lot of is degrees. Much more than the standard quota, and circles are not bound to have just three hundred and sixty of them here."

"I see," said Charlotte, shivering her shoulders out of Frogmore's grip. "It's very...very nice."

She wished she could have kept the awe out of her voice, but it was impossible. The house was very impressive, beautiful and huge and elegant. And even if the house had been a shack, the way Frogmore had spirited it out of nowhere was in itself magnificent.

"Welcome," said Frogmore in a grand, sonorous voice, "to

Frogmore. My ancestral home. Or at least, a version of it," he added, with a little self-deprecating gesture of one hand.

He smiled.

"You are safe here," he said.

Charlotte wished she believed him.

But then, what choice did they have?

21

C old. His toes were cold.

Why were his toes cold?

Matt surfaced through layers of dream and confusion, swimming up out of the darkness.

The darkness was so warm and pleasant. He didn't want to come up. Certainly not to any place that contained cold toes.

He struggled, tried to push himself further down again. But it was no good.

There was a pressure on his chest now. His lungs burnt. His toes were blocks of ice. Not just his toes. His feet. His legs. His *body*.

Then the pressure came again, thumping into his chest and...

...and Matt was vomiting, coughing, hacking, water streaming out of his mouth and nose. His gut burnt, his lungs burnt, his legs were stiff and frozen and soaked to the bone.

He rolled over, an instinctive movement, tumbling out of the warm clutches of unconsciousness and onto the black, sodden wood of the pier.

All at once, the sound came back, the crashing of the waves and the scent of the ocean, salt and rotting fish.

He gagged. More water came up, burning his throat.

Had he swallowed the whole of the ocean? Where was he? What the hell was...

He caught sight of NotCharlotte, laid out on the slick decking next to him.

She was laying quite still, silent, deathly white.

And a...a *creature* crouched over her.

There was no other way to describe it.

It was humanoid, about eight feet tall, long and exceedingly thin. The creature's legs were backwards-jointed, and as it crouched there over Charlotte's body, the wind whipped at its strange, elegant clothes and straight dark hair. It wore thick multi-faceted spectacles and a well-tailored jacket of some ancient design, with flared sleeves and bright brass buttons. The sun was peeking out from behind a cloud, and flared red-golden off the creatures strange, waxy skin.

As he watched, it crept forward on long arms, groping for her, reaching for her...

Before Matt knew what he was doing, he was up, leaping for the creature, meaning to pull it away, get it off of her. But before he could reach her, a word leapt through the air, a command shouted out like a whip.

"Wait!" the voice commanded, and there were strange resonances there, odd harmonics. It sounded like three voices talking at once, and it seemed to leap straight into his mind and short-circuit his limbs, pulling him up short.

He stood there, swaying, the world spinning around him.

Then a hand was on his shoulder, helping him down - not unkindly - and laying him back on the wet decking.

"Too fast!" the voice came again, though this time without that strange weight, the odd harmonics. Now it was just a voice, and Matt realised who it was.

"June!" he said, half turning to see the old woman. She stood above him, frowning, her one good arm holding him firm. "What's...what's *that* thing!"

He gestured fearfully at the creature. But to his great relief, the tall, thin figure was not eating NotCharlotte. Instead, he was leaning down, pumping his fist rhythmically against her chest, bang, bang, bang...

Then NotCharlotte was sitting up too, seeming to vomit out the whole ocean, just as Matt had done a moment before.

It was June, Matt realised. *She must have saved me. Saved us both. Got us out of the water, pounded on my chest until I came back to life...*

Only that was clearly impossible. June was an old woman - however strange and tough she was - and of particular note was the fact that she only had one working arm. That she could crouch over him and thump his chest hard enough to get him vomiting the water from his lungs, get his breath moving again...well, that was believable, just about.

But the last thing he remembered had been the slow, inevitable shutting down of this body, somewhere deep beneath the waves. It was impossible to imagine June leaping in and fishing them out - both of them! - Before leaping back onto the pier herself, and performing life-saving CPR.

Which meant...

Matt looked again at the strange newcomer.

He was crouched over NotCharlotte now, supporting her elbow, rubbing her back, whispering something soothing into her ears. He was, Matt realised for the first time, soaked to the skin.

"It was you," said Matt. "You got us out."

He had whispered the words, whispered them under his breath, not really meaning for them to be heard, just saying them because the world was making less and less sense, and anything he could do to try and anchor it was, he had decided, a potentially useful tool.

But the creature tilted its head, long ears twitching.

"Oh, indeed," said the creature. "No surprise there. I didn't really have much of a choice."

Then it frowned, removed its strange, multi-faceted spectacles, rubbed them thoughtfully with a especially ragged-looking corner of its robe, and replaced them on his long, thin face.

"That is to say, I actually had seventeen major choices," the creature added. "Though really, thirteen of those choices would have involved Interferences that the Court have not permitted me to use. Of the remaining four, leaving you both to drown seemed rather cruel under the circumstances, not to mention disastrous in the long term. So, as you can see, leaping into the sea wasn't so difficult a choice to make, after all."

The creature gave him a sudden, startling smile, displaying row upon row of sharp, black teeth.

This was such an alarming sight, that Matt briefly considered running away and jumping back into the sea, though he discounted this quite quickly when he tried, experimentally, to rise and felt a wave of nausea and vertigo wash through him.

"Oh, please don't be alarmed on my account," said the creature, noticing Matt's suspicion. "The teeth are quite harmless, I assure you. A hold-over from another life, you might say. I don't have much call to use them these days."

Matt stared at the creature, trying - by force of will - to make the Universe stop being weird and start making sense.

It failed.

"He won't eat you," clarified June.

"Oh," said Matt. "Good. Splendid. That's good to know."

There was a sad wet sneeze.

In the excitement of meeting a strange man with black teeth who promised not to eat him, Matt had forgotten all about NotCharlotte.

Only it hardly looked like her at all any more. Not the tough, impossibly strong super-woman who had led him away on this crazy adventure. Not the abrasive, determined fighter from a strange other dimension, who had just leapt them across vast expanses of water.

No.

This Charlotte wasn't any of them, and it wasn't his Charlotte either, with her twinkling eyes, and life pulsing in ever movement.

This Charlotte looked broken.

She sat there, soaked and shivering, hair running in sad, drooping streaks to her back, eyes downcast, undone.

She sneezed again, and Matt blinked.

Even her sneeze sounded defeated.

Before he knew what he was doing, he was by her side, one arm around her shoulder, the other brushing her cheek.

"Charlotte?" he asked, unable to keep the worry from his voice.

For a moment her eyes remained downcast, silent and impassive.

Then she looked at him, and that was almost worse.

"It's gone," she said simply.

"Gone?" asked Matt. "What's gone?"

NotCharlotte looked as if she thought shrugging despondently might be a good idea, but apparently didn't even have the effort to do that.

"The link," she said. "The link to the Chaos Drive. It's been snatched away."

Matt was aware of June and the tall stranger exchanging a glance, though the words didn't mean anything to him.

They didn't sound very positive, though. He was quite sure this wasn't good news.

He hesitated, trying to formulate a question big enough to take in the entirety of his confusion.

"We should get her in," said June. "She's freezing, look at her. She'll catch her death out here."

"Get her in?" asked Matt, looking around at the desolate, deserted pier. "In where?"

"To my parlour," said the tall stranger, as if it were obvious. "That is why you are here, is it not? To meet with me, so you can obtain the things you need."

Matt looked at NotCharlotte. He wished she would wake up, come back to herself and start helping him make out what the hell was going on.

But that wasn't going to happen, he realised. She kept her eyes fixed on the ground, unaware of the shivering that gripped her whole body now, apparently not caring about what decision was made or how it would affect her.

"*You* are going to help us get it?" asked Matt. "I thought that June was the one..."

"Don't you listen, boy?" interrupted June. "This was all perfectly clear when we worked it out last week. I agreed to help you, I agreed to do what I could - and we agreed a price, too, and you better not have forgotten that."

"I've not forgotten the price," said Matt, who hadn't forgotten it, despite really, really wanting to. "What I mean is, well, who actually is this guy? And what's he here for? No offence intended," he added quickly, remembering all those sharp black teeth.

"Oh, none taken," the creature assured him. "I would be surprised were you not to ask."

"But first, we get her inside," said June firmly.

And there was nothing Matt could say to that, because it was so obviously true.

NotCharlotte had stopped shivering now, and when Matt helped lift her to her feet, she was lighter than he would have thought possible.

"Follow Ninian," ordered June. "I'll come after. Have to make sure we close things properly after. Careful where you step!"

The tall stranger led the way across the slick, wet decking, and Matt followed, Charlotte propped up against one shoulder. She was moving her legs now, she was walking where he led her. But she didn't really seem to be looking where she was going. Her mind hardly seemed to be in the world at all.

The wooden slats creaked alarmingly under his feet, and Matt made a point of noting where the tall stranger stepped. They walked along the centre of the rotting pier, past rows of broken-down huts and stalls. They had been little shops, he realised, sweet shops and entertainments, the kind of thing that still existed on the Palace Pier, all the many and varied ways that the Pier had contrived to separate tourists from their money. There was no glass left in any of the windows, and most of the doors were gone, too.

Then the tall stranger stopped in front of one especially run-down looking frontage. This one did have a door, though half of the wall was gone. Inside, it was dank and gloomy. It was so dilapidated, in fact, that Matt wasn't entirely sure that it qualified as 'inside'. It looked, in fact, much more like a piece of 'outside' that had ideas above its station.

"We're going in there?" he asked. "That's meant to keep her warm?"

"Oh, yes," said the tall stranger. "Indubitably."

Matt frowned, thinking that if anything sounded dubitable, this was it.

The creature put one long, nimble hand into the pocket of his waistcoat, and withdrew an enormous bundle of keys. Matt blinked. There had not, he was quite sure, been anywhere near enough room in that slender pocket for the great bunch of keys.

"Aha!" said the creature, selecting a thin black key, and sliding it into what remained of the door.

He turned the key, pushed the door open...and vanished.

Matt stared suspiciously at the space where the creature had been a moment before.

"Is this some kind of trick?" he demanded.

"No," said June firmly. "It's no trick. It's just magic."

Then she shoved him in the small of the back with her good hand, and Matt stumbled forward, trying not to trip. He raised one hand and...

...And he was suddenly inside, passing through a thick oaken doorway and into a large, airy room, illuminated by candles of black wax. Perhaps thirty chairs were arrayed around a circular table of dark, varnished wood. All kinds of intricate runes were painted and carved into the surface. Shelves lined with odd-looking artefacts and uncanny devices crowded for space, and on the walls were mounted a variety of weapons and armour, skeletons, flags, small unlikely-looking vehicles, and a hundred other things too strange and unusual for Matt to name. The room was floored with wooden panels of the same rich, dark design as the table.

It was all splendid, of the highest possible quality, and Matt found that his mouth was going dry as he stared at it.

It was all so completely strange that he forgot almost at once that the way the room had sprung out of nowhere was, itself, an act of acute strangeness.

"What...what *is* this place?" he asked.

"Welcome to my workshop," said the tall creature. "This is where I do the majority of my work, carry out most of my consultations." He paused, and glanced around a little sheepishly. "Sorry for the mess," he added.

Matt turned to NotCharlotte, an unbidden smile on his lips.

This was *wonderful*. He couldn't say why exactly, and part of him knew he should have been running in terror from the weirdness of it all, and yet...

"This place is incredible," he said. "Did you know that we were coming here?"

But in his excitement, he had quite forgotten that something was wrong with NotCharlotte. Now, as she stared past him, not responding to his question, no hint of wonder in her eyes, the truth came crashing back to him.

"What's wrong with her?" he demanded of the tall creature. "Is she sick? Has she got hypothermia?"

"It's much more complicated than that," said June, appearing through the door out of a patch of drear Brighton sky, which flared briefly into being behind her, then vanished as she stepped fully into the room. "She's untethered. She's a target."

"Untethered?" repeated Matt. "What the hell does that mean? Is it dangerous?"

"Yes," said June. "Very."

Matt looked from June to the stranger and back again.

"Well, hadn't we better *do* something?" he demanded.

"Oh, yes," said the tall stranger. "That's why we've come here."

June helped NotCharlotte into a chair. She tensed, as if she were going to resist.

"Shush, now," said June, her voice firm and businesslike, but not unkind. "You better let us do this, if you know what's good for you."

NotCharlotte opened her mouth, but her eyes were blank; if she had words ready, they decided not to come.

"If that's what you want," said NotCharlotte, and the indifference in her voice made Matt's heart ache.

"What are you doing?" demanded Matt. "What's untethered?"

"It is rather a complicated problem," said the tall creature, sliding into the seat next to NotCharlotte and taking her hand in one of his. "We must act swiftly. Now that the link has been severed, she has no way of keeping your layer of reality from honing in on her. It will know she is wrong. In fact, it already knows. It is probably best for all concerned if you retreat to a little distance. This is rather a delicate business, and I understand you are rather a normal creature."

Matt felt something inside him harden.

Since this version of Charlotte had come barrelling into his life, things had taken on a surreal, unlikely aspect. Not only had he found out that his world was only one of an infinite number, but he was also expected to believe that he and everyone he loved existed, really, in some kind of story. And that wasn't even mentioning the variety of extremely weird things he had seen with his own eyes, up to and including this tall, backwards-jointed stranger.

Matt was many things, and he had put up with a lot of things, but he found that being called 'normal' really was the last straw.

"Stop," he said, and there was such flat determination in his voice that both June and the tall stranger froze in the act of soothing NotCharlotte and turned to stare at him, as if seeing him for the first time.

"Now you listen to me," said Matt, his voice quiet, but brimming over with barely-controlled rage, "I might not have superhuman strength. I might have limbs of the standard length, and all of them bend the right way. I might even never have gone to any other worlds. But I've seen an awful lot in the last few days, and all things considered, I think I've taken it pretty well. And if you think I'm going to let you do some strange and eldritch thing to my...to my *almost*-wife, you've got another thing coming."

He glared at them, switching from one to the other until they both - astonishingly - dropped their eyes.

"Good," he said. "Now. Answers."

The tall creature licked his lips. Matt noticed - with almost no surprise - that his tongue was long, forked, and purple.

"I see," he said. "Well, time is very much against us, so perhaps you will accept the abbreviated version. Charlotte is untethered, and that is dangerous because..."

"Wait," ordered Matt. "I don't know your name. What's your name?"

The creature blinked, his eyelids sliding in from the corners of his eyes in an odd little staccato.

"I'm terribly sorry, how rude of me," said the creature. "My name is Ninian. I am of the Bracken Court."

"Fine," said Matt, tucking the phrase, 'Bracken Court' away in his mind, in a folder titled, 'weird things to ask about later, when it doesn't matter if knowing the answers raises another ten questions'. "Tell me about what you mean. Why is she untethered? Why does that even matter?"

Ninian steepled his fingers.

"Charlotte is...from a different layer of reality," he said. He spoke slowly, as if choosing his words with great care. "But I'm sure you know that already. She doesn't belong to the same layer of reality as you. Her resonance is all out of synch with the rest of your world."

"Yes, I know all that," said Matt. "She's from a different story. A different version."

A frown passed over Ninian's face, and he exchanged a glance with June.

"Don't worry," said June. "It's just her frame of reference. With her, it's all about stories."

"Oh, I see," said Ninian. "Yes. Stories. I have heard such things before. How fascinating."

"Didn't you say time was a factor here?" Said Matt.

"Yes, I'm sorry," said Ninian. "Anyway, the thing is, when someone strays into a different layer of reality, they have to be careful. Every layer has its own resonances, its own predilections. Just by coming into your world, Charlotte has set things vibrating in odd ways, has set odd things to happen."

"Well that's hardly her fault," protested Matt. "She didn't ask to come here. Any more than my Charlotte asked to be taken off to...to wherever she is."

"No one's calling it her fault," said June. "All we're interested in here is facts. And the fact is, Charlotte doesn't belong to the same layer of reality as you, and your layer of reality knows it."

"And while we are focussed on facts," put in Ninian, "it behooves us to be clear about where we are now."

"I am perfectly bloody *behooved* about where we are," snapped Matt, unable to keep the frustration from his voice. "West Pier, Brighton."

But he knew as soon as he said it that this wasn't true. There was no way this splendid room, with its tall, dark candles and wide, varnished table was located in the same reality as the broken-down pier.

"No," contradicted Ninian patiently. "When you stepped through my door, you stepped out of your layer of reality, too. You are in my parlour, and that exists somewhere quite different."

Matt put his head in his hands, squeezing his eyes shut against the headache that was pounding at his temples, trying to get in.

"Right," he said. "And what layer of reality are we in now, exactly? A world of fairies and goblins, perhaps? Or if I walked outside, would I see golden spaceships being driven by the Norse gods?"

"Oh, we are in neither of those realities," said Ninian helpfully. "No, those realities are still a little way off from here. Actually, if you opened the door, you could come out in any number of realities, depending on the spin I projected. That's the beauty of my parlour. You can think of it as something like one of your elevators. A convenient way of travelling from here to there and back again."

"So you're...you're kind of *between floors*?" asked Matt, who found to his surprise that this was going into his brain a lot more easily than he had expected. The last few weeks with NotCharlotte must have stretched him, to the point where accepting such things was possible.

"Precisely," said Ninian, smiling widely and displaying rows of his splendid black teeth. "And if you opened the door without any spin at all being put on it, you would find yourself in a wide, white land of empty potential. A place between realities, if you will. A potential place, where it's easy to construct such half-realities as my parlour, if you know there trick of it."

Matt nodded, and started to ask another question, but at that moment, NotCharlotte slumped forward onto the floor.

Before Matt could act, Ninian was at her side, gently sliding a pillow under her head, a hand laid soothingly on her arm.

"Please, master Matt," he said, not looking at him. "It really is imperative that we act quickly. She is untethered, as I've said. She needs help."

Matt hesitated. Even now, he was reluctant to give the go-ahead for the strange creature to do gods-knew what to his almost-wife. But what choice did he have?

"Do it," he said.

"Thank you," said Ninian.

Using his quick, nimble fingers, he plucked various mysterious objects from about the room. Matt recognised some of them, or thought he did: some chalk, a thin white candle, and - improbably - a pair of fluffy dice. But there were several others that looked like nothing he had ever seen before. He noted with interest that, though several of the objects appeared to be made of metal, none looked as if they contained a trace of iron.

"What's he doing?" Matt asked June, as Ninian quickly arranged the objects in a rough circle around where NotCharlotte lay on the floor.

June sighed, gritted her teeth.

"It's difficult to explain," she said.

"Try," demanded Matt. Now Ninian was using the chalk to draw a shape on the floor around her. His movements were confident and precise, and an odd geometric pattern quickly emerged on the dark wooden floor.

"Fine," said June. "Look. Did you ever wonder about her...her strength? About the way she could pick you up without seemingly any effort? The way she found *me*? The way she could smell out strangeness?"

"Of course I did," said Matt. "I even asked her. Several times."

"And what did she tell you?" Asked June.

"Augmentations," said Matt. "She never would say more than that. I assumed she meant she had...oh, I don't know. Some kind of futuristic implants. Special robot parts. Carbon-fibre muscles. Something like that."

He waved a hand vaguely in the air. On the floor, Ninian had finished drawing the strange shape around NotCharlotte. Now he crouched over her. He began chanting something in an odd language Matt did not recognise. The syllables themselves seemed rich and vibrant, somehow, to drip with meaning that eluded him, but which nevertheless hovered enticingly, just out of reach. The shadows thickened around them. The thick black candles flickered and strained against the darkness.

"Augmentations?" June barked a laugh. "Well, her little joke, I suppose. It didn't matter what she called it, not really. The point was that you just accept what she was doing, without questioning too deeply."

"Why?" asked Matt. "What was it she was doing, really?"

June shrugged.

"Channeling power," she said simply. "Channelling energy from another level of reality. From the level of reality she was from."

"Channeling energy?" said Matt. He felt slightly hurt for his mundane level of reality "But...but how is that possible? Is her layer of reality so much more...more powerful than mine? That she can just snatch power from it and overwhelm my silly little world?"

"It sort of is, actually," said June. "But that's not how she did it. No, she couldn't channel weirdness directly from her reality any more than you could channel normality from yours, were you in her reality. No, she could channel power in because of the device."

"The device?" Repeated Matt. A phrase echoed around the back of his head, something NotCharlotte had said a few minutes ago. What was it? For a moment the words eluded him, then he snatched at them. "The Chaos Drive," he said.

"Yes," said June. "It's good to see you have been paying attention at last."

Ninian had stopped chanting now, though he continued mumbling something beneath his breath. The air had grown still, pregnant. Matt felt oppressed, as if to speak now was wrong, somehow, an insult to forces gathering around them, forces he could almost perceive.

Still, something prompted him to press on. He had to know.

"But what is it?" he demanded in a hiss. "This Chaos Drive...thingy? What does it do?"

June was silent for a long moment, staring at Ninian, staring at NotCharlotte's face as it danced under the flickering candlelight.

"She would say it's a machine for re-writing stories," said June at length. There was just enough irony in her voice for Matt to understand that June herself would never have phrased it in such a way, though quite what she would have called the Chaos Drive if *she* had made it, Matt could only guess. June paused, bit her lip thoughtfully. "She told me the machine channels energy from the raw forces on one side of Story," she said the words carefully, as if experimenting with ideas she was only just getting the hang of. "The way Charlotte phrased it, reality - every layer of reality - hangs between two opposing poles, two sources of antagonistic energy, competing against one another. Order and Chaos. It's the friction between these forces in which stories - in which realities - exist."

"And she made a machine that - what - tapped energy out of the chaos?" Matt frowned. He wasn't sure how healthy this all sounded, let alone how plausible. "How the hell did she do that?"

"Oh, it wasn't her who made the machine," said June. "Honestly, it's a wonder how little you know of her world, given that you've spent weeks with her. I got all this in just a few hours. And you were *there* when she told me."

Matt shook his head.

"Please excuse me if all this is rather new to me," he said, sarcastically. "Multiple worlds and machines that run on pure story might come naturally to you, but I'm used to seeing that kind of thing in *Star Trek*, not living it. I need a bit of a run up to get my head around things like..."

But Matt cut off. He stared, amazed, at what was happening to NotCharlotte.

Abruptly, as if appearing out of nowhere, a golden thread was visible. It emerged from her belly, a thick twine of sparkling incandescent energy, wavering in the air. It was like a huge, ephemeral umbilical cord.

"What," asked Matt in a low, urgent voice, "the hell is that?"

"What does it look like?" replied June. "It's the tattered end. The broken tethering. The thing that used to connect Charlotte to the Chaos Drive. It was wrenched, broken, cut loose earlier. Haven't you worked that out yet? That ...*skipping* of reality? When you were in mid-air, leaping towards the pier?"

"That was impossible," said Matt idly, remembering the huge height Charlotte had jumped them to, the incredible power in her legs.

"Of course it was," said June. "One more impossible thing, made possible by the energy of the Chaos Drive. Charlotte was able to channel power - well, she would call it *narrative potential* - in any case, she was able to channel it from her connection to the drive, to...to re-write the substances of your story. To change reality, if you want to put it in much more sensible terms," June added with a sniff.

On the ground, Ninian made a pass with one slender hand over NotCharlotte's midriff. Her body jerked. She cried out, her back arching, her teeth clenched in a grimace.

"Stop it!" cried Matt in alarm. "You're hurting her!"

"Shush now," said June, grabbing his shoulder. "He's only doing what has to be done. The tethered end has to be removed. It's putting her in danger, terrible danger. Putting all of us at risk, for that matter. Ninian has to remove it, and quickly."

"But, but..." said Matt weakly. "But why? What harm can it do?"

"Now that the cord has been cut, Charlotte can't call on any reserves of narrative potential to reshape reality," said June, as if it were obvious. "That means she can't jump over tall buildings in a single bound. That means she can't lift you up with one hand and spank your bottom with the other. And," she added, turning to look at Matt, eyes boring into him like dark coals, "and most importantly of all, it means she can no longer twist reality around herself, to make a shroud, to stop your level of reality from realising what is going on."

NotCharlotte writhed on the ground. She wasn't screaming any more, but her breath was coming in sharp, shallow gasps. She was obviously in pain.

"Why would this level of reality care?" Matt demanded.

"Reality cares very much," chided June. "Why, of course it does! Each layer of reality has certain conventions, certain expectations."

Matt looked at her blankly, trying to force her words to make sense. But it was too much. He had accepted seven impossible things before breakfast; perhaps his quota for barminess was filled for the day.

June sighed.

"Or, as Charlotte would put it, the story doesn't like that it's being messed with," she said. "Does that make any more sense to you? She's been playing havoc with the story, and keeping herself hidden from it with the same powers she's been using to manipulate it. Now those powers have gone, and her means of concealing herself has gone, too. The story - the layer of reality, it doesn't matter what you call it - will find out, and when it does, it will come for her. It will try and expel her like a body expelling a splinter. And that trailing cord, that silvery stub of a link that remains from her connection to the Chaos Drive - that stands out. It's like a sign hung round her neck saying, '*I'm not from around here and I've been filling your mundane world with magic - come and get me!*'"

Matt screwed up his face. He felt as if the carpet was being ripped out from under his feet - again! If all the things June was telling him were true, then the way NotCharlotte had explained it to him was…

"She lied to me," said Matt. "She didn't say anything about any of this. Not to me. She was…" he waved a hand. "All she talked about was shields and beacons."

"Ah, well," said June. "I'm sure she had a good reason."

"But what possible reason could she have?" asked Matt, but his voice was drowned out.

Ninian was chanting again, his voice growing louder, more keen, more commanding. The tattered golden cord was taut and fraying now, whipping about in the air like an angry snake.

Suddenly Ninian lunged out and grabbed hold of it. He held it in both of his long, sinuous hands. He strained. He screamed. NotCharlotte screamed, too.

The light flickered as if an unseen wind was blowing from nowhere into nowhere.

Then there was a wrenching. Matt had no other way to describe it. The cord had not been attached to him, but he felt the parting of it as keenly as if it were him that it had been tied to.

He screamed too. It seemed like the thing to do.

For a moment the cord hung there, silvery-golden-red in the dancing candlelight.

Then it dissolved in a puff of nothingness.

The candles shook, flickered, went out.

Darkness ruled the room.

From the floor, NotCharlotte gave a groan.

Matt dashed forward. He felt her in the darkness. Her hands were cold and limp, but when Matt gave one a squeeze, she squeezed him fitfully back.

"Are you okay?" asked Matt. "Is it over?"

"It's over," said Ninian. He sounded tired, but rather pleased with himself. "The link has been severed. She can't draw on the Chaos Drive any more, of course. But my understanding is she could not do that anyway, not since the link was taken by another. But in the circumstances, that hardly matters."

"I agree," said June, pulling up a chair and sitting down painfully. "The danger of immediate discovery has passed, at least for now."

"Yes," said NotCharlotte, sitting up. She looked around carefully, one hand out to steady herself, as if only now really seeing where they had taken her. "It's gone."

But she didn't sound happy. Not at all.

"That's it," she said softly. "I've lost. There's no hope of getting back now. We are done."

As soon as she spoke, as soon as she sat up, a storm of emotion welled up in Matt. She was alive. She was well. She was - apparently - capable of coherent conversation again.

And she looked so broken, so achingly hopeless. He wanted to go to her, to comfort her, to tell her that everything would be okay.

And yet...

"You lied to me," he said. He tried to keep the words from coming out petulantly, but it was no good. He couldn't help it. He felt petulant. What was more, he felt he had a *right* to feel petulant.

NotCharlotte sighed.

"I didn't mean to," she said. She didn't look at him.

"Yes, you did!" said Matt. "That was exactly what you did! You didn't tell me anything about this...this *Chaos Drive*. You told me we had to find something to shield ourselves. You said we needed to get a signal out, a signal back to your reality. And all the time you were carrying around shield and a link yourself! All the time! Why didn't you tell me?"

"I wish I could have," said NotCharlotte simply. "Don't you think I wanted to? But I couldn't. It was vital you didn't know the truth."

"What?" spluttered Matt. "Why? That doesn't make any sense!"

"Because you are a *part* of your own world," put in June. "You're bound up in it, bound close."

Charlotte was nodding.

"If I had told you the truth, the story would have known at once," she said. "It would know exactly what to look for. It would be able to untangle the glamours I put over the tendrils from the Chaos Drive. And I would have been expelled. And then I would be lost, and you would never have gotten your Charlotte back."

"It was vital she told you just enough for your layer of reality to know something was amiss," put in Ninian. "But not so much that it could realise exactly how Charlotte was the source."

Matt stared from one of them to the next. They all looked so composed, so earnest. Part of him felt the need to hold on to his anger, to cling onto his outrage. It felt so clean and righteous. And yet...

"So...so the story knew about you?" asked Matt. "It knew all along?"

"Yes," said Charlotte simply. "Yes, it had to. It's such a mundane little story - no offence meant! - but there's no room for weirdness here, no room for the strange."

"So much iron," said Ninian mournfully. "It's everywhere. It's in the *sea* even. I got mouthfuls of it when I fished you out. It stung."

"What have you lot got against iron, anyway?" ssked Matt. "Perfectly good metal. Very good at not breaking."

"Indeed," agreed Ninian. "So I have heard. But it is also very good at...at pinning reality to a set shape. At making things certain."

"Some things *are* certain," countered Matt.

"People in inward-facing worlds always seem to think so," said June. "Like ours. With this much iron about, that often seems the only possible truth. In fact, that's how inward facing worlds *become* inward-facing in the first place: too much iron getting thrown around, nailing the world in place, erasing the possibility of anything else..."

"Anyway," went on NotCharlotte, "the very fact of me being in your little iron story stuck out like a dragon on a ferris wheel. My only chance was to obfuscate enough of the circumstances that the story couldn't work out exactly how to expel me. If it had grabbed a hold of the link from the Chaos Drive, it could have tugged me out in an instant. That's where all the talk about shields and beacons came in. It's been so focussed on that, it missed the easiest way to get rid of me."

"You made her awful sore though," said the odd little man in the corner. "You might not have meant any evil by it, but you lot have put her quite out of sorts."

Matt nodded. This sounded sensible. He looked at the others. They were nodding, too.

"But the story must see I had no other choice," said NotCharlotte to the strange little man. "After all, what was I supposed..."

Then she stopped.

She blinked.

"Who," she said carefully, "the hell are you?"

Matt stared at her.

Why was she asking who the little man with the mismatched eyes was?

He had always been there, hadn't he?

He was...

Matt blinked, too.

Something weird was going on.

Something even more weird, that was.

"Yes," said Ninian. "I must say, I am most impressed by your ability to insinuate your way into my parlour. You quite fooled me, for a while. A neat little tricking of reality. It was most difficult to perceive that you have, in fact, not been here forever."

"Thank you kindly, sir," said the man with the mismatched eyes. He wore a battered, dusty hat on his head, and was dressed in faded blue jeans and a plain, white shirt. He had a long, drooping moustache, and his hair was...it was odd. As Matt watched, the man's hair flickered between colours, lengths, styles. But the really odd thing was, the moment the hair changed, it was difficult to remember it ever having been different. It was as if reality itself were stretching, trying desperately to appease the flickering whims of the newcomer. Just looking at him made his eyes feel as if they wanted to melt out of their sockets.

The man slipped off his chair, and put a hand to his face, stroking his greyish moustache. His other hand went idly to a golden star-shaped badge he wore on his shirt.

"I must say, it was a tricksy job," the man went on. "A most well-constructed little bubble. It took me quite some time to understand her. But I spoke about why I wanted to come in, and I listened to what she told me, and I made certain pledges. I won't hurt you. None of you. Not here. I promise."

"That's all very nice," said NotCharlotte. "But my previous question still stands: who the hell are you?"

The man straightened up. Next to Ninian, he looked almost like a dwarf; yet there was something in him, a stance, a certainty, something which made Matt believe at once that if it came to a fight, there would really be no contest here. The newcomer was *powerful*. Matt was quite sure of that.

"Oh, terribly sorry, ma'am, terribly sorry," said the newcomer. His voice was light, almost melodic. "My name's Norwood. Norwood Ginnell."

He smiled, and it was a pleasant smile, with no malice or boastfulness.

"I'm a Sheriff," he went on. "A Sheriff of the Folds. Of the Order, I should say. We've been looking for you. You've been causing us a whole heap of trouble."

"Oh," said Charlotte.

She looked mortified.

"Bugger," she added.

"The Order?" Asked Matt. "Are you some kind of...of monk, or something?"

Norwood Ginnel gave a laugh, light and clear. The smile on his face seemed genuinely amused.

"More of a something than a monk, friend," he replied. "And - as I say - I'm a Sheriff more than anything."

"A Sheriff?" repeated Matt, blankly. "As in, strolling around a dusty gold rush town, laying down the law, shooting varmints, that kind of thing?"

"More or less," said Norwood Ginnel, agreeably. "Though the dusty gold rush town is the whole Storystream, the main law I uphold is that of Order, and the varmints are..."

"Me," said Charlotte, in a small, broken voice. "Us. Anyone who meddles in the structure of stories."

Norwood was nodding at her, stroking his long, drooping moustache. He did not seem angry, but there was something uncompromising in those fizzling, mismatched eyes.

"You," he agreed, then gave a long sigh. "Oh, you've been

leading us Sheriffs a merry dance for a while now. Twisting stories this way and that, bending them to your whims, carrying off all sorts of things that didn't rightly belong to you."

"I'm...I'm sorry," said Charlotte.

"No, you're not," said Norwood amicably. "You and your team made a merry little game of things. What's more," he added, leaning forward and lowering his voice conspiratorially, "there were a few of us - Sheriffs of the Order, of the Folds, I mean - who noted the kinds of folks you were messing with, and didn't think too badly of it."

Charlotte looked, eyes suddenly filled with hope.

"You mean..." she started to say, but Norwood shook his head sadly, holding up one tough, leathery hand to forestall her.

"Now, I don't want to give you no false hope," he said, carefully. "What you've been doing - you and your companions - well, on a small scale, a few of us were prepared to look the other way, so to speak. But what you've set in motion now..."

His blazing, mismatched eyes roamed around the room, looking from one of them to the next.

Norwood gave a whistle, and shook his head.

"Well, let's just say things have got out of control," he finished, solemnly. "It's high time for us Sheriffs to step in."

Charlotte looked down.

"He took it," she said, almost whispering. "He took the Chaos Drive. He's going to..."

"He's going to do many terrible things," Norwood agreed. "Such devices always fall into the wrong hands, sooner or later. Which is why we probably should have intervened sooner, but..."

He looked up searchingly, as if trying to find the right phrase.

Then he shrugged and grinned at her.

"We liked you, I suppose," he finished.

Then he clapped his hands together, and stood a little straighter.

"Right," said Norwood, with the air of someone finally preparing to get down to business. "Time to get on with things, I suppose."

Something crackled in the air. Matt had the impression of immense energies being gathered, forces that he could not see circling and swirling and making ready to flare into being.

Matt moved quickly, instinctively

To his surprise, he found he was standing protectively in front of NotCharlotte.

Norwood looked at him mildly.

"You're not going to, er, kill us, are you?" Matt asked, awkwardly.

Norwood gave him an astonished smile.

"Kill you?" he repeated. "Why, bless me, no! No, of course not!"

Matt sagged, relief flooding through his veins.

"Good," he sighed. "For a moment there, I thought..."

"I'm just going to seal you off," Norwood went on amicably. "Place y'all in a sterile little bubble. Somewhere you can't get up to any more mischief, while the Sheriffs of the Folds put this mess to rights."

Matt frowned. That didn't sound quite as benign as Norwood's tone would suggest.

A howling noise began to rise. It came from the floor, from the roof, from the very fabric of reality.

"Wait," Matt said, voice rising against the crackling of strange energies Norwood was harnessing. "A little bubble? Sealed off? But I need to find..."

"Don't worry," said Norwood, and his cheerful voice was amplified somehow, so it overcame the now hurricane-like wind which swirled around them, scattering papers from Ninian's table, making the strange items rattle and whistle on the walls. "You'll be quite safe there."

"Where, though?" shouted Matt, but the wind was so loud he couldn't hear his own words.

Norwood did, though.

"Somewhere totally isolated," said Norwood. "Behind a Quarantine."

The crackling of vast energies was unbearable now. Matt covered his ears with his hands, and screamed.

Everything went black.

❧ 2 2 ❧

"**M**ore salmon?" asked Philip Frogmore.

Charlotte looked up from her revere and blinked, trying to work out what he was talking about, trying to hide the thoughts that had been rushing through her head, to stop them spilling onto her face.

She looked around guiltily. The servant proffered a plate of thinly sliced smoked salmon. It looked and smelt completely delicious, just like every other item in this elaborate feast.

The thing was, Charlotte wasn't hungry. She should have been. She hadn't eaten properly for many days - not since the night of her wedding, in fact, and that had been - what? - more than three weeks ago, probably. Since then she had been kidnapped by a horrendous frog-based alien race, chased by ginormous beasts, hunted through the ghastly landscape of Froghearth, and finally saved - or was it kidnapped again? - by this strange Frogmore person, and taken to a fluffy white land of empty potential.

She hadn't had a solid meal during that time. She should

have been hungry enough to eat a horse, and still ask if they had any likely looking ponies for afters.

And yet...

And yet, something didn't ring true about Philip Frogmore. For some reason, Charlotte just couldn't let her guard down. And as long as her guard was up, she found her stomach was turning summersaults, and nothing seemed to settle there.

"Come on," said NotMatt, his mouth half-full of some kind of exquisite concoction of duck eggs and fine herbs. "You really need to eat. And it *is* delicious."

It was good to see that NotMatt was talking again, that he was seemingly back in the world. The problem was, most of his vim and drive seemed to have melted away. He talked about the food being delicious, but there was no room for smiles on his face. He glanced around, he seemed to be taking in his surroundings, listening to what Frogmore was saying...but Charlotte wondered. He seemed deflated, somehow. To have lost his drive. To have lost his hope...

Which meant that staying safe and alive was now up to her. She couldn't rely on NotMatt, she had realised. It was all on her.

"Well, a little then," she said, reaching for the plate the servant was holding. He looked familiar, somehow. Had she seen this one before? Maybe that was why. The house was full of servants, lots and lots of them, all youngish men with firm, regular features and ready smiles...but their eyes were blank, and they did not seem capable of answering any of her simple questions.

And they all seemed to look so familiar...

She took a small slice of salmon and cut herself a piece. It tasted delicious, as advertised. But she found she just couldn't focus on the sensation.

"As you can see, I only eat the best," Frogmore was telling her. "Why not, when it is mine for the taking?"

"Absolutely," said Charlotte. "Why not. But tell me, Mr Frogmore..."

"Philip, please," protested their host.

"Tell me, Philip," amended Charlotte, stifling a sense of distaste at using the man's first name, "how did you get all this...this *stuff*? I thought the Place Between Stories empty, completely empty."

"Yes, that's a good question," said NotMatt. He was frowning, as if trying to think through a thick fog. "How do you make all this? I thought that it was easy to make things here, but difficult to get them to keep their substance."

"You heard right, Master Mathew," said Frogmore, and he bowed his head slightly in NotMatt's direction. "And were I to simply be conjuring this food up from the nothingness of this place, it would indeed be bland and unsatisfying. But these are *not* freshly-minted half-real platitudes, as I'm sure you can tell. No, my larder is stocked daily, and from the very best sources in the whole of the Storystream."

Charlotte tried to catch NotMatt's eye, but he was looking down, playing with the food on his plate.

"So...you make excursions?" NotMatt asked. He was frowning, as if his thoughts were coming slowly, and there was a slight thickness to his words. "Out into...where?"

Frogmore shrugged, and threw an olive into the air.

"Everywhere," he said simply, and smiled. He caught the olive in his mouth, chewed, and spat out the stone. "Anywhere," he went on. "The Storystream is broad and wide, and it is teeming with delicious things. To someone with my...resources, it is a simple thing to drop in wherever I will. To simply grab the very best, to keep my larders well stocked. In fact, I don't even have to make the trips myself much anymore. I have so many helping hands."

Charlotte glanced around, at the many servants that crowded into the grand room. Once again, something tugged at the corner of her mind. Why did the blank-eyed servants all look so familiar?

She shook her head. For some reason, this place seemed less and less comfortable. She was even beginning to half-wish she was back in Froghearth, and that had been a desperate, desolate place, filled with angry froglings who wanted nothing so much as to kill her. Which said something about how uncomfortable Frogmore was making her feel.

No, it was high time they were getting gone from here. And if NotMatt wasn't going to be the one to get them home...

"That must be...very nice for you," said Charlotte, trying to sound both friendly and businesslike. "But the fact is, mister...ah, I mean, *Philip*...the fact is, this isn't really the life for me. I have another life to be getting back to. I have a *husband*, even, and I'm sure he's missing me as much as I am him. I think we need to talk about what we are going to do next."

NotMatt was frowning again, as if he were trying to make sense of what she was saying.

"Well now, let's not be hasty," he said. "It is very...it's very *comfortable* here. And we don't want our host to think us rude..."

What is wrong *with him?* thought Charlotte.

Something was going seriously strange with NotMatt's thought processes. It had all started on the giant mushroom, with that weird shifting sensation. That was when he had seemed to lose himself.

And yet...and yet he had only started seeming so...so *slow* since they had come here, to Frogmore's mansion.

"No, not at all," said Frogmore, standing up quickly, and fixing Charlotte with a smile that would have been friendly if it were not for the cold light in his eyes. "My friends, I have kept you too long at dinner. I only did so as I assumed you must be famished after your ordeals, although I see now that was a mistake."

"No, I didn't mean..." began Charlotte, worried that Frogmore saw through her, worried that he could sense her mistrust. What would he do, she wondered, if he knew what I really thought of him? She hated to admit it, but they really were at the man's mercy right now.

"You are more hungry for something else, I see," went on Frogmore, talking over her. "You are hungry for revenge. Trust me, I know that hunger. Know it very well."

"Revenge?" said Charlotte. "I don't know about that. I just want to get home and..."

But now Philip Frogmore was striding forward, putting one arm around NotMatt's shoulder and leading them all away from the table. As soon as they left, the servants were swooping in, apparently without needing to be told what to do, cleaning the plates, clearing the tables. It was as if they were so attentive to their master's will that he he didn't need to utter a word.

"Oh, but I'm sure you *do*," said Frogmore. He was talking to both of them, but he was leaning on NotMatt, his lips mere inches from his ear. "Yes, revenge against the vile Frog who stole so much from you. Who *kidnapped* you! Who would have sacrificed you to his dark gods in the name of entertainment..."

Charlotte could see NotMatt's back tense and tremble.

"Revenge," he said. "Yes. Indeed. Revenge...that is what is needed."

"He took your lady," said Frogmore. "He took your lady, and he took your...pet. But that wasn't all. Oh, no. He took your device, too. Your special toy. And without that you're..."

"Nothing," whispered NotMatt. His eyes were downcast, but his voice trembled with emotion. "I am nothing."

For a moment, Charlotte was too shocked to speak. How could this be NotMatt? This snivelling, broken creature - this wasn't the same man who had fought off the monster, who had defied King Toadflaps! This man was...was something else. Something unsettling was happening here. She was sure of it. She could tell by the way she was becoming unsettled.

"But you don't have to be," said Frogmore earnestly. He was leading them down wide corridors, deeper into his sprawling mansion. "No, not if you take a stand. Not if you fight back."

A buzzing began to build at the back of Charlotte's head. It was all too much. It was too strange, she felt too off balance. She followed behind, feeling as if Frogmore had almost dismissed her, as if he were focussing all his energy on NotMatt. She felt that she had to do something, to break the flow of his words. But what? And how could she concentrate with this buzzing growing in her ears?

"Fight back," echoed NotMatt. He stopped, shoulders hunched. He glanced at Frogmore. "Yes. Yes, I should fight. I need to fight back. I need to *kill* him."

NotMatt said the words as if there should be venom there, but the funny thing was, there was very little force there at all. Instead, his words sounded strange, stilted. Almost as if they weren't his words at all.

Charlotte opened her mouth to protest. How could they fight back? How could they even go back to the Frogopolis, to contend with the power of this Chaos Drive, in the sweaty, slimy hands of Head Frog 127?

But at that moment, the buzzing lanced upwards. It seemed to come from every corner of the world, and yet Charlotte knew with complete certainty that it was really only coming from the inside of her own head. She gasped. It was too much. She needed to sit down. She needed to be alone, to think things through.

"The bathroom," she managed to gasp. "I need to...to use the bathroom. Please."

Frogmore blinked at her. For an instant, he stared with such uncovered hostility that Charlotte almost took a step back. Then he was all smiles again, was taking her by the arm, passing her over to one of his many servants. This one had brownish hair turning to grey and had a broad, pleasant face. But, just like the others, there was something unnervingly familiar about him.

"Of course, my girl," Frogmore crooned at her. "Here - boy! Take our guest to one of the restrooms. And wait for her. We don't want her...getting lost. Then meet us in the...armoury."

As his lips formed the last word, he made a horrible little slurping laugh.

"Yes, yes please," said Charlotte, mentally filing the term, 'my girl' under the heading of, 'patronising bilge for which revenge is owed', and wishing she could come up with some way of deflating Frogmore. But the buzzing in her head was too much. She had no room in her mental space for fighting, for standing up for herself. She had to be alone. She had to think...

"This way, please," said the servant in a pleasantly bland voice. He led Charlotte down more passageways, seemingly an endless supply of them, always melting out of the next wall. Charlotte found herself wondering how big the manor was. Frogmore (the house, not the person) was certainly huge...but then, if she understood properly what Frogmore (the person, not the house) had been saying earlier, was there really any limit to the place? Or did it just unfold endlessly into the potential space of the Place Between Stories?

The servant came to a halt. They were standing before a

palatial bathroom made of perfect worked marble of various colours. It was quite the most splendid bathroom Charlotte had ever seen.

"I will wait here for you, my lady," said the servant. "Please do not hesitate to call me if you need anything."

"Yes, yes I will," said Charlotte, struggling to speak through the buzzing in her head. Now it had grown so loud, so intense that it seemed to be filling the entire world. "I mean, I won't. Need anything, that is. I'm sure. Just...just...I'll be back."

And she stumbled off into the bathroom before the servant could reply.

Inside, she found herself surrounded by mirrors and huge, spectacular sinks. She walked to the one furthest from the door, splashed her face with cool water, and then examined herself in the mirror.

She looked pale and her face was drawn.

She had hoped the buzzing would calm down with a little solitude, but it just kept building, building, building...

She squeezed her eyes shut, tried to make it stop.

It was no good. It was overwhelming. It was too much, like a scream building deep in the middle of her skull.

She opened her eyes. She was panting now, and her face was covered with sweat.

She looked at herself again in the mirror.

She really was pale and strange and...

...and it wasn't *her* staring back.

It was someone who looked a little like her, but it certainly wasn't her.

She could tell by the eyes, which were big and yellow, and by the smile. She wasn't smiling, but the reflection was. It wasn't a nasty smile. If anything, it was trying to be friendly, reassuring. But the problem was, it was difficult to be reassured by a face in the mirror that wasn't yours, no matter how nice their smile was.

And anyway, the main thing that told her it wasn't her reflection was neither the eyes nor the smile.

It was the fur.

She was quite sure she didn't have fur. Quite sure.

And certainly not that much, thick and soft-looking and dark.

Actually, it quite suited her. She thought she looked pretty.

"Hello?" asked the reflection. "Charlotte, can you hear me?"

Charlotte looked around, as if expecting someone to be positioned just behind her, the person the reflection was really addressing. Of course, the bathroom was empty. She was on her own.

She realised the buzzing noise was gone. She shook her head. It felt...clean. For the first time in ages. Her thoughts were sliding properly now, uninterrupted.

"What the hell is going on?" she asked, not because she was really expecting an answer, but more because she felt like expressing to the Universe exactly how baffled she was.

The reflection took a deep breath.

"Matt lost his connection to the Chaos Drive, which means he hasn't been able to channel power to influence reality," it began. "I nearly managed to get to you, but that bastard Frogmore swept in at the last moment. *His* machine is more powerful than I thought. Much more powerful. And I can't get to Matt any more, since his brainwaves are being interfered with, which I can tell you noticed, too. Then there's the business with the Sheriffs of the Order. They've got involved at last, like we always knew they would. Things are hotting up. So I decided to try to get through to you, instead. It looks like it's down to us, kid."

Charlotte blinked.

She hadn't really been expecting an answer. She certainly hadn't been expecting one that made sense.

Well. Almost made sense.

She blinked again, catching up with the last bit.

To her further surprise, she found she didn't mind being called 'kid'. Not by this person, whoever they were. It was much better than Frogmore calling her *girl*, anyway.

"Right," she said, uncertainty. "Actually, that's good to know. About Frogmore, I mean. I was...I *knew* we shouldn't trust him. But...but what can I do? We're trapped here, I'm sure of it. He's not just going to let us go..."

"Listen to me," cut in the reflection. "We don't have much time. I haven't got the power to communicate for long. That place is too well shielded. You have to play the fool. You have to make him think he's won you over. Bide your time. There will be a chance. I'm sure of that. There always is."

Charlotte frowned. How was it possible that her reflection knew all this? Especially that bit about there always being a chance...?

And then she understood.

Of course, she knew.

Really, who else could it be?

"EB," she said. To her surprise, there wasn't even a hint of uncertainty in her voice.

The reflection's smile widened.

"You got it, kid," it told her. "Now, hang on in there. I'm going to try to get to you, to make things right. But you're going to have to be ready. You won't be able to expect much from Matt from here on. You're on your own, I'm afraid, at least for now."

Charlotte shook her head, suddenly alarmed.

By herself? How could she do this by herself? She wasn't

even from this *reality*. Come to that, she wasn't even sure she knew what *reality* meant anymore...

"Wait!" she said desperately. "How can I do that? How will I know what to...oh."

Because even as she was saying the words, she realised that her reflection had changed.

Now it was just herself staring back at her. Her eyes were brown, as usual. The fur had gone.

EB had been right. She really was on her own.

She took a deep breath, and splashed more water on her face. At least the buzzing in her head had gone now. It must have been linked to the incoming communication from EB. At least she could think clearly now.

"Come on," she told herself. "You can do this. You can."

She walked back outside, to where the servant was waiting for her.

She fixed him with a bright, nonchalant smile, the kind of smile that said, 'hi, I've just had a perfectly normal time in the bathroom, a time which hasn't at all involved talking to weird semi-reflections of myself, bringing me dire warnings from another dimension'.

"Nice place," she said. "Come on. Let's go."

The servant led her off through the maze that was Frogmore. She followed at a discrete distance, chewing her lip, wondering vaguely what the hell she was going to do.

Lay low? Blend in? Don't let Philip Frogmore know that she was on to him?

Sure, but how was she going to do that, without letting the man push them off in whatever direction his dire fancy dictated? And judging from what Frogmore had been talking about before she bowed out, it would involve combat of some sort. Though why on earth would Frogmore want that? To send them to war with Head Frog 127 and the Frogopolis? It seemed like a strange goal. What was he set to gain from it?

At that moment, Charlotte caught a strange light glimmering in a corner of her eye.

She stopped dead in her tracks, turning her head. To her right, a half-open doorway gave into...well, it looked almost like some kind of chamber. She took a step forward, peered in...

Inside, the room was dark. A single comfortable seat sat facing a desk, and on the desk sat...

...It was a box.

A simple metal box.

There were bright flashing lights scattered all over it, and a keyboard attached to the base. It was the flashing lights that Charlotte had caught a glimpse of, painting the side of the room in flickering colours.

She took another step. She couldn't say why, but she was intrigued. This felt...this felt *important* somehow.

Now she could see there was a patch of the machine where something had been removed. It looked like there had been a big, round button. The metal underneath was pale and scratched. Above the place where the button had been, there was a screen. As she watched, sequences of numbers and words scrolled past. The buttons pulsed faintly.

Was it...some kind of computer? Running some strange software?

She made to take another step, and then a hand was on her shoulder.

"You shouldn't go in there, my lady," said the servant.

His voice was quite even and pleasant, but the grip on her shoulder was strong. It gave the impression of a much deeper well of gripping that could be called on, if the gripee didn't do the decent thing and be gripped properly.

Flickering her eyelids in what she hoped was a winsome and disarming manner, Charlotte gave a little laugh and took a step away from the room with the strange machine.

"Oh, my, those lights make me all *faint*," she said, hating herself just a little bit. "You don't mind if I hold on to you to steady myself?"

She put an arm around the servant, and forced herself to do an impression of some simpering, silly woman. The kind of woman who was quite happy being called *girl* by someone like Philip Frogmore.

To her surprise, the ruse worked.

"Not at all, my lady," said the servant, the unfriendly species of grippiness being replaced by a much more reassuring and supportive sort of grip. "Perhaps you ought to sit down for a moment? I can easily summon medical attention if you so wish?"

Charlotte let herself be sat down in a convenient couch. She could still see the machine flickering away.

"I don't think that will be necessary," said Charlotte. "It's just those lights! They are so...so *pretty*. Took me by surprise. Err. What are they?"

The servant frowned. He looked torn.

"We are not supposed to talk about the master's Heart," he said reproachfully. "Such a matter is not for polite conversation."

Frogmore's *heart*? This was getting more and more weird.

"But surely you can tell me *something*?" she tried. "After all, I'm not some spy, I'm...oh!"

And she cut off, because as she had spoken, the servant had glided across to the room containing the flashing lights, and pulled the door shut.

But as the door had swung shut, the light had hit his face in just such a way, his chin tilted at just such an angle, that Charlotte had seen it.

It was obvious.

How had she not realised it before?

"Of course," she muttered, trying to keep her voice level

while the realisation shot through her, as implications began to click into place like falling dominoes. "How silly of me. Let's find the others..."

The face was different, of course. But then, that made sense.

She compared the face of this servant to her recollections of the others, all the other servants of the house of Frogmore, waiting tables, cleaning up, fetching things,

All blank eyed.

All so polite, and so stilted, and so strange.

It wasn't that they all looked alike, exactly. And again, that made sense, too.

"I will take you to the master," said the version in front of her, the one who had been taken and tamed and - she assumed - made to play the part of servant, probably with no more memory of what he had been or how he had come here than a faint flickering, a sometimes intuition that somewhere, somehow, things had been different.

This one had his chin. That was it, she thought, as he led the way through the twisting passageways of Frogmore.

She remembered another with his eyes. And another with his nose.

Different versions, all slightly different.

But different versions of the same person.

The person Philip Frogmore was out to get, again and again and again.

He was collecting them, she realised.

But why? Why the hell would anyone do something so...so *mad*?

Then they passed under a wide trellised arch into a courtyard, and Charlotte's mind stuttered and stopped working.

How would it be possible to continue thinking normally when you arrived suddenly in a place like this?

"Ah, Charlotte, my girl," said Frogmore in his horrible oily voice. "I see you made it back from your adventures to the toilet unharmed."

He gave a laugh, and cocked the shotgun he was holding in one hand.

It was a huge and rather horrible shotgun, adorned with totally unnecessary spikes and ugly-looking skulls and things. But it was nothing compared to the weapons arrayed around the rest of the courtyard.

Guns and knives and grenades. Flame-throwers and assault weapons and bows and arrows. There was no consistency. They looked like they had been harvested from a hundred different worlds, a million different stories of death and destruction. Which, of course, was just where they had come from, she supposed.

"What do you think?" said Frogmore, proudly. "When I told you about my men scouring the Storystream for food, I hadn't really told you the half of it."

"They are very," managed Charlotte, in a small voice. "That is to say, this all looks very...death-y."

"That's rather the point," said Frogmore happily. "Can't fight a war without weapons. And with these weapons, that slimy Frog bastard doesn't stand a chance! Well, unless he had some even *bigger* weapons, I suppose..." he added, nonchalantly.

And then Charlotte realised that the worst thing about this courtyard wasn't the weapons. Not by a long way.

She glanced around.

One of the servants was holding a plasma gun. Another was swinging a huge Morningstar experimentally.

And then there was NotMatt. NotMatt was standing with the others, holding a rather quaint-looking revolver in one hand. He had a slightly bemused expression on his face, as if part of him couldn't understand what he was doing here or why he wasn't stopping.

And the worse thing wasn't all the servants holding the weapons, either.

It was that now, glancing from the servants to NotMatt and back again, it was already growing hard to tell the difference.

Somehow, Frogmore was stealing NotMatt's will.

Somehow, another version of NotMatt from the infinite store of versions the Storystream had to offer, was falling under Frogmore's influence.

And surrounded by an army of brainwashed Matts, what the hell was she supposed to do?

Frogmore smiled at her. It was a smile that said he wondered if she had worked things out yet, and that he didn't care one iota if she had.

"Matt!" hissed Charlotte, ducking away from Frogmore and dashing to NotMatt's side. "Come on! We have to go!"

"Oh, my sweet girl," said Frogmore, not hurrying, not seeming at all alarmed by her actions. "There's nowhere for you to go. Nowhere at all."

And as NotMatt turned to look at her with the same bland, empty eyes as the other servants, she realised Frogmore was right.

🦋 23 🦋

"**P**ull!" shouted King Headfrog, and the decrepit old groundsman released the trebuchet.

The kree gave a shriek as it was catapulted into the air. It really was a most silly beast, King Headfrog reflected, as the vast creature sailed up into the air, limbs falling ineffectually, making a kind of frog-ish mooing noise. If they looked ungainly on land, they looked even more ungainly in the air.

King Headfrog took aim, titling the huge plasma rifle through careful degrees, tracking the flight of the beast. He saw a pleasing parallel between the predatory way he moved the gun, getting the helpless beast firm in his sights, and the way in which he had locked on to the whole of the Frogopolis, taken the measure of it like a vast, bovine creature...and pounced.

"Hah!" shouted King Headfrog as he squeezed the trigger. An instantaneous burst of pure white light leapt out from the barrel of his gun and struck the flying kree full the in the chest, dissolving it instantly into a rain of fine green mist.

"What a shot!" he congratulated himself, thrusting the

gun behind without looking. At once, one of his countless frogling attendants rushed forward to take the weapon.

"Perfect, your majesty," congratulated the ancient frog who had released the beast.

"Perfect?" chided King Headfrog. "Why, of course it was! What were you expecting, Toadflaps? That I would wobble and flail as if I were as incompetent a shot as you?"

King Headfrog glared at the decrepit groundsman. The ancient, flabby frog coloured and began examining his hands.

"No, not at all, master," stammered Toadflaps. "I just thought..."

"I care less than a penny for your thoughts," said King Headfrog brusquely.

He wondered vaguely how much the old frog remembered of how things used to be. Was there some shadowed, echo-memory of the old order of things? It seemed that no one but him remembered the way reality used to sit, before he had altered things with the Chaos Drive. Certainly, the court never slipped up. None of his attendants had made the mistake of referring to him by his old name, of adding that demeaning little '127' at the end, of forgetting the appropriate sobriquet of 'king' at the beginning. Well, nearly no one...

No, all they seemed to remember was this glorious new reality, this lovely new order of things that he had sculpted for himself, using the power of the alien device.

And it *was* powerful. So powerful...

King Headfrog shook his head scornfully and walked away from the enfeebled, disgusting Toadflaps. Enough hunting. It was time for him to meet with his counsel, and determine how things in the Empire stood.

He strolled across the grass, flanked by his powerful, deadly, and utterly loyal FrogGuards. They each stood over eight feet tall, powerful, muscular genetically-perfected soldier frogs of the highest caliber. Not that he needed protecting, not really. No, he was well-loved throughout the Frogopolis, not even the lowliest frogling would want to hurt so much as a patch of scarring alopecia on his bald head. And there was really no risk of assassination or attack from one of the lesser galactic civilisations. No, the Frogopolis was a juggernaut, it was *the* Galactic juggernaut, other civilisations frayed and quailed beneath the power of the Frogopolis, and no alien race would dare to attack him. He was safe, and really the only reason to have the elite FrogGuard by his side was vanity - it soothed his pride to surround himself with such perfect, deadly specimens of the Frog race.

He was escorted into his sleek frog-shaped spaceship, saluted the captain of the FrogGuard, and launched himself up into the stratosphere. As the engine pulsed in a reassuringly powerful growl behind him, King Headfrog felt the last traces of a nagging tension leave his body. Now that he was alone again, he allowed himself the comfort of retrieving the Chaos Drive from his pocket. Not that it mattered, not that there was any risk...but he did not like to withdraw the beautiful thing when there was anyone else nearby. It was his secret. It was his splendid toy, and he would not share it with anyone.

The enchanting rainbow play of colours glittered and refracted around the sleek internal surfaces of his ship. It was good to see the device again. Not that he had felt separate from it - indeed, since that first day of synching, he had never felt really separated from it. His mind flashed back to that first encounter, the first brushing of his mind against the alien device, the way the alien had tried to stay attached...and the soaring feeling of triumph as he had yanked it loose, and plugged it into his own consciousness.

Outside, the atmosphere shaded through tones of gold and purple as the ship lifted him effortlessly out of the planet's gravity well. He liked to spend his leisure time back on the home planet, hunting, carousing, generally lording it up. But when it came to the business of running the Empire of the Frogopolis, King Headfrog liked to do it in style, from his vast orbital command ship. That was where he was headed now.

He thought idly on how long ago that first day seemed now, when he had first plugged in to the Chaos Drive, when he had first begun to understand the power of the thing, the ease with which he could use it to re-write reality itself. It amazed him that the aliens had had so little vision. How could they have used the device for such lowly aims? To rob a planet here, to confound a pursuit there...they really were stumbling, foolish creatures, quite lacking in imagination. After just a few days of being linked to the machine, King Headfrog had realised the unbelievable potential.

Anything.

He could change *anything*.

If he didn't like the way a conversation had gone...he could change it.

If he didn't like the way his top lip hung down, or the exact swamp-green shade of his eyes...he could change it...

...and if he hadn't cared for the way he had been a mere commander of one of the King's fleet, instead of supreme leader of the Empire of the Frogopolis....

Well.

He could change that, too.

The ship gave a pleasing little bleep, announcing that they would soon be docking with *The Pondwater*. His old command was now a vast orbital hub, a huge ring reaching all the way around the solar system, arcing around the sun itself. That had been one of the more taxing uses he had put the Chaos Drive to. It had involved reorganising vast quantities of matter, sucking huge reserves of carbon and hydrogen and elemental metals from the hearts of various stars, conforming them into endless bulkheads and computer terminals and living quarters. But the mere redistribution of matter was nothing much in itself - the real task was in re-writing history and galactic geography - which was, of course, nothing short of re-writing reality itself.

Doing this on such a vast scale, King Headfrog had realised, took a little time, and often left him with a headache, with a slight, unsettled feeling, almost a shade of guilt, as if he had done something not quite sensible, not quite discrete. But he always pushed such feelings away. After all, the power was his to command - and he would use it!

The ship gave a small shudder as it docked with the huge orbital craft. There was a reeling sensation as the artificial gravity field shifted to include the smaller ship, and then a hissing noise as the airlocks equalised pressure.

King Headfrog's elite command counsel were waiting for him as he disembarked.

He smiled as he took in their green, sweating, beautiful faces.

Of course, his command counsel were all female, assembled from the most stunning lady frogs the Frogopolis had ever seen. With their long, drooping legs and damp, faintly fetid smell, the assembled command counsel were quite the most erotic group of frogs King Headfrog had ever seen or even imagined.

Which was natural, of course, because - in a manner of speaking - imagining them into existence was exactly what he had done.

"Ladies," said King Headfrog, beaming at them. "So good to see you again."

"The pleasure is all ours," crooned Lady Marshleaf, who had spectacular dirty grey skin and a daring splash of red pigment on her bald head which only appeared during the mating season. "Please tell us you have arrived to make passionate love to us all for the next year, and not to discuss drear politics again?"

"Alas, the lovemaking must wait," said King Headfrog, leading them to the spherical command chamber, from whence every aspect of the Empire of the Frogopolis could be directed. "At least, for a little while. The matters of command must first be attended to."

A disappointed sigh went up from the command counsel.

"Oh, you're such a tease," complained the Countess Tad Poleena, in her sleek, exotic accent, wriggling her narrow hips so that they dislocated and relocated enticingly.

"The empire comes first," said King Headfrog nobly. "Now: report!"

He listened with satisfaction as they told him of the state of the empire: an uprising quashed in the horrid little alien world of Mars, a new class of warship freshly designed by the boffin frogs of Reglin VII, a request for peace from an underwhelming and wholly inferior galactic-level civilisation on the far side of the central Black Hole.

King Headfrog nodded and gesticulated, directing the Empire, making his orders known.

"...and then, of course, as soon as they lay down their arms, we annihilate them, to the last stinking alien," he concluded, outlining his plan for a pesky peace-loving race of morons who happened to have sole access to a urgently-needed store of rare radioactive isotopes.

Not that conquering and enslaving them was strictly necessary, of course - with the Chaos Drive, he might just as easily have fabricated the substance himself, or have relocated it to a star system well within the existing sphere of influence of the Frogopolis.

But where would the fun be in that?

A round of applause went up from the assembled command counsel. King Headfrog bowed his head and modestly lapped up the adoration. It was his due. After all, he *was* completely fabulous.

He raised his hand to signal for a pause in the applause...

...and realised it had stopped already, a moment before he had willed it.

He frowned, glancing round for the cause, and his eye alit on the door leading off from the command centre to his private chambers.

It was open, and someone was glaring out. Under that steely gaze, the assembled beauties of the Frogopolis were wilting like daisies under a blowtorch.

It was the princess, of course.

It was Frogmella.

King Headfrog felt his heart skip a beat. She was so beautiful. Even more lovely than he had remembered. It had been a few days since he had last seen her, and she had refused his requests to attend the counsel meetings, up to now.

"Darling!" he boomed out, shoving the assembled members of the command counsel aside in his haste to reach her. "You have decided to attend! I am glad. I thought that..."

"You thought that I wasn't speaking to you," said Princess Frogmella in a stern, cold voice.

The silence in the command chamber deepened. King Headfrog felt waves of anger washing off the assembled female frogs. They were outraged that anyone dared speak to their king in such a way.

Any one of those beautiful frogs would die for me, he thoughts. *More than that: they would kill for me, too.*

And he knew, also, that the only thing that stopped them falling on Princess Frogmella and tearing her limb from limb was that they knew the princess was - unaccountably - still in his favour.

"Would you like us to...help the princess back to her

chambers?" asked the Countess Tad Poleena, in a hopeful voice.

King Headfrog slowly shook his head. They didn't understand his restraint, they never could. It was impossible. How could he explain it to them? That would mean telling them everything - about the Chaos Drive, and the nature of reality, not to mention the fact that he had re-written everything, including their own brains - and this was clearly impossible.

No.

He would have to deal with this the way he always dealt with it.

"Leave us," he said. His voice was low, but he didn't need to issue the command twice. He never did.

As the chamber emptied, as the assembled beautiful female command frogs issued out, King Headfrog held the gaze of the Princess Frogmella. Her eyes were dark and stormy, full of hatred and resentment.

Of course they were. How could they be otherwise, when he had allowed her to keep her memories of the way things had been before? She was bound to resent him, and the fact that she could do nothing, absolutely nothing about it just made her hate him all the more.

"So you've changed your mind?" he asked, when the chamber belonged just to the two of them. He tried to keep all traces of hope from his voice, but it was no good. His voice betrayed him, there was a little quaver there, a small dimpling in the words. He couldn't hide from her how much he wanted her by his side.

"Don't you know that already?" she taunted him. "Can't you see it in your alien machine?"

And the truth was he could, if he had wanted to look. He could have seen into the fold of her mind exactly as easily as he could have commanded it. Of course he could. He just didn't want to, that was all.

A frown passed over his face, and for a moment he struggled to understand, yet again, why he let her keep her old memories. Such a risk. Such a terrible risk..

He looked at her, the elegant, enticing lines of her face. For a moment, the lines seemed to *blur*.

He almost fancied that for an instant he was staring not at fresh green flesh, but at...at *fur*...

Which was of course ridiculous.

He shook his head to clear it, and the feeling passed. What was he even wondering about? He found he could not quite put his finger on it.

He just knew that she had asked him if he would ever mess with her head. Why did she have to keep asking him that? Surely she knew the answer.

"You know I would never do that," said King Headfrog, coming hesitantly to her side. "Not to you."

He reached out a hand, but she backed away, turned her shoulder to him.

It was quite the most enticing thing she could have done. No one turned away from him these days.

"Well, aren't I privileged?" she told him sarcastically. "Aren't I just the lucky one?"

It was odd, he thought idly. Even though her words were biting and harsh there was something...almost *relieved* about her body language. *Amused* even.

Which didn't make any sense.

King Headfrog shifted from one foot to the other. This wasn't going as he had hoped. It never did, and yet he kept hoping. He had to. After all, he loved her. He loved her with every ounce of love in his heart, which was to say, actually not all that much, but still just about enough to stop him doing anything especially nasty to her.

Whenever he spent any length of time away from her, the feeling seemed to wain a little. He found himself wondering why he did not just get rid of her; or, if he really did want her as much as his heart told him, then why not simply re-write her mind and be done with it?

But always, when he returned to her side, it was like this.

"Darling, please," he found himself saying in a voice that was not quite his own. "You know I care for you. You know I want us to be...to be...well, to *rule* together. Wouldn't that be splendid?"

She turned to face him, and his heart soared as he saw the look on her face, the tears in her eyes.

"I want that too," she told him quietly. "Of course I do. It's just...if you'd only let me share the power of the Drive...just a little touch..."

And once again her hand was reaching for him, her slender, nimble fingers mere inches from his pocket, from the place where the Chaos Drive rested.

Let her have it, a voice said in his head. And it had to be his voice, of course. It sounded like him. It must be his. *Just share power a little. That's all she wants. She loves you. She wants to rule this galaxy with you...*

Of course that was what he should do. It was so easy, so simple. He should let her take the Drive, and then their love would be complete...

But he was turning away, ignoring the voice, ignoring the shrill tearing noise coming from what passed for his heart.

"No," he said, and his voice was colder than he meant it to be. "Not that. You should know not to ask me that."

He faced away, half-crouched over the precious thing. He didn't want her to touch it, didn't even want her to see it.

"But *why not*?" she demanded in a hiss, and there was such frustration in her voice, such strength that for a moment King Headfrog found he barely recognised her.

He glared at her, and there was a moment as their eyes met when she understood that she had gone too far. She tried to call it back with a smile, to soften her words, but it was too late.

"Why so desperate?" he demanded. He took another step back. Now she was on the other side of the central command table. Around them, hundreds of view screens showed a constant stream of images from every corner of the Frogopolis - some showed peaceful scenes of life in the subdued worlds of the Empire, but others showed the waging of wars and the putting down of rebellions. In that flickering light, King Headfrog found that the Princess looked suddenly untrustworthy. Something in her face screamed deceit.

She pursed her lips tight, hesitated, seemed on the verge of telling him something, something important.

This was it.

He knew it. She kept secrets from him, terrible secrets. He had always suspected...

His mind flashed back over their days together, over the encounters, over the meetings with that other frog he trusted less than any other. And suddenly his thoughts coalesced.

He knew.

"You've...you've..."

He found he was too angry to say it. The words burnt the back of his throat, refusing to be said.

She looked at him. Now she seemed worried. She understood that he knew.

"You've been having an *affair*," he said, finally managing to get the words out.

For a moment she blinked at him, a blank look on her face.

"What?" she said, and her acting was so good it almost fooled him.

Then he remembered the times he had seen them together, the way they had behaved, the little looks that passed between the two of them.

"Glob," he said with simple venom. "That bastard Glob. It's him, isn't it? You've been seeing him behind my back."

A look of surprise passed over her face, vanishing as quickly as it had come.

"An affair?" she repeated, almost to herself. "You suspect me and Glob of having an...affair?"

"Do you deny it?" he squawked at her. "It's so obvious. You always give him meaningful looks, you always protect him from me. You always...*how dare you*?"

But it was no good. The princess had reacted in the one way he hadn't anticipated.

Denials he would have been ready for, and outrage would have been easy.

But laughter...

She was laughing at him.

Not the high, trilling, polite laughter of a well-bred lady, but deep guffaws that rose up from her belly and tumbled out her mouth in great peels.

She waved a hand, as if she could dismiss his righteous accusations with such a simple gesture.

"Oh, my little king," she chuckled at him. "Of all the things you could choose to worry about..."

He stomped his foot in outrage.

How *dare* she speak to him like that?

"I am not *worried* about it," he told her. "I just want you to know that I've found you out! Yes, and it won't go on! It will stop at once. And Glob..."

"Yes sir?" said Glob, materialising as if by magic in the doorway. The huge, fat frog looked at him with his slow, stupid eyes. All at once, King Headfrog found that he felt uncertain.

Could the princess really love *this*? This wretched excuse for a frog, with his ungainly waddle and stench of a low-class breeding pit?

But if she didn't love him, then why was she always inter-vening on his behalf? She had always pushed for him, always, for a promotion, for more control...even - gods be good - even to let the wretched chief of security keep his old memories, his old identity...

Why would she do that? Why, if not for love?

"Why - are - you - *here?*" demanded King Headfrog through gritted teeth.

"A pressing security matter has arisen..." Glob started to say.

"No it hasn't," said King Headfrog, cutting him off. "If I had wanted one of those, I would have arranged it myself."

And this was true. Since ascending to complete control of this reality, King Headfrog had made a point of having pressing security matters arise with fair regularity. What good was it being the leader of a vast warlike Empire, if the galaxy didn't give you an excuse to exercise your fists once in a while?

But on this occasion, he had not used the Chaos Drive to will any such thing.

Which meant that Glob must be wrong, of course.

"I have *not* been having an affair with Glob," said the princess. She looked at Glob and gave a nod. He nodded back. "I simply see in him an...ally. Someone who could help you. Someone who could help *us*."

King Headfrog looked from the princess to Glob and back again.

Was it possible?

Was it simply that she saw something in the sly, vile frog that he had missed?

"Help us?" he demanded. "Help us *how* exactly? There is nothing that is a threat to me, nothing! Every star in this galaxy, every atom in the Universe is *mine* now! Don't you see?

That's where we are now, that's what I have achieved! I am the master of all! I can undo any threat with a *thought*!"

The princess looked unimpressed.

"There is much about these Universes that you are yet to grasp," she told him. And as she said it, something funny happened to her voice. It lasted only a second, but Headfrog frowned. It sounded like several voices speaking at once, like harmonics sliding up and down the spine of the Universe. She smiled at him. "Let me teach you," she said, and there was an urgency in her voice now, a pressure, and it was as if she were throwing everything she had, every last ounce of influence, spending it all on an effort to sway him. "Just consent to share power, and I will teach you all the secrets you never knew the Universe was keeping from you."

Uncertainty burnt him. He wanted her. Wanted her so badly...

And this talk of secrets...What if she was telling the truth? What if there *were* secrets, little holes in the glory of his plans, things that would undermine and overthrow him...

He teetered on the edge, his hand reaching into his pocket, on the verge of withdrawing the Chaos Drive, on the verge of simply handing it to her and being done with it.

He closed his eyes.

He took a deep breath.

And then he made up his mind.

His heart - his narrow, twisted heart - just couldn't keep up the fight any more. His scheming, twisted mind was too strong.

The suspicions were too great. The risk was too big.

Maybe she loved him, maybe she didn't.

Maybe she was faithful...and perhaps she was not.

And maybe, just maybe, this talk of secrets was all a lot of hot air.

He wheeled away from the two of them, from Glob and

the Princess. He didn't need to press a button or utter a word. His mind was linked to the Chaos Drive, and the decision itself was enough.

Reality *flickered* and//

//and when King Headfrog turned back, the two of them were in chains. He saw their eyes widen, the disbelief rolling around their faces. He could have knocked them out, he could have killed them, even.

But no.

This was more pleasing to him.

Glob stared stupidly at the chains that bound him, heavy dark metal that hadn't been there an instant before. Which was to be expected. King Headfrog might have let him keep his memories, but he certainly hadn't told him anything about the Chaos Drive or how it worked...or what it could do.

The Princess, though...

It only took her an instant to realise what had happened. Headfrog saw it in her eyes, those beautiful, stormy eyes. They opened wide in understanding.

"How *dare* you?" she hissed, only this time this hiss was deep in her throat – closer to a growl – and there was something strange about it, too, something he had not been expecting. "You will undo this at once..."

And again her voice strained against strange harmonics, sliding up against one another; and the words seemed to leap straight into his mind, short-circuiting his brain. It battered against him, a force of unbearable mental influence, like a hot, dry wind blowing sand into his face. King Headfrog felt his will wilting under the assault, under a last desperate attempt to control him//

//and he slammed his mind shut, tearing power out of the Chaos Drive, pushing the uncanny influence away.

There was a shower of sparks that burst from a ring of nothingness between the two of them, then the Princess was flying backwards, a scream tearing from her lips, smashing into a metal bulkhead and spinning away. Blood was on her face and power crackled around her, an awful discharge of some unseen energy and Headfrog gasped, because he hadn't meant to do that, he hadn't want to really *hurt* her, and//

//and then she wasn't the princess anymore.

The command centre was silent and still. Headfrog could hear his breathing, feel his heart hammering in his chest. He walked towards where she lay, the figure that a moment ago had been the princess.

It was humanoid still, a shape full of lithe power, suggestive of danger even laying there, floored, prostrate and giving of a faint smell of singed fur.

But it was no princess.

It was no frog, even.

It wore a battered leather jerkin, well-worn and tough-looking, and trousers made of the same material. But really, these clothes seemed less than necessary, as the whole body was covered with a lustrous black fur. It looked elegant despite the fact that it was smoking faintly.

"No," said Headfrog, a mounting horror threatening to wipe aside every last ounce of control. "No, it can't be. You *died*. I saw it. I *saw* it..."

And in the privacy of his head he added: *and for how long? When did this deceit begin?*

The figure groaned, and rolled over to face him. The chains hadn't held, Headfrog could see. Whatever power this...this creature had brought to bear had melted away that figment of reality which Headfrog had sought to impose. But that didn't matter, not now. Headfrog could see at a glance that he had won, that he had used the power of the Chaos Drive to overcome every last mote of energy this strange creature had somehow stored up inside itself.

The figure on the floor sighed. It moved slowly, as if every inch of flesh ached. It pulled a cigarette from an inside pocket, inserted it between long feline teeth, then flicked its claws together, to make a spark.

It inhaled deeply, then breathed out a plume of smoke.

"Didn't anyone every tell you about my lives?" said the wretched creature. "I get nine of them."

Headfrog jerked forward and battered the cigarette away with a snarl. The creature stared at him impassively.

"You tricked me," said King Headfrog. "How did you...how *dare* you..."

He stuttered to a stop, unable to get his words out past the outrage that choked his throat.

"I've been doing what I could, yes," said the cat, mildly.

EB, thought King Headfrog. *The vile thing is called EB. What a stupid name for a stupid beast.*

In the background, something started beeping. King Headfrog ignored it.

"Well it hasn't worked," said Headfrog. "You tried to influence me. You tried to make me...to make me *love* you..." There was a revulsion in his voice now, a horror. He thought back over the time he had spent with the princess, about the thoughts he had had of her, of the lust, the longing...

"Yes, that wasn't much fun for me either, believe me," said the cat. He sounded unbearably debonaire. "But needs must, and all that."

The distant beeping noise was joined by a second, similar noise. They brushed up against one another disturbingly. Headfrog pushed the sound away.

"You...I bet you helped the aliens get away, too," said Headfrog, a sudden suspicion forming in his mind.

"I did what I could, yes," sad EB, seemingly without a hint of shame. The feline was frowning now, though. Something was bothering him.

Good.

He must be realising, at last. That was it. The damn cat was realising the damn fool mistake it had made to mess with *him*, to try and fool *him*.

He would pay. Oh yes. And no amount of begging would save him, not now, not after this...

"Your death will be exquisite," Headfrog told him. "You tell me you have nine lives? Good. I'll arrange nine deaths, and none of them will be quick, none of them will be gentle..."

"Yes, well," said EB, as if brushing away a minor point of protocol, "we can deal with that in due course. But right now, I really do suggest you let me..."

"Let you go?" cut in Headfrog. "I just bet you do! But I won't. No, your influence on me is gone. You spent it. You're all used up."

The air was saturated with beeping now. King Headfrog realised he was shouting to make himself heard.

"Let me help you, I was going to say," said EB reproachfully. "After all, you've made rather a mess of things. I knew you would. No restraint, no finesse. You took the Chaos Drive and used it to the hilt, and didn't think twice about the consequences. Now, I'm afraid, we are all going to pay the price for your intemperance. Unless you listen to me, that is."

Headfrog opened his mouth to laugh...and it was then that he realised how dark the room had grown.

He looked around.

The display screens had almost all gone blank. The flickering stories they had been telling of life and conflict in the thousand worlds of the Frogopolis, the pictures they had been painting of all the planets in the dominion...they were gone.

Even as he watched, a dark fizzling screen descended over the last of the displays. As it did so, yet another warning klaxon added its voice to the cacophony of beeps and buzzes, bleeps and clashes and alarms.

What was happening? Was it war? Was the Frogopolis under attack?

But how was that possible?

He would have felt such a thing through the Chaos Drive, and he had felt nothing from that direction, nothing at all for...

And then he realised.

Ice crept up his back, he felt his mouth go dry. In his chest, the thing that passed for a heart stilled for a moment, lurched, continued...

The Chaos Drive was telling him that things were...empty.

There was a space where the Universe should be.

A blankness, something he couldn't claw past.

It felt like...

"There's a wall," he said aloud. There was horror in his voice. Desperately, he sent out tendrils of influence, trying to claw at it, trying to push the blackness away.

But it was no good.

He could feel it pressing tight, a darkness covering his perception of the Universe. It was as if the Universe itself ended just beyond the walls of the command centre. Beyond that he felt...nothing.

There was a tearing lurch, and all the noise shut off at once.

That should have been better, he should have been able to hear himself think, but it was not.

No, the quiet was just another form of blankness, another wall placed over the universe, imposed on him.

But imposed by *whom*?

By his side, EB got slowly to his feet, and brushed himself down. Then he strolled over to where Glob had stood, silent and still, waiting. The feline creature began working at the chains, loosening the bound frog.

King Headfrog knew he should stop him, knew that he should push the cat down again, blast him, kick him, *kill* him...and yet, he did nothing.

It seemed so pointless.

The problem of nothingness was so much bigger.

"It's not a wall, not exactly," said EB. "The people putting it up wouldn't use the term 'wall' because that would hardly do justice the multitude of different dimensions this obstruction works in."

"What do they call it?" King Headfrog found himself asking. The nothing was very close now, it was all around and pushing tight.

"A quarantine," said EB grimly. "The Sheriffs call this kind of thing a quarantine. Did you really think you could use the Chaos Drive so freely? Reality is made of stories. And stories have guardians."

EB turned and flashed him a dark smile.

"It's a very dangerous thing to annoy the guardians of stories," he said grimly. "Stories have a way of fighting back."

❧ 24 ❧

Matt sat in the whiteness and trembled with anger.

He had thought the anger would have started to subside by now. If anything, it was worse.

The things she had said, the excuses she had made...

They kept swirling round his head, intruding on his thoughts, stopping him focussing.

Making him angry.

"I fear you have failed again," announced Ninian. He sounded completely calm. There was no chastisement in his voice, there wasn't even a hint of reproach.

Which was annoying.

They had been trying for so long. It was Matt who kept failing. It was Matt's fault they were still here.

And yet Ninian was somehow still as patient as mountains.

Perhaps he didn't care, Matt reflected. After all, he had more or less hired the creature. What would it matter to him how quickly they got going? The price would be owed either way.

Matt glanced over at the strange, gangly creature. Ninian looked back at him, the odd crystals in his spectacles making his dark eyes seem huge and jagged. Out here in the stark brightness of the Place Between Stories, Ninian looked more weird than ever. His finely tailored coat whipped about in a wind that blew from nowhere into nowhere, and which didn't touch the skin or cool the face.

Matt found himself wondering once more if he preferred owing the debt to Ninian. It was all the same really. June had never really been asking the price for herself - she had simply been telling them what Ninian wanted. Now June was gone, spirited back to her own world by that strange Sheriff, Norwood Ginnel, and he supposed she had accomplished what she had set out to.

After all, Ninian *had* sold him his help, and here they were.

Around them, the dark blankness of the Quarantine crackled alarmingly. They were keeping as far away from it as possible, which Matt thought was sensible. But still, they had to get closer than he would have liked. Ninian had started by explaining it in long, complicated equations that Matt couldn't even begin to understand. But what it came down to was: they couldn't do what they needed to do if they were near to Ninian's parlour. If they tried making the hole anywhere near an existent reality bubble - near to Ninian's parlour, for instance - the narrative resonances would leak, and their attempt would fail. Hence they had to get as far away as possible, and in the context, that meant they had to get as near to the quarantine as they dared.

But it still wasn't working.

It didn't matter that Ninian's parlour was just a tiny dot agains the vast whiteness of the Place Between Stories. It just wasn't working.

And it was Matt's fault.

"No, really?" snarled Matt. He kicked a tuft of nothingness, which was completely unsatisfying to kick on account of it not hurting at all. Matt wanted to feel something. He deserved pain. It was his fault they hadn't managed to break out yet, to burrow down. He was the only one who could save his Charlotte now, the only one who seemed to *want* to save her.

And that made him think again of the *other* Charlotte, of NotCharlotte, of how weak and afraid she had been. And that made him more angry than ever.

"You must try and calm yourself," said Ninian. His voice was annoyingly reasonable. "Perhaps it would be best if we return to my parlour for a time? We could discuss our failure with the others. They may be able to give useful suggestions."

Matt glared up at the strange creature. He was beginning to get a feeling for the odd way Ninian's mind worked. It certainly didn't work in a human way, which made sense because Ninian certainly wasn't human.

"We are not going back there," said Matt firmly. "Besides, you heard what she said. She's not leaving. She's doing exactly what the Sheriffs asked of her. She's a coward."

And he thought back on the way her lip had trembled, on the way her blue eyes had filled with tears. Norwood Ginnel hadn't even needed to make any threats! As soon as the Sheriff had mentioned that the Order knew what Charlotte and her friends had been doing...that was it. She fell to pieces. It was disgusting, really. She had pretended to be so strong, to know so much. And all the time, she had neglected to mention the really important part.

The part about her being a criminal.

The part about the whole mess being her fault...

"If that is the way you feel, sir," said Ninian with absolute politeness. "I am, as we have discussed, now in your service. I will do what you think is best in this matter."

"Thank you," said Matt. He stretched his neck, closed his eyes, tried to concentrate. "We'll go again in a moment. Just let me clear my mind."

But clearing his mind was the one thing he couldn't do. It was impossible. His mind was full to bursting.

He opened his eyes.

"You know what really makes me angry?" he asked rhetorically.

"I can identify seven reasons for your current emotional distress," said Ninian promptly, who - Matt was beginning to realise - had very little understanding of what a rhetorical question was or what you hoped to achieve by posing one. "The most prominent reason is probably all the lies."

Matt glared at Ninian.

Then he nodded.

"Yes," he said. "Absolutely. It's the lies. Only she didn't call them *lies*, did she? No, she called them *economical truths*."

But they *were* lies.

The part about them needing to shield themselves from the Story was a lie. The truth was that *NotCharlotte* needed to shield herself from the Story, because if the Story found out she was there, then it would have told the Sheriffs.

Because NotCharlotte was Wanted.

Wanted and considered Dangerous.

For crimes against the Storystream. And dangerous was right. He knew that. He had found that out for himself.

"I can't believe she was doing something so *stupid*," he said out loud. "So...so *reckless*. So selfish."

"You should believe it," said Ninian, a faint hint of reproach in his voice. "She admitted as much herself."

"No, I mean..." Matt spluttered, shaking his head. "I mean, I know she *did* it. It was her machine. This Chaos Drive thing...It's just...to use it....To use it again and again, even after things like this had happened before, even when they all knew the risks..."

And he trailed off, because it just seemed such a huge crime, how were there even words for it?

NotCharlotte and her friends had played about with forces they didn't fully understand and couldn't even half control, and the upshot was, his world had been torn apart. And he had lost the person he loved.

And they had done it all for *money*!

The thought made him so angry he wanted to scream.

So he did.

The scream was loud and sharp and full of fury.

There was a flash of colour as a bolt of lightning leapt from Ninian's eyes. It shot out, striking the scream and//

//And suddenly a small, cross-looking dragon whelp was flapping about their heads.

Matt putt his head in his hands.

"Not again," he muttered.

"Squark," said the dragon whelp, before launching a pillar of tepid flame into the nothingness.

"Sorry," said Ninian. "I thought it best to be ready. If you had only managed to focus your emotions then, it might have worked."

Matt shook his head. Then he concentrated on the dragon whelp.

He thought about his anger, visualised it as a flower starved of light, drained of water, focused on pulling away all the energy that had given the thing life//

//and the manifestation of his anger melted away, falling back into the hollow substances of the Place Between Stories, from which it had been made.

It was strange.

Twenty four hours ago, and he never would have believed that he - he, Matt, who was born in Lichfield, who drove an old Volvo with only one working window – he never would have believed that he would ever, *ever* be capable of creating a small dragon out of pure anger.

The notion would have made him turn summersaults out of sheer amazement.

But now...

They had been trying for hours, Ninian using every ounce of his skills, every mote of his strange powers, trying to weave substance out of Matt's imagination. Such a thing was possible here, in the Place Between Stories, this echoing chamber of potential, where the difference between thought and substance was the difference between two sides of the same coin.

And yet they had failed.

And failed.

And failed again.

Matt lacked focus. He had produced manifestations of his fear, of his guilt, of his panic. And now – of his anger, too.

But he had not managed the one thing he needed.

"I really think we should go back," said Ninian. "At least for a little while. Perhaps the Sheriff will return with more news. Perhaps..."

"No," said Matt. "Again. We go again. Now. Unless you have decided you don't want what I have to offer?"

Ninian regarded him for a moment, his long head titled to one side.

"Our bargain still stands, of course," he said at length. "I would not break it. I *cannot* break it. And you would do well to remember we sealed it, Firm and Frozen. You have a debt now, just as I do. There is no going back."

Matt nodded.

Ninian was right. Not that Matt had understood half of the ritual, nor could he read the contract they had both signed, the letters having been made out of a strange, fiery script that seemed to melt and change even as he looked at it. But he had understood enough to know that he was promising his services, in exchange for what Ninian could give him. Which was what had been arranged to begin with, back when Matt had still believed what NotCharlotte had told him, and had trusted the deal she had struck on his behalf.

It turned out it wasn't NotCharlotte that Ninian needed, and it had never been June who could have got them the things they had asked for. She had only ever been an intermediary. She had skill, oh he didn't doubt that. But when it came to passage through the Storystream - or through the *Grand*, as Ninian called it, whatever that meant - then the old lady did not have much power.

"The Bracken Court will have my service," Matt told Ninian. "Don't worry. I don't intend to go back on my deal, as long as you do your part."

"*Wishes*, sir," said Ninian. "We call them *wishes*. And you owe three of them."

"Three of three hundred, you won't get any unless you do what you promised first!" snapped Matt. "Now - are you ready, or not?"

Ninian tilted his head again.

"You know that is not quite correct, sir," said Ninian. "That is not the nature of things. Reality in these matters is quite different. In another place, we have already left to fulfil your wishes. The Grand is vast. There is room for endless iterations to exist side by side."

Matt shook his head.

"No," he said firmly. "Not this again. Not now. It's too...too confusing."

"You cannot expect me to change the nature of reality," observed Ninian.

"I can ask you not to mention it," countered Matt.

In the silence that came next, Matt and Ninian regarded one another. Finally, Ninian gave a small nod.

"As you will," said Ninian evenly. "I am ready."

"Good," said Matt.

And he concentrated.

He pushed it all aside, the hate, the frustration. All the fear and the anger. The memory of the lies he had been told, the journey he had been on, Brighton Pier in the rain and June's shop, everything...

And then, to his astonishment, it worked.

His mind was empty.

The lightning leapt from Ninian again. It was a gift, Matt knew, some special quirk of Ninian and of his people, something the stranger had developed in himself, worked on over countless years, grown strong at, until it was his speciality, the power he brought forth for his people, for the Bracken Court - whatever that was - and which could be used, in the hollowness of this place, to craft figments from the nothingness. Figments...and passageways...

But it would not work unless there was something for it to work on, and that was where Matt came in.

Who else but him?

The others had not seen his Charlotte, after all.

And that was what it came down to, of course.

Love.

He held the nothingness in his mind - the empty space, the blankness - because what was nothingness if not a door? A door between here and there, which was exactly what he needed. And then, holding it firm, he did what Ninian had told him, coaxing her image from the darkness. It was her face he conjured, but not just her face - it was the smell of her, the way she moved, the energy that animated her life and mind, it was the whole of her, every inch and moment.

It was love.

For a moment, they could see nothing.

Then the empty part of his mind flickered, sparking off the lightning, and forming//

//a door, opening above them, swinging into the blank air of the Place Between Stories not ten feet from the dark, crackling energy of the Quarantine.

And through the door...

Matt cried out.

He saw her.

He saw Charlotte, his Charlotte, the *real* Charlotte!

And she was hurt, and afraid.

Terribly, terribly afraid.

She crouched in some dark place, and though no rope bound her, Matt could see at a glance that she was constrained, imprisoned; that something bad was happening to her.

The image wobbled, flickered, seemed to lose its force.

"No," Matt gasped, fighting to keep the panic from his mind, fighting to keep it from spilling out and engulfing his consciousness, from ruining the portal.

Sweat burst on his brow. Panic washed at the corners of his mind like an unquiet ocean, storming against the shore.

The image stabilised. It began to become real.

It was close now! It was working!

He had done it. He had done it. He had//

//A hand grabbed his shoulder, and his concentration was broken and//

//And the image of Charlotte was gone.

There was an instant of crackling energy, as the lightning forking from Ninian's eyes struck only chaos and tumult. Strange half-seen shapes gained semi-reality in the air above them, writhing shapes that were half emotion and half substance and nothing at all...they burst and flickered, colours and shapes...and then faded, unmade.

And then it was gone, and Matt had failed again.

He turned, furious.

Who had spoilt things? He had been so close!

NotCharlotte.

Of course.

The blue-eyed NotCharlotte stood trembling before him, head shaking back and forth, desperation clear in her face.

"Stop it!" she told him. "You have to stop it! You can't do that, you can't.."

And he would have hit her if he could, would have slapped her for what she had just done, for what she had stopped him doing, hit her even though he knew that would be wrong...But he was suddenly weary, bone-weary, too tired to stand.

He stumbled backwards, half fell into the soft nothingness of the Place Between Stories.

For a moment, no one said anything. All that could be heard was the crackling of the Quarantine, sparkling blackly, a barrier encircling this portion of the Place Between Stories, with Ninian's parlour at its centre.

"You must stop it," said NotCharlotte again, and there was no force left in her words.

Matt shook his head, looked at her with disgust.

Then he looked away.

He was too tired now. Too tired for anger.

"Go," he told her, and there was no harshness in his voice, just emptiness. "Haven't you done enough? Just go."

"You can't do this," NotCharlotte said. "Didn't you hear what Norwood told us? This place is Quarantined. *We* are Quarantined. The Sheriffs are dealing with this. They are resolving this problem."

"This problem that you made," said Matt.

NotCharlotte didn't say anything. The silence began to grow heavy.

All he had seen her do since the Sheriff turned up was cringe and cower, give in and roll over. And be calm.

He didn't want her calm.

Because in the back of his mind, an idea was forming. A desperate idea. But desperate ideas were all he had left.

"It's not about being brave or being a coward," NotCharlotte told him. "It's about not giving the Sheriffs an excuse to...to get rid of us. If we want them to give us a chance, then we've got to do what they say."

"You didn't care much about what the Sheriffs wanted in the past," said Matt. He weighed his words with just enough venom. "If you had cared about that, I would be with the woman I love. This is all your fault."

For a moment, he saw a flicker of annoyance cross her face. She pushed it down, smothered it at once. But he had seen it. It gave him hope.

"I'm sorry about what happened," she told him yet again. He could feel anger in her voice now, bubbling below the surface. Her face looked calm, contrite. But her eyes...

"So you keep saying," said Matt. "If you were sorry, you'd be helping me to get her back. You think you can just charm your way out of this. That if you act like a good little servant, the Sheriffs of the Order will forget about what you've done. But they won't. You're in trouble."

"What do you know about the Sheriffs?" she snapped at him. "You don't know the first thing about them. But I'll tell you this: now that they've found me, I'm going to do what they want, because that's the wise thing to do. They are *dangerous*."

Matt shrugged.

"Why should I trust you now?" he asked her. "Why should *anyone* trust you? Anyone who trusts you ends up broken. Isn't that what happened to your friend?"

NotCharlotte jumped up, eyes flashing.

She doesn't like being reminded of that, thought Matt.

"They're *not* broken!" hissed NotCharlotte. "They're just missing. And it wasn't my fault! EB had fixed the Drive, he had spent ages making sure it was in synch..."

Nearly there, thought Matt. *Just a little bit further...*

"I wondered when you'd get round to blaming someone else," he said aloud. "Who's fault is it this time? Mine, perhaps? Maybe I was sending out psychic rays that interfered with your precious Chaos Drive. Whoever's fault it turns out to be, I'm sure it won't be yours."

Her lips trembled. Her eyes blazed.

"No!" she was shouting now, standing up and screaming at him. "No, it's not *your* fault! It was that bastard Frog! I don't know how or why, but I can *feel* it!"

Inside, Matt was smiling. It was so easy. Why hadn't he realised it before? She had buttons, the same as everyone else. All he had to do was *push*.

And the final touch, he thought.

"Yes, yes, whatever you want to tell yourself," he said, turning away from her. "It was nothing to do with you. It was the fault of the Frogs. And your precious Sheriff will sort everything out. So why don't you just do what you're good at, and leave your friends to die alone in the darkness?"

And that was it.

That was enough.

NotCharlotte screamed.

It wasn't just anger.

It was rage, and fear, and self-loathing. It was all the bad things she had been pushing down, hiding from everyone, probably hiding from herself.

The emotions opened out and poured towards him.

And in the Place Between Stories, strong emotions had a tendency to *substance*.

"Now," said Matt, nodding to Ninian.

273

He didn't know how he knew what to do, he could just *feel* that it was right.

After all, he had not been strong enough on his own. Even when he projected everything he had, the image of his Charlotte had been shaky and insubstantial. It had collapsed in a moment, and he doubted he could have focussed it enough to give them time to get through.

But now it wasn't just *his* emotions he was working with. The torrent of feelings NotCharlotte had hurled at him was potent. He knew it would work. He *knew* it.

Coloured lightning shot from Ninian's eyes, arcing across the space between them. And Matt split his mind in two.

One half he kept blank, as blank as the night between the stars.

And with the other half of his mind, he visualised her.

Charlotte.

His Charlotte, as she had been a moment ago, as she had been when they last saw one another, as she had been all the days of their lives together, luminescent and special.

The portal opened, as he knew it would.

If shimmered, unstable.

He could see her once more, his Charlotte. But this time the portal would not fail.

This time, he would force the jaws of the Universe apart using the torrent of emotions NotCharlotte had sent barrelling towards him.

Time seemed to slow. There was so much of it. There was all the time in the world.

He felt...right, somehow. Supercharged. Like this was what he had been made for, like this was what he had been waiting for all his life...this *conducting*, of emotion and energy, of possibility and time and of space.

He felt the mass of anger, of despair and fear. It burnt

though the air towards him. He could *see* it, he could actually see it, carving a deep furrow in the nothingness.

He *twisted*, marshalling it all, guiding Ninian's power, using it to direct the portal that was opening.

The colours were sharper, the image cleaner and clearer. Charlotte. He could see her...and she could see him.

His mouth opened, a smile forming on his lips. There was wonder in her eyes, a sudden leap, a light when before there had been only darkness...

And then the portal lurched.

There was a moment of shimmering, of fading certainty.

No, was all Matt had time to think. There wasn't even the possibility of shouting a message, of crying out. It all happened too quickly.

Then the view through the portal was changing, being yanked away by the force of NotCharlotte's emotions.

He hadn't counted on that. Hadn't even considered it.

Why should he, when all Charlotte had wanted to do was stay here, hiding in the Place Between Stories?

Wasn't it?

The new place visible through the portal was bright, so much more vivid and light than...well, than anything. It was hyper-real, in some ways. As if there was more weight there, more solidity than was usually allowed in the Universe.

Matt caught a glimpse of small, dark creatures, fur-covered but quick-moving.

And with sharp teeth.

They had lots and lots of sharp teeth.

There were mounds of something, too, glimmering rainbow mounds of strange sloppy somethings, but Matt didn't even have time to really wonder what they were, because the whole world was lurching.

It was like a sneeze, a sneeze taking place all around them, the ground and the sky, the Universe itself sneezing and inverting and//

//and then they were all tumbling through, spilling out to leave them in this new place, with the piles of glimmering stuff to be seen in every direction. Further off, there were huge, dark towers of used-up junk.

Matt scrambled, desperate. They had to get back, because the only place this trick would work was in the Place Between Stories, because that was the only place hollow and empty enough for emotions to be forged into figments of reality. Ninian had been quite clear on that.

But when he looked back, he was just in time to see the portal shimmer and vanish in a puff of nothing.

They were standing in this new place, this strange hyper-real land of rainbow glimmerings.

"Where," said Matt, "the hell are we?"

But at that moment there was a rushing, withering noise, like a great, terrible wind...a *hungry* wind. The creatures were rushing towards them, rushing from every corner, scurrying faster than he would have thought possible.

And where they were no longer seemed to be the priority.

The priority were those teeth, spinning like chainsaws, bright and sharp and so, so hungry.

✭ 25 ✭

Charlotte didn't pay any attention to the approaching footsteps, on account of how engrossed she was in gaping.

She had been gaping for several minutes now, non-stop and with a good deal of intensity.

She had seen him. She had seen Matt.

Not NotMatt who she had been on the run with, and not one of any of the countless number of other NotMatts that drifted through the vile mansion of Frogmore, devoid of emotion or willpower.

No, it was *her* Matt.

He had appeared suddenly, a vista opening on the wall of her chambers.

They hadn't said a word, but understanding had flashed between them, hope.

She didn't know how he had done it or what had gone wrong, but the fact was there now, levering open the jaws of despair that had clanged shut around her, whispering to her that there was still a reason to keep fighting.

There had been others with him. A strange, tall creature, rake-thin and *wrong* somehow.

But that creature hadn't been the odd one.

No, the really odd one had been the other version of her.

Who else could it have been? She knew that face, she was used to seeing it every day when she looked in the mirror.

And since there were no mirrors in this comfortable prison in which Frogmore had locked her, she had known at once who the girl was.

It was another version of her, presumably the version that belonged with the NotMatt she had been travelling with.

So Matt was with this other Charlotte.

Good.

Of course that was good.

She would be looking after him, she would be protecting him.

Wouldn't she?

The footsteps drew closer. They echoed around the soft, pink wallpaper, soaking into the various sofas, beds, and other comfortable furniture. The chambers were exceedingly nice, if you liked places that didn't have any doors.

Charlotte had never imaged a prison so comfortable.

And what was worse, what was more terrible than the thought of this NotCharlotte not looking after her Matt, the most terrible thing, so terrible she could hardly bring herself to examine it was...

...What if he decided he liked her?

What if Matt liked the other Charlotte more than he liked her?

Impossible. Stupid even to think it...

But then, she couldn't *stop* thinking it.

And now she wasn't sure what she would even do first, if the portal re-opened, if she could reach Matt.

She assumed it would be to run up to him, throw her arms around him, and give him a huge, wet kiss.

But then, there was just the outside chance that what she would do first would be run up to the other Charlotte and punch her in the nose.

The footsteps came to a halt. There was a grinding noise. It sounded a bit like a key rattling in a lock, only the key would have to be made of stone, and the lock would have to be made of another, bigger stone.

The noise was quite at odds with the soft glamour of the room.

Charlotte shook herself.

It would do no good if whoever it was came in to find her engaged in a prolonged gaping session. If it was one of the brainwashed Matts, then probably she would get away with it. Though she couldn't be sure. What if they reported it to Frogmore? She was quite sure he was checking up on her, however busy he was in the 'preparations' - as he called it - for whatever horrible thing he had planned for them next.

But then, it might be Frogmore himself, and Charlotte had come to realise the man was worryingly sharp.

Of course he was sharp. He was cunning and ruthless and...and he had them in his power.

There was a creaking noise, and then one whole wall of the chamber swung open as if on oiled hinges. A man strode in. He was dressed in a sort of militarised version of the Frogmore Serving Man outfit, with camouflaged trousers and a green vest, a smart black beret and an armband showing the crest of House Frogmore - a frog and a unicorn combatant on a field of chequered black and gold.

Behind the man, a sparkling concordance of lights danced and shimmered. Charlotte caught glimpses of a thousand worlds, landscapes and moonscapes and storyscapes half-forming out of the Chaos substances of the Storystream. She had thought it wonderful, incredible when she had first seen it, when Frogmore had first taken them off on his mad dash through the Storystream, leaving the Place Between Stories behind them, a fading memory of simple, empty space. She had asked him for an explanation, despite her promises to herself not to ask him for anything. Frogmore had laughed his horrible oily laugh, and told her that this is what it looked like to skirt the skein of a million stories, to dart, nimble as lightning through the ever-evolving geography of the Storystream - or rather, through this one backwater part of it, a fraction of a fraction of the smallest, tiniest portion. Even that much was bigger than the mind could hold.

Frogmore was hunting for things. He was scouring the Storystream for weapons, the very best, the most deadly, the most potent weapons. It was the way he lived, he had explained. His scouting parties were not just out to collect food. His was not a narrow mind, and there was no end to his ambition.

The figure stepped into the room, and Charlotte realised that even this spectacular view didn't give her even a hint of wonder anymore. Now it just gave her vertigo.

"Shut it off," she said, shielding her eyes with a hand and scowling at the newcomer. "Stay if you have to, but please close the door."

"Of course," said the man in a courteous, neutral voice. There was a clanging noise, and the burning light of a million stories shut off.

"There," said the man. "Is that better?"

Charlotte nodded, and it was only when she looked at him again that she realised the newcomer was NotMatt - the NotMatt who had been - until recently - her friend, her saviour, her co-escapee.

"Much better," she told him. "So he sent you to me? That's risky, isn't it? Surely if he wanted something from me, it would have been safer to send one of the fully dominated versions."

"I am fully dominated, I assure you," said NotMatt. If anything, he sounded rather pleased. "I am here to serve Lord Frogmore's commands, as are we all."

Charlotte raised her eyebrows.

"Lord Frogmore, is it?" she asked. "He was just a 'sir' last time I looked."

"He has decided to promote himself," said NotMatt. "We all thought it was a splendid idea. Lord Frogmore is a very special person," he added, a hint of reproach in his voice.

"Oh yes," agreed Charlotte. "Very special. I can't argue with that."

She sighed, Why was she even doing this? What use did it serve, to take her frustration out on NotMatt, to try to get through to him? There was nothing to get through to, not anymore.

"What does he want?" she asked quietly.

"The time draws near," said NotMatt. "Lord Frogmore has decided you should be by his side as things begin."

Charlotte felt a thickening in her throat.

"Already?" she said, too quickly. "How can he be ready? I thought there were thousands of...of you..." she finished lamely. She still hadn't got her head around talking about Matt as a pleural entity. She had found the idea of two Matts quite disturbing enough.

"There are," said NotMatt simply. "And now that we are all armed..."

Charlotte noticed for the first time that a gun hung at his belt. It was an ornate pistol, with a varnished handle of dark wood and a splendid brass barrel. But though there was something almost ornate about the thing, there was a weight to it, a certain indefinable aura that seemed to scream danger.

"All of you?" she said. Her eyes didn't leave the gun.

Thousands of Matts, all armed and dangerous, all brain-washed and willing to die for the man who had ensnared their minds.

This wasn't her Matt, and neither were any of the thousands of servants who were about to be sent screaming into war...

But war is what it would be, and in war people died. Probably lots of people.

It didn't matter which version of Matt this was. He shouldn't die. None of them should die. Not like this. She had to stop it, she had to stop Frogmore.

"But the world is cut off," she said, grasping desperately for something, some reason why the war must wait. "Frogmore said so himself. The Sheriffs have sealed him in. Head Frog 127 or King Headfrog or whatever he is calling himself now."

Charlotte was still trying to get her heads around all the bizarre things Frogmore had told her. She had barely managed to come to terms with the existence of multiple versions of herself, with a Universe made of stories, with a hateful frog-based race of aliens who had set themselves the mission of hunting her down as some kind of deranged sport.

But Frogmore's revelations had been more bizarre still, and she was still reeling from them, still trying to lever open her model of the Universe and fit all these strange new pieces inside.

Sheriffs of the Order she could just about understand. After all, she had seen one - the hugely tall figure of Indigo Shuttlecock, striding into Froghearth just as they fled it. But it turned out Indigo Shuttlecock was so keen on barrelling into that world because these Sheriffs - these guardians of Order, guardians of the integrity of stories - these Sheriffs were worried about the Chaos Drive. King Headfrog had been playing mayhem with the structure of his story, tearing it apart from the inside as he sought to rearrange things into a conformation which suited him.

And you couldn't do that, Frogmore had told her.

Not if you wanted to keep below the radar of the Sheriffs. Matt and Charlotte and EB might have been the ones who made the Chaos Drive, but they had been surprisingly subtle in the way they had used it. At least, that was what Frogmore had told her, and she couldn't see a reason for him to lie about that.

About lots of other things, she was sure he was lying. But that had the ring of truth.

Now, though, King Headfrog was making a frightful racket. If the Chaos Drive had originally made a noise like a small bell rung faintly at long intervals, King Headfrog was making a noise like a drum kit falling down a mountain.

He was the least subtle creature ever to have got his hands on a device for undermining the substances of reality.

Of *course* the Sheriffs had taken notice.

"They have established a Quarantine, yes," agreed NotMatt. "The story of King Headfrog has been sealed off from the rest of the Storystream. Even trans-narrative creatures of great potency would have trouble breaking through. And King Headfrog has only a small machine, one he is not fully synched with, one of which he only understands the hundredth part. He will not get out. He is trapped."

NotMatt smiled, a pleasant, gentle smile.

"But we can get in," he said. "Lord Frogmore is...exceptional. He is capable of incredible things. You will see."

Charlotte frowned. There was something there, something in what he had just said...

She couldn't quite grasp what she was missing.

"You will see for yourself," said NotMatt, and he reached forward, grasping her by the shoulder.

Charlotte started back. Before she knew what she was doing, she had slapped him round the face.

There was a moment of silence. NotMatt stared blankly at her. If he was surprised by her action, if he felt any pain, he didn't show it.

"Don't touch me," she told him. "I couldn't bear that."

"But you must come," said NotMatt reproachfully.

"I'll come," she said. She didn't see that she had an option. "Just...just don't touch me, okay?"

She knew it didn't make sense, exactly; but being touched by NotMatt under the sway of Frogmore would be just like being touched by Frogmore himself.

NotMatt indicated the door, and Charlotte led the way cautiously out and along the gangway. She kept her eyes firmly on the floor as she walked, trying to shut out the incandescent brilliance of the Storyscape. It was overwhelming, like walking through the heart of a star.

With every step, she felt herself slipping away. Her mind was breaking into a million pieces; the Storystream was too vast and too strange to hold within the confines of her consciousness.

Out of desperation, she forced herself to speak.

"You never finished your story," she said.

"Story?" he repeated. He was keeping pace behind her, careful not to touch her...but also not so far away that he couldn't reach her easily if she decided to try to dash away.

The Storyscape swirled and flashed. She felt a noise that was not a noise building around them, a bone-deep thrumming, an awful weight crushing the coherent narrative of her mind.

"Of EB," she said. She felt like she was shouting, but she knew that she was barely whispering the words. She forced herself to go on. "Of Bournemouth. Or the place that looked like Bournemouth but wasn't..."

There was a silence from NotMatt. It went on for so long that she thought he wasn't going to answer her.

She turned, expecting to see him just coming on after her, a blank look on his face. To her surprise, he had stopped. He was staring out into the swirling Storyscape as it flashed around them, but he wasn't seeing it. She was sure of that. His eyes were far away. There was a puzzled look on his face, as if he were trying to remember something, trying hard.

A wild hope fizzled up in her chest. Somehow, in the reflected light of a million stories, he looked almost like NotMatt again.

"Bournemouth..." he repeated, slowly.

"Yes, yes," said Charlotte, trying to keep the excitement from her voice. "That was where he went, remember? EB. A long time ago. You told me. He fell through the portal, and..."

"And it looked like Bournemouth, but it wasn't," said NotMatt. There was a rising certainty in his voice. "Yes. Yes, I remember. We went looking for him. Not just me. Me and you..."

He trailed off. He looked at her, carefully.

Then he raised a hand - slow, gentle. It came towards her face. Charlotte thought she would flinch away, but no - this wasn't a hand that was moved by Frogmore. This was NotMatt's hand, moved by NotMatt's mind, by a defiant flickering of his own will.

He touched her face. His had was warm and surprisingly soft.

"Not you," he said slowly. "She was almost you. But you are not her."

There was such sadness in his voice, such loneliness, that Charlotte felt her heart lurch.

She put her hand to his.

"No, not me," she told him. "But we will find her. Together, we will."

NotMatt paused. He titled his head, as if listening to an inner voice, one far off and difficult to catch.

"He was...on holiday there," he said at last.

Charlotte frowned. That didn't make sense.

"Holiday?" she repeated. "Who? EB?"

But Matt shook his head.

"No, not him," he said. "No, EB had just found his way there. He had sniffed it out. Cats have their ways, you see. They can move through the smallest of places. No, EB had just gone looking for him, because the man had been kind to him. He had been feeding him, a special food. He wanted more of it. Even then, he knew what was happening. He knew that he was changing. He wanted more."

Charlotte shook her head, hoping that the words would make more sense after being rattled around a bit.

It didn't work.

"EB was...changing?" she said. "What food? Found who?"

NotMatt smiled. His eyes were far away.

"The janitor," he said gently. "That's what he called himself. Very modest, really. He is much more than that. He's in charge of...of very important things. Where would we be without him?"

"And he was...on holiday in Bournemouth?" said Charlotte, trying to clarify the situation.

Around them, the gangway gave a faint moan. The flickering of the Storyscape gentled.

"Why not?" said NotMatt. He sounded a little affronted. "Everyone needs a holiday. Even the janitor - Rosewater, that's his real name - needs a holiday. Where would you go, if you were a trans-narrative being of almost limitless power? Where would you go, where you could really put your feet up, and hope not to be bothered by the endless flotsam and jetsam of the Storystream?"

"Um," said Charlotte. "Bournemouth, I suppose."

"Exactly," said NotMatt. "That was where he had gone. A version of it. An empty version. He conjured it up for himself, a little nominal dimension, unpopulated by anything of any real solidity. He wanted to be alone. Just for a bit. But EB found him. He had been calling on Rosewater for some time. That's what we hadn't realised. Rosewater had taken quite a shine to him. He had been feeding him. Feeding him little titbits, little morsels. He must have known what would happen. He isn't a fool. Not Rosewater. He must have known."

The light around them had settled now. They were standing once more on a viewing gantry. There was no hum or sense of movement. Frogmore Mansion had come to a standstill. Something was still tugging at Charlotte's mind, something NotMatt had said earlier. But there was so much to take in. She couldn't focus. And now that they had stopped their headlong dash through the Storystream, she knew that time was running out. She could sense it.

"Rosewater?" she repeated. It was an odd sort of name. And, "Food? What food? What do you mean?"

NotMatt opened his mouth...and then the footsteps came.

Charlotte turned around.

Philip Frogmore was there, striding dramatically along the gantry towards her. He was dressed impeccably. A fine hat with a luxurious green feather in it, a silken waistcoat, purple trousers well-pressed and tailored, and soft, leather gloves. Around his neck hung a large, dark gemstone. There was something about it, a brooding weight. It glimmered blackly, like storm-clouds forming up at the edge of night. Charlotte's eye was drawn to it. It seemed familiar, somehow.

But if Frogmore's garments were elegant and sophisticated, there was nothing elegant about his expression.

He wore a snarl, his lip curled up, fire in his eyes.

"Mathew?" he said sharply. "You were meant to bring her to me, not stand here dawdling..."

Then he must have caught something in NotMatt's eyes, some looseness in the way he stood, for he paused for a moment, frozen, alarm flashing over his face.

Charlotte looked at NotMatt.

His hand, she noticed, was inching towards the butt of the gun that hung at his side. His fingers were moving slowly. There was something in his eyes, some vitality, some inkling of his old self.

I've done it, she thought. *It was EB, that was all it took! Just memories of his old life, just...*

His hand reached the gun, gripped the butt.

He unholstered it and brought it to bear in one fluid motion.

But not at Frogmore.

At her.

"I'm sorry, my lady," said NotMatt, his voice distant and mechanical once more. "You must go with Lord Frogmore."

Charlotte found she couldn't look at him. Her face was burning.

How could she have let herself hope? How could she have believed that she could get through to him, that she could break Frogmore's hold?

She kept her eyes on the floor, and walked in the direction NotMatt indicated. Frogmore walked ahead, quite relaxed once more.

He led the way into a big, bright room that bristled with monitors and displays.

And Matts.

Matts were everywhere.

They all wore ridiculous skin-tight white jumpsuits, embossed with the Frogmore coat-of-arms on their chests. They scurried everywhere, working away, tapping things into consoles, reporting to one another - a steady, businesslike hive of activity.

"As you can see, we are nearly ready to begin," said Frogmore. He waved a manicured hand at his assorted command team. "It is a lot of work to organise an assault on the scale I have planned. I couldn't possibly do it by myself. That's where these chaps come in."

A few of the Matts looked up briefly from their work and gave respectful salutes. Frogmore waved them away.

"But...but why?" asked Charlotte. "What purpose does it serve, to send all these...these versions to war? I've seen the weapons those horrid frogs have. These...these versions will just *die*. Why not just zoom away? It doesn't make any sense!"

"Oh, my dear," said Frogmore. "Of course it doesn't make any sense to you. You don't understand me. Not where I'm coming from. Not what I've been through, or where I want to go. You shouldn't even try."

Some of the screens showed views of the Frogopolis. These screens looked hazed and disrupted, showing fuzzy, unclear images of planets teeming with frogs, of spaceships and barracks, of the whole military might of the Frogopolis. The images flickered and blurred, covered in a snowstorm of static. It was the Quarantine, she realised. It was preventing clear readings.

But Frogmore was still able to see something, which was surprising in itself. Hadn't the story been sealed off? How was Frogmore able to see inside?

Her eyes drifted across the screens. Not all were fuzzy. Most, in fact, were not. They showed views of the inside of Frogmore, she realised. Only the house was nothing like it had been - or perhaps Philip Frogmore had only ever let them see the faintest, furthest corners of the mansion, for truly the place was huge, more fortress than dwelling. Her eyes flickered from screen to screen, tasking it all in, and her mouth slowly fell open in amazement.

Hanger upon hanger she saw, great hollow loading bays filled with machines of war – tanks and planes, hover-ships, artillery, horrible things she didn't even have names for, things she had never seen before, but which had obvious military applications.

"Oh, I have not been idle," said Frogmore. His voice was warm and smug, cloying like rancid cream. "The depths of the Storystream have all manner of riches to plunder. For war is rife, my dear. It is everywhere, sown into the fabric of the universe itself. Stories of war abound; they run on conflict, after all; and big or small, conflict is something I mean to use."

Charlotte began to shake her head, as if she could deny the truth of his words. But it was pointless. Everywhere she looked, another screen displayed the marshalling might of House Frogmore.

In one bay, she saw a battalion of manticores. Another bay contained giant space-eagles, each harnessed and saddled, awaiting only riders to mount and swoop off to war.

A third bay contained...

Charlotte frowned. She squinted at the screen. Surely, she was wrong? Surely it couldn't be...

"Unicorns?" she asked.

"Indeed," said Frogmore. "Fine beasts. Deadly at close quarters. I have always been fond of unicorns."

"It will never work," she said. She tried to put some scorn into her voice, but she sounded so small in this vast place, so weak. "All these weapons...all these beasts...it doesn't matter. The story is *sealed*. You can't get through. You just can't."

"We shall see," said Frogmore. He was handling the large gemstone that hung from his neck. Once again, Charlotte thought how familiar it looked. Her eye was drawn to it. She peered, as if she could fight back the shadows, as if she could see deep within...

And then, to her surprise, she *could*. There *was* some kind of light in there, in the depths of the dark gem. Several lights, flickering and dancing, so small and frail they looked like the echoes of light that might have existed a million years ago.

But it was familiar, achingly familiar. Where had she seen it before?

Frogmore was looking at her. He had gone very still. He was examining her face, she realised, working out where her eyes were pointing, trying to discern the thoughts that were running through her head.

She didn't know how, but she suddenly knew that the gem was important to Frogmore. Important...and meant to be a secret. She was not supposed to know about it. And if Frogmore thought she *did* know about it...well, whatever reason he had for keeping her alive, for gloating over her, that reason would evaporate.

She had to make him think she suspected nothing.

"It's your gloves, isn't it?" she said. She didn't know where the words came from. They just came out, a desperate ploy she was sure wouldn't work.

A look flashed over his face, a sneer of hatred, of outrage.

But she saw the other look, too.

The one that had appeared and disappeared so quickly, she would have missed it if she hadn't been hoping for it.

Relief.

"The gloves?" he said, turning away.

"It's how you control them," she went on. "You're like a...like a puppet master...I didn't see you wearing the gloves earlier, but they must have been in your pocket or something. It must be how you're managing it. Matt would never do this. You've been bending his mind. Bending all their minds. And now I know how."

Frogmore sighed, and turned back to face her. The look off resignation he wore was very good. Charlotte almost would have thought it real, if there wasn't something around the eyes, a dark laughter.

He's sneering at me, she thought. *He's addicted to being in control, to playing people. To using them. He thinks he's doing that to me now.*

"Oh, you are sharp, aren't you?" he said. "I can see why he likes you. You see clearly, it seems. Very well then, I'll tell you. What harm can it do now?"

Charlotte kept her eyes carefully on his face. She could feel the jewel pulling at her, trying to snag her gaze.

"You'll never win," she found herself saying. "It doesn't matter how many tanks you've got, how many weapons, how many...unicorns..." she faltered, shook her head, and went on. "None of that matters. I've seen the frogs. I've been *hunted* by them. You've got a few hovercrafts? They've got *spaceships*. A fleet of them. You've got manticores? They've got *Tony*. He's five times as big and five times as scary."

She neglected to mention that Tony was probably either dead or still recovering from the punch that had floored him.

"And how many soldiers have you got?" she went on, before he could interrupt her. "A few hundred? A thousand? The frogs have millions. *Billions*. They have whole worlds of soldiers, fanatical, loony soldiers ready to die for their kingdom. It's pointless! You'll never win."

Frogmore stared at her for a moment, then burst into laughter.

"Win?" he asked. "Why on earth do you think I want to *win*?"

She blinked.

Of all the answers he could give, she wasn't expecting that one.

"Well, of course you want to win," she said. "Isn't that...I mean, surely that's the *point* of going to war?"

Frogmore shrugged. Then he pointed from screen to screen.

"In Landing Bay One, there," he said. "You see all those figures, getting into hover ships? There's five hundred there."

"Five hundred men?" said Charlotte. "So what? I've already told you how many frogs there are."

"Five hundred *Matts*," interrupted Frogmore, with sudden vehmnance in his voice. "Not men - *Matts*. Five hundred of the vile, cheating, stinking creatures. All plucked from their stories. All carefully gathered and dominated."

Charlotte blinked, caught off-guard by the unexpected malice.

"You must really hate him," she said.

"Oh, yes," said Frogmore. His eyes grew narrow, seemed to burn with an inner light. "Not just him. *Them*. All of them. Every version of him. Every single one."

"But...but why?" she asked.

"Because they're all the same!" he snapped. "They're all liars! They're all cheats! That's how they're *made*."

He lunged forward, caught her by the elbow, led her down through the chamber and past rows of monitors and servile attendants. She was so shocked by the move - and so fascinated by his unexpected venom - that she didn't even try to resist. She had the sense that he was telling her something he had been holding back, something that had been burning in his belly like poison.

"You see them?" scoffed Frogmore, as he brushed past a group of Matts, each staring intently at their display screens, typing in numbers, coordinating the impending assault. "You see them all? I've done my research, I've spend my share of time scouring the Storystream. I didn't want to make any rash decision. At first, I couldn't believe it. But after a while, I couldn't argue with my results. With my research."

He had led her to a console that sat in the heart of the room. He flipped a display into position, tapped out some commands. The screen lit up, showing a gradually rotating, three dimensional rendering of...

...Of Matt.

Or rather, as some kind of amalgamated, ideal Matt.

The face was too smooth, the expression too bland. But it was unmistakably him.

"Here, you see?" said Frogmore. There was a manic edge to his voice now, an instability that he had kept well-hidden until now. The rendering zoomed in, filling the whole screen with a representation of Matt's brain. Groups of neurones lit up as they fired in glittering patterns. Charlotte couldn't make sense of the activity, of course, though it seemed Frogmore could. Or thought he could.

"I modelled them extensively, you see," he went on. "I had to find out. After what he did to me, after how he *humiliated* me, I had to find out *how he worked*. It was vital, you understand."

"Vital?" said Charlotte, trying to keep up with the torrent of words. Then she shook her head, meaning filtering through. "You modelled him? How do you mean? How did you..."

"Vivisection," said Frogmore primly. "It had to be done. There was no other way to be sure. And I *had* to be sure."

"Vivisection?" repeated Charlotte, pulling away from Frogmore at last. "You mean you...?"

"I dissected them, yes," he said. He was looking at her face, but Charlotte had a sense that his mind was elsewhere, settling on whatever unknown wrong Matt - some version of Matt - had done him, whether it was real or imagined. "Oh, a conventional, simple view of morality might say I was wrong to do so, but we both know better, my dear, and there's no point clinging on to outdated notions."

Revulsion was running through her blood now, twisting her mouth into a scowl.

On the monitor, the brain of Matt - of all Matts, every single version - rotated endlessly. How many Matts were needed, she wondered, for Frogmore to construct this model?

"You killed them," she said hoarsely. "You hunted them down and ripped them apart to make this...this..."

"Oh, don't be so dramatic!" said Frogmore. "Of course I didn't kill them! I *couldn't* kill them! That was half the problem!"

Confusion filled her.

Couldn't kill them? What did he mean? And if he hadn't killed them, then how could he have made this model?

"You still haven't grasped the rules, have you?" said Frogmore. He had calmed a little now, the fervour that had animated him losing dominance. His voice held a hint of sadness.

"Rules? What rules? I can see that you're a bastard. That seems like a pretty obvious rule."

To her surprise, Frogmore chuckled.

"I am, at that," he said. "Yes, I can't seem to help it. I always am. For there are countless versions of me, too. Naturally, there are. Oh, not as enlightened as me, not with the power I have at my fingertips-" here he wiggled his fingers dramatically, making his white gloves dance like worms. "But versions of me, all the same. At first, I thought I might get some help there, that they might take me in, be of some use to me, but no."

He sighed again.

"What did he do to you?" asked Charlotte.

"He won," said Frogmore, simply. "Oh, not in a big way. Just a silly way, really. He...ran down my ideas. Disproved my theories. Nothing awful, you might think. Nothing unfor-givable."

"He...ran down your ideas?" said Charlotte. "And for that you want to kill him?"

"Not just him," tutted Frogmore, annoyed. "You really have to pay more attention. *Them*. All of them. They're like a plague. A sickness. The Storystream is replete with them. Vile things. Always cheating, always claiming silly little victories. He's the *hero* you see. He *has* to win. All my life, all my existence I thought I was a main character, a master of my own fate. It turned out I was just a heel. A villain. Not even a very good one."

He sounded melancholic again now, though there was something poised to his words, as if he had rehearsed them many times.

"And that's the way it always is," he went on. "Across the Storystream, as far as I can see in any direction...he's the hero. I'm the villain. Not just in the little story where he first *humiliated* me. But everywhere. So what help could I get from the other Frogmores? They're all villains, too. They're all *losers*. If I went to them, I could only lose. I worked that out a long time ago."

"Lord Frogmore?" came a voice from the gantry above them.

"Yes, what its it?" demanded Frogmore. "Can't you see I'm in the middle of revealing my evil plan?"

"Sorry, Lord," replied the Matt stationed on high. "You asked to be notified when all the units were in position. They are."

"Very good," said Frogmore. "You may go and attach your-self to one of the boarding parties. Make sure your gun is loaded and you are ready for combat."

There was a clatter of activity from the room as Matts everywhere left their stations and departed to join their units.

Charlotte felt a rising sense of dread. It was nearly time. She was doing no good here, none at all. She couldn't alter anything, she couldn't stop the suicidal attack from going ahead.

She had to do something. She had to stop him, to stop this madness...

"You're thinking about how you can stop me," said Frogmore slyly. "But you can't. You don't even understand the game."

Charlotte gritted her teeth. She wanted so badly to just thump him.

I could do that, she decided. *All his bodyguards are gone. It's just me and him...*

But he was taller than her, and bigger than her. She was unarmed; and she was sure someone as mistrustful as Frogmore would have various weapons hidden about his person. Perhaps he even had other mechanisms in place, hidden guns, something that would pop out at a single command from him and zap her to pieces.

No, attacking him wouldn't do any good. If she were to have any chance of helping, she would have to be clever. She would have to learn more

"Then enlighten me," she heard herself saying. "You're right, I don't understand this game you're playing. Not at all. But I know one thing."

Frogmore gave a little titter, looked at her with amusement.

"Oh, yes?" he said.

"Yes," she said. "I know that you can't kill me, either."

It was a bold move. If she were wrong, she might just tip him into proving it to her there and then.

But she was rewarded by a scowl, a darkening of his face that was hidden a moment later by an insincere grin.

"Very good," he told her. "You're not just a pretty face, after all."

"If Matt is a hero, then so am I."

She spoke with more confidence than she felt.

"Exactly right," said Frogmore primly. "And what do you think would happen if I were to try and kill you?"

Charlotte felt weightless. Relief flooded her.

He couldn't hurt her! Of course he couldn't! She thought of stories that she had heard, that she had read and seen. She was the hero! There was no *way* he could kill her!

"It wouldn't work," she said. "I don't know how...maybe...maybe the weapon would break. Maybe an emergency would develop..."

Frogmore started ticking things off on his fingers.

"Or I would be betrayed by one of my underlings," he said. "Or I would have a seizure, or I would be boarded by space-pirates..."

He smiled thinly.

"It's all happened before," he said. "Every one of those little get-outs, those *deus ex machina*, things that could only happen to a hero. Every time I tried to kill one of the vile creatures - or one of you, for that matter."

Charlotte let out a laugh. It was so obvious, really. Why had she ever been afraid?

"Well, it's all a waste then, isn't it?" she said. "The whole thing. You can't win. The hero always wins. The hero always triumphs."

And Frogmore smiled again, and said, "No."

The word echoed around the command centre. It was totally empty apart from them now. All the Matts were gone. Every last one.

Uncertainty gripped her once more.

The monitors showed the machines of war were well-manned. The unicorns were chomping at the bit, ridden by splendidly-armoured Matts. The hovercraft hummed ominously.

"But...but you just said..." said Charlotte. "You just told me...we're heroes...heroes *win*."

"They might win," said Frogmore. He tilted his head. "There is one other option."

"What?" demanded Charlotte. "What can a hero do, apart from win?"

Frogmore turned away, striding over to a monitor. He picked up a transmitter, toying with a red button on one side of the device.

"That depends," he told her. "I wondered...maybe a hero could become a villain. That would be nice. That would be *sweet*. I was going to do that, at first; but it turns out that reversing narrative momentum in such a way requires a great deal more power than even I possess. So, what could I do? Not reverse narrative momentum, but simply...*adjust the terms*..."

He looked at her, eyes keen, as if daring her to understand him.

"I can't kill Matt any more than I could kill you," he went on. "After all, he's the hero. But what if he were a *doomed* hero? A doomed hero, sent into pointless war against an over-powering enemy, not cognisant of his own fate, led there by an overweening abundance of pride...tell me, my girl: what happens to heroes when the story becomes a tragedy?"

And she understood.

Her eyes widened.

"No," she said, very softly.

The word echoed around the empty chamber.

Frogmore held down the button, and spoke into the transmitter.

"Begin the assault," he commanded.

❧ 26 ❧

In King Headfrog's darkened command ship, lights began to come back on.

His head had been in his hands, and he had been contemplating failure.

But now...

The screen in front of him was clearing. It was as if a mist were being blown away.

It showed a view of his own command centre, as seen from the outside. Around it, various horrible-looking warships of the Frogopolis circled and drifted, aimless, order-less. They knew they were meant to protect their King. But their king had stopped sending messages...

King Headfrog licked his huge lips.

Was it possible? Was his power returning?

Hesitantly, fearing for what he might find, he reached out a tendril of thought towards the Chaos Drive...and felt it pulse back at him.

It was there. It was back!

The Universe was back!

Not all of it, perhaps, but the part that mattered. He

could feel the Chaos Drive, and he could see the immediate surrounds of his ship.

Far off, deep in the bones of the world, there was a tearing noise, something more felt than heard. King Headfrog was dimly aware of the alien feline creature. It was screaming something; it sounded worried.

King Headfrog ignored it.

Around the room, screen after screen was lighting up.

"They are coming back to me," King Headfrog said. "I knew they were *weak*, these guardians you spoke of. They cannot stand the might of the Chaos Drive. Of *my* Chaos Drive!"

Then something flashed on one of the screens.

It was like a...a tear, a rift. The Universe sheared open, and beyond it King Headfrog could see...

...Dots. Lots of dots. All coming towards him, moving fast, growing...

A nasty suspicion tickled at the back of his mind.

"Is that a...Unicorn?" he said aloud.

And then the wretched cat was at his side, staring at the screen.

"He's got through," said EB, and his voice was flat and full of horror. "He's overcome the Quarantine. He's ripping it to shreds..."

"Who has got through?" demanded King Headfrog. He flicked a control on the monitor, and the view zoomed in, and he saw...

It was him.

The alien, the one who had given him such a merry chase.

Matt.

His eyes flickered.

He frowned.

Was that...*two* Matts?

His eyes flickered again.

Not just two. Lots of them. Lots and lots.

They were everywhere. Flying manticores, riding in space-tanks. A war fleet of Matts.

A joy filled him, a savage joy that was full of rage and the love of blood.

"They have come, then," he said. "That one thinks he can test me. But I will destroy him. I will destroy them all!"

EB was shaking his head.

"No," he muttered. "My friend...he would never...and he *could* never...not even the Chaos Drive could tear down a quarantine, could go against the Order..."

King Headfrog gave a laugh.

"You see, cat?" he said. "It seems you don't know everything. Perhaps you don't even know anything..."

There was a beeping noise, and a door slid open, revealing a cohort of his elite close-combat frogs. Metal implants and bio-synthetic weapons poked dangerously out of every limb. They clattered into the room, glowering at EB, towering over him.

"Should we...dispose of this one, my grace?" croaked the leader.

King Headfrog gave a little wave.

"Oh, no," he said. "I couldn't possibly have that. This one must be kept here - under guard of course. He must watch this failure. That other one, too," he added as an afterthought, gesturing to where the thing that had been Glob twisted and shivered on the floor.

If EB had emerged quickly from the shell of the Princess that he had hidden within, whatever it was that had invaded Glob did not have that strength or determination. There was no solid form, only an oozy, gelatinous mass of frog-flesh and ill-defined features. He looked more like a chrysalis now than a creature.

Still, King Headfrog did not want any nasty surprises.

"Bind them both," he ordered curtly. "Bind them and guard them, keep them in a corner over there...but make sure they have a good view!"

As his elite guard bundled EB away, something flashed again on the screen, drawing his eye. A snow of static descended over the view. King Headfrog had the strangest sense of bodies, huge bodies rushing towards the rent. He could only half-see them. They seemed bigger than worlds, bigger than the mind could understand...but at the same time they could fit into the view on the screen, as if somehow diminishing themselves, allowing their bodies to slide within the narrow dimensions of what passed, in this instance, for reality.

"The Sheriffs," gasped EB. "They've come themselves! They're fighting it!"

But fighting it or not, King Headfrog could see at a glance that they were not finding it easy.

They strained and strove, thrusting themselves into the rent, trying to seal it back, trying to rebuild this *Quarantine* EB had spoken of. There were lots of them, more than he could count. They seemed to flicker in and out of reality as they danced around the rent, tried to stop the armada of Matts coming through. They darted back and forth, parrying, trying to weave the Quarantine back together...but every time they tried to get a hold on it, the thing shook and tore as if it were being savaged.

That bone-deep thrumming noise came again. It filled him with a dark joy. Something was trying to tear the Quarantine apart, and he felt an instinctive accord with that force.

"Tell me, cat," said King Headfrog, not taking his eyes from the battle that raged on the screen, "what manner of force could oppose, these, ah, *Sheriffs* of yours? They are the guardians of stories, so you said."

There was a long pause before EB answered.

"It must be...something like the Chaos Drive," he said, and his voice held a hint of injured pride. "But stronger. It would have to be stronger. The Chaos Drive couldn't break apart the Quarantine."

The battle surged and raged. Now the Sheriffs had the upper hand. The Quarantine was closing again, dark knots of nothingness swimming together. The force that battered it from the far side was becoming more desperate, more fevered.

King Headfrog felt as if he was poised high above the world. He could feel the power of the Chaos Drive, thrumming at the back of his mind like a magnificent engine, finely tuned, just waiting for him to call forth its fury.

"It's almost over," said EB, and there was relief in his voice; and it was that, that note of relief which made the decision for him.

After all, King Headfrog reasoned, if the cat wanted the Quarantine to stay, he must do everything to get rid of it.

Anyway - how was he to join his enemy in glorious combat if he could not reach them?

King Headfrog focussed his thoughts - and then from silence to a purr, from a purr to a scream, from a scream to a thunder that filled his whole mind, he unleashed the power of the Chaos Drive.

He shot a beam of influence straight into the heart of the Sheriffs, to the mote of clear space around which the Quarantine was re-sealing. He was the Chaos Drive, and the Chaos Drive was him; a lance of pure thought, pure willpower - the will that the barrier should be removed.

Then there was a mingling, a joining, force on force - and he tasted it in his mind, a bitter steel tang, an influence like his but greater, far greater. He recoiled from it, regrouped, observed with his mind, picturing things in a great multitude of dimensions, picturing them how they actually stood, out there in space that was more than space, the rift that was more than a rift.

The Sheriffs were becoming aware of him. He could feel them. They had given all their thoughts to defending their work from this assault from without.

A mistake.

King Headfrog grinned, and channelled yet more power into the disintegrating Quarantine.

❧ 27 ❧

I t was funny, thought Matt, how teeth focussed the mind.

A moment ago, all his mind had room for was his rage, his disappointment, his fury at NotCharlotte for having twisted the path they took, for allowing the portal to open somewhere else.

Now, however, all his mind contained were teeth. Lots and lots of teeth.

The creatures were everywhere. There were hundreds of them, thousands. They were small, dark creatures, roughly spherical, with no discernible legs.

And then there were the teeth, of course.

The teeth were prominent.

They formed a rough circle: sharp, gnashing teeth. Worse, they seemed to rotate around the head - assuming the creatures had a head, of course, and were not just made of body - grinding and salivating, buzzing alarmingly.

"Um, where are we?" he asked. He tried to keep his voice level, but there was a brittle sheen to it that bespoke of great fear, possibly of a level up to and including trouser-wetting.

"Oh," said NotCharlotte. She sounded more surprised than afraid. His mind took this as a good sign, while sending a cautionary note to his lower extremities not to entirely discount the trouser-wetting thing for now. "We're here."

Around them, a broad, gently rolling land tumbled away to infinity. It was not all ephemeral nothingness like the Place Between Stories. Nevertheless, it still held a sense of being not quite real; or perhaps it was *more* real, somehow, than the places he was used to.

The landscape was scattered with decaying piles of junk - he could make out hollow, desiccated carcasses of creatures great and small, towers that had the look of the once-magical and now-defunct, spaceships with no vim, drooping and used-up. And everywhere - as ubiquitous as the teeth-monsters, it seemed - there were the piles.

Piles of glittering, glamouring, flickering, shimmering multicoloured *something*. They stood in little pyramids, gelatinous and strange. A non-noise came from them, something in the earth and in the mind, a humming, trembling sort of sound.

It felt...

Potent, somehow. Full of potential.

"Where...where have you brought us?" Matt asked.

NotCharlotte shook her head.

"I didn't mean to," she said. "I couldn't help it. It was your fault! The things you were saying, those horrible things! I couldn't stop thinking of him..."

Matt frowned. He looked around, half expecting to see some annoyingly superior version of himself strolling up to meet them. But there was no other humanoid in sight. Just the creatures. They were growling now. He felt a sense of rising tension. They were getting ready to pounce...

"Where is he, then?" Matt demanded. "This other version

of me, this Matt you're trying to get back to, that's so much more important than my Charlotte. Where is he?"

NotCharlotte didn't answer.

Instead, she sat down, head low, defeated.

"I think the answer is quite obvious, is it not?" said Ninian. He was looking around with great curiosity, and no hint of alarm.

"What answer?" growled Matt. "Where he is or where we are?"

"Both," said Ninian. "The answer is: your cat is not here. After all, he *was* trying to rescue you, and it makes no sense at all that he would still be here, the place of his birth and of his rebirth. He was here, and that is why your mind was drawn here - but he went away."

"Excuse me," said Matt. "I know we are about to be ripped to pieces by these strange little furry teeth-balls, but I would very much appreciate not being in the dark as I am torn apart."

The others exchanged glances.

"We're down below," said NotCharlotte.

Matt frowned.

"Below?" said Matt. "Below what?"

"The Universe," said Ninian helpfully.

"You can get *below* the Universe?" said Matt. "Isn't the Universe, well, everything?"

"I suppose that's a matter for philosophers," said Ninian reasonably.

And then the creatures were coming.

Slowly at first, inching forward in little wiggles, the creatures were moving towards them. He shifted backwards, and found that the three of them were pressing tighter and tighter into one another, being herded in on all sides.

Matt could hear the buzzing of their teeth...

"What do we do?" Matt hissed.

NotCharlotte shrugged.

"Nothing we can do," she said. "Just have to hope he turns up. He usually does, when there's an unscheduled delivery."

They were close now, only a few feet away, a few seconds away...

"He?" said Matt. "He who? Deliveries?"

And then the creature was on him, and Matt just had time to think that 'Deliveries?' was an especially dumb word on which to end his life, when...

"Stop that!" came a voice, high and clear, and sounding slightly cross.

There was a moment of suspended time, and then Matt realised to his great relief that he had not, in fact, been eaten.

He opened one eye.

The furry creature was about a hand's width away from him, slavering and slobbering...but resisting, somehow, falling down and ravaging him. It was as if some invisible force held it at bay. Matt looked around. Everywhere, other creatures were arrested in similar acts. One was even hanging in the air about three inches from Ninian's nose. Ninian was studying it with obvious interest.

"That's it, that's right, get back!" the voice came on. "Silly girls! These aren't for eating. At least...not yet."

And then the owner of the voice came into view, emerging from behind one of the piles of glimmering strangeness.

He was a tallish, pleasant looking man in a light-coloured suit. He had straight, sandy hair, and a slightly confused half-smile on his face.

The creatures seemed to wobble, torn between the command and their eminent desire to engage in savaging.

The newcomer put his hands on his hips.

"I'm not joking!" he said sternly. "Now: back! There's plenty of other stuff to be eating. Now - off with you!"

The creatures seemed to deflate, and then they were scuttling away dashing off to somewhere distant...but not too distant, thought Matt, for he could still hear the grinding of their teeth, a little closer than he would really like for comfort.

"Well! There. That's jolly good," said the newcomer.

He stood, looking at them, taking them all in. There was nothing hostile in his gaze, though when the newcomer looked at him, Matt felt as if he was seen right into, as if every atom and thought were weighed in the balance, understood, and put back in place, carefully, kindly, even. But not without a great deal of thought, all happening very quickly and below the surface.

"I'm Rosewater," said the newcomer. "I don't often get guests - well, not the sort that aren't used-up and ready for processing - and I can see that you are *not* ready, whatever my Munchers might want to believe."

"Ah, Munchers?" said Ninian. "Is that what the creatures are called?"

"Indeed, Munchers!" said Rosewater. "Another name to take back to the Bracken Court with you. You are fond of names, are you not?"

Ninian blinked. It was strange, Matt thought, to see him startled.

"Why, yes," said Ninian. "Names and numbers and many other things interest me. But I wonder that you know where I'm from."

"Oh, I have visitors from the Court all the time!" cried Rosewater, quite hearty now. "Now, let me see...when was it old Fifian came calling? It can't have been longer than a few thousand cycles, give or take."

Ninian titled his head, pondering.

"Fifian was before my time," he said at length. "Though he did leave some remarkable writings. Yes. Now that I think on it, that is why all this is so familiar."

"Oh, he was a gentleman and a scholar," said Rosewater. "I was rather touched when his time came. He left me a bottle of good gin in his trouser-pocket, quite unused, quite full of substance and not strictly speaking within my remit to keep. Still," he added with a twinkle - "we must allow ourselves *some* leeway."

"This *is* the land under the Universe, then?" asked Ninian.

"It is many things," answered Rosewater, "and it goes by many names. You might call it that, though you might equally call it the Land Below Stories. That's what my charter says, anyway, so it must be good enough."

"You mean," said Matt, who felt that he might just catch up with things if the Universe would stop turning summer-saults around him, "that this is...this is *after* things? Are we dead? Is this *heaven*?"

"Not *after*, my good human: *under*," said Rosewater, not unkindly. "As in beneath. As in, the place where things filter down to when they are used up and ripe for recycling."

"Oh," said Matt, not certain if he should be happy or disappointed or just satisfied to be getting answers at last. "Then I'm not dead?" he added, to be quite sure.

"Not in the least," said Rosewater, raising up a hand as if to forestall him. "And before you ask, I don't have the faintest."

"Faintest?" asked Matt. "Faintest what?"

"Idea," said Rosewater. "About what comes after. Not my department, I'm afraid. That's for the administration to decide, and frankly, I'm not even sure *they* know what the plan is, sometimes."

"Do they not?" asked Matt, rather confused by this little speech, but feeling as if he should say something.

"Oh, more often than not, in fact," went on Rosewater, taking a few steps closer. "You know, just the other aeon, I applied for..."

And then he stopped short, for he had seen NotCharlotte at last, where she crouched, half-hidden behind the others.

"You!" cried Rosewater warmly. "You should have told me you were coming! What are you crouching down there for?"

NotCharlotte let out a sigh, getting slowly to her feet. There was a wobble in her stance, an uncertainty.

Then Rosewater was poking Matt under the chin.

It was a soft sort of a poke - quite the most polite poke he had ever been recipient of - and he could tell at once that Rosewater wasn't the sort of gentleman who was very used to poking people.

"Aha!" said Rosewater. "I knew I'd never met you before, but I see now why you're so familiar!"

He looked at NotCharlotte, an eyebrow raised, his face one big question.

"What on earth is going on?" he demanded. "Charlotte, are you in a mess?"

For the longest time, NotCharlotte didn't answer.

Then she dropped her arms to her side and let out a sigh.

"It's all gone wrong," she said, and her voice sounded small and broken.

"How so?" asked Rosewater.

NotCharlotte took a deep breath

Then she told him.

❧ 28 ❧

On Frogmore's command deck, Charlotte watched as more and more power was brought to bear on the Quarantine.

She stood a little way off, careful not to let her eyes wander to the gem at Frogmore's throat.

I could leap forward and just grab it, she thought for the hundredth time.

And maybe it was true. Frogmore was hardly paying her any attention. His face was locked in a scowl, his teeth bared, his eyes glaring at the display.

She could feel it, somehow: the vast power of whatever Frogmore's device actually was. It hazed the air around them, it made reality itself feel thin and hot and dangerously liquid.

I could jump forward, snatch the jewel away, and then...

But that was the problem.

What *would* she do then?

Even if she managed to get it before Frogmore could stop her, and even if she managed to dash away into the bowels of his mansion...well, it was *his* mansion, not hers, and she was quite sure he knew every inch of it. He would run her down in moments.

It might be different if she thought she could work out how to use the power, too; if she could be confident that, in holding the jewel, she would be able to use it to bend reality in the way Frogmore was doing...well, if that were the case, she needn't fear anything. She could shift things how she liked, she could turn Frogmore into a gentleman, or a tulip or...or whatever. She could stop this stupid war before had even begun.

But how in the name of all things normal does one go about using a reality-shaping machine, anyway?

Charlotte didn't know.

So don't try and use it, she found herself thinking. *You don't need to use it. You need to* destroy *it.*

And she bit her lip so hard she tasted blood, because she would bet her last breath that destroying something like that wouldn't be easy. You'd probably need to throw it into a volcano where it had been forged, or find some kind of cunning, secret flaw in the way it had been designed or...or something. Something else that made sense in *stories*.

She thought the word with disgust. All at once, she realised she was sick of stories.

"It won't be much longer," said Frogmore, in a surprisingly calm voice. "I can feel their little barrier buckling, you know. It is most glorious. I've wanted to get one up on the Sheriffs of the Order for quite some time."

Charlotte shook her head in frustration. If it wasn't bad enough that this tall twit was set on destroying endless iterations of the man she loved, if it wasn't enough that she had been kidnapped and manipulated and was being made to watch something suspiciously close to the end of days, if all that wasn't bad enough...

"Do you have to keep talking in riddles?" she demanded.

Frogmore frowned, glanced at her, and appeared to pause in the act of manipulating shadowy forces beyond the ken of mortal kind.

"What?" he said. "What do you mean?"

Charlotte sighed severely.

"All that," she said. "Everything. As if it's all bloody self-explanatory. As if a million versions of us is normal, as if I should understand everything."

She sighed again as she saw the blank look on his face.

"Start with these Sheriffs," she said crisply. "You've mentioned them before. But what the hell *are* they? Why do you hate them?"

"Oh," said Frogmore, the puzzled look on his face briefly giving way to disappointment. "You know, for a moment there, I thought you had a little fire in you. Something that would have been interesting to play with. But, no. Just normal, everyday ignorance."

He turned away from her.

She opened her mouth to ask again, then stopped.

She ran back over what he had said. That was interesting. And she realised the important thing wasn't what these Sheriffs were or were not, and it wasn't even why Frogmore hated them. From the brief time that she had known him, she realised, it was quite probable that Frogmore hated most people. At least, hated the ones who didn't do what he wanted, hated the ones he couldn't manipulate, couldn't toy with...

No, the important thing had been that she had, briefly, very briefly, got his interest. She had pulled his attention away from the task he was focussed on, she had got him focussing on her. And there had been a nasty light in his eye, something playful, something taunting and vile.

He's addicted to being in control, she thought once more.

And then, hot on the heels of that thought: *it's a weakness. You can use it.*

But how? How on earth could she use something like that against him?

She didn't know.

But any little weapons like that might prove useful.

There was a sharp, creaking noise. It sounded like glass cracking, getting ready to break.

She shifted her weight from one foot to the other. Frogmore's hands were stiff at his sides, white gloved fingers stretched out tight. Sweat was on his brow...and the jewel at his throat glittered red as fire.

Again, she had the sense that she had seen something like that fire before. Not the jewel itself, perhaps, but something like it...

Frogmore span to look at her in triumph. She dropped her eyes as he turned, more out of instinct than conscious thought, not quite knowing why she was doing it. Now she was staring at his gloves.

Out of the corner of her eye, she saw the flicker of a smug smile on his face, and knew that she had scored a point. Oh, he liked the idea that she was mistaken. It made him happy. It made him feel *in control*.

"It's breaking," he said.

She blinked, not understanding.

Then the cracking noise came again, louder this time, and her eyes were drawn back to the monitors.

On each screen she saw it, shown from a hundred impossible angles. No longer were they displaying the armoured might of House Frogmore. No longer was she watching the arming and armouring of an army of Matts. No. What she was looking at now was...

...weird.

Very, very weird.

To say it was a wall would be to glorify every wall in the real world that she had ever seen. The thing on the screens was so much bigger than a wall, so much grander. It was made of glimmering colours and crystalline light and of pure, petrified will. Somehow, the screens were displaying something that existed in more than the handful of familiar dimensions. They were showing something that was trans-real, that was *supra*-real.

And though she was looking at the monitors, she realised she was *seeing* it in a much more profound way, in a way that stretched beyond sight, as it stretched beyond every other human sense. It existed just beyond the skein of the world.

"The Quarantine," she breathed, not really knowing what the word meant - other than it meant this thing, this incredible, powerful, vast construct which stretched from the beginning of *here* to the end of *there*, purer than rainwater, vaster than the confines of the skull, and stronger than the wrath of gods.

And it was breaking.

"You're tearing it down," she said, and she found her heart was echoing to an unheard sound, the sound of something breaking that should never, ever be allowed to be undone. And it felt like her own heart was breaking with it, and her eyes were suddenly full of tears. "How are you doing that?"

"Oh, it's easier than I thought, my dear," said Frogmore, a nasty lightness in his voice. "You see, I've got help. They weren't expecting that."

"Help? From who?" she asked.

"From that fool, 127, of course," said Frogmore. "He wants this fight as much as I do. As I knew he would. It was one of the reasons I selected him. A perfect villain - much more villainous than I - to whom I sacrifice my poor doomed heroes..."

And at that moment, several things happened.

The first was that Charlotte felt a warping, a bending in the air; then an absolute stillness, balanced for a perfect moment...and finally a great *rush* in the very fabric of reality, and she knew that the Quarantine had broken.

The second was that the monitors were abruptly not showing the barrier anymore – for the barrier was gone. Instead they displayed the horrible might of the Frogopolis, revealed to them across the solar system, spaceships and space tanks, war-frogs in heavy-armoured space-suits, and guns, guns, guns – guns beyond number, guns trembling with a bloody suppressed excitement, an arrested will, a waiting, brooding, *neediness* to fire, to fill the world with bullets and plasma and death.

The third thing happened inside her head.

She understood.

She remembered.

The jewel at Frogmore's throat, glimmering redly, glittering with power. She knew where she recognised it from. The machine. The device she had encountered after her meeting with EB. The machine she had not been meant to see – the keyboard and the display, and the wriggling lines of power and code.

With the hole – the space where something should go – the jewel. *That* was where it came from. From the machine.

And an intuition was suddenly on her, a knowledge that she could not explain any more than she could doubt – the thing at Frogmore's throat was not the machine itself, not the source of Frogmore's power, not the heart of his ability to control reality or bend the mind of Matts.

No – it was simply the remote control. It was how he *channelled* the power.

If she stole that, if she destroyed that – well, it might set him back for a few minutes. It might mean he had to find his way back to the machine and interact with it directly - but it would not break his power.

No.

To break his power, she would have to break the machine.

The Heart of Frogmore. A glittering, glimmering box. So diminutive and strange.

The source of all his power.

Then she nearly smiled - though she knew she must not, because the game she was about to play was very risky, and hinged absolutely on Frogmore's vanity, on the foolish cruel clockwork of his mind.

On his addiction to being in control, to playing people.

If he thought for even one second that she knew the real source of his power, then what she was about to try would never, ever work.

If he thought that she *really* knew how to hurt him, he would never, ever let her get away.

And that was the way she would get away from him, she realised. She would get away from him, because he would *let* her get away. Because it would be more fun for him. It would be irresistible to him, the opportunity to gloat, to win again, to laugh at her stupidity.

And thinking this, and realising she had no time either to hesitate or to contemplate her plan, acting purely on instinct, Charlotte moved.

She jumped forward, silent and determined, reaching out for Frogmore, as he stood, a smile on his lips, gazing out at the screens, unleashing his army, willing it to pour forth.

Even as she rushed through the air towards him, she saw it on every screen - the airlocks were opening. The army of Matts was released.

And even as they poured from Frogmore mansion - a huge thing, home and fortress and machine of death that projected into the dimensions of Frogspace as a vast spacecraft, made for war and destruction - Matts on space bikes, Matts in rocket ships, Matts on unicorns and manticores and dragons - even as they poured out to join the enemy, Charlotte struck.

Her hands moved as if in slow motion. She watched as they rose towards the jewel at Frogmore's throat. She watched as he became aware of her, as his eyes flashed towards her, a look of shock on his face as he thought she would make a grab for the red device...and then she watched as her hands continued moving, missing the jewel entirely, grabbing instead for those silken white gloves.

Frogmore's eyes lost their concern, as she had known they would.

They filled instead with a hooded, laughing anticipation.

And he let her take them.

Of course he did.

He practically held his hands out for her.

After all, what could be more fun for him, what could give him more scope for gloating, than letting her believe she had stolen the source of his power, letting her believe that she had won?

"No!" he cried. "Stop! Come back!"

But though she could hear his footsteps clattering after her, though she could feel the panting of his sour breath in her hair - she knew that he would let her get away.

She did not look back.

She ran, and ran, and ran.

And then, when he had let her get away, when he was - she was quite sure - already plotting and laughing to himself, working out the best way to play with her, she stopped running, and looked around, and began to work out the route she would take.

The mansion of Frogmore was huge, a vast place with seemingly endless rooms, endless corridors.

But it was not infinite. Not really.

And she was confident that if she put her mind to remembering, she would find it.

The hidden room, with the machine, the vulnerability.

The Heart Of Frogmore.

Charlotte let herself smile. There was hope. There was a chance. She would do it, she would destroy him, she would...

There was a distant explosion. The floor trembled beneath her.

She realised - to her horror - that this distant corridor, deep within the vaults of Frogmore mansion, was quite as well provided as the command room itself. Even here, there were monitors and displays.

They showed that the battle had been joined.

They showed flares of fire and plasma, and the smashing of ships, the engulfing of unicorns in balloons of flaring destruction.

The death of frogs...

...and of Matts.

She felt her smile fade.

However quick she was now, it would not be quick enough.

They were dying already.

The Matts were dying heroic deaths.

Frogmore was winning.

But he hasn't won yet.

She took a deep breath. And she ran.

❧ 29 ❧

NotCharlotte finished her story, and the Place Below Stories was silent. Not even the distant buzzing of Munchers could be heard, and Matt wondered again how exactly the creatures were linked to Rosewater - for linked they must be, to be so completely still and silent while their master was listening with such rapt attention.

"I see," said Rosewater at length.

It was not a good sort of *I see*, Matt thought. There was a whole weight of sadness in those two little words. He didn't know what exactly he had been hoping for - help, maybe; an answer; a hint as to something, anything that might work, that might allow him to get back to the woman he loved.

Those two little words put an end to that.

"So I thought, perhaps *you've* seen him," said NotCharlotte, her voice strained. "EB, I mean. After all, he must have come here. He must have. That's what happens, every time. Isn't it?"

Rosewater nodded slowly at that, but the expression on his face was still grave.

"Indeed," he said, and though there was a faint smile at

the corner of his mouth now, it was a sad sort of smile. "It must. Every time, for it is bound up in the way he was changed."

"Well, then you must have seen him," said NotCharlotte. "Something like that wouldn't have just passed you by!"

"My dear," said Rosewater, "this is my realm, and *nothing* that passes here, passes me by. But that does not mean I have the time or energy to dedicate myself to every atom of it. Yes, now that you mention it, he did come back. I remember. I noted his coming."

"Well, then!" said NotCharlotte, relief flooding her voice. "And where did he go?"

"Away," said Rosewater simply. "I felt him come, I glanced over, I saw him. I even gave him a little wave. But there was a new shipment coming in, lots to be directed. He did not look to be in any trouble..."

"Didn't look like he was in trouble!" broke in NotCharlotte, a hint of desperation in her voice. "Rosewater, when did you *ever* know that one to look like he was in trouble?"

Rosewater leant back, and gave a sad little chuckle.

"Yes, you're right there," he sighed. "Ah, that was one of the things I first liked about him. Do you know, the first time I met him, I was having a little holiday, and..."

"I know, I know!" cut in NotCharlotte. "I was there, remember? But what about *now*? What about this situation? Isn't there *anything* you can do?"

"Do?" said Rosewater, as if to do anything was the most ludicrous suggestion in the whole world. "Why, of course not! No, not if what you say is true, not if the Sheriffs are involved, and there's a Quarantine, not to mention that you've let yourselves lose the Chaos Drive..."

"Lose it?" snapped Charlotte. "Weren't you listening? We didn't lose it, it was *stolen*! Honestly, sometimes I think that..."

Matt shook his head. He felt their words washing over him, as if he were not really there, as if the fact of him being there meant neither one thing nor the other. He was so sick of that feeling. Of being ignored, of being unimportant.

The frustration bubbled in his chest like lava in a volcano.

"Stop it!" the voice cried out.

It was a high voice, thin and clear and full of impotent rage.

It took Matt a moment to realise it was his own.

To his surprise, the others *had* stopped talking. They were staring at him.

Matt was so shocked that this had worked, for a moment he didn't know what to say next.

He took a deep breath.

"Look," he said, trying to keep his voice from cracking, "I know that this is very stressful for everyone. But please, try to understand. All of you are, to one degree or another...well, *strange*."

He thought that might have been a mistake, but then he realised they were all nodding.

"Yes, well," he went on, "I'm *not*, you see. Strange, I mean. I'm not from a weird parallel dimension where I'm a space pirate with a talking cat. I certainly don't have an army of voracious floating fur-balls and a whole realm to call my own. And I'm not a...a..." he faltered, looked hard at Ninian, then licked his lips, momentarily at a loss.

"A wandering scholar of the Bracken Court, used to travelling through the endless dimensions of the Grand," put in Ninian helpfully.

"Yes, one of those," said Matt. "The point is, I'm not *any* of those things. For you, this sort of weird nonsense is like bread and butter. It's like rain after a cloudy day. But for *me*..."

He waved a hand vaguely, taking in the rolling, ephemeral

realm, the piles of glamouring potential, the endless rotting junk of the Place Below Stories.

"All I'm trying to say is," he concluded, feeling suddenly self-conscious, "I would really appreciate feeling included."

There was a long, pregnant pause.

Matt wondered if he had said too much. What if Rosewater didn't like being referred to as strange? Surely, this wasn't the sort of...of *creature* he wanted to annoy. What if he made a quick, brutal gesture with his ebony stick, and the next thing (and the last thing) Matt knew would be the buzzing of thousands of little teeth?

"Oh, that *was* well put," said Rosewater, with what looked to be a genuine smile on his lips. "I must say, I do like you. You're so much like the other one, but more...what's the word? *Normal*."

"You see, that's just what I mean!" said Matt, emboldened by the fact that he had not been eaten, and determined - therefore - to press his point until it was understood. "Half the things you say are like riddles! They're like little in-jokes, things I don't get!"

"My apologies," said Rosewater. "You're quite right. Very rude of me. I do rather take all this for granted. Normal is what's normal for you, and all that. To me, this all seems very natural. But, please - I will make an effort, I promise. Now - how can I make things better?"

"Well, that's...that's good of you," said Matt, caught rather off balance. "Just...just..."

And then words failed him, because it was suddenly all too much to take in and explain, all the hints and half-understood things.

Luckily, Ninian came to his rescue.

"I imagine there are seven things that are currently bothering you," said the odd, tall creature, peering down at him through his crystalline spectacles. "To answer them briefly in turn: EB came back here after he was killed, because this is the place to which he was bound. He was bound here, because our friend Rosewater took a shine to him, and gave him a stock of that manure to eat."

Here Ninian gestured towards one of the piles of glamouring strangeness.

"After he ate that, he was changed," put in NotCharlotte.

"It's raw potential, after all," said Rosewater.

"When we first found him," said NotCharlotte, "*My* Matt and I, I mean - we knew something was changed. He had always been clever, but after eating this stuff..."

"It was in his eyes," said Rosewater, a distant, dreamy look on his face. "Oh, yes, I knew I shouldn't have given it to him, but even before he had a bite, I could see in his eyes there was something, some rare intelligence, an understanding..."

"And after EB ate the manure, everything changed," said NotCharlotte. "He could...he could *shape* things."

"Of course he could," said Rosewater, tilting his head curiously as he looked at Matt. "You do see that, don't you?"

And to his surprise, Matt found that he could. Looking at the piles of the stuff, the glimmering and strangeness, the air of raw power that thrummed just beneath the skin of the world...It made anything seem possible.

"Yes," he answered, quite surely. "I don't know why it would be that way, but I can see...or rather, I can *feel*..."

"It's because of what that stuff really is," said Ninian in his soft, helpful voice. "It's pure, recycled power."

"What sort of power?" Matt asked.

"*Narrative* power," said NotCharlotte. "Raw story-stuff, recycled, washed clean and pure and ready to make new stories."

"Or to reshape the world itself," said Rosewater. "I wanted to...I needed to give it to him, somehow. It wasn't clear to me why that was the case. But then, that's the way of things, sometimes. And that's true whatever the Sheriffs of the Order think. Order isn't the only force in this Universe, or even the best one. It isn't as simple as that."

"He was changed," said NotCharlotte. "But he was still EB. He was still our *friend*. He was just...just *more*. He knew more, he understood more. And he could *change* things. He could make things, too."

"He made the Chaos Drive," said Matt, understanding flashing through him. It wasn't a question, but NotCharlotte was nodding anyway.

"Yes," she said simply. "He did. And Rosewater let him."

"Oh, I shouldn't have, I know," said Rosewater. "It wasn't in keeping to my charter, as the Sheriffs were at great pains to point out. And yet..."

He gave a small, helpless gesture, as if he could have resisted such a thing as easily as he could have resisted the proper unfolding of the whole of existence.

"The Sheriffs left us alone," said NotCharlotte. "They turned a blind eye. It was easier than going up against Rosewater. Our friend here is quite the power," she added.

"Oh, tosh," said Rosewater, looking flattered. "There are certainly much more potent entities than me in the Universe. There are at least two of them, I'm quite sure of it."

"They ignored you," said Ninian. "As long as you were careful. But you *don't* have the Chaos Drive anymore. And the one who holds it now is *not* being careful."

Something changed in the atmosphere around them, and Matt had the strangest feeling. It took him a moment to realise that it was the feeling of not being a mile behind everyone else when it came to understanding what the hell was going on.

"Yes, yes..." said Rosewater, and there was something new in his voice, and a frown on his face, an air of, if not confusion, then at least of uncertainty. "The frogs. You did mention that. I wonder..."

And then Rosewater was striding off, away through the endless gentle folds of the Place Below Stories.

"Wait!" shouted NotCharlotte. "Where are you going?"

"Come along!" Rosewater called back over his shoulder. "I think the time has come to do a little research."

NotCharlotte hurried after, and a moment later they were all trotting after Rosewater, hurrying to keep up.

"I thought there was nothing to be done!" Matt said.

"Oh, I'm quite sure there's nothing we can do," said Rosewater. "From what I understand, things are quite, quite hopeless."

Matt felt something leaden twist in his bowels. For a moment, he had been quite sure that they were getting somewhere, that Rosewater was leading up to telling them how they could change things, how he could get back to her, how everything could be right again...

But no.

Of course not. Rosewater wasn't full of vim because he thought he could *help*. He was just full of vim because he was *Rosewater*. Matt was getting the feeling that Rosewater would be helpful and optimistic if he were in the midst of a discussion with a shark about who should eat whom for dinner.

The Land Below Stories was broad and vast. The air was very clear, and Matt had the sense almost that he could see for ever. Wherever he looked, in any direction, the realm seemed to unfold before him in endless crystalline splendour. He could see things in the deep distance - piles of discarded story-junk, used up and battered - looking smaller than atoms, but in aching sharp focus.

The little group had become strung-out. Up ahead, Ninian was striding with his long legs, keeping pace with Rosewater. They looked to be in rather animated conversation. Matt couldn't decide which of the two tall creatures was weirder; he supposed they had lots to talk about. Glancing over his shoulder, he saw that Charlotte brought up the rear. She was walking nearly as fast as the others, but she kept glancing around, as if constantly on the look-out for something.

Up ahead, Rosewater and Ninian had come to a stop. They were standing by what looked to be a huge bookcase. It was so wide that at first glance it looked like it was a wall stretching off into the deep distance. It was at least a seven hundred feet tall.

Matt turned around to see what NotCharlotte made of that, and was just in time to see her vanishing behind a hill of piled junk-stuff.

He glanced back to the others.

Ninian was now holding the bottom rungs of a huge ladder, while Rosewater ascended into the more distant heights of the enormous bookshelf. He was already half hidden from view behind a small bank of clouds. He didn't know how long it would take them to do whatever it was they were doing, but he was quite sure he wouldn't be able to help.

Moving carefully, he walked back across the Land Below Stories, until he was standing directly before the pile of junk into which he had seen Charlotte vanish.

Up close, the tower of junk looked rather sad. There were bit of machinery, odd pieces of armour, even what looked to be fragments of an old house. But everything seemed washed-out and used-up, dry as bone and lacking utterly any lustre or potential. It was, he found, rather difficult to stay focussed on the stuff - there was so little pull to it, so little interest, the eye automatically unfocussed and swam away.

But near the *bottom* of the tower...

A sort of small passageway opened up between the stacked junk, a tunnel that went downwards into the earth.

But it was not dark at all, as if the substances of the Place Below Stories were such that a kind of background light existed everywhere, a default state, in the way that every other place had the darkness.

He hesitated.

He should go back to the others. He knew it. Why go wandering off after NotCharlotte, after everything that had happened? And when it was possible, just possible that Rosewater was even now devising some king of cunning way he might get back to his own Charlotte...

And yet...

He stepped into the tunnel. The air was cool and still. It didn't *feel* like the sort of place where horrible seventeen-mouthed monstrosities would be waiting to rip him apart...but then, if the last few days had thought him anything, it was that he really didn't know anywhere near enough about monstrosities in general, or about their lurking habits.

He glanced back towards the enormous bookshelf. Ninian was standing, bracing the foot of the ladder. Matt tilted his head back to find where Rosewater was.

And back.

And back some more.

Then he saw him. Rosewater was about two hundred and fifty feet up. And still climbing. Little wispy clouds were forming about his legs.

He looked back into the un-darkness, listening carefully.

At first, he could hear nothing. Then it came to him, at the very edge of perception, a tiny whispering noise, so faint and fragile he wondered if he were simply imagining it.

He should go back.

He knew he should.

And knowing that very well, Matt moved forward anyway into the tunnel.

30

It wasn't a sound. It went deeper than mere sound.

King Headfrog felt the whole Universe stretch and scream about him...

..a tearing, rending noise, as if the very fabric of reality was compromised...

...and then the Quarantine broke.

He felt it as the sudden absence of resistance, a great, welcome, endless *compliance*.

There was a moment of suspended stillness, and then the two parts of the Universe were coming together, those two factions which the Sheriffs had strived so hard to keep apart. They smashed like huge waves in a wild sea, rushing forward and intermingling in a joyful, fierce chaos...

And then the war was joined.

On every screen in his command centre, it could be seen. The Matts had come. They flew on their manticores, on their space ships, in their power suits. Lasers blazed, plasma coiled and ripped through the void, unicorns reared and charged, somehow completely unbothered by the lack of atmosphere.

Oh, it might have been frightening, King Headfrog

reflected, to some other Frog. To some lily-livered, snivelling excuse for a warrior. To some old toad of a king.

The Matts *did* charge fiercely, and their machines of war were surely splendid and deadly.

But King Headfrog was the glorious leader of his people, the one who had demonstrated the skill and cunning, the pure raw *control* necessary to rest reality, to redefine it, to will it as he saw fit.

And he was not alone.

All this had happened in the time it took him to draw a breath: the collapse of the Quarantine, the dismay of the Sheriffs, the assault of a million Matts.

Now, as King Headfrog breathed out, he reached out with his mind, redirecting the flickering tendrils of influence, refracting them through the glory of the Chaos Drive, making his will felt throughout the Frogopolis.

And the Frogopolis answered his call.

All around his orbital hub, ten thousand waiting hatches slid silently open. Ten thousand deadly fighter ships poured forth. They were shaped like sleek and deadly Frogs, metal poison sacks beneath the cockpit from which deadly streaks of magnetically-accelerated rounds would leap.

On the surface of his home world, a million launchpads tilted to readiness. Ten million engines leapt to life, rockets beyond counting preparing to shoot into the atmosphere, to do glorious battle with his foes, to fight for him, to die for him, yes...and to kill for him.

"No," came the voice from the floor. It was hollow and broken, a breath.

King Headfrog grinned down at EB, where he lay bound hand and foot.

"I am sorry, my lord," said one of his elite close-combat frogs. "Would you like me to cut out his mouth?"

"No, that will not be..." King Headfrog began. Then he

paused. "Wait, did you say you could cut out his *mouth*?" he asked. "Surely you mean his tongue?"

The elite combat frog shrugged.

"Either would work very well, my lord," it told him.

"It would, at that," agreed King Headfrog. "But no. I want him to watch this. I want him to see his friends die. And I want to hear what he has to say about it."

King Headfrog enjoyed the malice in his own voice. This...this *cat* had dared to pretend to be his own would-be queen! To be the beautiful Princess Frogmella! When he thought of that, he wanted to tell the guard, yes, yes, cut out his mouth, cut the whole thing to pieces!

But no.

A less bloody revenge would be so much worse.

So he would let the cat watch.

On the floor, the creature that had been Glob kicked and wobbled. There was even less of the old chief of security there now, King Headfrog noted. But whatever metamorphosis the cat had planned was clearly not working. The ugly, dripping thing was amorphous and horrid.

He turned back to the screens, just in time.

There was a moment of frozen waiting, an anticipation, a stillness so clear that King Headfrog could see the snarls on the faces of individual Matts, could see the glinting eyes of his frog pilots, could sense the coiled readiness of a whole world about to make war.

And then they clashed.

Jets of plasma shot out, disembowelling his fighter ships, sending sheets of fire roiling up the whole breadth of his orbital command ship. Lasers darted like sudden, hard sheets of metal, miles long, impaling his missiles before they properly left the atmosphere, raking across the shields of his command module, melting and boiling his fighter ships instantly.

But the battle wasn't one sided.

His first wave of fighters smashed into the fleet of Matts, sending deadly flashes of super-accelerated projectiles through the ranks, melting them like plastic toys under a blow torch. And then his ships were through the first rank, breaking and weaving among them, and chaos reigned supreme. He saw close combat, his pilots jettisoning from doomed ships, roaring through the void in power armour of their own. He saw unicorns impaling his warriors, and his warriors breaking necks even as they died. He saw manticores roaring and flailing as they were torn to pieces.

He saw...

He saw...

He saw...

The battle was glorious and all-engulfing. It filled his mind to bursting, a joyous rage that made his heart beat and his breath come quick, that filled him with something close to ecstasy.

Behind it all, he had the sense of the Sheriffs retreating - and well they might! For had he not overcome them? Overcome them, as he would overcome every force in the Universe that dared oppose him?

But the glory of battle was all about him, and he could not bring himself to care.

And then with a final inversion that felt like the last piece of tatty carpeting being pulled from under the feet of the world, the Quarantine was gone completely, and the two realities were joined.

King Headfrog gaped.

The battle raged on all but one of the screens in the command ship, and King Headfrog did not look at any of them.

Why would he want to look at any of those screens, when the *real* foe had just honed into view?

The enemy ship was big - nowhere near as big as the orbital hub his *Pondwater* had become - but much bigger than any of the puny attacks ships that had been sent at him.

Of course it was bigger.

It was where all those ships had come from. He understood it now. This ship, this mother-vessel had been hidden up until now, kept behind the last shreds of the disintegrating Quarantine.

But it was hidden no longer. It was...

It was ugly, for a spaceship.

It was ungainly, wide and uneven, looking more as if it had been grown than if it had been made, with spurs and corridors, whole spiralling wings that looked as if they had been slapped on as an afterthought. And then, was it even really a spaceship?

King Headfrog wasn't sure. Parts of it looked as if they were...were bits and pieces of some grand country estate, not suited to combat at all. He thought he made out pools and tennis courts, patches of lawns, a spread of little gazebos. He peered closer, nudging the view on the screen with his mind, zooming in.

Was that a flag flapping in a wind that shouldn't properly exist in the vacuums of space?

He peered closer.

He recognised it, he thought. If he could just think what it was he was looking at, just remember where he had seen it before...

The flag flapped closer. It filled the whole screen.

King Headfrog's mouth went dry.

He knew what he was looking at and where he had seen it before.

A frog and a unicorn, combatant on a field of chequered black and gold.

It was him.

It was the man who had come to him, who he had protected...and who had betrayed him.

The man who everyone had called the Prophet.

Philip Frogmore.

So that was who his enemy *really* was.

He should have known.

King Headfrog manipulated the screen with his mind, flashing across the exposed areas of the enemy ship, taking it all in, trying to gauge its readiness for battle...and trying, most of all, to catch a glimpse of the man himself.

A deserted command deck; battlements and launch pads empty, their combat ships already launched; the whole ship seemingly hollow and ripe for the plucking.

And then King Headfrog saw him.

Philip. The Prophet.

He was stalking down a long corridor, seemingly oblivious to the carnage going on around him, mind and will focussed on chasing...chasing someone.

King Headfrog didn't care who the man was chasing, didn't care at all.

No, the important thing was that Frogmore was distracted.

Now was his chance.

Now was the time to strike.

"Gentleman," he said, not taking his eyes off the screen. "Prepare my personal launch and my power armour. Make sure all your weapons are primed and combat-ready. And bring the prisoners," he added, almost as an afterthought. He smiled, a horrible, mad smile. "It looks like we will be going on a little jaunt."

31

The tunnel had a smooth, even floor. As Matt moved forward, the opening behind him faded from a hole to a pinprick, and then finally to nothing. But still, he found that he could see. A faint whitish light seemed to emanate from the very substance of the Place Below Stories, casting soft illumination.

At first, he ran one hand along the side of the tunnel, thinking it might help him keep his bearings. But there was something unpleasantly absent about the stuff that made up the wall, something hollow and washed out, so he snatched his hand back, though he couldn't stop himself from looking. He saw fragments of a thousand different realities, crushed together and mouldering, as if the glue that held the very shape of existence together had melted. The little pieces of physically recognisable things weren't so bad - swords and guns, trees and plants, organic things and made things and deadened, hollowed, haunted things. No, worse by far were the things that weren't really things at all. They had been present on the surface all along, he realised - present and wound inside the piles of junk, though he hadn't noticed them, for they were subtle. But down here, in the un-dark-ness, they could hardly be ignored.

They were coiled inside the walls of the tunnel. The words, the endless whispering - that was part of it; the words of endless broken stories, torn fragments flapping in a non-existent wind, whispering Tellings of themselves to nobody. Then there were the other elements - things that existed in dimensions Matt was not usually aware of, but which he found he could now sense. He felt folds of broken characteri-sation ripple around him, pull and tug against him in a wistful chaos of half-understanding. He felt the sodden weight of undone narrative inevitability, unspooled from a thousand ravaged tales, useless and sad and half unknowing. And under-neath it all, a sediment of used-up tone, a tired maelstrom of background sensibility blowing like a dust unseen across the dry ground.

Stories.

Endless used up, broken down stories.

Stories awaiting the cleansing teeth of Rosewater's munchers...

The tunnel opened abruptly into a sort of cavern. It was lighter here, too, as if the background luminescence of the Land Below Stories was concentrated here, and Matt found that he was blinking.

Along one wall of the cavern, a number of brilliant, vivid paintings were hung. At least, he thought they were paintings at first, bright paintings hung on tall canvases, depicting various scenes of battle and mayhem. But looking closer, he realised they were far too vivid and realistic to be mere paint-ings. They were more real - almost - than reality itself. The images seemed to *strain* out at him, as if longing to be born. And then he realised that he recognised the figures in most of the images.

Of course he did. Most of them contained him.

Only, if he looked more closely, he realised it *wasn't* him. It was him how he could have been, if he were about 70% more dashing and grand and dangerous. He looked from one image to the next. In this one he held some kind of space-blaster, pointed viciously at a nine-mouthed alien. In this one he was piloting what looked like an especially fast and deadly kind of war ship. And in this one...

In this one he was with Charlotte. Holding her. Kissing her.

Only it wasn't *his* Charlotte.

It was her, of course.

NotCharlotte. The other Charlotte.

This was where she belonged, he realised, this was where she came from, this other world, full of danger and spectacle, a space-heroine from another version of reality, a better version, a *superior* version.

He had a sudden, deflating sense of himself, of what he must look like to her...and worse, more disabling, a realisation: NotCharlotte was missing someone, too.

She was missing her version of him, every bit as much as he was missing his version of her.

Which he had known all along, of course he had...but he had never properly *felt* it, not in the solid, aching way he felt it now.

He looked again at the images, saw the warmth of love that they felt for one another, and then glanced away, embarrassed suddenly, ashamed, as if he were looking at something unspeakably private, something he had no right to see.

And all at once he felt the anger he had held for her vanish, the frustration and rage and hate all blown away, as if by a fresh breeze.

He understood. She was like him. Of course she was.

All she wanted was to get back to where she belonged.

He looked again, and saw what he hadn't noticed before.

In every image, the versions of Charlotte and himself were not the only human creatures present. In fact, they were not even the most prominent. Every image contained another shape, a humanoid shape, slender and strong, and invariably laid out in a posture that seemed to indicate either extreme distress or terminal stillness.

He looked more closely. Yes, definitely *humanoid*, if not quite human...

The ears were too big and pointy.

He felt a smile creep across his face as he realised who the figure must be.

EB, he thought, knowing deep down and at once that he was right. *That's who it is. EB. So* that's *what he looks like...*

"What is this place?" he wondered aloud.

"It's where he dies," said NotCharlotte, achingly clear in the strange un-darkness. "Where he comes to, I mean. Every time we've lost him. Every time he's been killed, this is where he's drawn back to..."

Matt jumped about six inches in the air, and did his best not to squeal.

"Oh," he said in what was meant to be a flat, unimpressed voice, but which was entirely spoiled because it was three octaves too high.

She was sitting on a small ledge at the far end of the cavern, holding what looked like a sheath of rolled up papers in one hand.

Matt's brain caught up with what his ears had registered.

"Wait, what?" he said. "Every time?"

NotCharlotte nodded.

"It's sort of...sort of written into things," she said. "Don't ask me why. It's just the way our story started to fall, after EB did what he did. After he ate that bloody *stuff*."

Matt moved down the cavern, past image after image. He stopped in front of one, his eye having been caught by something. He tried to focus on what it was that was different, but couldn't bring his mind to bear. There was just too much going on, too many questions...

"Written into things?" he asked. "What do you mean?"

He gazed at the image in front of him, looking at the silvery outline of EB. Only it wasn't the EB he was used to seeing from the other images. In this one, the shape seemed much more, well, *normal*. There were no pointy ears, there was no sense of fur or tail or sharp front teeth...

"Stories have a certain shape," sighed NotCharlotte. "It's just the way of things. It's not like...like *absolute*. There are various possibilities. But, you know, when you have two main characters who are in love, and a third character - a sort of plucky friend, say, or perhaps a child - well, there are certain *shapes* that the story tends to fall into."

"How do you mean?" asked Matt, not taking his eyes off the picture.

"Either he would be wounded," said NotCharlotte. "You know, the first thing that would happen is that he would get sick, become unwell...and then we'd have to go on a quest to the third moon of whatever to find some rare herb that would save his life..." She waved her hand in vague, bored circles in the air. "You know the sort of thing I mean."

"Right, yes," said Matt.

"Yes," said NotCharlotte. "He would be killed by some horrid alien villain, and his death would be the motivating fire that set us so firmly on extracting some kind of strikingly poetic revenge." She smiled thinly. "It was all terribly romantic at first...but it got a bit tiresome after you had been through it fifty or sixty times."

The words seemed to be coming to Matt from a great distance now. He was so firmly fixated on the image, determined to work out what was wrong, why it seemed to important to him. He moved away from the silvered image of EB, taking in the rest of the image, seeing if there were any other clues...

"Rosewater helped us set it up," said NotCharlotte. "Right after that first meeting, when he explained what eating the manure *meant*. When we were first getting used to the idea, to EB's new shape. Rosewater told us something of the shape of stories, and that he would always be drawn back here when he died. That he would sing himself back into existence here; and then, all he would have to do was wait, wait until the dynamics of the story we were in had proceeded enough that he might leap back in, without upsetting things too much."

EB's new shape, Matt repeated in the fluttering chaos of his own mind. He didn't know why, but the phrases seemed to resonate with him. He had moved on from the silvered shape of EB, and now he was regarding the image of Charlotte. It was strange. This version of her looked different, somehow. Different from both his own Charlotte, and from the one standing next to him. Her eyes were brown...but there was something different about her posture, about the set of her face...he couldn't put his finger on it...

"How do you mean, leap back too soon?" he asked vaguely.

"You can't have characters resurrecting themselves willy-nilly," said NotCharlotte. "It undermines the whole arc of the story, makes mince-meat of the motivations. So he'd have to wait until we'd, you know, dealt justice to the race of horrid alien fiends who had killed our beloved friend, etcetera etcetera. Then, when we'd moved on far enough, when that little chapter was behind us - wham! That was fair game, and EB could jump back in and join us. At least, until the shape of the story meant it had to happen all over again. It got tiresome pretty quickly."

Matt frowned.

"Wait, are you saying he should be here? That he's been *killed?*"

NotCharlotte gave him a surprised glance.

"Killed?" she repeated. "Yes, of *course* he's been killed by now. Bound to have happened."

"Then," said Matt slowly, "if what you've told me is right, then surely he can't just leap back in while all that stuff's unfinished. Doesn't he have to wait until, well, until you've defeated the Frogs and been reunited with your version of Matt?"

"Absolutely," said NotCharlotte. "And that's what's worrying me. EB *hasn't* waited. He's not here. Which means he has broken the rules."

Matt was still staring at the image.

Something in the far corner of the image caught his eye. It was an animal. A small animal.

A small animal with black fur.

It was a cat.

"Oh," said Matt.

He didn't say it loudly, but there was a weight to the word.

"What is it?" asked Charlotte.

"It's EB," said Matt flatly.

"Another death," shrugged NotCharlotte, looking at the image. "Just another death, amongst a great many others."

"Are you sure?" asked Matt. "Do you remember this one?"

"Of course I do," said NotCharlotte, half frowning. "I bloody well should do. You tend to remember when one of your best friends is killed, even if it's happened lots and lots of time before. Although..."

And she trailed off uncertainly.

Matt pointed.

"That's not you though, is it?" he asked.

NotCharlotte followed his finger.

"No," she said after a moment. "I'm sure of it. She's someone else. Another version."

"And she's not my Charlotte, either," said Matt.

"Are you sure?" asked NotCharlotte.

"Oh, absolutely," said Matt. "Quite sure. Number one, her hair isn't right. She's never worn her hair like that. And she's a bit taller in this version, too."

"And number two?" Charlotte asked.

Matt sighed.

"And number two, if this had been *my* version of reality," he said slowly, "I'm sure I would have remembered it. I don't have a cat, you see. And there, at the back, you can see EB. That's him, curled up in the background, looking quite markedly un-transformed, and very catty in the traditional sense. But most of all," he went on, "I don't remember being zapped and sucked out of my life. Which is quite clearly what has happened to the Matt in this version."

There was a pregnant pause.

"Ah," said NotCharlotte. "You're right. That's not EB. That's you. That's a version of *you*."

"But...but *why* would that happen?" Asked Matt. "I haven't eaten any of that manure stuff. Have I?" He added, suddenly worried.

But NotCharlotte was staring intently at the image.

"This version of you didn't die," she announced. "Look, he's walking along, quite unconcerned. Bit of a spring in his step too, it looks like. No, this version of you didn't die. He didn't come here under his own steam. He was *summoned*."

"Summoned?" said Matt. "By who."

NotCharlotte didn't answer. She was looking down at the sheaf of rolled up papers in her hand.

"You know," she said slowly, "I think we need to get Rosewater to have a look at these."

"What are they?" asked Matt.

"I found them through there," said NotCharlotte, nodding to the far end of the cavern. "That's where he leaps from. Where he jumps back in, enters our story again. These papers were on the floor. They are pages."

And then NotCharlotte was brushing past him, moving back towards the tunnel, and then racing, faster and faster and faster, back the way they had come, back up towards the open expanse of the Land Below Stories.

They raced up through the tunnel, and back into the bright land beyond.

They arrived just in time to see Rosewater slamming a huge volume down in frustration.

"Gone!" exclaimed Rosewater, sounding outraged "I can't believe it! It hasn't happened before; it's unheard of!"

"It is missing?" said Ninian, tilting his head to one side. "The entry you were searching for?"

"Look!" said Rosewater, holding the book up. It was a huge volume, thick and covered in dust. But though the binding was heavy and gnarled, when Rosewater sprang it open with one hand, Matt was astonished to see that the individual pages were so thin and fine they almost seemed like cobwebs. They blurred past, thousands of pages, hundreds of thousands, more than the one volume could possibly have held...and then they stopped, for Rosewater had thrust a finger downwards with unerring accuracy, splaying the book open.

Matt saw that there were two pages missing. He could see the jagged rip marks near the spine, where the pages had been torn away.

He blinked.

He turned towards NotCharlotte, but she was already moving, her hand coming up with the sheath of papers she had found in EB's cavern. She let the papers go, and they floated down a few inches, then were abruptly snatched up by the book itself, tendrils of gossamer webbing reaching out from the torn leaves, grabbing at them, pulling them back, and...

And with a flash of un-light, the book was whole again.

"Oh!" exclaimed Rosewater, looking from NotCharlotte to the book and back again. "What...where did you find those?"

NotCharlotte told him.

"But I can't read them," she added. "What do they say? And why did EB take them?"

"I don't know why he took them," said Rosewater, rather darkly. "But it was a most grievous thing for him to do. Why, these books are *mine*! He shouldn't even have *touched* them, let alone damage them!"

"But what *are* they?" asked Matt. "The books, I mean?"

"Friend Rosewater explained it to me just a moment ago," said Ninian helpfully. "The bookshelves are part of his Charter, in a way. They are a record and a prophesy and an invoice, all rolled into one."

"An invoice?" asked Matt.

"Yes," said Ninian. "He gets deliveries from every part of the Grand. From the *Storystream*, I should say. It's an awful lot to keep track of. That's what the books are for. They are a record, an accounting, a list of every ounce of substance that has come to him or is yet his due."

There was a thoughtful silence.

"You mean," said Matt carefully, "there's a record in this library of everything that's happened?"

"Oh, yes," said Ninian. "Or that will happen. Then again, in a way, the whole thing *is* Rosewater. An extension of him. And what's more, only he can read it. He brought us here because he thought it might help, you see. He thought he could look up something about this Head Frog creature, about where he came from, and why, and so on. Only, when he did that, we found that it was cross referenced with someone else. Some chap called, ah..." Ninian primly lifted his spectacles off his head, and polished one crystal glass, looking thoughtful. "Frogmore, I believe. *Philip* Frogmore. Seems this chap is important. Vital, even, if we are to understand what's been going on and how to help. Only, when we tried to look up *Frogmore*...well, the pages were missing..."

"Not anymore," said Rosewater, and if the anger in his voice was fading, there was still a certain stiffness there. He peered closely at the pages, eyes skimming over a dense, ornate script which Matt felt he might almost understand, if only he had a little longer to stare, to decode...

But the longer he looked at it, the more sure he was that he would *never* understand those words, not if the Universe itself were to grow old and cracked, not if there were time enough for the stars to go out.

"Oh, it's not really letters," said Rosewater. "They just look like that - like words, letters - because that's the closest thing your mind understands. They exist in rather different dimensions, really. I advise you not to stare too closely."

"Really?" said Matt, who was quite busy peering, too. "Why's that?"

"It has a tendency to make people catch on fire," said Rosewater casually. "Oh, not everyone. Just some people. After a while. I mean, it's fairly safe. You'd probably be fine. Just, you know. Fair warning."

There was heavy pause, and then the only person looking at the book was Rosewater again.

"Can you, um, translate it for us?" said Charlotte.

"Oh, yes," said Rosewater. "That almost never results in combustion. It says..."

Rosewater's eyes flickered over the pages. After a moment, his brows raised a little.

"My, it appears to be two small stories," he mused aloud.

"Interesting. Yes, now that I think about it, that does sound familiar."

"You mean they've..they've already come down here?" asked Matt. "They've been recycled?"

"What?" said Rosewater, not looking at him. "Oh, no. No, they aren't due yet. Not for a goodly while. They are still out in the Storystream, floating around, being told, interacting in small ways, echoing..."

His voice trailed off, and he picked idly at a nail.

"It seems they aren't due to me for a fair few cycles yet," he went on. "No, this volume of my library is just an accounting of one aspect of the Universe. My due, but in a latter age. These stories have a lot of Telling to be done before they are done and Told."

"But what are they about?" prodded Charlotte.

"Oh, they are about this Frogmore fellow," he said. "Well, Frogmore and..." He ran his fingers up and down the text, as if making sure of something. "Yes, and another version of you."

"Of me?" asked Matt.

"Indeed," said Rosewater. "It seems the two of you are tied together in some way. Hmm."

Rosewater scratched a few calculations in the air around him, the others watching as figures and formula danced in bright un-light, fizzling madly in nothing, then bursting back out of existence when Rosewater had seemingly got an answer.

"Yes, it looks like a fairly typical agonist/antagonist pattern," he went on. Then, when Matt continued to stare at him blankly, he added, "This Frogmore fellow was the baddy. This other version of you was the goody. They defined one another, in a way. Look, here's a translation if you're interested."

Rosewater ran his hand over the book, and cast off a

shimmering tracery of the page, which solidified into two small stacks of papers, which NotCharlotte picked up.

"I can read these versions," said Matt, peering over her shoulder. Then he looked nervously up at Rosewater.

"Is it, uh, safe?" he asked

"Of course," said Rosewater. "They are quite diminished. Not an ounce of raw story-stuff in them. No risk of combustion."

Matt peered at them.

The first was titled *I Want To Believe*.

The second was called *Dry Ink And Empty Pages*.

He skimmed through them, and began to understand what Rosewater had meant.

"So...so this Frogmore guy really doesn't like me," he said at length. "This other version of me, I mean."

"Correct," said Rosewater. "And what is more, it appears from the second story that he actually managed to get his hands on some kind of trans-narrative device. A machine for shaping stories, for moving plots around. Which is quite a deep shame. Such a device in the hands of a two-dimensional villain..."

He shook his head.

"Sometimes, I do wonder what the Pheasant is thinking," he added. Then he shrugged. "Still, she knows best, I'm sure."

Rosewater gave a sigh.

"Well, I do hope you've found that helpful," he said. "Please feel free to have a bit of a rest before you go."

Matt looked at him blankly, not understanding. Then he felt it break on him, like a huge, dark wave.

Rosewater wasn't going to help them, after all.

"But...but you've *seen* that we're in trouble," he protested in a small voice. "I thought you said it was *bad*, to have a villain like this Frogmore guy, roaming around with powers like that."

"Oh, it is!" said Rosewater, very sincerely. "It is awful. Very dangerous. Who knows what might happen?"

"Well, then!" said Matt. "Don't you...that is, can't you do something to stop him?"

Rosewater looked scandalised.

"Stop him!" he repeated. "Of course not! That's not in my charter at all! No, if he's been bending things with this plot device of his. That's not *my* job to police. That's what the Sheriffs of the Order are for," he added, rather primly.

A sudden suspicion formed in Matt's mind, a flash of intuition.

"You don't like them, do you?" he said. "The Sheriffs, I mean. Why?"

Rosewater gave a little harrumphing laugh.

"What I feel about the Sheriffs is neither here nor there," he said in a carefully neutral voice. He did not meet Matt's eye.

"You don't like them," pressed Matt, sure of it now. "Why else would you let EB exist? Why else would you let him make the Chaos Drive? The Sheriffs don't like that, not one bit. They were quite clear on that point when they threw us into their Quarantine!"

"Yes, well," said Rosewater. "I couldn't stop them doing that, not after Head Frog got his hands on it. Not after he started reshaping things so brazenly. They might not have an appreciation for the balance of forces in this Universe, but things like that can't be ignored."

There was something here, Matt knew it. There was something that could help, something he could use...

It hovered at the edge of his understanding, just out of his reach. If only he could grasp it, he sensed that he could help her, could get to her, to his Charlotte...

And yet it didn't make sense.

"Oh, just tell us why you hate them, won't you?" he

snapped, his frustration momentarily getting the better of him. "You know something! Why won't you..."

But Rosewater was changing. He was tall, suddenly, much taller than he had been a moment before, taller than Ninian, bigger than houses, filling the whole world.

"Enough," he said, his voice as hard and cold as stone. "I have indulged you all because I am fond of Charlotte. But I did not let you into the heart of my realm so you could snap and whine, so that you could blame me and make demands. I have my own duties, and I have been neglecting them. You speak of things of which you know little, vanishingly little. There are other forces in the Storystream than raw Order. You would do well to remember that."

Matt was aware of NotCharlotte standing next to him, shouting something up at Rosewater, words he couldn't hear. But it was too late.

Rosewater had made his decision. He had gone, and the three of them were alone in the vast, bright emptiness of the Land Below Stories.

32

"You know, you shouldn't write me off so quickly," said Philip Frogmore. "I really am a hell of a guy, once you get to know me...."

Charlotte didn't move. Her teeth were pressed tight together in a grimace, her whole mind focussed on easing the breath in and out, slowly, steadily...quietly.

She was crouching behind a bank of monitors. On the other side of the large, empty chamber, Philip Frogmore was advancing. She could hear his footfalls, slow, deliberate.

And he knew she was there. He had seen her duck in this way a moment earlier, another false turn in her mad dash, desperately trying to find the way back to the banks of flashing lights, to that special, central room...to the Heart of Frogmore, to that elusive room she had thought would be no great trouble to find.

She had been sure she would remember the way. The mansion was huge, of course it was; but still, she had thought it just a matter of directions, of lefts, rights, and more lefts.

The problem was, the geography of this place was unstable.

It was only after a seemingly straight corridor had led her back to Frogmore for the third time that she understood. The internal dimensions of the mansion were in flux. It was like trying to navigate through someone else's nightmare.

"It wasn't nice of you to take my gloves," came Frogmore's voice once more. There was an amused, mock-angry tone to it now. "Didn't anyone ever tell you that? To steal is wrong, my girl! Well, you're still coming to terms with this situation. I don't blame you. It's just..."

But his voice was momentarily drowned out by a huge, distant explosion.

Charlotte used the cover of the noise to jump up and scuttle a few more feet, keeping well below the obscuring line of a huge desk, and make a dive towards a thick metal door. It was red, and had a big yellow cross painted across it. Through a central rectangle of glass, Charlotte saw stars twinkle. Then something flared, brighter for a moment than the sun, and then faded in scintillating fragments to a plume of dust, and Charlotte realised what she was looking at.

An airlock.

Not an escape route, not for her. Not a route that might lead to the central place she was trying to get to - quite the reverse.

She was peering out into deep space, watching the flashes and carnage as Frogs and Matts fought and died in the unkind void.

If she only had some time to think...

"Wow, that was a magnificent one!" exclaimed Frogmore in his unctuous voice. "You really should have seen that one, my dear. Five of those frog-ships vaporised in one go. Excellent. Of course, it took the sacrifice of a good number of my own soldiers. Good men, bravely giving their lives. But still...that is the point, rather."

Charlotte could hear the leer in his voice, could see the oily smile in her mind's eye.

It made her angry, so angry...

...but what could she do?

She had no gun, no knife, no weapon at all.

All she had were these stupid gloves! These finely-made but entirely worthless gloves, and the knowledge that Frogmore was only stringing out the chase because he enjoyed it so much, enjoyed the feeling of power, of thinking he knew something that she did not...

She froze mid breath.

A smile spread across her face.

It would be risky. If she had miscalculated, it would all be over, and she would be back in his power.

But then, what choice did she have?

She took a deep breath.

If this was ever going to work, she was going to have to let go of any hint of doubt. It would only work if she were to project absolute confidence.

Philip Frogmore would never get drawn in if he thought for a moment that she didn't believe it herself.

It was all about power, for him. All about knowing something more, about being right when he knew you were wrong, of the sly manipulation, the too-late revelation...

She pulled the fine gloves onto her fingers. The silk felt cool and splendid against her skin, so delicate that she almost found she could believe the lie.

She focussed on the feeling, willed herself to go with it.

These gloves were special. They were powerful. They were *magic*.

The she opened her eyes, and rose smoothly to her feet.

She forced herself to smile.

It wasn't a smile she was used to smiling.

Not a pleasant smile, not a friendly smile.

This was a wicked smile, full of every ounce of knowing delight she could muster.

It felt strange on her face, like someone else's dirty clothes.

But he had to believe that she believed.

Otherwise it would never work.

"I see you've fallen for it," she sneered. "You've come along, just as I wanted. You're out of time, Frogmore."

To her great, silent amusement, Philip Frogmore gave a little jump as she swung up from her hiding place. She saw a sequence of expressions flash across his face, one after another, like clouds zipping past on a windy day. Real fear first, the kind of fear bullies always harbour. But it was gone in a moment, replaced by confusion, then delight, and then - a mere moment later - by a sort of thin, false fear, an obvious act, part of his game.

When she saw that expression of false fear, she felt herself relax. She knew the game he would want to play.

"Not the gloves!" Frogmore cried. "Oh, take them off! Oh, you shouldn't be able to do that!"

He was hamming things up dreadfully. He was so sure of his own superiority, so certain that he was the one holding the strings.

"I worked it out, you tall twit!" she cried. She flicked her fingers dramatically. "I saw the way you moved, the way you directed things. I knew where your power came from...and what I had to take to steal it!"

She gestured with one hand, indicating Frogmore, fingers stretched out, beckoning, as if drawing him to her...

Oh, it was a delicate thing. She had to give him time to decide how he would play along, to make him complicit in his own deception - and all the time, he had to think that she was the one being deceived.

There was the barest pause, a heartbeat between her

gesture and the glint in his eye which meant he had decided to act in the way she had predicted.

Frogmore's clothes crumpled around him, as if in the grip of a giant, invisible hand, and he was pushed along the floor towards her. If she hadn't been looking for it, she never would have seen the sparkle in the red jewel he wore at his neck.

"No!" he yelped, and it was nearly convincing.

"Come here, you dog!" cried Charlotte.

It wasn't about what she would really do or really say, if the power really was hers to command. It was about what *Frogmore* imagined she might do – and that, of course, was limited by his ability to imagine what he would do himself.

Charlotte held out a hand, pulling tight on his ear – but not too tight! Too tight and he might actually get angry, might decided to end things, to teach her a lesson there and then.

"Mercy!" cried Frogmore. "I will bring them back, all of the Matts! I will undo all of this, I promise, I..."

He was cringing at her, but she could see his eyes glinting at her, shining out from behind that mask of fear. They looked amused. He was enjoying this.

She knew she wouldn't have long. He would tire of the game before it got much further. Already, she could tell he was building up to the reveal, to his moment of reversal, the climax of what he thought was his trick: when he would show her it had been him with the real power, all along.

There would be no second chances.

They were beside the airlock.

It would work. It had to work.

It had the necessary poetic element, she thought. He would be unable to resist the obvious, horrible inversion she was offering him.

She reached out one gloved hand, and slapped the control panel. There was a hissing noise, and the inner door of the airlock slid open. With her other hand, she pulled Frogmore after her, stepping inside.

Now they were both in the airlock, the inner door sliding shut behind them. The design was strange, for the walls and bulkheads here were made of some kind of semi-transparent substance, so that she could see the whole, horrible battle unfolding around them.

Plasma leapt, laser beams slashed the void, and everywhere, everywhere the war raged in the terrible, silent stillness of space. For a moment she faltered, uncertain, unsure.

What if he didn't act as she anticipated? What if he simply let her die?

But with every second, more Matts died, more versions...

...and Charlotte realised it didn't matter.

At least she had tried.

"I'll keep the air," she told him. "Enjoy deep space, you bastard!"

She slapped a command console , and the outer airlock slid open.

There was the rushing of air, a tearing noise so loud she could hear nothing else.

There was a single, jarring moment when the escaping air tugged at them both.

Then the jewel at Frogmore's neck glimmered...

...And they were somewhere else.

❦ 33 ❦

"So...what do we do now?" asked Matt.

Around them, the bright emptiness of the Land Below Stories thrummed and shimmered. It was bright and friendly, and quite, quite empty.

Matt hadn't realised at first. He had been too busy being appalled to wonder very much about what the Munchers were up to, scooting in from every angle, grabbing piles of junk and of the Manure, and trundling off with it. He had been far to upset to worry what they were doing or if he should try and stop it.

Now, of course, he knew exactly what they had been doing.

They had been getting rid of everything Rosewater might want.

Getting rid of it, moving it away, so that Rosewater might erect his own kind of barrier.

"It's...a little like the Sheriffs' Quarantine,"said Ninian presently, sounding rather impressed.

He was walking in a circle around where they were standing, seeming to move no further than a few strides away.

"What?" asked Matt. "What do you mean? I can't see..."

And the trailed off, because he couldn't see much of *anything*.

Somehow, in the few moments since he had last been aware of a Muncher, everything had gone.

Everything.

Not just the piles of manure near where they were standing, not just the nearby piles of junk...but really everything. There was not anything to be seen in any direction, not even in the deep distance. The huge, hulking bookcase had gone, as had the ladder. Even EB's mound and tunnel seemed to have vanished.

"Oh, it's not *quite* the same," said Ninian. He stopped walking for a moment and looked thoughtful. "I can...almost *taste* the difference. There's a tang about this trick. It has something of that glamouring strangeness to it, something wild..."

He trailed off.

Matt let out a long breath. It was the sort of deep, well-controlled exhalation usually reserved for moments when what you really want to do is hit someone over the head with something heavy and satisfying.

"Can you please," he said in a carefully neutral voice, "refrain from admiring what that bastard has done? Perhaps we could concentrate instead on finding our way back to the woman I love? Preferably before she is disemboweled."

He glanced over at NotCharlotte, hoping she would catch his eye, hoping she might agree. But NotCharlotte wasn't looking at him. Instead, she stared thoughtfully into the distance, then got up and started walking in a little circle around him, also.

"He's not really a bastard," she said, still not looking at him. "You know, in all the time I've known Rosewater, he's never once turned his back on me when I've really needed him."

"Oh, is that so?" asked Matt sarcastically. "Well then, why didn't he just magic up a portal and zoom us through to the others? If he's like the - what? - the second most powerful being in the Universe? That's what he said! If he's so powerful, why doesn't he help us?"

Matt waited for Charlotte to answer him. Instead, she just kept walking round and round in circles. Every now and then, she crossed in front of Ninian, who had - annoyingly - also resumed walking.

"He said a few other things," said NotCharlotte. "He talked about quite a lot, really. About his Charter. About what he was allowed to do, and not do. About the Sheriffs, and what he thought of them."

"Yes, fine, okay," said Matt. "Perhaps he's not usually a bastard. Maybe he did go on about all that stuff. But what does it matter?"

No one answered him. There was a moment of stillness, and Matt found himself overcome pure unreasonable rage. He was here, waiting, wasting time, trying, *trying* to get to her...and these...these *idiots* were just *mucking about*.

"I said *answer* me!" he snarled, unable to keep his feelings in check any longer, and launching himself furiously towards Ninian, who happened to be passing in front of him at that moment.

Only Ninian *wasn't* passing in front of him. As soon as Matt moved, the dimensions of the space seemed to shift sickeningly. Suddenly, Ninian was floating high above. But he was standing quite unconcernedly in the nothingness, because it wasn't in fact nothingness, not thin air - just the same bright substance of which all of the ground here seemed to be made.

Matt felt his world spin vertiginously. He looked back,

and realised that the others were not walking in a circle either. Instead, they were both hanging above him, floating in the nothingness...only, they weren't above him *in the same direction*.

Because there were a lot more directions than there had any right to be.

Matt span around again, trying to force the dimensions of the place to make sense.

And kept on spinning.

There appeared to be far more degrees here than he was used to.

The world swam sickeningly, and Matt's eyes took the very sensible decision to close themselves without any kind of executive order coming down from the higher centres.

"Urgth," he said.

Things were better with his eyes shut. With his eyes shut, he could pretend that he was somewhere normal, as opposed to somewhere that seemed to have at least seventeen extra dimension, not to mention well over two thousand degrees in a circle.

"Very apt," said Ninian, sounding much closer than he had seemed a moment ago. "That is exactly how any normal being should be feeling, under the circumstances."

Matt took a steadying breath, then sighed.

"At the risk of sounding depressingly repetitive," he said, "where the hell are we? Now, I mean. As opposed to the weird, bright place where old stories go to be recycled," he added. "Which, I must admit, I suppose I was starting to take for granted."

"Oh, we are still in the Place Below Stories," said Ninian reassuringly.

"Oh," said Matt. "Good."

He thought about opening one eye again, then decided he wasn't quite reassured enough to do that.

"Then why has it gone so...so *gloopy*?" he asked instead.

"It is as I said," said Ninian, a hint of reproach in his voice. "This is like the Quarantine the Sheriff's made, it's similar in purpose. But the execution...well, it is quite spectacular, really. I must say, I've never seen anything like it."

"He's folded us in," said NotCharlotte. "That's why the dimensions seem wrong."

Matt's eyebrows rose.

He gazed out at the brightly distorted world. Now that he was beginning to understand what he was looking at, he wasn't so completely nauseated by it.

"He's...he's *broken* his own realm?" asked Matt. "Just to keep us here? That does sound a bit bastardly. You have to admit it."

"He hasn't broken his realm," said NotCharlotte, from the far side of the area of folded space. She wasn't looking at him, was apparently walking further and further away...and then abruptly appeared at his elbow.

"He's just *folded* it," she went on, sitting down on the other side of him. "Folded it back on itself, tucked the dimensions inwards. I'm quite sure his realm is perfectly safe."

"Indeed it is," said Ninian, seeming to step in front of Matt from at least five directions at the same time, and coalescing seamlessly into his usual shape and form. "I can feel it thrumming out there, not far away at all. The thickness of a shadow, I would say - though it is quite unreachable. A fine piece of work. Rosewater really is a craftsman. He has..."

But Ninian cut off abruptly.

Matt and NotCharlotte looked at one another.

"What is it?" Matt asked. "What's wrong?"

"Do you...do you see *that*?" Ninian asked.

Slowly, very slowly, his hand came up, so she was pointing away from them.

But there was nothing *to* see.

"See what?" said NotCharlotte. "It's all emptiness here. It's all - oh!"

For Ninian had moved so quickly, with such reptilian suddenness that the others both jumped in alarm.

But instead of moving in the direction he was pointing, Ninian jumped backwards...

...and flitted through the strange, kaleidoscopic dimensions of the place...

...and appeared opposite them, darting out of the folded space, hands outstretched, and grabbed - something.

"I have it," said Ninian.

He kept his hands closed tight as he walked back to them.

"What is it?" asked NotCharlotte

Matt was sweating. He could hear a faint buzzing emanating from the thing clutched in Ninian's hands.

But Ninian was shaking his head.

"Stories," he said. "Stories - that's the way you see things?"

He was looking at NotCharlotte, who shrugged, then nodded.

"That other thing you sense," he said. "That buzzing, throbbing thing. I think I know what it is."

"Have you worked something out?" asked Matt. He felt a faint stab of hope.

"I believe so, yes," said Ninian. "The Sheriffs work with Order, that is clear. But Rosewater is in the middle, so to speak. He does not restrict himself to one end of the spectrum. He works with the whole thing."

"Chaos," NotCharlotte said softly. "Rosewater has made this Quarantine out of Chaos."

As if the word itself had some power to unsettle, Matt found he was shivering. His mouth was suddenly dry. A wind blew, softly, strangely, in that empty place in which there was no other *where* for a wind to blow to or from.

Something stirred in him, something that was small and

delicate, and which he hardly dared to look at, in case it turned out not to be what he thought, after all.

Hope.

"Chaos?" Matt repeated softly. "What...what do you mean?"

"Chaos is the other prime force," said Ninian. "It is the other fundamental, the counterbalance. Without it, the Universe would be dry and perfect and quite, quite dead."

"And no story would ever exist," said NotCharlotte. "Stories balance between the two, you see. Between Order and Chaos. That's what EB used to say. He said that was how it worked, the Chaos Drive. By tapping into the Chaos, by using it as a fulcrum..."

"No wonder the Sheriffs hate it," said Matt. He sighed. "Bloody stories," he added.

"It does not matter how you frame it," said Ninian, helpfully. "Stories are just a paradigm, a reference point. The Bracken Court know that the Grand is balanced between these forces, too, though we have different names for them."

"Yes, but what does this *mean*," Matt wanted to know.

"In itself, who knows?" said Ninian. "It may mean nothing other than that Rosewater is powerful indeed. But that's *not* the only thing. There's also *this*."

He held up his cupped hands.

Then slowly, very slowly, he opened them.

Inside, there was a blackness.

Not just the absence of light and colour, not just something dark.

This was *black*, pure jet black, so black it was like a gap in the fabric of reality itself.

"Is that...what I think it is?" asked Charlotte.

"Perhaps," said Ninian. "I would even guess what you might call it, though I've seen one before, and I knew it by a different name."

"What is it?" asked Matt.

Ninian smiled at him, through rows of sharp black teeth.

"It's a Plot Hole," he said.

NotCharlotte was smiling.

"Rosewater *did* want to help us," she said. "He couldn't do it himself, because he can't take sides like that. He has to be seen as neutral. So he did this, instead. He put us here, in a fold of space woven through with Chaos, and left us the Plot Hole. It's perfect. He might as well have given us a portal opening to anywhere."

And there was that word again.

Chaos.

As NotCharlotte said it, Matt felt something throb in his chest.

It was good news, it was exciting, it was tremendous...

...But why did he feel so scared?

"That hole," said Matt, pointing to the ring of pure blackness that was now dripping from Ninian's outstretched hands, seeming to boil and run, enlarging quickly to something the rough size and shape of a doorway. "What...what does it do?"

"It's a passageway," said Ninian. "A way of linking different levels, different realities. It bridges places that would otherwise never meet."

Matt felt himself relaxing. Obviously, the Plot Hole would be enough. They would simply open a portal, that was all, a doorway. They would step out of this twist of space, and step into the place where his Charlotte would be waiting for him, and he would be just in time to save the day.

They didn't need to mess around with that Chaos stuff. They didn't need to even *think* of it.

But Ninian was shaking his head.

"Normally, yes, of course we would do that," he said. "But the Sheriffs have erected their Quarantine. It is a force made of pure Order. I do not think a Plot Hole would be allowed to exist in such a context."

NotCharlotte was nodding.

"So we're going to circumvent the Quarantine the only way that's possible " she said, and Matt felt his skin turn to ice. He knew what she was about to say.

He had known it, really, from the first moment he had heard that poisonous word.

She smiled at him, a happy, half-crazed smile.

"We're taking a trip through the Chaos," she said.

❧ 34 ❧

The void that had been ringing her lungs dry had gone.

Charlotte felt a wave of relief rush through her. There wasn't much that was more pleasing than the sudden realisation that your eyeballs *weren't* about to boil off into outer space, after all.

Then she caught sight of where she was, and the relief turned to elation.

The doorway.

The doorway she had been looking for.

The doorway through which she could see the machine. The simple metal box. The rows of flashing lights. The place where something was missing, a circular blank patch. She could feel waves of oily, dark power rolling off of the thing. It was intoxicating, like the smell of lightning in a thunderstorm.

It had worked! She had manipulated him, tricked him into taking her here, to the one place she was desperate to get to, the one place she had no way of finding herself.

The Heart of Frogmore. The device which made all his dark machinations possible.

What better way to get him to take her to the Heart, than to try to take him far away from it?

But there was no time to congratulate herself - she had to act right away!

And the door to the room was open! How lucky was that? She had been sure that Frogmore's servant had closed and locked the door, had been certain opening it would be a major obstacle.

She sprang towards the door, wondering what would be the quickest way to destroy the machine. She didn't have anything to hit it with, or any liquid to pour over the thing, which would have been her first choice. Then again, maybe she should simply fall on it and start ripping apart the lights with her bare hands? The box itself looked sturdy enough, but the lights and wires looked flimsy and vulnerable. She would fly at it, she would pull it apart, she would sit herself down and get to work...

...except the chair was full already.

Of course it was.

Where else would Philip Frogmore be sitting?

She barrelled in through the open doorway, careened wildly towards the machine And still she thought it might just work. She would slam into the machine, she would break it as it broke her body, and she didn't think for a moment that the price would be too high.

And then she stopped.

She didn't slow and slide. She didn't change her mind, or hesitate.

She simply stopped, hung in the air, not able to move a muscle, not even able to breath.

Philip Frogmore was staring up at her, eyes blazing scorn and amusement.

The jewel at his neck flared bright.

"You didn't really think that would work, did you?" he asked with quiet venom.

She tried to move her mouth, but there was nothing, not even a flicker.

An ache began to build in her chest.

"Oh, please," he said, languid in his chair. "You are not sly. You are not subtle. You have none of the qualities you would need to outwit me."

Charlotte's eyes bulged. The pain in her chest was building, a burning need to breath. But it was not so sharp as her anger, her sudden fury at Frogmore, at his words and at his actions, at everything he stood for.

In the distance, seeming to come from almost infinitely far away, Charlotte was dimly aware of a deep, dull, clanging noise.

Frogmore tilted his head, one eyebrow raised.

"What's that, my dear?" he asked. "You want to say something? How terribly rude of me. Please, feel free."

He waved a hand in her direction. The jewel at his neck glimmered, and the force that held her chest and mouth was suddenly gone.

Charlotte sucked down a lungful of air, then another.

She glared at him.

"I might not be sly," she told him. "Or terribly subtle, not compared to you. But that doesn't matter. Other things count."

The air around them shimmered. Far off, there was a percussive, pulsing noise. She didn't know what it meant, but it hardly seemed important right now.

"Count?" said Frogmore idly. He looked away, lifted the jewel from his neck, and held it for a moment. "Count in what way? In life? In the pursuit of happiness? As a way of convincing yourself that you are a good person?"

"All those things!" spat Charlotte. "Loyalty! And love! And...and doing what is best for everyone, even if it means the worse for you!"

"Ah, you mean *sacrifice*," said Frogmore. He laid the jewel down carefully, placing it into the small blank space in the machine. As he did so, all the lights that adorned the device shimmered bright. The smell of ozone grew stronger.

"Yes, sacrifice!" agreed Charlotte. "It doesn't matter if you stopped me, if you knew what I was trying to do. Sooner or later someone *will* beat you. They will do it despite any odds you can stack against them, because people are *good* because they will be willing to sacrifice everything, sacrifice themselves, just for the chance to take you down!"

"My dear," said Frogmore, stepping gracefully to his feet, "I am quite counting on it. Sacrifice is very important to me. But let us not talk of this now. It would be rude, what with our new guests arriving."

Charlotte felt herself twisted around, shoved by the same force that held her body tight.

She was just in time to see the corridor outside dissolve in a blast of plasma.

❦ 35 ❦

What was left of the rooms they moved through looked very much like an approximation of hell. King Headfrog rather liked it.

The heavy plasma weapons of his guard worked wonders like that. They had made short work of the thick metal bulkheads, of the automated lasers and other defences offered by this strange vessel. Globs of red-golden metal dripped and pooled from the half-devoured superstructure of the vast machine.

He swept forward grandly, flanked on either side by his elite combat frogs, sleek, well-muscled warriors who embodied every virtue of his noble race. They did not look like mere thugs - not like that traitorous idiot Glob - no, these were what *real* frogs looked like. They moved like dancers, stepping lightly, dangerously through the melted, flaring wreckage.

There was nothing to fear at all from that stupid man, that *Prophet,* who had pretended to offer so much, and who had then attempted to betray him so completely.

Nothing to fear at all, he told himself.

Yet as they swept deeper into the curious craft, as they went past floor after floor filled with a bewildering mixture of horrible-looking weapons, he began to feel...uncertain.

It was not a conscious decision, but King Headfrog found that he was lagging further and further behind, letting his elite combat Frogs lead.

Which was only wise and just, of course.

After all, he was the King. It would not do for him to appear too eager, when he swept down like lightning and made the killing blow. No, it would be far more dignified to stay just a little back, to appear a few moments after his troops, just in time to see the look of astonishment sweep across the Prophet's face, that moment when he realised he had lost...

"Realised you'll be safer back here with us?"

The annoyingly debonaire voice cut through his thoughts like a chainsaw. King Headfrog scowled at EB. The feline was manacled and chained, was flanked on either side by two especially dark-eyed elite combat frogs. King Headfrog thought the blasted creature should at least have the decency to look cowed.

But he didn't. Not a bit of it. He walked as if the chains were marks of office.

"Shut up," snapped King Headfrog.

EB gave a little shrug.

"I don't blame you," he said amicably. "Whatever device this guy has, it has to be something pretty special. To go up against the Chaos Drive, to reshape reality like this...well, who knows what you'll find when you finally get to him. Which I am sure you will do eventually," he added after a moment's pause, with a perfectly indifferent yawn.

"Oh, we will find him soon, you can be sure of it," snapped King Headfrog. He put a hand to his chest, felt the reassuring pulse of the Chaos Drive. He had felt the strange, hostile pressure of this reality from the moment they had boarded. The feline was right, though he was loath to admit it. Whatever force the Prophet possessed, it was potent. He could feel it working against the power of the Chaos Drive, smothering it, pushing it down. Every little reshaping of reality he made here was harder. Not impossible, no, just - just more *expensive*.

"Oh, I *am* sure," said EB. "He wants to see you again. Why else would he have let us board?"

"He knows *nothing* of our coming," King Headfrog snarled. "Don't you think I saw to that?"

He opened his jerkin a little, just enough for the faintest tracery of light to spill out. It was like the sun peeking from behind a cloud. The raw potency of the Chaos Drive was something wonderful.

"I can *feel* where he is," went on King Headfrog. "I can feel him lurking at the rotten heart of this ship, like a worm in a withering apple. We will be on him soon."

EB smiled thinly.

"You sound like a mouse," he sighed, "rejoicing over the lump of cheese he has found, discarded carelessly on a spike, wondering idly what all the coils and springs are for."

Then the voice of his captain crackled in King Headfrog's earpiece.

"Sir," said the captain. "We are outside the chamber. We can see the target. Do you want us to eliminate?"

"No," said King Headfrog. "I want to enjoy this. Light up the corridor. Use the heavy plasma weapons again, as you did to break us in. Be careful not to hit him...but tear the corridor outside to pieces."

There was a half-second of silence...then the world lit up in a fury of light and heat and sound. A hot wind blew back at him, superheated air expanding from the site of the devastation. King Headfrog swept it aside with a flick of his mind, the Chaos Drive pulsing at his breast.

And then it was done, the weaponry turned off, and King Headfrog was gazing hungrily into the abraded ruin at the heart of The Prophet's ship.

The whole area had been swept clean. Monitors, doors, walls even - it was all gone, leaving only the floor and ceiling, creaking ominously as they cooled.

King Headfrog smiled. He felt every trace of doubt swept aside. The Prophet - *Philip Frogmore* - could not hope to stand against his might! How could he have ever let himself feel afraid? No, he had no business feeling afraid. This was his moment. And he would enjoy it.

He strode forward, pulses of pure energy flickering from the Chaos Drive, cooling the floor as he strode along it, the abused metal creaking.

He was pleased to see his orders had been executed well. Not even a scotch mark showed on the door, amid the wreck and ruin of the surrounding structures.

He caught a curious flashing light, reflected in the margins of the room. He saw a leg floating in the air, and thought for a moment that the Prophet had much more shapely ankles than he remembered.

Then he realised it wasn't the Prophet.

It was *her*. The alien female. One of the ghastly little creatures that had fled from him back on Froghearth, that had been so irksome. His smile broadened. Oh, this would be delicious.

He was dimly aware of an unexpected silence behind him. A small part of his mind wondered what his elite combat Frogs were doing, and why they weren't following as close on his tail as usual. But he didn't really care. He felt the power of the Chaos Drive pulsing at his breast. Nothing could harm him here. His power was complete.

The alien female was hanging in the air. As he watched, she rotated fully to face him. He caught the fear in her eyes.

Then King Headfrog saw him.

The Prophet.

Philip Frogmore.

The tall, thin man sat languidly. He had an infuriating expression on his face, as if he had summoned King Headfrog, and was having the good grace to pretend not to be annoyed at how late he was.

"Prophet," King Headfrog forced himself to utter the sobriquet in a cold, disinterested voice. "So nice to see you again. You've been quite the annoyance. You've almost made me stretch myself."

But to King Headfrog's annoyance, The Prophet didn't so much as quiver. Instead, he gave a thin smile.

"Ah, 127," said Philip Frogmore. "So nice of you to join us."

There was a moment of stunned silence.

He had *dared*! The man had *dared* to call him by his old number! What cheek! What gall! What...what...

But words failed him. His outrage was too keen, and without realising it, without stopping to consider what he was doing, King Headfrog put a hand into his pocket, and withdrew the Chaos Drive.

It was incandescent.

It was a shimmering thing of endless, boundless beauty - so bright it hurt to look upon, so wonderful it hurt to look away.

King Headfrog raised it high, and felt a well of endless power line up beneath his very soul.

"You do *not* address me like that," he said simply. All thought of restraint was now forgotten.

King Headfrog felt his mind kissing against the endless

potency of the Chaos Drive. Then he directed a stream of influence towards his enemy, and let out a scream.

He didn't seek to direct the flow of influence, to shape reality in any set way. Instead, he let the pulsing heart of the machine darken beautifully, and a beam of pure UnTelling shot forth.

He wouldn't alter the Prophet, wouldn't bind him hand and foot, wouldn't strip him of his skin or take his eyes.

He was too angry for that, too angry by far.

No, he would simply wipe him clean.

Write him out of this reality.

The beam of unTelling shot out of the Chaos Drive, darting towards Philip Frogmore like quicksilver, faster than thought.

It hit something.

Something hard and stern and unspeakably, unutterably awful.

There was a moment of suspended time, as King Head-frog felt his blast flutter against something far more powerful, feebly, like a small heart bleeding out.

Then with a sound like the shattering of worlds, his hold on the Chaos Drive was broken.

❧ 36 ❧

Charlotte should hate him, she knew. But the creature looked so sad and pathetic now, so bereaved, it was difficult to not feel a little pity, too.

King Headfrog was a king no longer.

Philip Frogmore had undone it with a thought. Charlotte had caught the glimmering of the jewel that was the heart of his device, and those finely tailored clothes were siphoned away, filtering into themselves and emerging as torn, dirty rags.

Head Frog 127 looked around, bleary eyes full of horror.

"What...how..." he stumbled, unable to comprehend what had happened.

"Ah, 127, so nice to have you back in your place," said Philip Frogmore. "Good of you to bring me the little toy. Though you will have to have it back before long."

Head Frog 127 barely dared to breath.

"...back?" he said, his voice so quiet Charlotte could hardly hear him.

Philip Frogmore held the Chaos Drive up, as if examining

an interesting piece of jewellery. The brilliant, glimmering intensity of the thing had faded to almost nothing. Only a faint reddish pulse showed through.

"Fascinating," he said at last. "More or less what I had been expecting, from everything I'd felt. Quite powerful, really."

Then he tossed the Chaos Drive idly in the air and caught it again, as if it were a trinket from a cracker.

"Nothing compared to mine, of course," went on Frogmore, with a quick, oily smile. "Which I knew from the start. Then again, it didn't have to be anywhere near as powerful. Just powerful enough to make the conflict possible. To make the danger real. To give a cause in which my troops would be able to sacrifice themselves heroically..."

There was a clattering from beyond the room, and a moment later a group of wicked-looking, hard-eyed frogs came into view. They held an assortment of weapons, varied and menacing and horrible. And in their midst walked EB.

She recognised him at once, even though they had never met in the flesh. He was as lithe and strangely handsome as he had been in her vision. But though he walked with unconcern, head unbowed, Charlotte sensed a weariness in him; and when their eyes met, she saw sadness there, defeat.

And then she understood.

They had lost.

For all her efforts, all her desperate, foolish plans to fight back and win the day - they had lost.

They had lost from the start. Everything had been going according to Frogmore's plan, from the very beginning.

Her eyes darted back to Head Frog 127. There was a momentary hope in his face, a sudden, stupid dream that his guards had come to protect him, to win him back his device and his power.

They had not.

"The prisoners are secure, my liege," said the captain, addressing Frogmore.

"Oh, good," said Philip Frogmore. He smiled thinly at EB. EB did not smile back.

"So nice to see you again, my feline friend," said Philip Frogmore. "Where was it again? That place I nearly had you? Last time I got *very* close."

"Flibbidiwibbit," said EB scornfully. "You never nearly had me."

"No?" said Frogmore. "Perhaps you didn't realise it, then. But I've been close before, very close. This chase has gone on much longer than I had planned. You've thwarted me before; you didn't manage it this time."

"This time's not over yet," said EB evenly.

"But it is, I'm afraid," said Frogmore. He waved a hand...

...the banks of lights at his desk glowed out, momentarily brighter than anything, brighter than the Chaos Drive had been at its zenith...

...and the wreckage caused by King Headfrog's attack was undone.

They stood now in a vast, open hanger, smart and ornate and perfect. Frogmore sat at his desk still, flashing lights and central jewel, but there were no surrounding walls, and he gestured up at a thousand screens, blazing in ultra high-definition.

And on the screens was - stillness.

Silence.

Ships hanging in the void. Manticores and unicorns and Matts beyond number, stretching into the far distance - and arrayed against them, the equally vast might of the frogs.

Head Frog 127 was looking from screen to screen.

He looked defeated.

"My fleet is as mighty as yours," he said at last, trying to force some certainty into his voice.

"Oh, but it is," agreed Philip Frogmore. "Quite completely. Quite exactly. They are balanced. Perfectly."

Head Frog 127 looked confused.

"You might win, Prophet," he said at last. "But it will only be because you cheated. Because you stole my prize, snatched it from me. Give me back the Chaos Drive, and I will show you what frogs are really made of!"

Philip Frogmore smiled, a smile that was at once sharp and nasty, but also completely, utterly sincere.

"I do hope you will," Frogmore said. "Not that I am so very interested in what Frogs are made of. But it would be splendid to see what all *my* troops are made of."

He flashed a triumphant look at Charlotte. A horrible thought was occurring to her.

He's not going to do it, she told herself. *Of course he's not. He's won, he defeated that horrid little Frog. He's not going to...*

"Why don't you show me?" said Philip Frogmore.

He flicked his thumb.

The Chaos Drive sailed up into the air, described a small arc...

...and landed in Head Frog 127's outstretched hand.

A light sprang up from the Chaos Drive, particles of luminescent dust, like a billion tiny stars, an aurora of a galaxy...

...a flash, vivid purple and green...

...and King Headfrog was back, no snivelling, wretched frog, but a king returning rightfully to his throne.

He stood before them, a little broader and more muscular than Charlotte had remembered. She realised he must be feeling insecure.

"Oh, I *will*," promised King Headfrog. "I will. You can be sure of..."

But he didn't complete the sentence.

Charlotte felt the pulse of command wash out from King

Headfrog, a nearly-physical thing, a wave of pure, hateful influence.

And on the monitors, the war was once again joined.

Unicorns charged forward, impaling spaceships.

Spaceships banked wildly, darting beams of light into Frogmore's army of slaves.

And everywhere, everywhere she looked - Matts died.

Charlotte wanted to look away. She wanted to scream.

But she could not shut her eyes, and no scream would come.

She felt her gorge rising.

And then something caught her eye.

She glanced towards EB, where he stood, forgotten for the moment.

No one apart from Charlotte was watching him They were all far too consumed by the carnage playing out on the screens.

But EB wasn't watching the screens.

He was watching something else.

Then she realised what it was that had caught her eye.

It was EB's hair, his beautiful black fur. It was standing on end.

He looked like he had walked into a thunderstorm, like he was standing beneath the biggest electromagnet ever made.

But he didn't look scared.

His eyes were fixed on a portion of seemingly empty space, a little way behind the others.

Charlotte's eyes darted to the place EB was staring, then back to EB, then to the empty space again.

Only it wasn't *quite* empty.

There was something wrong with it, something strange. The colours were...wobbly.

She looked harder.

It wasn't just the colours now. It was the lines that defined the portions of the room, it was the solidity of the space itself.

It was vibrating, sure and steady.

And it was getting more powerful.

A sudden, stupid hope filled her, something she could not explain to herself or to anyone, an elation, blind, unreasoning.

She looked back to EB, and now he looked at her, and she felt an understand spring suddenly between them.

EB gave her a small, secret smile.

Then he mouthed something silently at her.

Be ready.

❧ 37 ❧

Inside the bubble, things made sense.

Don't look beyond. Don't look outside. Definitely don't let yourself fall outside.

That was what Matt told himself.

The problem was, that to not look out was completely impossible.

They crouched in a shell of contained normality - the little piece of balanced reality which they had brought with them, and in which they now huddled, staring out at the awful beauty of the Chaos.

It was a maelstrom.

The space through which they were moving was not a space, any more than it was a sound or a smell, a colour or a liquid, even a dimension, nor any type of substance that fell inside the categorisable order of things.

Matt screamed, and the scream became a flock of small white birds which were also an echo of Sundays from his childhood in England, and also something falling and what it felt like to fall and the colour something had when it dropped, and Matt felt his mind breaking under the strain of ecstatic discombobulation, and longed for it to stop, and longed for it to break at the same moment, which it did, exploding into a patchwork quilt of a thousand sounds no one had ever heard before which all tasted unaccountably of tulips, and he leant out to smell them, leant to breath in the everlasting scent of springtime in flower, and and and...

...and a hand was on his neck. He was being pulled back inside the bubble.

He gasped. He had been about to fall out, and hadn't even realised.

"Look at me!" NotCharlotte commanded, voice urgent, blue eyes glinting like tiny shards of ice.

Matt tried to do what she said, tried to keep his eyes fixed on her. But it was so difficult. He wanted more than anything to turn, to let himself dissolve into the wonderful, messy unknowing of the Chaos...

"I do advise holding on," said Ninian mildly, and then his long, quick fingers were encircling Matt's neck from the other side.

There was a moment of balancing. Matt felt that he still might do it: tip back into the Chaos and let himself dissolve in the endless bubbling substance from which the Universe was made...

Matt closed his eyes, and pictured her face.

No. Not today. He would not let go...

And then the crisis was past, and Matt opened his eyes.

Ninian's hand slid away, but NotCharlotte kept hers on his neck, massaging it gently.

Matt was thankful for it. This was so strange, so unbearably, impossibly alien.

It was like sliding through a scream as big as everything.

"How...How much longer?" he managed to gasp.

"Not much further," NotCharlotte told him. "Ninian, can you hold the bubble?"

Matt wished very much that he could. The only reason they had survived so far - in this awful rush of Chaos-space, this broiling, liminal place through which Charlotte was leading them - the only reason they hadn't boiled away to nothing, was the structure of normal space that Ninian had erected around them.

"Time is strange here," said Ninian, a little reproachfully. "In theory, I should be able to hold the structure until last Tuesday. Which might sound alarming, but I assure you that hasn't happened yet."

Matt felt waves of nausea rolling up. The thought of this bubble collapsing was sickening.

"That is...singularly unhelpful," said NotCharlotte dryly. She wasn't looking at Ninian though, nor really fully concentrating on him.

Instead, she was peering out into the flashing hyper-ways of the endless Chaos, steering them, straining forward, searching for...

"There!" she burst out suddenly. "I can *feel* them! I can feel..."

And then she faltered, and her smile swam away.

"I can feel EB," she said. "But Matt...*my* Matt..."

She trailed off.

"I'm sure he will be there..." Matt started to say.

But at that moment, the bubble slammed into something as hard and unforgiving as pavement.

There was a reeling sensation, a bouncing, a turning back, as if the Chaos itself was clutching at them, jealous, unwilling to let them go.

NotCharlotte snarled, her jaw set and eyes blazing.

"No - you - *don't*!" she growled

There was a moment of suspension, and Matt felt as if he were a sweet-meat, something infinitely small caught and balanced between two forces that were inestimably vast.

Then NotCharlotte won, and the Chaos let them go.

They slid out of Chaos-space, reality sucking back in around them until they stood once more on firm ground. Ninian gave a sigh, and Matt felt the ghost-echo of the bubble that had kept them safe drifting away like pollen on a breeze.

Elation filled him.

They had done it! They had got through the Chaos, and out the other side! They were *here*...

...And then he saw where *here* was, and felt the bottom drop out of his world.

They were in large, wide deck, filled with monitors showing scenes of vicious space combat. He couldn't help but notice in passing that several of the screens showed close-up shots of people who looked uncannily like him. Some of them were riding on unicorns, which was rather strange.

What was more unsettling was that they kept dying.

Some were blasted by lasers, some were blown to smithereens, some were ejected from their dying unicorns, only to die themselves in the unforgiving vacuum of space.

The next thing he noticed was that the room, though huge, was not empty.

There were lots of people here, many of whom looked both exceedingly ugly, and horribly, proficiently violent.

They also, he could not help but notice, appeared to be frogs.

Bipedal, well muscled frogs, with great soggy lips and deadly yellow eyes.

And they were all armed to their back teeth.

Then he noticed that they were not all frogs, after all.

There was a tall, supercilious man there, too. He was the only one sitting down, but this gave an impression not of subservience, but of nonchalant dominance, like a king on his throne - only this throne was simply a chair made of moulded black plastic, and set before a desk of odd, flickering lights.

There was a cat there, too.

A bipedal cat with black fur and quick, intelligent eyes. The cat was the only one looking at them.

EB.

And then, before he could make sense of any of it, he realised that EB *wasn't* the only one looking at him.

There was a girl there, too.

A woman.

She had brown hair and beautiful brown eyes, and she was floating in the air just behind the others.

Matt felt a sob rising in his chest, an elation, an almost unbearable need to cry.

It was Charlotte.

The real Charlotte, *his* Charlotte.

The one he had been looking for since all this madness began.

Their eyes locked on one another, fierce, unbelieving.

He opened his mouth to shout to her, to tell her how much he loved her, how he had missed her.

And at that moment, one of the frogs - taller and dressed more grandly than the others - turned and caught sight of Matt and his friends, and all hell broke loose.

❈ 38 ❈

King Headfrog saw the male alien, and knew at
once that he had been betrayed.

The Prophet had tried to trick him, yet again.

It was almost enough to make him smile.

The waiting was over. It was time to act.

He peeled his awareness away from the war being waged
outside the ship. The war *inside* was much more important.

At the same moment, he channelled every ounce of influence through the Chaos Drive. He knew now that the
Prophet was stronger, far stronger. Whatever device it was
that he had, it far exceeded the might of the Chaos Drive.
There was no hope of beating the Prophet head-on.

No, his only hope lay in striking first.

The command he sent alerted his elite close-combat frogs
that they were needed. This was swiftly followed up by a
shield of protective force that hazed the air around them. He
wasn't sure how long it would work, but hopefully it would
keep the Prophet from getting at his frogs, at least for a few
seconds. A few seconds might be all it took.

Then King Headfrog was spinning around, bringing his own ornate blaster up.

To his delight, he had a clear shot. He could see that Frogmore hadn't yet noticed what was going on. He still had a lazy, supercilious look on his face. King Headfrog had the man in his sights. His finger tightened on the trigger, trembling.

But he did not pull it.

A moment's confusion ran through him. He could not stop his eyes shifting, moving back to the human that had given him so much trouble.

Only he didn't look quite right. He looked softer, somehow - though there was clearly something hard in his eyes. King Headfrog still had time to shoot Frogmore. His eyes had moved, but not the gun,

An anger was rising in him, hot as molten iron. The human.

Yes, the creature had given him such a horrible slip. This one deserved punishing.

Even though he knew it was the wrong decision, a strategic mistake, he couldn't help himself.

The gun slipped to one side, and now King Headfrog had the human male in his sights.

He squeezed the trigger.

39

Charlotte saw him.

Matt. Her Matt.

He had arrived, he had come for her. He had...

...he had another Charlotte.

The woman looked quite like her, Charlotte thought. The eyes were different, the stance was more confident, but still...

A pang of jealousy shot through her, sharp and hard, quite unfair and absolutely irresistible.

Here she was, being suspended in mid-air by the nefarious will of a vile pan-narrative villain, having been chased and terrorised, nearly killed more times than she could count...and all the while, Matt was galavanting around with some other version of her! It was enough to make her scream.

And to her surprise, she found that she could.

Whether it was because Frogmore was too busy directing the war outside, or if he had simply grown complacent, it was impossible to tell. Either way, Charlotte realised that her voice was hers once more.

She opened her mouth to tell Matt what an idiot he was...and she saw the blaster.

King Headfrog was pointing it straight at Matt.

Matt had seen the gun. So had the others who had appeared with him. But no one could do anything about it. Everything was happening in slow motion.

Matt was about to die.

Charlotte screamed.

It was a good scream. It was wild and frightened and frightening. It made everyone jump.

It also alerted Philip Frogmore to what was going on.

Then everything happened at once.

King Headfrog fired his weapon. But at the last moment, he jerked it back towards Frogmore.

Frogmore was leaping to his feet, the jewel from his device once again in his hand. It flared, and a shield of pure influence gleamed around him. The jolt of light from King Headfrog's weapon leapt into the shield, and was transformed into a small explosion of colourful butterflies. They flapped around the scene, adding to the chaos.

The Chaos.

Even as Charlotte thought the word, she felt her eyes drawn. Back to Matt, and past him, past his strange companions - to a place that was...*different.*

The air there was hazing. The very substance of space seemed to bubble and writhe. It made her eyes sore just to look at it...but it was beautiful, too.

They had gotten here through that place, somehow. She knew it instinctively. Just as instinctively, she knew that it was dangerous, horribly dangerous.

Then other weapons started to flare, faster than she could count, faster than she could make sense of.

The Frogs were fighting one another. She saw one huge brute, spiked shoulder pads and a wicked sword of fizzling light, turn towards King Headfrog, a brilliant, empty light in his eyes. She could feel the waves of influence dancing off of

Frogmore, could sense the invisible battle of wills being waged.

A moment before the brutish frog could run King Head-frog through, another huge fighter leapt on him, bearing him down. There were shouts and screams; the discharging of blasters and the clash of hand weapons, and the air was full of the scent of burning frog.

Then Matt and his friends were charging in to the fray. She didn't know why, it was a foolish thing to do, none of them looked anything like fighters - except maybe the other version of herself, she admitted grudgingly. She couldn't even see any weapons.

But that didn't stop them. They came on, and then -

- and then Charlotte realised they weren't trying to fight, they were trying to get to her.

To rescue her.

She realised with sudden hope that it might work - the others were too distracted, too busy fighting one another! They had forgotten about her, both King Headfrog and Philip Frogmore.

Matt was almost at her. Their hands reached for one another...

...and with a silent explosion, Frogmore won.

The pulse of power he sent out from his own device was like a detonation.

Charlotte felt it cut through the ribbons of influence from the Chaos Drive, leaving them in tatters.

Matt slammed straight into a wall of invisible force. It separated them.

Charlotte turned to glare at Frogmore, who stood just a few inches away. He gave her a sweet smile.

In the silence that remained, Charlotte saw that all the elite combat frogs had been won over. They stood now in a grim half-circle around their King, fingers on weapons, ready to obliterate him.

Charlotte turned back to Matt. He was so close.

She strained again, but the barrier between them was thick and cold, like a slab of invisible ice. There was no hope of getting past it. Frogmore was throwing a huge amount of influence in that direction, keeping them apart.

She leant back, muscles giving up, going slack...

...and her body rocked back in the other direction, moving freely towards Frogmore.

The barrier in that direction had gone. Frogmore must have strengthened it one side, at the expense of weakening it at the other.

She stared at Frogmore, wondering if he had seen, if he had realised.

But Frogmore was not looking at her.

All his attention now was focussed on King Headfrog.

"Really, 127, when will you learn?" said Frogmore. His voice sounded bored, but Charlotte could feel the hate vibrating just beneath the surface. Philip Frogmore had not appreciated the surprise attack. He had only just won, she realised.

"I am just better than you, don't you see?" went on Frogmore. "I gave you a chance to serve me, to do willingly what I require of you. But it seems I will need to alter you more fundamentally. It isn't ideal, but then, you have already helped me accomplish much. We have wiped a great many Matts out already. When we begin again, it won't take us long to delete the ones that remain."

With the final words, he shot a horrible wet smile past Charlotte, straight at Matt.

Her Matt.

The Matt she loved, the Matt who she had been trying to get back to, who had come to find her.

And Frogmore was talking of killing him as lightly as he might talk about eating a trout for supper.

Charlotte snapped.

Her leg snapped out. It passed through the air, unimpeded by any form of barrier from Frogmore. Her foot sailed straight past his groin (which was a tempting target) and missed his face (which she told herself she would get next, if given another chance), and struck directly in the place she was aiming.

His hand.

His long, effeminate hand.

The hand which held the jewel.

Philip Frogmore gave a yelp.

His hand went up...and the jewel was lost.

It flew into the air, up and away, hit the floor and bounced off down a corridor.

Philip Frogmore stared at her, a mixture of unbelieving hurt and bottomless hate in his eyes.

And then the invisible force that had held her aloft was gone, and Charlotte was on him.

Her fist connected with his nose, with a satisfying wet noise. She bore him to the ground, and Frogmore went down as if he were made of mud.

He was not used to fighting, she realised. How long had it been, she wondered, since he had had to do anything himself, without the boundless power of his own machine?

She grinned down at him, a wild, terrifying smile, a smile of victory.

"How - do - you - like - *that*?" she asked.

But she didn't have a chance to get an answer, because at that moment the world exploded again.

❧ 40 ❧

Matt saw Charlotte bear the tall man to the ground, and a moment later he felt the barrier that had held him dissolve.

He was dimly aware of shouts and cries from both his companions and from the awful looking frog-creatures, but he had no time for them. He saw Charlotte strike the man, once, twice, and again, and was amazed by the sheer strength in her arms, by the fury of her blows.

That was *Charlotte*.

That was *his wife*.

The pride that filled him was so large, there was no room for anything else, not fear, not anger, nothing at all.

He looked back over his shoulder, a huge, grin on his face, wanting to share the moment with his companions.

And the grin died on his face.

Ninian and NotCharlotte were being squeezed together, compressed by an invisible force. But though he couldn't see the force, he could see clearly where it was coming from.

The leader of the frogs, the one who a moment ago had been so clearly defeated, now stood proud. In his hand was a device which had to be the Chaos Drive, a swirling, glimmering thing.

He tried to say something, to shout a warning to Charlotte, but there was no time.

The creature who held the Chaos Drive glared at him. His eyes were baleful, a force of sheer hate. Matt felt taken aback by that hate. The creature didn't know him, had never seen him before...or had he? The thought flashed through Matt's mind that maybe, just maybe the other version of him had been playing havoc with this frog in some way.

Good, he thought.

He didn't like to judge books by covers, but if this horrible frog-creature had been a book, he would have been horrible and gnarly and bound in human skin.

The frog raised his gun, and fired.

But not at Matt.

Instead the frog pointed the weapon at Charlotte.

His Charlotte.

There was no time to think. Matt just moved, muscles springing, body hurling itself through the air instinctively.

The bolt of energy struck him in the side in mid-leap, sending him spinning. The pain was intense, like nothing he had ever imagined. It was like being boiled and frozen and beaten, all rolled into one.

But Matt would have gladly gone through it ten times - or a thousand - if that was what it took. He didn't care about the pain, because - even as he was knocked from his feet - he understood that the bolt was meant for Charlotte, would have hit her squarely in the neck if he hadn't gotten in the way.

He whipped around, his body flipped by the energy weapon as easily as if he were a kitten. The back of Charlotte's head spun into view. He just had time to realise what was happening, and then their heads connected.

Hard.

It was like smashing into a brick wall.

She grunted and fell forward, and Matt went sprawling on top of her.

The world swam crazily about him, consciousness flickering, on the verge of fading out.

Through the dim haze of pain, he was aware of the tall man - Frogmore, was it? - scrambling back and away, getting to his feet and dashing off.

He knew that he should run after him, that he should not let the man get away. But his body didn't seem to be working properly. There was a great numbness in his side now, worse by far than the pain, and his fingers and feet - even his lips - felt strange. He couldn't control them properly. The smell of scorching meat was on the air, and it took him half a moment to realise it was the smell of his own burnt flesh.

Then another shape barrelled over him. A sleek shape with dark fur, humanoid but infinitely more supple and full of grace than any human Matt had ever met or could even imagine.

EB.

The feline landed, and turned his momentum into a roll - not a moment too soon, for the whine of a blaster was in the air again, and more energy bolts shot past Matt, grazing the ground where EB had been a moment before.

"Come back, damn you!" The frog-creature cried. Matt looked at him, and saw he was on the verge of setting out in pursuit. But then the frog King hesitated, glancing from the tangle of Matt's captured friends, back to Matt, then to Charlotte, and finally to the now-deserted corridor down which EB had sprinted, in pursuit of Frogmore.

Then he turned back to Matt. He smiled.

The ugly frog gestured, and Matt found himself tugged

irresistibly across the chamber, thrust into the tight-held ball of his companions.

His vision was starting to go grey at the edges. Thoughts were coming more sluggishly.

He knew it was important to get free, he knew that this was bad.

But it didn't seem quite so urgent, somehow.

He stopped struggling. It wasn't doing any good.

Slowly, gently, Matt's vision dimmed to black.

✾ 41 ✾

King Headfrog knew he should just end it quickly, but that was against his nature.

He enjoyed the finer things in life - and to him, the finer things included revelling in the torment of those who had opposed him.

Like these horrible aliens. Like their horrible companions.

He looked at them now, the three humans and the hideous tall creature. He was squeezing them into a tight, tangled knot. The way their limbs interlaced, the way their bodies creaked and strained...it was pleasing.

"You see?" he said. "There's no getting away from me. Not with this."

He tossed the Chaos Drive up into the air and caught it again. It sparkled magnificently, luminescent threads and embers trailing in the air. He felt the power of the thing pulsing out at him, a dark heart he could not see. It was intoxicating.

King Headfrog moved closer, stepping over the corpse of one of his elite close combat Frogs. It was a shame they had all died. Some of them had proven exceedingly loyal. The way they had killed and died for him was almost touching. He made a mental note to punish Philip Frogmore for this additional insult. First he would kill these enemies...then he would hunt down the Prophet.

"It's not yours," said one of the humans. Her voice was icy cold. It was the female alien - one of them, rather, as he noticed without much surprise that the two human females looked quite similar. Humans tended to look the same to him.

"Really?" he asked her disdainfully. "Then who does it belong to?"

"Me," the alien rejoined. She had quite startling blue eyes, King Headfrog noticed. Those eyes might almost be pretty, if the rest of her head wasn't so hideously un-froggish. "You stole it."

"My dear, I didn't *steal* it," King Headfrog corrected her. "I merely liberated it. It was so sick of being bound to you, you and that...other one. It came to me with such joy. It knew a *real* master when it felt one."

King Headfrog watched as the alien snarled, tried to wrench herself free of his influence - but to no avail. He held her tight with the merest flick of his mind. She would never get free.

He gave a snort, and tossed the Chaos Drive into the air again...

...and staggered, as a wave of influence whipped out of the alien, raking the air between them, grasping hungrily for the Chaos Drive, so that it hung in mid air, caught for a moment in perfect balance between them.

The blue-eyed alien screamed.

"It - is - not - *yours*!"

The Chaos Drive wobbled, moved towards her....

Then King Headfrog snarled. He had let her live too long. He would not make such a mistake again.

He focussed his will, reached out for the Chaos Drive, and *pulled*.

The orb of light trembled in the air between them, then slowly, inexorably it moved towards him.

He could feel her influence failing as he drew the thing back. It felt beautiful, like ripping her fingers one by one off a high ledge from which she dangled.

The alien screamed. He took pleasure in it.

Then her influence was broken. The Chaos Drive snapped into his hand.

King Headfrog grinned. He had broken out in a cold sweat, but the struggle had been good for him. His blood was up. He felt alive.

For a moment, he wondered if he should simply take the humans prisoner, take them back to Froghearth, to enjoy at his leisure.

But, no.

That would be foolish. He had already indulged himself too much.

They would simply have to die, now, with no further spectacle.

It was a shame. He enjoyed spectacle, especially when it was happening sharply to someone else.

He gave a sad smile.

"Well, that will have to do," he told her. "I would say this isn't personal and that you shouldn't take offence. But it is. And you should."

He lifted the Chaos Drive, and fed orders to the thing. It began to pulse ominously, preparing a killing blow.

"Goodbye," he said.

Then he struck.

❧ 42 ❧

Charlotte saw the Chaos Drive fill with light. A terrible sound was on the air, a bitter howling that hurt her ears.

She saw the other Charlotte grit her teeth, gather herself, preparing to try again.

Charlotte understood what was happening. She could sense the back-and-forth pull of influence. She had felt it before, dimly, when she had been fleeing with NotMatt, when she had sensed this vile frog-creature rip the power away from him. Now it was a thickness in her mind, something thrumming on the very edge of the visible world.

But she knew it was hopeless. NotCharlotte was not strong enough.

A light kindled in the Chaos Drive, bright and deadly. It was painful to look at. Charlotte turned away...and there was Matt. He stared into her eyes. He looked so sad, broken...

It was so unfair. To have been separated, and to have been looking so desperately...and then to find each other, only to be killed a moment later, splatted by a ludicrous tyrannical frog, before they even had time to properly say hello...

She reached out, forcing her hand agains the web of influence that bound her, and took Matt's hand in hers...

...and a jolt of power shot out.

It was like a fresh wind, blowing from a happy place.

It was like hope.

Not understanding quite what she was doing, Charlotte reached her other hand towards NotCharlotte.

The blue-eyed version of herself looked puzzled for a moment...then she held out her own hand, and their fingers touched, intwining.

A power swelled within them.

And Charlotte was not just Charlotte anymore.

She was...more.

She was Matt. She felt the ache in his heart, and the loneliness, and the fear. She could see out of his eyes, and - with a spiralling sense of vertigo - she realised that she was watching herself, seeing her as he saw her.

She looked bruised, and angry, and hurt. She was crumpled and dirty, and looked more tired that she had thought possible.

But she was beautiful, too.

She had never imagined that she was so beautiful.

The world swam.

She was herself and she was him, and she was NotCharlotte, too.

And she understood what she - they - had to do.

Their minds moved as one, just as the Chaos Drive let loose a beam of crackling energy.

The bolt shot through the air...and melted to nothing in the combined heat of their minds.

King Headfrog looked appalled. He was staring at them with bulging eyes, lips drawn tight, a snarl on his huge, wet lips.

The Chaos Drive shuddered, began to move towards

them.

Charlotte felt elated. They *all* felt elated, all thinking and feeling and sensing as one. They were something more than human.

Yes! This was it! They would win! They would...

...King Headfrog gave a cry.

A wave of psionic force roared from him. It flared, a furnace, a forge, an irresistible landslide of white-hot willpower.

She felt her mind begin to buckle, and screamed, and//

//and Matt felt Charlotte's scream coming out of his own lips, could feel the slipping, sliding dread as the Chaos Drive was wrenched once again from their hands. He looked around desperately, searching for something, for anything they could use. He saw Ninian, pushed further back than ever, excluded from this echoing battle for mastery. But Ninian had never been synched with the Chaos Drive, and could not help.

At first it had seemed they would win. But even as he had thought it, he had sensed the answering thought from NotCharlotte, sliding into his mind as easily as if they were part of the same great circuit: there was still too much distance between them. They were similar, but they were not the same. It would not work. Even linked together, as close as they could get, they were not strong enough...

King Headfrog was laughing now, wildly, horribly. He knew he would win. Any moment now, the last of their resistance would fail.

They were all going to die.

Matt found himself thinking of Rosewater. Well, if their story was about to end, at least he had a good idea where they might end up. The Place Below Stories, washed out and used up and ready for recycling.

Or was that right? Would he end up there? Or was that

only his story? Would his story go on without him, while his soul was flashed away to some other place...

All these thoughts shot through his mind in a moment, far quicker than it takes to tell, and without him wishing to think them at all.

He was sure there was an order to it. A system. Probably he should just submit himself to it, to the order that ran the Universe...

Matt felt like he had been slapped in the face.

A memory.

Rosewater again, speaking harshly to them, just before he abandoned them.

There are more forces than Order in the Universe. You would do well to remember that.

He had assumed Rosewater had been talking about how they could get here, to rejoin Charlotte, and he had been.

But what if he had meant something else...?

Not daring to think on it, hardly daring to hope, Matt pushed his mind towards the others, forcing the thought towards them, the faintest stirrings of an idea//

//and Charlotte blinked, catching the idea in her mind, feeling it resonate between the three of them.

NotCharlotte took up the thought, echoed it back to them, louder, more certain, more joyfully.

It would work. It *had* to work.

But at what price?

She shook her head. There was no time to think of prices.

Doing nothing would cost them everything.

Charlotte cast her eyes to the corner of the chamber, to the place where Matt had appeared.

For a moment, she could not see it. Her eyes scanned savagely, desperately, searching for a sign, looking for that one point where...

She saw it.

The hazing of the air, the flitting, flickering, uncertainty of raw, untrammelled Chaos.

It had not closed.

The margins were still open.

Opposite them, King Headfrog roared This was it. The final assault. They could not stand it, not on their own, not with the differences that still existed between them.

Charlotte, Matt, and NotCharlotte moved as one. Their minds lashed out towards the Chaos. They grappled at it, clawed at it, pulled back the boundaries...

...and the Chaos flowed in.

❧ 43 ❧

King Headfrog cried out in triumph.

He felt their minds buckle, knew they were about to shatter like fine porcelain under the hammer of his own great consciousness.

Only they didn't.

Something flickered in the corner of his vision, hazing and strange.

Then the aliens *did* shatter.

But it was not in the way he was expecting.

King Headfrog screamed. A rush of freezing heat tumbled from the far side of the chamber. Reality was broken. The thing that seeped in was dark and brilliant. It shone like the combustion of a million yesterdays. It rippled across the floor, turning it to soup, to pancakes, to the smell of bitter tears on the cheek of of of...

King Headfrog staggered as the Chaos washed in.

It blew through them, and between them, and into them. It blinded and scoured and shrieked, apocalyptic, unstoppable.

It was everything.

And then it was receding, the pressures of reality having equalised, and King Headfrog stood, gasping, gaping at the place where his three adversaries were standing.

But there were only two of them now. One male, and one female.

They looked...different, somehow.

Was it their eyes? They glinted, changing, now as bright blue as ice, now as warm brown as molten chocolate.

It didn't matter.

Whatever had happened, one of the three was dead.

Now there would be no struggle at all.

He would crush them like insects.

He reached for the Chaos Drive...

...and there was nothing.

No link. No influence. Nothing at all.

King Headfrog gaped.

This was wrong. There had been a mistake.

Dumbly, he reached out again.

He could see the Chaos Drive, lambent and brilliant, like the dream of a waterfall. But he could not *feel* it.

Slowly, moving as if they were one, the two aliens raised a hand each.

The Chaos Drive came to them.

King Headfrog stared, aghast.

How was this possible?

As he watched, the aliens turned to one another, ignoring him. They each held the device with one hand. Their other hands were linked.

He could see love shining in their eyes, love for one another, a horrible, selfish love from which he was excluded, from which he would always be excluded, for there was nothing like this for him, not ever, not in any version of reality he could possibly imagine.

His lip trembled.

Well, then.

If not for him, then no one could have it.

King Headfrog reached down slowly, unsheathed the blaster from his holster.

The Chaos Drive was a weapon. That's what it had always been: a big gun. The biggest.

But the humans had been so focussed on the Chaos Drive, they had forgotten about other weapons.

King Headfrog raised his blaster and squeezed the trigger.

✢ 44 ✤

Matt gasped. Power rushed through him and around him.

He looked down at his feet, saw them telescoping out below him forever, to a floor a million miles away. At the same instant, they were no distance away at all. He was a mote, an infinitely small speck of existence in a vastness that was beyond comprehension. He was the Universe, and everything that moved within it.

As he breathed, he not only felt his lungs fill, but every other lung - the lungs of a million Matts, a billion, concertinaing off into infinity and back again, trembling, echoing just beyond the vale of this reality.

It was tremendous.

It was like riding the edge of a breaking wave, a wave that was bigger than the ocean, bigger than the cosmos.

The Chaos had washed in, had cast aside the vibrating motes that kept them apart, that separated one aspect of his existence from every other version. He could feel them, the thickness of a shadow away...he *was* them. Memories began to ripple through his mind, memories and perceptions, an unstoppable torrent of them. For a moment he struggled, terrified of losing himself amid the explosion of Selfness. Then he let go.

He was every Matt, in every version ever told. And he was himself.

He glanced at Charlotte, and knew that she understood, too. He watched her eyes flicker - green, blue, brown, violet, faster, faster still, splicing through sequences of colours he had no name for. The world seemed to ripple around them. He looked at her and//

//and Charlotte looked at Matt and laughed. It felt so good, to welcome them all back. All the versions of herself. All the myriad potentialities of herself. She knew them, knew them intimately - for she *was* them, just as they were her.

She beckoned with her mind, and the Chaos Drive sprang to her. She felt a tiny ripple of hurt as King Headfrog was cast out. Then the Chaos Drive was with them, and the Universe seemed to open up, every mote and instance.

She glanced at Matt again...and her smile faltered, just a shade, for she could sense that in the whole infinite array of him, there was yet something missing.

She concentrated.

What was it?

Not one, but *two* somethings.

Two versions of him were missing. They had not been called through the Chaos, they had not coalesced with the rest of him. That was strange...that was disturbing...

She tried to sense more, but it was no good. There was simply too much to take in.

It did not matter.

She pushed the thought from her mind.

Now was not the time to worry about such little things.

Now was the time to deal with this *thief*.

She looked back at King Headfrog, and was just in time to

see him pull the trigger of his silly little weapon. Not that such things mattered. She could sense the whole expanse of this reality – down to the movement of every atom, the vibration of every electron, the spin of every quark. In another frame of reference, she could sense the wisps of Telling and narrative inevitability, swirling round and about the singularity they now inhabited, just as she could understand the same thing in countless other frames, perspectives beyond counting.

But the frame didn't matter.

What mattered was that she had felt King Headfrog's finger squeeze the trigger before she ever saw it, just as she had felt the flow of thoughts through the cruel smear of his neurons that passed – if she were generous – for a brain. She knew his intentions, understood every inch of them.

And they were ready.

She reached out for Matt//

//and Matt grasped for her, and together they sang a song, a trembling soprano into the Chaos. And the Chaos responded.

Even as light ignited in the muzzle of King Headfrog's gun, even as a beam of energy began to reach for them – slow, slow, a glimmering, glistening thick treacle of energy, tied to the strict laws of cause and effect which held the whole Universe to account – Matt lashed out with his will. He felt Charlotte move with him; and underneath them, the billions of other versions of themselves moved in perfect syncopation, and the Chaos Drive responded.

A hole opened up, a perfect dark sphere. It sprang into being an inch from King Headfrog's nose...but also an inch from every other atom which belonged to that wretched level of reality, to that silly and vicious *story*.

And before he could scream, before he could so much as breath, and as the first faintest light of understanding started in his eyes, the sphere of perfect darkness flickered, swallowing up King Headfrog and every other part of his stain, and carried them far away, wrapping that wretched dimension in unbreakable knots, and delivering them to themselves, inward facing and alone, forever more.

❧ 45 ❧

Matt listened, but there was nothing to hear.

Silence.

King Headfrog was gone. Froghearth was gone.

On screens all around, empty space sparkled, a beautiful, boiling void.

The frog ships were gone, and the only craft that remained were the empty vessels belonging to Philip Frogmore. There were spaceships of a thousand types, combat vessels and heavy bombers, wickedly armed and armoured - and all of them were without pilots now, for the Matts that had steered them had been sucked in, and now echoed in his own mind.

He looked at Charlotte.

"We did it," he said, his voice seeming huge in the silence.

Charlotte looked back at him. Her eyes were cycling colours, her features flickering and unstable. Matt realised he must look the same way.

To feel the infinity of other versions of himself, thrumming just below the surface was...unsettling.

The Chaos was strange and furious, powerful beyond the ability of King Headfrog to comprehend, let alone resist.

But it was dangerous.

Matt knew that instinctively, could feel it clawing at the corners of his mind.

It was time to put the Chaos back in its box.

The thought flashed between them. She understood.

Matt let out a breath. He felt raw, as if he had been tap dancing barefoot on the surface of a neutron star, as if his skin was alive with pure, untrammelled electricity.

He reached inside himself, meaning to shut off the Chaos he had caused, meaning to cut the strings that bound him to every other version of himself.

Nothing happened.

❧ 46 ❧

Charlotte reached inside, and cut off the Chaos.

For a horrible moment, there was nothing, no response.

It was like trying to grip a shadow. The Chaos slipped through her fingers.

Then something shifted. It was like an infinitely heavy rock grinding on the bones of the world.

It was so difficult, so painful...

But she had to go through with it. If she didn't, she would end up with her mind spread across a million million versions of herself. There was no choice, really.

Charlotte screamed.

The scream went on for an instant and a lifetime and for the entire thickness of the Universe.

Then it was done, and Charlotte stood in a sudden, startling stillness.

She could still feel the Chaos thrumming all around her. It had leached into the world now, and she couldn't shut it off. But she had shut it off *in her*.

There was a reeling sensation, as the countless other

versions of her fled, back into the infinite echoes of reality from whence they had come.

There was loss, an infinite sadness for all the other things she could have been.

But at the same time, she was glad, because she was herself again. She was Charlotte, and she knew the parameters of her mind.

She glanced to one side, and saw that NotCharlotte had coalesced out of the Chaos, too, and was standing next to her. They looked at one another, and smiled.

Then she turned, meaning to look at Matt, to share the smile with him...

...and the smile died on her face.

Matt stood before her...but it wasn't *her* Matt. No, this was still a flickering composite, a glimmering multitude of shadow-selves.

He had not let go.

"What's wrong?" she asked, anxious. "Let them go. Just be yourself again."

Matt didn't answer.

❦ 47 ❦

Matt forced the panic down, closed his eyes, and let his mind expand. He reached out with the Chaos Drive...

...and felt the spreading influence of the Chaos.

It was shooting out in every direction, spreading like a sickness.

And he understood.

They had called the Chaos, and the Chaos had come.

But it wasn't some obedient dog, it wasn't some servant that would do his every bidding, then return at his word.

Oh, no.

The Chaos had been waiting, for so, so long.

It had always been there, layered on the fabric of this reality, layered to one side of it, pressing, always trying to get in.

Now it had been given a way in. It was propagating through the fabric of reality. He felt it flash past planets, past countless suns, take in worlds beyond number.

And in every place it passed, it gnawed away the boundaries, undoing the barriers between the real and the unreal, the more-than-real...

Reality could not survive such an onslaught.

But why couldn't he let go? How was it Charlotte had managed to come back, to dissolve the countless iterations of herself, to come back to herself - while he could not?

"What...what's happening?" he asked.

"Just what I wanted to happen, of course."

The voice was light, and posh, and horrible, insufferably arrogant.

Matt looked up. Philip Frogmore was standing there, perfectly at ease, a lazy smile on his face.

❧ 48 ❧

Charlotte jerked back.

Where there had been only empty decking, Philip Frogmore now stood, tall and languid. At his feet was the curled up form of EB. He looked as if he had been beaten. Badly.

Then another figure moved, coming out of the shadows at Frogmore's side, and Charlotte saw...

Matt.

Only this version looked empty-eyed, heartless and hollow and strange. He was dressed in the uniform of Frogmore's personal guard, the insignia of House Frogmore sown onto his expansive gold shoulder pads.

"Matt," said the woman next to her.

It wasn't a cry, it wasn't a shout. Charlotte looked at NotCharlotte, at the anguish on her face, the longing.

And she knew.

These two versions belonged together. And now they were together again, at last.

But something was wrong.

NotMatt turned his hollow eyes, gave NotCharlotte a long, slow look.

There was no recognition there.

"Oh, he doesn't remember you, my dear," said Philip Frogmore, almost apologetically. "No, he doesn't remember much of anything. Apart from the desire to serve me, of course."

Philip Frogmore held something up.

Charlotte felt something squeeze inside her.

The gem. The Heart of Frogmore.

It pulsed faintly, and she saw an echoing pulse dancing in NotMatt's eyes.

Charlotte looked back to her Matt - to the Matt that was *every* Matt, still expanded and joined through the Chaos. But something was wrong. He was fraying at the edges, as if minute particles of who he was were burning away, scorching off into the vast seething nothingness/everythingness of the Chaos.

He was being pulled apart. The Chaos was claiming him.

Why wasn't he letting it go? Why wasn't he coming back to her?

Then Matt was raising the Chaos Drive. He was holding it straight in front of him, pointed at Frogmore like a gun. Which was what Frogmore had called it earlier, wasn't it? When they first met him.

Hope flared up inside her.

Of course!

That was why Matt was holding onto all the versions of himself! He wanted to keep the coherence, to keep control of the Chaos Drive - so that he could blast Frogmore to smithereens.

She looked at Frogmore, and waited for him to vanish, to disintegrate, to be cast away to some far-flung reality.

But nothing of the sort occurred.

Philip Frogmore smiled.

❧ 49 ❧

Matt focussed his mind, and sent a bolt of pure, fearsome undoing from the Chaos Drive, straight into the sanguine, arrogant face of Philip Frogmore.

Only he didn't.

His mind twitched. The Chaos Drive pulsed, rotating slowly.

Why...why wasn't it working?

He looked in confusion from the sparkling brilliance of the Chaos Drive, to Frogmore...to the gem that pulsed in his hand.

And he understood.

He didn't *want* to destroy Frogmore.

There was no time to resist, no possibility at all.

A jolt of influence shot from the gem and struck him full in the forehead, and before he could turn, before he even really understood what was happening//

//he was standing at Frogmore's side.

Matt looked down at his body, at the smart, outlandish

outfit he was now wearing. The gold shoulder pads were especially spectacular, he thought.

There was a reeling sense of vertigo as the memories belonging to the other Matt slid and settled in his mind. He remembered lurking in the darkness, watching EB chase his master. He remembered grabbing the gemstone, retrieving it from where it had slid when Charlotte had kicked it away. He remembered the way he had called, doing as his master bid him, distracting EB at a vital moment, giving Frogmore the chance to turn the tables.

And he remembered the way EB had looked, astonished, betrayed, as he had helped to beat him down.

And the worst thing of all was that he felt no guilt.

He knew that he *should* feel guilt. He knew that EB was his friend, that EB had trusted him.

Still, it had been necessary.

And now, here they stood, at the very brink.

Everything was going according to plan.

He turned and smiled at Philip Frogmore, his glorious master.

"I am ready," said Matt – said every Matt, for now they were all bound as one, as the Chaos cast aside all barriers, and the concertina was complete. "What do you need of me?"

Frogmore smiled back at him.

"I need you to be a hero," he said.

❧ 50 ❧

Charlotte saw NotCharlotte start to move, and before she had time to think, she was moving too.

Whatever Frogmore had done to Matt - to all the Matts - did not bear thinking on. It must simply be fought.

She had then sense of them jumping together, and for a split second she thought it might even work. Frogmore didn't seem to be reacting at all. Her fist tensed. She would punch him and kick him and tear him. She would scratch his face and pull his hair and...

...and Matt made a gesture, and a wall of air caught them, suspended like flies.

NotCharlotte made a noise, an inchoate roar of rage.

"Oh, hush, my dear girls," said Frogmore, brushing some invisible dust from his lapel. "There's no point crying about it now. It is almost done. Better to let it happen."

Charlotte looked at Matt, desperately searching for something in his eyes, some glimmer of who he was, of who he really *was*.

"You give him back!" NotCharlotte was yelling. "He's not yours! Let him go!"

Philip Frogmore gave Matt a significant look, and suddenly a gag appeared in NotCharlotte's mouth.

"Oh, I think the Universe needs him more than you," said Philip Frogmore. "Don't you think?"

And Charlotte went limp, because she suddenly understood.

She felt the hollow place in the fabric of reality, the place where the Chaos hazed most strongly, the point where it had broken through into the world.

And she sensed, even now, the bitter, burning edge of the Chaos, marching faster than thought across the Universe, melding and undoing, turning everything it touched to a maelstrom, a shattered rainbow of possibility and nonsense, as every possibly version was sucked into the advancing singularity.

She may have stepped back from the brink, she may have undone the singularity in herself – but that had not been enough. Not while Matt remained, an infinitely dense point of confluence, twining the infinite versions of the Universe together.

And there was only one way of undoing it.

"Oh, no," she said, so softly it was barely a noise.

She shook her head.

"No, no, no..."

"You understand," said Philip Frogmore. "Good. The Universe is doomed now. We are only here, sharing these words, because we are held in the palm of the singularity. All around us, the Universe is being invaded. The Chaos has gotten in. There is only one way of getting it out."

"The singularity must be destroyed," came a voice Charlotte did not recognise. It took her a moment to realise it was the tall creature, the one who had arrive with Matt. He was looking at Philip Frogmore through a pair of crystalline spectacles. He did not look worried, or angry. Just interested, in an academic way.

"Yes, master Ninian, it must," said Frogmore. "How nice it is to meet someone who sees things clearly. And perhaps you can enlighten us as to what would happen if the singularity is *not* destroyed?"

"Then the Universe will collapse into Chaos," said Ninian helpfully. "This has been a theoretical possibility forever, of course. How fascinating to see it played out! When the doorway was first opened, when the Chaos was first called, there was the option of simply closing the door. As Charlotte did when she let herself collapse back into her composite versions. But now it has gone too far. It won't *let* Matt collapse back. The only way out is to destroy his coherence entirely."

Philip Frogmore turned to Matt, as if everything had been decided.

"Well, there you go, then," he said, in a friendly voice. "Aren't we lucky that this has happened to *you* though, Master Matthew? For anyone else, that would be a tough choice. But for someone as *heroic* as you - why, to make the ultimate sacrifice is practically in your DNA."

Charlotte stared at Matt, willing him not to do it, willing him to resist.

Moving slowly, but without a moment's hesitation, Matt lifted the Chaos Drive aloft, twisting it, turning it, until it pointed, like a gun, at his own head.

❧ 51 ❧

Matt saw it all.

It was so simple, so obvious.

The Universe would be destroyed, destroyed entirely.

Unless he closed the singularity.

He looked at the Chaos Drive, glittering in his hand. It was beautiful.

But Frogmore was right. It *was* a gun.

Matt glanced at Ninian. The tall creature looked back at him, dark eyes unreadable. He was right, Matt knew. He could sense the Universe breaking apart under the onslaught of the Chaos. And he knew that he, Matt - the confluence of Matts - was what was giving the Chaos its way in.

He looked sadly at the two Charlottes. He remembered both of them, remembered them perfectly. Their smiles. Their little jokes, their warm eyes, all the precious moments.

He didn't want them to end.

But there was no choice.

Matt stoked the fires of the Chaos Drive with a thought,

felt the power in it start to grow, brighter, brighter, like an igniting star.

It would be quick. There would be no pain.

He looked at EB - his friend, who he had betrayed. He wished he could tell why he had done it, he wished he could explain everything.

But there was no time.

Then something glinted in EB's eye.

Matt frowned.

EB was looking from Matt to a shape on the floor, and back again.

Matt knew he shouldn't hesitate - he felt the weight of Frogmore's mind on his own, pushing him, urging him on.

Still, he resisted, somehow.

An extra moment wouldn't hurt.

He followed EB's gaze, and saw a shape on the floor.

It was a large something, gelatinous and oozing; it looked rather like a body wrapped in thick layers of jelly.

Matt quested towards it, his curiosity piqued. What *was* that thing? Why hadn't he noticed it before?

And then, as his mind touched on the shape, he felt an answering pulse of...of *something*, calling back to him from inside.

It was calling to him, with words he could not quite make out.

But he recognised the voice.

Of course he did.

It was his own.

❧ 52 ❧

Charlotte saw Matt hesitate, she saw him looking - not back at her, but at the shape on the floor, the bundle, the chrysalis-thing that had lain unnoticed since the moment King Headfrog had arrived.

They had all forgotten about the torpid, globular thing on the floor.

Glob, she thought. *Yes, that was what King Headfrog had called it. Glob. It had been - what? - one of his soldiers?*

Charlotte looked at Philip Frogmore. His mouth was frozen in a smile. There was the shadow of concern in his eyes.

He was worried.

And with that realisation, a desperate, wild hope sprang up in her again.

Her eyes darted back to Matt, then back to the shape on the floor.

It twitched.

It twitched again.

Charlotte watched, unmoving, hardly daring to breath.

The thing on the floor exploded.

❧ 53 ❧

Matt raised a hand to shield his face. The stuff that exploded from the shape on the floor was gelatinous and cloying, a thick viscous fluid that coated them all from head to toe.

When he lowered his hands he saw...

Himself.

The chrysalis was gone, and the version who stood there instead was slim and composed.

Matt quested with his mind. This version was...it was the last of him. The last version, the only one that had not been drawn into the singularity that he had become.

"Hello, Frogmore," said the newcomer. His voice was higher than Matt expected, younger. "I wish I could say it was good to see you again."

"Mathew," said Philip Frogmore. His voice was hard as ice. "Well, I should have expected a cheap, sneaky trick like this. Still, you're just in time. I wouldn't have had you miss your own suicide."

Frogmore gestured, and the newcomer screamed.

❧ 54 ❧

Charlotte flinched.

Even though his voice was different, even though he was younger and slighter, he was the same.

To see him in pain hurt her, too.

Not meaning to, not even consciously willing her hand, Charlotte leant forward. Their hands touched.

Mathew looked up at her, and for a moment the pain slid away from his features, and then//

//she felt his mind.

Through some joining she could not understand, she felt him whispering to her.

It is nearly time, my love. The words came soft and warm as summer rain.

Charlotte felt tears pricking her eyes

It's not me, she told him. *I'm not...I'm not...*

She wanted to tell him that it wasn't *him* she loved, not this strange new version, and not the version she had been traipsing round the Universe with, nor any of the million million other versions of him.

It was *Matt*. It was *her* Matt. The one who had been taken. The one she could not get back to, however hard she tried.

You are.

The reply came to her, calm and certain.

You are for me, as I am for you. Across all the versions. Every version.

She was dimly aware of Frogmore gesturing with his gemstone. Though he was only a few feet away, he might as well have been on the other side of creation. He seemed so unimportant now.

But I just want him, Charlotte wailed. *I just want him back.*

Mathew smiled at her, and his eyes were sad and old.

It all depends on you, he told her. *The choice will be yours.*

Charlotte tried to ask him what he meant, to scream at him that she didn't understand, that she didn't want to understand, but//

//but the link was broken.

She felt something grasping at him, sucking at this new version, this iteration which dared to resist the pull of the singularity.

Mathew closed his eyes. He looked very peaceful.

Then a wind blew, and he was gone.

❧ 55 ❧

The newcomer flickered...

...diminished...

...appeared, Matt sensed, within his own composite.

He felt a new web of memories settle inside himself, and suddenly he understood.

It was his fault.

Or rather, Philip Frogmore thought it was his fault, which came to the same thing.

He remembered the way he had scorned Frogmore, embarrassed him, back when they were both just figments of a small story.

Philip Frogmore hated him.

He had always hated him.

He *would* always hate him.

Nothing he could do would change that.

"There is no more time for talking," Frogmore was saying. His voice had lost the playful, mocking edge of earlier. Now it was hard.

Desperate.

Hungry.

"No more talking," echoed Matt. He felt Frogmore's will descend again, stronger than ever. He would do it. He *had* to do it.

He sensed the tearing blade of the Chaos, slicing the universe from bow to stern. It was unspooling. Everywhere was coming apart.

It had to be stopped, and there was only one way to do that.

He had to kill himself, so that the Universe might live.

He moved the Chaos Drive to his forehead.

"Do it," urged Frogmore. His voice was low, his words insistent. "Do it, now. There's no other way. I told you: the Chaos Drive is a gun. Ever since it first appeared, it has longed to be used."

Still, Matt hesitated. Something held him back, a force pushing against the rising, urgent commands that came from Frogmore.

His head was hurting now, pounding.

It felt like he was being crushed, that he would be pulverised to nothing.

Matt started to scream.

✲ 56 ✲

Charlotte watched as Matt put the Chaos Drive to his head.

She was powerless.

He would kill himself, kill all of himself.

And she would be alone.

And then the tears came. They rose up from some deep place inside, drowning her, filling her eyes, gagging her mouth.

She was alone, she was all alone.

She was...

...a hand slipped inside hers.

It was warm, and strong, and gentle.

She looked up.

It was the other her.

NotCharlotte.

She had tears in her eyes, too. And pain so deep it could drown the world.

It was like looking into a mirror.

And Charlotte understood.

A peace descended on her, so beautiful and still it left an

emptiness ringing in her ears. The world seemed frozen in place around her. She saw Philip Frogmore, where he stood, eyes blazing, will bent on the man she loved. She saw Ninian, head tilted, still more curious than concerned.

She saw EB on the floor where he had been let fall, still, silent...but with eyes open, and hope in them.

And she saw Matt.

The man she loved.

All the versions of him.

It was so simple.

All this time, she thought. *All this time, I was trying to get back to him, and he was trying to get back to me.*

She looked at the other Charlotte, at NotCharlotte, and they both smiled.

And all this time, NotCharlotte thought at her, *it didn't matter. Because we were together.*

Because the versions of us are the same.

She could no longer tell if the voice in her head was her own.

They are all the same. We are all the same. The memories, the details; these are not important.

Charlotte quested with her mind.

She felt the tendrils of her thought brush against the Chaos Drive, kiss it, entwine and stroke and stoke it.

It was like embracing an old friend.

Charlotte opened herself, calling out, calling them again.

And the other Charlottes came.

They slipped in from the shadows and from the others places, from every corner of every versions, sliding into place, reforming...

...and then she was Charlotte again, a second singularity.

The Chaos roared around them, and time slipped back into the world.

"It *must* be fired!" Frogmore was screaming. His face was

very close to Matt's. "It is a *gun*, damnit! It appeared in the first act: think what Chekov would say!"

Charlotte smiled.

She knew what she had to do, and she knew the price.

"Chekov is a character in *Star Trek*," she said scornfully.

Frogmore's eyes darted up at her. She saw them widen, as he realised what she had done, what she was about to do.

She saw his fingers tense on his jewel, felt the first wave of power wash towards her, to try and influence her, to control her in the way he was controlling Matt.

But Frogmore *couldn't* control her. The device had been designed to hold Matt's mind, every version of him.

But not hers.

Charlotte reached out and took the Chaos Drive.

She held it, suspended in the singularity that was her, in the raw, tumultuous wonder of the endless iterations of her soul.

Then she crushed it to dust.

❧ 57 ❧

M att looked into her eyes.

He looked into all her infinite eyes.

They were so beautiful.

Blue eyes, like lapis lazuli. Green eyes, like jade in the shadow of evening.

And brown eyes.

Her brown eyes.

He understood what she had done, the sacrifice she was making, making for both of them, for all of them, for every inch of this fragile, delicate Universe

I love you, he had time to think. He felt the thought snake out, refracted by the Chaos Drive, felt it answered by Charlotte, echoed and redoubled and sent out again, sparkling and splendid.

And then the Chaos Drive shattered, and Matt was torn apart.

❧ 58 ❧

It was like being a firework.

It was like being a sun.

Charlotte felt the ignition inside herself, felt the whiplash hand of Chaos, passing through every atom of who she was - of who she *could* be - felt every version ripple and seethe and//

//and then she was flying across the Universe, expanding at the speed of thought, the endless versions of herself hurtling back to their own realities, their own parallel levels of existence//

//only they were *not* as they had been.

None of them were.

The Chaos Drive had shattered when they were bound in singularity.

Nothing would ever be the same again.

She felt the countless memories of a million million versions of herself fragmenting, rearranging, crossing and recrossing like strands of DNA exchanging information with themselves.

A wind blew in her mind, a rising wind, that rushed, louder, louder, louder, until//

❄ 59 ❄

Matt screamed.

The versions of himself were trying to fall back, to fall apart, mixed and endlessly, hopelessly changed.

The Chaos Drive was gone. The force was gone, the force that had woven him together, that had allowed the singularity to form up. His endless versions *had* to fall away.

And yet they couldn't.

Something was grasping for them, pulling them, trying to stick them together.

It was Frogmore.

Matt could sense him straining, desperate, forcing more and more energy through his glowing gemstone.

"No!" Frogmore was screaming. "No, come back! You can't leave! I forbid it!"

But it was no good, it was hopeless, like trying to hold together the fragments of an exploding star with sticky tape.

"You...*can't*!" Yelled Frogmore, and his scream became a howl, and...

...the jewel exploded.

There was a moment of shock, of stillness.

Matt just had time to see the appalled look on Frogmore's face.

Then the wind took him.

There was nothing to resist it anymore.

Matt felt himself scattered, felt the versions of himself falling away from the singularity//

❧ 60 ❧

//**A**nd the singularities were gone//

   //and the doorway that had opened the Universe to the Chaos was closed//

//it slid and buckled, desperate, like a dying tentacle, severed from its body, thrashing, urgent//

//and the seething edge of Chaos was undone. It fell back from the Universe, and the Universe was resealed around it. And//

//Everything went dark.

❦ 61 ❦

Charlotte blinked her eyes open.

A white expanse lay over her.

It was so pure and empty, like a vast blank page, the first line waiting to be written.

She took a breath. The air smelt faintly sweet, like the first taste of spring as the year turns.

She looked around. She was in a gently rolling land, soft grass tickled by a slow wind. At the margins of the land, the sky was blue. A little way off, a roughly spherical thing glimmered and swam. It was faintly green, and full of sparks and half-glimpsed things.

Not knowing why, not really thinking at all, Charlotte felt a slow smile creep onto her face. This place felt...it felt *safe*. She tried to remember the last time she felt safe...

...and that was when the problems began.

As soon as she peered backwards in her memory, she began to get into trouble.

She remembered the wedding, of course, the dancing, all the fun...

But she also remembered the attack on their ship. The Frogs coming after them. The desperate attempts to flee.

She frowned.

She remembered being taken, a prisoner, to Froghearth, to a combat pit, facing a horrible monster...and she also remembered leading Matt through the Lanes in Brighton, looking for someone to help, to help her get back...

The world swam in front of her eyes. The Universe vibrated oddly. It was like looking at the world through two sets of memories, trying to triangulate a position in reality from various points which couldn't possibly make sense...

"Hello," said Matt. "What's wrong with your eyes?"

He was sitting up next to her, looking at her blearily.

There was something...odd about his face, though.

He looked so familiar, and yet so *strange*. She tried to put her finger on it, and realised she couldn't.

All of him was different, and all of him was the same.

"My eyes?" said Charlotte. "Nothing. They look fine to me."

"Yes, but you can't *see* them," Matt pointed out.

"I know," said Charlotte, annoyed at how reasonable this sounded. "I mean, they look fine from the *inside*."

"Oh," said Matt. "Well, from the outside they look different. From each other, I mean."

"Surely they do," said a voice from behind them. It was an odd sort of voice. It was full of gravel and chalk, an old voice. Yet it was full of life, too; it had strange harmonics. "Eyes generally are one of the first things to change. Windows to the soul, as is said."

Charlotte turned. The owner of the voice was standing a few paces back from them. He had a hang-dog demeanour, as if he felt slightly sheepish about the mere fact of his existence. He was of medium height, but was so slight that he had the appearance of being much taller. He wore faded blue jeans and a crumpled white shirt. On the shirt, a golden badge poked out, like the sun peering out from behind clouds.

"Who are you?" asked Charlotte, then stopped short, because she remembered suddenly that they had already met. Of course they had. On Brighton pier, in Ninian's parlour. It was the Sheriff of the Order, the one who had insinuated himself into their reality.

"Ya'all shouldn't feel bad about it," said the Sheriff, his grey moustache twitching solemnly. "It's always a bit flibbity, letting the pieces of yourself settle back together. *Especially* when they didn't all used to be together to start with."

Charlotte opened her mouth to ask what he was talking about, then choked on the words as a long lock of flowing black hair exploded from his previously bald head.

"What...why did *that* happen?" asked Matt.

Norwood Ginnel stared at him blankly for a moment, then chuckled.

"Oh, pay that no mind," he said, brushing the question away with a wrinkled, tanned hand. "Just something that happens to someone like me, is all."

Even as he spoke, the black hair settled into a neat quiff for a moment, before rolling back like retreating tides and leaving him completely bald.

"Someone like you?" said Charlotte, who found she had regained the rudiments of speech. "What, you mean a Sheriff?"

She was concentrating hard on not letting her head implode from the weight of two sets of memories. She knew very well what a Sheriff of the Order was. Of course she did. She had spent much of the last few years trying to evade them, along with Matt and EB. The Chaos Drive had put them on the map the Sheriffs had of what the Storystream should and should not contain, even if they remained only a small footnote. On the other hand, she had a competing - and apparently completely valid - set of memories that were screaming at her that she shouldn't know what a Sheriff of the Order was, even if she *had* met this particular one before (which this set of memories was equally sure she hadn't).

"Not exactly," said Norwood, his smile settling a little. Did she imagine it, or was there a note of sadness in his voice? "No, I mean someone who wanders. Someone who makes a habit of visiting other stories. They have a way of rubbing off on you. But this might *look* extreme," he went on, indicating his ever-changing hair, and winking at her with an eye that - she suddenly realised - was also constantly changing colour, "but believe me, I've gotten away *very* lightly. I've dropped into many and many a story; that's why they call me the *Wandering* Sheriff. Between you and me, it's not a few of my colleagues think I must be *mad* by now!"

He gave a sudden, alarming laugh, shrill and high, and completely, insanely sincere.

Charlotte wondered for a moment if this might be a good time to run, but before she could really process the thought, Norwood had stopped laughing, and was looking again at them with such warmth, that she found she was not afraid of him. Not at all. Even if he was a little bit mad.

"You mean...we're starting to have other stories leach into us?" said Matt. He was looking quite worried now. "You have to know, we never meant for anything *nasty* to happen. With the Chaos Drive, I mean." His words were tumbling out over one another. "We thought it was just a bit of fun. We never took anything from anyone who didn't deserve it," he finished in a rush, then clamped his lips together.

Norwood blinked at him. It was a good blink, long and slow and rather banal. It would have made Charlotte think Norwood was rather stupid, if she hadn't already decided he was pretty sharp indeed under it all.

"Oh, we ain't coming after *you*," said Norwood, and Charlotte thought he was probably enjoying this. She found she didn't begrudge him that. After all, things had got rather out of hand.

"That's a relief," she said. Then a worrying thought hit her. "Wait, what about EB? Do you mean you're going to blame *him*?"

But Norwood was already waving his arms slowly at her in negation.

"No, that's *not* what I mean," he said. He thought for a moment. "Not that it wasn't mooted, you understand. Not naming any names, but some of the other Sheriffs really wanted to throw the book at that damn cat!"

"But you're not going to?" Charlotte pressed.

"Nope," said Norwood. He frowned, his hair flickering up suddenly into an angry red mohawk, vivid as fire. "Probably wouldn't have, even without the petition we received from Rosewater. Which did *not* go down well, I might add. Rosewater meddling with Order business."

He let out a long sigh, as if calming himself. His hair swam back down, becoming long and silvery and straight.

"Anyway, the point is that *none* of you are being blamed for this mess," he said. "You'll find your cat quite unharmed, when you get back to him."

"*Someone* is being blamed then?" said Matt.

"Of course they are!" said Norwood, staring at Matt as if he had gone stupid. "My, don't you ken what nearly happened here, boy? The Chaos was set loose! Stories set to the flame, iterations pulled out of their natural homes, things directed in ways that were fundamentally squiggly! Of *course* someone is going to be punished!"

"Good," said Matt, leaning back with a smile of his own. "Bet I can guess who."

"Me too," said Charlotte. She found she was smiling.

Norwood returned her smile. His eyes glimmered.

"Want to see for yourself?" he asked.

Matt and Charlotte nodded.

Norwood turned and led them across the gently rolling land. As they walked, she felt that they were descending. Something struck her as odd about that, but she couldn't quite place it.

They came to the rough sphere she had spotted earlier. It was glimmering and strange. Peering at it, Charlotte had the strangest sensation. It was as if she were looking at something that was both huge and tiny at the same time. There were sparks there that might have been suns; there were shapes that were either huge cities or motes of dust.

"Is that...what I think it is?" she asked, trying to keep her voice level. It was difficult to keep the thing in focus. It swam and flowed, as if it moved on several more dimensions than Charlotte could perceive.

"Yup," said Norwood Ginnel simply. "Most certainly. Here, let me slow things down. Translate them a little..."

He waved his hand, and the sphere seemed to coalesce, to drip in on itself. Charlotte had the sense that Norwood was dragging it, forcing it to redefine itself into terms that she could understand. And then...

...then Charlotte was looking at a system. A central sun, with planets spinning around it. One planet was more prominent than the others, a vast, sprawling mess of cities and marshes and industrial districts. She recognised the huge arena where she had been prisoner. A way off, she saw the huge mushroom they had been chased up what felt like a million years ago.

"Froghearth," she said, her voice full of disgust.

"Indeed," said Norwood. "The story of the Frogopolis, the Frog empire. Back again, as it should be. Set to run right, all compromising elements removed or smoothed back to Order."

Charlotte found her eye wandering across the solar system. Small metal things glinted in the void. Spaceships. Somehow, she found her eye drawn to one in particular...

...and instantly, the view zoomed in on this, until it seemed to fill the whole world. An ugly, creaking war ship, badly made and poorly maintained. She peered closer and...

...and now she was staring at what looked like an access tunnel underneath one of the huge, creaking engines which powered the ship. She could almost smell the foul stench of scorched fuel, could almost taste the acrid, burning air. A shape was creeping and squeezing itself through the maze of tunnels and access ramps. An unhappy shape. She saw sweat beed on its head, saw the lips fixed in a permanent scowl.

"King Headfrog," said Matt, with - it had to be said - a rather malicious satisfaction.

"Not quite," amended Norwood. "Not *King* Headfrog, not anymore. He made himself that with the Chaos Drive, which - I might add - you very kindly destroyed, saving us the trouble of having to do so."

"So he's...what?" said Charlotte. "Head Frog 127, again?"

"Nope," said Norwood happily. "King Toadflaps punished him most vigorously for his recent escapades. He tried to steal away with the King's own daughter, don't you know?"

"Ah," said Matt happily. "Yes, that does sound about right to me. Exactly the sort of sneaksome, underhand thing that git would do."

"Yup," said Norwood. "So now he's Engineer Frog 127, second class. I thought the title rather suited him."

"Agreed," said Charlotte. She found she was enjoying herself. She knew she should probably feel a little guilty about *how much* she was enjoying herself, and made a mental note to reprimand herself later for exactly how un-guilty she actually felt. "Now," she went on, "what about the other one? I'm looking forward to seeing Frogmore even more than this idiot. I hope you've done something fitting with him."

"Ah," said Norwood, seeming to deflate. "Well, I can only say I agree with you there. I would very much like to see him getting what he deserves, too."

Charlotte's smile slipped, just a little.

"What?" she asked, hoping desperately that she had misunderstood Norwood. "You don't mean he got away?"

Norwood nodded his head sadly, eyes downcast. Even as she watched, his hair drooped down into a wet little comb-over.

"Wish I could say how," he told her. "We've had a long confabulation about the matter, the other Sheriffs and I. But we don't have any answers. Not *how* he got away. Not *where to*, either."

"But, no, that's not *possible*," put in Matt. "I was there! I could *feel* his mind, pressing in on me. It was horrible. I could feel that...that *device* he used...and I could feel it when the energy snapped back into it when the Chaos Drive detonated! It was blown to smithereens, I'd swear it!"

"I know," said Norwood. "I saw it too. We all did. We thought he was as good as ours. And yet..."

"And yet he got away." said Charlotte.

She stepped back from the sphere of light which was the story of the Frogopolis. Norwood waved his hand, and it fell away, sliding back into some strange, multi-dimensional play which Charlotte could not follow.

Suddenly, it didn't seem to matter so much any more. She felt a little sick.

"What are you doing about it?" said Matt.

Norwood blinked at him, frowning, as if rather cross at having been asked.

"Doing about it?" he shot back. "Why, we are doing *every-*

thing about it. Of course we are. What kind of idiots do you take us for?"

Matt scowled for a moment, then hung his head and shut his eyes.

When he opened them again a moment later, his face was calm again.

"I'm sorry," he said. "I just meant...well, it was *horrible*, feeling him on top of my mind like that. I just wish you had caught him, that's all."

Norwood frowned a moment longer, then burst into a sudden smile.

"Why, of course we'll catch him," he said warmly. "Don't you worry about that. We're *bound* to catch him, because we know exactly where he will strike. Sooner or later."

Matt looked at him blankly for a moment, then sighed.

"Of course you do," he said. "He's bound to come for me again. Sooner or later."

Charlotte put her arm around Matt.

"He'll come for *us*," she amended. "And we'll be waiting for him."

"And you won't have to worry about it at all," went on Norwood happily. "Because we'll see as soon as he tries anything, and we'll pounce on him!"

"You know," said Matt thoughtfully, "there's a word for what you're trying to use me as."

"I *do* know," agreed Norwood joyfully. "*Bait*. We thought you wouldn't mind, on account of how we have kindly dropped all charges against you, and agreed to send you back to your own story."

Charlotte looked at Norwood.

His eyes were so wide and open, his voice was so sincere. She genuinely thought that he didn't wish them any ill, none at all.

But at the same time, there was a hardness there, lurking

behind the oddity, behind the flickering colours and the changing hair.

There was something *unbending* about Norwood, which was strange, because on the surface the one thing he seemed to do all the time was bend. He was practically the embodiment of change. He was like seawater, ready to fit himself at any moment to whatever container was required. But she sensed that he could be as implacable as the tides, as strong and unyielding as the ocean.

Matt sighed.

"Fine," he said at last. He gave a smile, and Charlotte was happy to see his old twinkle had returned. There it was again. She had missed it, though she realised now she had never really left it, had never really left him.

They would be fine, she realised.

Of course they would. They had each other. What else mattered?

When Frogmore came again, they would be waiting. They would be ready.

"Wait," said Matt, as if suddenly remembering something. "What about Ninian?"

"Don't worry about him," said Norwood easily. "He's quite safe."

"Will I see him again?" asked Matt. His voice sounded a little strained. Charlotte thought he looked worried. He gave a little cough, and added, "Will we get the chance to, ah, say goodbye, I mean?"

Norwood shrugged.

"Who knows?" he said. "I can't promise anything, even if I wished it."

Matt made a sound that might have been a cough, and looked away.

"Now," said Charlotte, after a moment's silence. "You mentioned you were going to send us back to our own story?"

❧ 62 ❧

"**A**h, but which *is* your own story?" asked Norwood. "Can you tell me that?"

Matt opened his mouth to say that of course he could say what their old story was...then he stopped, confused.

He thought of their wedding night, the lights, the dancing. The smiling faces of all their friends. He thought of the life they would be going back to, the house they would return to, the jobs they both had.

And it wasn't enough.

It was right, but it wasn't everything.

So he thought of their ship, and how it had been destroyed by the frogs. He thought of the new ship they would build, twice as splendid, four times as fast as their old vessel. He imagined them standing once more on the bridge, Charlotte and EB and him, and of all the places they would visit, the adventures they would have.

And that wasn't enough either.

He tried to make the two sets of memories fall in synch, to make the two parallel versions of himself meld.

But it felt...strange. There were interference patterns flickering across the internal substances of his thought.

"I...yes, I see," said Matt, looking down.

This was...this was worse than he had imagined. He had thought they had *won*. He had thought it was all over now. That everything would be okay.

A hand squeezed his. He looked up, and saw Charlotte, gazing at him with her kind, mismatched eyes, which were wondrous strange and infinitely familiar at the same time, and he realised it didn't matter.

He squeezed her hand in return.

"We'll work it out," said Charlotte.

Norwood Ginnel nodded, as if he had known that would be the case all along.

Then the ground that they were standing on lurched, so hard that both Matt and Charlotte were abruptly on their backs, staring up at the arc of white-blue sky above them.

A thought occurred to Matt. Something he hadn't yet wondered about, on account of how much other stuff there was going on that he didn't understand.

"Norwood," he said slowly. "Where are we?"

Norwood's eyebrows rose.

"Why, ain't you worked that out?" He sounded genuinely mystified. "I thought the two of you was *sharp!*"

"I've got a guess," said Charlotte, coming back to her feet.

Now that Matt gave it some thought, he found one answer leapt immediately to mind. The homes of the Sheriffs. A place they had seen once from a distance, which EB had pointed out to them. A place they had tried very hard not to come into contact with, on account of them really not wanting to be arrested.

"Guess away," said Norwood.

"We're in the Fold," said Matt. "Of course we are! Where else would a Sheriff take us?"

Which explained why he had felt so safe here, Matt thought. The Fold was a haven, a place outside the hurly-burley chance and maelstrom of the Storystream. Of course, 'safe' for a small, vulnerable story had always meant something very different for a fugitive trio of space-faring reality pirates, who made their living jumping between stories - all quite illegal, as far as the Sheriffs were concerned - and hence had been somewhere that Matt, Charlotte, and EB had been eager to avoid.

Norwood looked at him in stunned silence, then burst out laughing.

"The Fold?" he repeated, wiping tears from his eyes. "Oh, that's good. That's priceless!"

"What do you mean?" asked Charlotte, frowning. She looked as if she might be on the verge of stamping her foot, at least a little. "Why is that funny? *Isn't* this the Fold?"

Norwood gave another peel of laughter.

"You're right and wrong at the same time," he told her. "The Fold ain't just *one* place! There's lots of them. Lots and lots. They're all a bit different, one from the other. But you're right: this is a Fold. The Wandering Fold. *My* Fold."

Matt looked around, as if seeing the place for the first time.

He took in the way the ground rolled away from where they were standing, and realised that it had seemed they had come down to this point when they moved previously.

"It's all downhill," he said.

"Yup," agreed Norwood. "'Course it is. It's only a tiny little Fold. Look, watch."

He turned and sprinted away from them, quickly vanish from sight as if descending an increasingly steep hill. Matt stared after him.

There was a tap on his shoulder.

"See?" said Norwood, giving him a wide, slightly manic smile. "You can circumnavigate it real quick."

"The Fold is a circle?" asked Charlotte.

Norwood tilted his hand.

"More of a seventeen-dimensional hypersphere that projects into the deeper fabrics of reality," said Norwood. "But basically, yeah."

"But what...?" Charlotte started to say, and the ground gave another lurch.

Matt managed to keep his feet this time. He glanced over one shoulder, and was just in time to see a rectangle of apparently banal blue sky twist in on itself...

...and then he was looking through to another place.

It was a wide, green-blue land, rather like the one they were in, but much, much bigger and grander. He caught a glimpse of what looked like more stories, glimmering and shimmering away like the one Norwood had shown them, the story of the Frogopolis.

"What...is *that*?" asked Charlotte.

"That there is the *Western* Fold," said Norwood. He sounded rather pleased with himself. "We thought it would be the best place for you."

Matt felt his eyes widening.

"You mean...we're not going back to our story, after all?"

"Of course you're going to your story!"

The voice shouted out of the hole that had appeared in the side of the Wandering Fold. It was clear and steady, not high, but with a generous helping of grit and gravel. It was the sort of voice, Matt thought, which would brook no nonsense. But it wasn't unkindly.

"Hell, Norwood, what you bringing me, here?" the voice came again. "I thought you said these folk were *smart*!"

Then a shape flickered in through the opening, and the owner of the voice stood before them.

She was a slim, tough-looking woman, with a youngish face, and fair, slightly grubby hair tied back in a sensible ponytail. Her hands were small and strong, and she wore the same faded bluejeans as Norwood, with a chequered shirt, upon which was pinned a bright golden star.

"Sheriff Shuttlecock!" cried Norwood, leaping forward and clasping her warmly by the hand. "It's good to see you!"

The female Sheriff returned the handshake, if rather less warmly. She gave a smile, but it was thin and rather curt.

"Norwood," she said, a little crisply. "I'm glad things worked out. For a while there, I wasn't so sure. But I ain't joking! I thought you were brining me people who *understood*!"

"Oh, I'm sure understanding is there," said Norwood easily. If he noticed the brusque way in which the new Sheriff was speaking to him, he gave no sign of it. "But they're only little people. And they've been through a lot; give 'em some time. I'm sure they'll work it out."

"Um, excuse me," said Matt, a bit annoyed at being talked about as if he wasn't there. "But we can hear you, you know. And we can speak for ourselves, too."

Sheriff Shuttlecock whipped her head to look him up and down, and Matt found himself taking a step backwards. Her gaze was so striking, it seemed to take him all in at a glance, every hidden nook and cranny of his inner world, and Matt had the unsettling feeling that she had understood him better in a matter of seconds than he would ever understand himself.

Then she turned her eyes on Charlotte, and he felt Charlotte's hand tense in his.

Sheriff Shuttlecock gave a thoughtful pause.

"Yes, well," she said, and Matt was relieved to find her voice seemed a little warmer than it had a moment ago. "I suppose you can, at that. I'm Indigo. Indigo Shuttlecock. Sorry for such a reception, but you've given us Sheriffs a rough ride. Unleashing the Chaos, indeed! If that weren't rash, I don't know what is!"

"We didn't have much of a choice," said Charlotte. "I'm not sure if you noticed the small matter of Matt nearly being wiped from existence."

"Oh, but that *would* have been a small matter," said Indigo Shuttlecock evenly, "if you compare it to the Storystream itself being flooded by Chaos."

The two of them stared at one another for a moment, unblinking.

Then Indigo gave a small, tight smile.

"But, hell, things worked out well enough," she said. "And that was largely on account of the choices you both made, at the end. Which is why we've decided to give you this chance."

"I thought you were putting us back in our story," said Matt.

"We are, you ninnyhammer," said Indigo. "Well, putting you back in *something*. We'll have to see how it takes, how it grows. Your case is...quite unusual."

"What do you mean?" asked Charlotte.

Indigo waved a hand.

"Look, this sure would be easier if I can just *show* you," she said.

She turned to Norwood.

"Sheriff Ginnel," she said formally. "I herby take receipt of this cargo. I endeavour to watch them and keep them safe, as per the Charter invested in me by the Order of Sheriffs."

"Sounds fine to me," said Norwood, rather less formally. "It's been nice knowing you folks. Mayhap's we'll meet again."

He raised a hand in farewell, and//

//and they were standing in a much wider world, watching Sheriff Norwood Ginnel and his small Fold through a tiny window in the far distance.

"Thank you," Matt started to say, but the hole was already closing, and Norwood was gone.

❦ 63 ❧

Indigo Shuttlecock led them through the Western Fold. It was much, much bigger than the Wandering Fold, with gently rolling slopes and hills.

"Is this real grass?" asked Charlotte.

"Sort of," said Indigo. "It might as well be. It's kind of the *story* of grass. The essence of grassiness. Which is why you see it that way. Same with the sky and the sun. Not meaning to be funny, but you're just little creatures here. You can't see this place the way it really is. So what you see is...well, a *version* of it."

Matt thought it looked wonderful, whatever it was.

They passed stories, lots and lots of stories. They shimmered and glimmered happily away, sending out pulses and fragments of things he felt he could almost taste, could nearly understand.

At last, they came to the river.

Matt had heard the noise of it, building from some distance away. It roared and tumbled, sending up a fine rainbow spray. It was spectacular, unlike any river he had ever seen.

"What's *that*?" he asked.

"The Storystream," said Indigo simply. "Leastways, the smallest, narrowest tributary. A projection of it. Now you two stay here. It ain't safe for you to go much closer."

Indigo strode forward and thrust her hands into the river, sending up a spray of glittering, kaleidoscopic colours. Then she returned. Something was dripping from her clothes and her hair. It wasn't water.

She held her hands out, and inside them Matt saw...

...he couldn't say.

It sparkled and swam, enticing, maddening, substances on the very edge of forming up into meaning.

"It's raw story-stuff," said Indigo, her voice quiet but clear. "Unformed. Unconstrained."

"What...what are you going to do with it?" asked Charlotte.

Indigo gave her a slow smile.

"*We* are going to do something new with it," she said. "You and I, together."

Not knowing quite what he was doing, acting almost without willing it, Matt raised his hands. He saw that Charlotte was doing the same thing.

As his hands entered the glamouring substance, Matt felt a shock pass through his body. It was like pure energy, pure potential. It was hot and cold, joy and sorrow, night and day, every pole and every splendid thing in between.

It was life.

It was story.

He understood suddenly, and looked at Charlotte. She smiled back at him, eyes warm and knowing.

It was *their* story.

Whatever they might make of it.

"I can't give no promises," warned Indigo Shuttlecock. "This ain't in the usual run of things. But then, *you* aren't in the usual run of things, either. We'll have to see how things go."

"I know," said Matt.

"It won't be your old story," said Indigo. "It won't be either of those."

"I know," said Charlotte.

"Then go in peace," said Indigo. "Blessings of the Pheasant be upon you."

"What?" said Matt, but the time for questions was over.

Light sprang up from the strange substance. It ran up his hand, to his arm, to his chest. He felt Charlotte's soft, strong hand in his.

They closed their eyes, and let the story take them.

✥ 64 ✥

"That was close, EB," said the Captain, letting out a long breath and looking at the scanner to make sure they hadn't been spotted.

The scanner - which picked up every broadcast on every known frequency emanating from the little planet near to which they had jumped - remained blissfully silent.

The Captain relaxed, and leaned back in her chair.

The fact that the chair was actually a sun-bed was neither here nor there.

EB hit a key that switched them to auto-pilot, swivelled to face her, and lifted his cocktail in salute.

"I assure you, it wasn't," EB told her. "If we had exited hyper-mega-space any later, *that* would have been close. As things stand, we are just close enough to enjoy a leisurely jaunt through real space. Time to relax a little, before going through all the stuff and bother of first contact."

The Captain shrugged, then lounged back on her sun-bed. Above them, the artificial lighting did a really spectacular job of imitating a blazing sun against a cloudless blue sky.

"Whatever you say, EB," she said. "You've got more experience of this than me."

"Not at all," protested EB, sliding comfortably into his own sun-bed, and casually flicking shades down over his eyes. "You've got just as much experience as me; it's just that now it's mixed in with lots of experiences of a totally different kind. You know - experiences to do with, ah, *going to work* and *watching television* and, ah..."

He faltered for a moment, struggled to come up with a third item, then gave up and waved a hand vaguely at the little blue planet rotating slowly on the view screen.

"Well, you know," he concluded. "Whatever other fascinating things you got up to in that other life of yours."

Charlotte nodded slowly, regarding the little planet.

Home.

She was going home.

But then, this ship was home, too.

She had two homes now, two sets of memories, two personalities, two existences which had been merged into one. It was all rather confusing.

But good. It felt good, too.

There was a beeping noise, and the hatch to the engine room slid open, disgorging the Crew.

The Crew consisted of one gentleman with dark hair, rather more liberally sprinkled with grey than once it had been, wearing finely tailored clothing that looked rather the worse for wear on account of being covered in greenish-yellow goo.

He stomped over to where the Captain lay lounging, did a little light fuming, then - when it became apparent that no one was going to comment on his appearance - decided to do so himself.

"I'm soaked!" he complained.

"So we see," said the Captain. "It was very brave of you,

volunteering to take care of the new star drive like that."

"I didn't volunteer," sulked the Crew. "I was press-ganged."

Charlotte raised an eyebrow.

"You volunteered to submit to a democratic election process whereby we were all assigned roles," she elaborated. "It's hardly fair to question the outcome after the fact."

The Crew glared from Charlotte to EB and back again.

Finally, deciding that he was on to a losing battle, he gave a sigh.

"Fine," he said, with a fair approximation of good grace. "But I *definitely* get to be Captain next time."

"Deal," said Charlotte unconvincingly, as Matt unzipped his bespattered jumpsuit to reveal bathing shorts, and lay down next to her on a sun-bed of his own.

He put his hand in hers. Her fingers felt warm and soft and strong. He played with the forth finger, the one with the ring. It was made of an exotic metal that had been mined from the heart of a long-dead dark star, using techniques and requiring specialisms that would boggle the most expanded mind, and was linked - via a subtle form of quantum entanglement - to the molecules of the ring he wore on his own left hand. It had cost rather a lot.

There was a period of contented silence.

"That new drive is a bit of a clunky thing," complained Matt. "Couldn't you have come up with something, you know, smoother?"

EB shrugged.

"That depends," he said, "on whether you'd like to incur the wrath of the newly-pacified Sheriffs of the Order, and risk opening the door to the Chaos once again."

Matt pondered on this for a moment.

"Nah," he said at length.

"That's what I thought," said EB. "So we are stuck with

hyper-mega-space, then."

"But...but will it always be so, so..." Matt searched for the right word. "Gloopy? When we jump, I mean."

"I'm afraid so," said EB, trying - not very convincingly - to hide a smirk. "That's the thing about hyper-mega-space. It's full of gloop."

Charlotte let out a long, satisfied sigh.

"Let's not worry about it," she said. "It's not every day you go on a honeymoon to a planet you've never visited before, while simultaneously returning to your home-world, which you have never left."

"True," agreed Matt. "This two-previously-separate-but-now-united-realities business is a bit tricky though, isn't it? I mean, how am I going to explain it to my mum, for instance?"

"You're nothing if not compelling," said Charlotte. "I'm sure you'll work it out."

Matt thought about this for a moment, then relaxed.

"I'm sure you're right," he said. "I suppose we should just lay back, take things easy, and bask in the fact that the Universe is not about to be destroyed. Or at least, not by us."

There was about five seconds of calm, peaceful silence.

Something began beeping.

EB moved to the console and examined the scanner.

"Hmm," he said.

It wasn't a reassuring sort of a *hmm*.

"What," said Charlotte, with a brittle brightness in her voice, "is that?"

"Could be nothing," said EB, without much conviction. "The scanner is picking up an odd energy signature."

"Where from?" asked Matt. He glared suspiciously at the planet on the display screen. "Is it Denmark? I've never trusted Denmark."

"It's not Denmark," EB reassured him. "In fact, it's not coming from anywhere on the planet."

Charlotte was leaning forward now. She was frowning.

"Where *is* it coming from, then?" she asked.

EB looked up at her.

"Behind you," he said.

There was a bone-deep thrumming noise. It wasn't quite a sound. It was something deeper than a sound.

Matt and Charlotte turned.

There was a door there, hanging in mid air about six inches from the floor.

It was made of old, gnarled wood, varnished and polished, and with a handle that appeared to be formed from a single, huge piece of amber.

The handle turned smoothly, and the door creaked open.

A figure emerged.

"Oh," said Matt.

"Hello again, good master," said Ninian.

He was every bit as tall and slender and strange as he had been. He wore a jerkin and trousers of an odd, shimmering substance, that appeared at the same time to be of every colour and of no colour at all. The material flared and slid about him as he moved into the room, drifting as if they formed a dream of clothes rather than clothes themselves. His crystal eyeglasses sparkled elegantly.

"Oh," said Matt again. He seemed currently unable to say anything else.

"Hello," said Charlotte, a faint, puzzled smile on her lips. "What...what are you doing here?"

"I've come to claim my half of our bargain," said Ninian, giving Matt a small, solemn nod. "My people are in difficulty. All the oracles and omens have led me to you, as we discussed when we last met."

Charlotte turned her head to give Matt a long, slow, unblinking stare.

It was the sort of *stare* that was in imminent danger of

turning, at any moment, into a *glare*.

Matt winced. He made something with his mouth that wasn't quite a smile.

He was starting to get his head around what was happening now, and thought he might be able to move on from *oh*.

"Ah," he said.

"Indeed," said Ninian, "it is vital that we make haste, for the Bracken Court cannot hope to survive for long."

"The Bracken Court?" repeated Charlotte.

"My people," said Ninian. "My home. There is a...a danger. It is difficult to explain. Factions are involved. The Faef are implicated. A whole swathe of the Grand is awash with the matter. Even the Caemph of Lunlock..."

Ninian trailed off, an abstracted glint in his eyes. He looked almost worried.

Matt wasn't used to Ninian looking worried.

It was worrying.

"In any case," said Ninian, with the air of someone determined to get through the difficulty without letting himself be broken by the details. "Things are unraveling faster than I feared. If there is now any hope of putting things to right, it is with your help. With your three wishes."

There was a long, rather awkward silence.

"You *did* promise," added Ninian, reproachfully.

Charlotte looked from Ninian to Matt, then from Matt to EB, then finally back to Ninian.

"Tell us what you need," said the Captain.

THE END

<<<<>>>>

AFTERWORD

Thanks for reading. If you enjoyed the story, please consider leaving a quick review e.g. on Amazon, Bookbub or Goodreads.

The Storystream is an odd series.

Keep reading for an extract from the next tale from the Storystream: the novella *All Quiet In The Western Fold*...

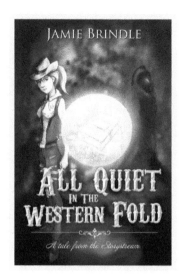

EXTRACT - ALL QUIET IN THE WESTERN FOLD

It was midnight in the Western Fold, and the stories were far too quiet. There was no susurrus of conflict, no flashes of tightly-wound plots clicking into place, no shocking revelations or grand resolutions. It was uncanny.

Sheriff Indigo Shuttlecock surveyed her anthology and frowned. She was relatively new to the job—she had been in her post for little over sixteen narrative cycles, which basically made her a novice—but she knew a problem when she saw one. Even from this distance, it was obvious something was wrong. Stories were not meant to be this quiet, especially in the Western Fold. That was her patch, a mixture of ghost stories, mysteries, and cheap thrillers. Typical rookie district —nothing too complex, nothing too literary, easy stuff, and if she had been happy to be given it when she graduated from the Academy, she was quickly becoming bored and eager for a promotion. So far, it had been almost too simple: textbook problems. She had had to find a hero who had accidentally wandered into the neighbouring story and got lost; a few of the simpler tales had contracted a disease that caused them to start using overly-complicated locutions. Nothing challenging. It had been a good rookie assignment, but not something a Sheriff could make a career of, not without becoming a laughing stock.

This, however...

She stared again at the huddle of little stories. They bobbed merrily, glistening orbs of lightning blue and burning red, curious folds of narrative potential wound up into those most elegant of sensical things: stories. They seemed completely oblivious to any problem. Still, Indigo knew there *was* a problem. No healthy story would appear so completely *calm*. Stories weren't *meant* to be calm. They ran on conflict, after all. Without conflict, there was no story.

Indigo smiled. Well, if there was a problem, she would deal with it. That was her job, after all. Maybe this would be the case that would make her career. Perhaps this was her chance for the promotion she had been looking for...

Time to investigate.

Indigo decided to start with *Blood Ties*. The silly little chiller was as good a place to begin as any. She concentrated on the twirling red-blue twists of narrative potential that composed the tiny story, letting herself fall into the dance. The loops of story became huge and swollen—or perhaps it was Indigo herself who shrank, who could say?—and soon she was inside the story, watching the comings and goings. The tale was spread out before her—characters, plotting, motivation, everything glimmering in perfect detail. After all, she was the Sheriff, and all the stories in her patch knew to do as she asked.

"Evening, Sheriff Indigo," said *Blood Ties*. The little story had personified itself as a small anaemic man with glasses and big teeth.

"Good evening, *Blood.*"

"Everything okay, ma'am?" asked the story.

"Not sure about that, *Blood,*" said Indigo. "Why don't you tell me how you're feeling?"

"How I'm feelin'?" *Blood* repeated. "Why, very well, thank you! Truth to tell, haven't felt this good for... well, not since I was first told!"

"Oh?" asked Indigo. She kept her voice nonchalant. "How's that, *Blood?*"

"Well, see for yourself!" said *Blood Ties*, spreading a hand to indicate his main characters.

Indigo looked at the three protagonists. They were smiling and holding hands.

"They look well enough to me," said Indigo.

"Oh, they're happy as anything!" said Blood. "That's just it. Usually they're at each other's throats by now!"

Indigo passed a hand through the folds of plot. It was true. The story was meant to revolve around a lover's quarrel. There were supposed to be hidden letters, the discovery of a mistress, a row that escalated to violence...

The three protagonists were dancing around in a circle. They appeared to be singing some kind of nursery rhyme.

"I see," said Indigo. "When did this start?"

"Difficult to say," said Blood. He looked shifty.

Indigo Shuttlecock narrowed her eyes.

"You do know that to withhold information from an officer of the Council is a serious offence?" she reminded him. "If I find you've been holding out on me, it could go bad for you."

The little story clenched his fists. For a moment, he looked as if he would say something.

Then he swallowed.

"I don't know nothin'," he said stubbornly.

Indigo stared at him.

"Fine," she said at length.

She let her concentration falter. The characters and plotting of the little story began to fade, shimmering back to the red-blue twists of narrative.

"What... what will you do now?" Blood called after her.

"Find someone who does know something," Indigo told him.

Maybe the next story would be more useful...

Read the full novella, *All Quiet In The Western Fold*...

BIBLIOGRAPHY

Tales from the Storystream

The Hard Blokes Of Sparta: The Princess In The Tower

The Hard Blokes Of Sparta: The Daemon In The Basement

The Hard Blokes Of Sparta: The Zombie In The Fire (currently being written!)

Star Frog 127 and the Chaos Inception

Space Raiders of the Frogopolis and the Chaos Singularity

All Quiet In The Western Fold

Of Blood And Iron

The Storystream Box Set

Storystream Shorts

The Gift

The Last Train

Red In Tooth And Claw

Modern Serpents Talk Things Through

Small Mistakes

Dust On The Crystal

A Clean Death

The Hard Blokes Of Sparta: The Relic In The Dungeon

Shards Of Chaos

The Fall Of The Angel Nathalie

The Land Before Life

The Land Before Life

Diminishing Returns

The New Life

www.jamiebrindle.com

For deals and updates, follow me on...

...BookBub

...Facebook

Tweet me @mazeman11

Lightning Source UK Ltd.
Milton Keynes UK
UKHW021018050321
379837UK00015B/2157

9 781914 186035